Only a Girl

Lian Gouw

Dalang Publishing

First edition

All characters in this book are fictitious, and any resemblance to real persons, living or dead, is coincidental.

ISBN: 978-0-9836273-7-1
Library of Congress Control Number: 2011931586
Dalang Publishing
www.dalangpublishing.com
California
Printed in the United States of America

Dedication

To the sisterhood of women with whom I share the joys, loves, hopes, sacrifices and pains that live in a woman's heart, that mold a woman's life.

Acknowledgments

I thank my teachers and editors. Without their guidance *Only A Girl* would not have arrived at the form it is in today.

I thank my friends, writers and non-writers. Their support sustained me during my writer's low times.

I thank Robert A. Kato for providing the author's photograph as well as the cover art.

I thank Nono Sutiknja for providing the photograph of the Tangkuban Prahu used to create the cover design.

Only a Girl

CHAPTER 1

Bandung, Indonesia/The Dutch East Indies, 1932

Carolien scooted deeper into the seat of the *delman*. A cold January wind rushed through the feathery leaves of the tall jacaranda trees lining the streets. She adjusted her woolen shawl to wrap once more around her neck and tried to relax as she was usually able to during her daily buggy ride home from work. Water drops cascading onto the canvas carriage roof sounded like a light drum roll. Pushing her hands deep into her coat pockets, Carolien rehearsed the question she planned to ask over dinner. She knew her mother and oldest brother would not be pleased and their attitude would set the stage. Carolien sighed. Why had she been born into such a traditional family?

The Malay driver clacked his tongue and flicked a whip lightly across the back of the horse as it trotted up the steep incline. They passed mansions surrounded by rolling lawns, colorful flowerbeds, and large trees. The late afternoon rain had left the streets dark and steaming. The outline of Tangkuban Prahu, the sleeping volcano, filled Bandung's northern skyline with the image of a capsized boat. Today, the familiar sight seemed ominous. Carolien shivered. She wasn't going to allow her boat to be overturned. Her boat was going to skim across the water with full sails.

All in all, she was fortunate. Her father had fallen into the good graces of the mayor of Bandung in the early 1900s, when he helped close a major opium den. He was shot during a raid, and the Dutch official not only saw to it that her brothers, Chip and Ting, received a Dutch education, he also helped them secure positions in the colonial government. Chip, the oldest, had moved the family into this exclusive neighborhood and made sure that Carolien received a Dutch education as well, but she chafed against his rule. Did being the oldest male in a traditional Chinese family give him the right to decide her life?

The buggy driver urged his horse into Koninginnen Boulevard.

"Stop at the gate by the big tamarind tree," Carolien said in Malay, pointing ahead of the buggy.

The driver reined in his horse under the sprawling canopy of the old tree. Carolien paid the driver and rested her hand on the heavy latch of the wrought-iron gate before lifting the lever to open it.

The barking of German shepherds welcomed her as she walked toward the house. Dusk had begun to fall and, one by one, lights flicked on behind the windows. The outside lights painted broken shadows of shrubs and trees on the whitewashed walls. Carolien walked up the wide steps leading to the porch that wrapped around the house. Her mother and brothers would most likely be sitting in the livingroom. Nanna, whose hands were never at rest, would have some bead-work. Her brothers would be reading the evening paper. Sue, her older sister, was probably in the kitchen overseeing the finishing touches of dinner. Married at 16, Sue had moved back home after her husband died in a typhoid epidemic and she was pregnant with Eddie.

"Hurry! Hurry! Get the door! Carolien's home," the myna bird squealed.

Carolien hung her coat on the coat stand in the vestibule, next to the ornate mirror. She put her umbrella in the old Delft blue umbrella stand as the young voices of her nephew and nieces drifted through the door along with a tantalizing mélange of scents coming from the kitchen. She knew going forward with her plan meant giving up this warm security. Could she do it? Would it be worth it in the end?

***

At dinner that evening Carolien scooted to the edge of her chair, her heart was racing. The light from the crystal chandelier reflected in the edged glass of the buffet doors. The rosewood of the altar table glowed with a deep warm sheen. Nanna quietly presided over the family dinner from her seat at the head of the table. The steam rising from the rice bowl carried the aroma of the golden chicken resting in a pool of coconut milk and turmeric, side dishes of braised tofu and stir fried vegetables.

Chip and Ting carried on a conversation about world politics and economics while the rest of the family remained silent out of respect. As the meal came to a close, Sue served the coffee and Carolien took a deep breath, smoothing her skirt. It was now or never.

"When can you receive Po Han?" Carolien's voice dropped to almost a whisper and she kept her eyes on her cup. She had not directed her question to anyone in particular, but everyone would know it was meant for Nanna and Chip.

The steadfast tick-tock-tick-tock of the grandfather's clock was the only sound piercing the sudden silence. If only she could come up with *one* thing her family would find favorable in Po Han.

Nanna excused her grandchildren from the table. The teenagers threw curious glances at the adults. Chip's two daughters, Emma and Els, rushed out. But Eddie lingered, looking at Carolien. She met her nephew's concerned look with a feeble smile.

"Does that mean he'll be coming alone, without an elder?" Nanna asked.

"I think so. He didn't say...." Carolien bowed her head and turned her water glass on its crystal coaster.

Sue put down the coffee pot and rejoined the table. "Is it true that he doesn't have any family other than that drunken grandmother? Why isn't the old woman coming with him?"

Carolien bit her lip. Things were playing out just as she had expected. She had hoped that her sister might support her, but Sue had spent a lifetime catering to the wishes of the family. She would never go against Nanna, Chip, or their younger brother, Ting.

"We sent you to Dutch schools so you'd be an asset to some decent man's household," said Chip. "Your education would enhance his position and, in turn, secure yours. A typewriter salesman has little security to offer."

Carolien crumpled the napkin in her lap. Chip never missed an opportunity to wield the authority that came from being the oldest son in a fatherless Chinese household. She threw her brother a sideways glance. It was no use arguing with Chip.

"I never agreed to take the risk that comes with exposing girls to the Western way of life," Nanna said turning to Chip. "I warned you against Lien's stubbornness."

Only Nanna called Carolien by her birth name. She had been named Ong Kway Lien at birth. According to Chinese custom her family name, Ong, came first. The teachers of the Dutch School for Girls had altered the name to suit their tongue and habit. Thus, Ong Kway Lien became Carolien Ong.

"You turned down good suitors," Sue said. "Why do you now want to marry someone who has neither a degree nor comes from a wealthy family?"

"I love him. I don't need a husband with a degree who'd treat me like an exotic household fixture." Carolien jutted out her chin. "Do any of you know what it means to be happy instead of just financially secure?"

A deep condemning silence met Carolien's outburst.

"Po Han says that if one is happy, all good things in life will follow—and I believe him."

Chip, Sue, and Ting remained silent, but Nanna spoke. "Happiness is peace. You won't find peace unless you are secure. And you won't find security in an unstable situation." She reached for the small silver bell by her plate and rang for Mundi, the native houseboy. Then she walked across the room to the Buddhist altar where she worshipped the gods and family ancestors.

Nanna lit a few bunches of incense sticks and placed them in the urns. The curling smoke carried her prayers toward the ceiling and Nanna turned to Carolien. "What do you know of love?" she asked her daughter. "Love is what stands through misfortune. There is love when a woman's loins have grown tired and a man still finds rest beside her." Nanna's words had such gravity that Carolien bowed her head. "Love is when a man chisels a cavity in a woman's heart and the woman fills the gaping hole with concern for his well-being." Nanna straightened her tall, wiry body. "Lien!" Carolien looked up and Nanna held her eyes. "After you've experienced any of this, then come and talk to me about love."

Mundi entered the room with a large wooden tray and began to remove the dirty dishes.

Chip leaned across the table toward Carolien. "I forbid you to see him again."

Carolien looked to Ting for support, but he looked away.

"Next time I'm at the club," Chip said, "I'll drop the word that my pretty, intelligent sister is ready to settle down, and that the man she chooses to marry is lucky."

Carolien rose. "You have no right to prevent me from seeing anyone. I'm thirty and you're not my father," she shouted, holding back tears.

"As long as you live under my roof, you shall respect your brother," Nanna said as soon as Mundi had left the room. Then she turned to Chip. "You're wrong to consider anyone who marries your sister lucky. The poor man will have a big headache!" Nanna left the room, the conversation was finished.

***

The next day Carolien left her office at noon. Ever since she and Po Han begun dating a few months earlier, they had spent the lunch hour in nearby Queen Wilhelmina Park, a green oasis in the center of Bandung's business district. Po Han was to meet her at their usual spot, a secluded lawn area surrounded by a tall hedge of vibrant red canas and partially shaded by an ancient tamarind tree. She glanced at her watch and peered down the path, recalling the morning Po Han stepped into her office to sell a new typewriter to her employer, Mr. Wachter. A flock of sparrows carried on a noisy dispute across the lawn. Po Han should be here soon.

After settling on a park bench, Carolien took out her sandwich and opened up the *Nederlands Indische Courant*, the Dutch newspaper that served the major islands of the Dutch East Indies. The front page issued the usual warnings regarding the effects of the worldwide recession on the economy of Southeast Asia, particularly the Dutch colony. Sukarno, the young native engineer known for being a strong nationalist, was making headlines again. He had recently been released by Governor General de Graeff after serving three of a four-year prison term for subversive activities. Carolien shook her head. The man was an outright troublemaker. Turning him loose would only allow him to stir up more. She moved her watch around her wrist. It was twenty to one. Po Han was supposed to meet her at twelve. He was usually on time.

Carolien started to walk down the graveled path. She paused by the statue of Jan Pieter's Zoon Coen, and listenend for approaching footsteps. The bronze image of the Dutch governor of The Netherlands Indies towered over her from his pedestal, casting a long shadow on the lawn. Carolien fingered the Dutchman's weathered metal toes. In 1619, Coen had given preferred status to the Chinese citizens of the colony, placing them under the ruling Dutch but above the native population.

Two Dutch businessmen halted their conversation as they passed her. One of them threw Carolien a curious glance. She met his gaze boldy, and when he averted his eyes she smiled. "Just because you're men and Dutch, don't think you can stare me down," she murmured as they walked away.

Gravel crackled under hasty footsteps and Carolien whirled around.

"Sorry for being late." Po Han pulled her into his arms. "Guess what?"

Carolien stepped back, looking around for possible observers. It was improper for a Chinese girl to be alone with a man she was not officially engaged to. "What happened? I was just about to leave."

"I took an order for ten Olivetties!"

"You made the sale!" Carolien grabbed Po Han's arm. She looked at Po Han's handsome sunburned face and tried to hide her giddiness.

"What's more, after I deliver the machines, I'll be photographing the typing room for Olivetti. If they like the shots, they'll use them in their brochures."

Po Han's mention of the future reminded Carolien of her family's decision. Standing on tiptoe, she straightened his tie and flicked some cigarette ash off his lapel. "Won't that be nice?" She wished she could muster more enthusiasm.

"Well, when can I see your mother and brothers?"

Carolien looked away, searching for words to deliver her bad news.

They started walking toward the street and, for a moment, there was only the sound of crackling gravel under their shoes. Po Han reached into his pocket for a pack of cigarettes and a lighter and Carolien watched the quick pulsing of his Adam's apple.

"They won't see you," she said as he drew the first drag of smoke.

Po Han inhaled deeply. He tilted his head slightly backward and let the smoke escape between puckered lips. "Did they say why?"

Carolien studied the shape of her manicured toenail, which showed through her open pumps. "Your grandmother doesn't show much respect for me or my family if you have to ask for my hand yourself."

Po Han crunched his half-smoked cigarette into the gravel.

"They must have found out about her beer habit," Carolien said.

They resumed walking, the persistent honking of passing taxis in the nearby street breaking into their awkward silence. "My brothers think that your job as a salesman isn't very steady," Carolien said when they reached the end of the park.

"Government positions don't hang off trees." Po Han took Carolien's elbow and, maneuvering between the cars, *delmans*, and bicycles, guided her across the street. They walked the short distance to Carolien's office without further conversation. A brisk January wind picked up and flared the skirt of Carolien's silk dress. "Can I see you tonight?" Po Han looked down on her, his hands stuck deep into his pockets.

Carolien threw him a desperate look.

"We need to talk."

Carolien caught the stares of a few passers-by. She rubbed an imaginary stain on the palm of her hand. "Okay," she said.

***

At the end of the workday Carolien walked to a window overlooking the street. The shouts of paperboys offering the evening paper dominated the cacophony of traffic noises. Carolien spotted Po Han as he strode across the street toward the law office where she had worked as a secretary for over a decade. She unlocked the door for him and they exchanged strained hellos.

"Well, what are we going to do?" Carolien perched on the edge of her chair in the deserted office. Her eyes were fixed on the pencil she rolled between her palms.

"Your family feels disrespected because my grandmother won't ask for your hand." Po Han leaned across Carolien's desk. "And my grandmother thinks your family is no good because they allow you to work in a Dutch office. She thinks you won't make a good wife because you're not at home cooking and taking care of a house." Po Han pulled Carolien out of her chair and held her at arm's length.

Carolien looked away. She wanted to be with him, marry him against all conventions, but how could she go against her family and their concern for her future?

"That's why they don't want us to get married, but it isn't them–it's us." Po Han eyes bored into hers. "What do you think? Do you want to be married to me?"

"There's a lot more to it than how we feel about each other," Carolien said slowly, unable to meet his eyes. "We'll be entirely on our own, you know. And if my mother and Chip don't agree, we'll need a dispensation."

Po Han crushed the half-smoked cigarette in a nearby ashtray. He grabbed Carolien by the shoulders and shook her gently. "But we'll have plenty to do with each other–we'll have a life together. And I don't think we'll have trouble getting a dispensation, you'll soon be thirty-one."

Carolien rested her head against his chest. "I'm scared," she whispered. "Will you take care of me, always?" Po Han stepped back and searched her face. For a moment he seemed stunned but then closed his arms around her.

"Yes, of course," he murmured into her hair. Please say you'll still marry me. We'll show them–your family and my grandmother. You will, right?"

She responded with a silent nod against his chest and he tightened his embrace.

"When? Let's set a date."

"On my birthday." She nestled her head into his neck and smiled. "I'll be thirty-one and we won't need a dispensation."

Po Han clasped Carolien in his arms. "July twenty-second, your birthday, will be our wedding day."

CHAPTER 2

Carolien felt a cool hand brush her cheek and she clutched her roll pillow tighter. She had spent most of the night tossing and turning, only falling asleep when the wind breathed cooler air, sometime after the night watchman had called three. Familiar morning sounds drifted into the room through open shutters, Nanna talking to Mundi, the myna bird yelling, "*Goeden morgen, mevrouw!*" Carolien squinted at the light.

Sue took a seat on the bed. Her eyes were red and swollen. "Are you really going through with it?"

Carolien stretched. She wasn't going to allow worries to bother her today. She swung her legs out of bed and walked barefoot across the room. The smooth floor tile felt cool against the soles of her feet. She tore a leaf off the wall calendar and read the next page out loud. "Friday, July 22, 1932. I'm thirty-one today and the law says I no longer need permission to get married. I can marry anyone I want–and I'm going to marry Po Han."

The white linen suit she had bought to wear at her wedding hung from a hook on the door. Carolien fingered a sleeve before spinning around. "Why can't anyone understand that all I want is to be happy?"

"Aren't you scared at all?" Sue clasped her hands together in her lap.

"Scared?" Carolien flung her nightgown on the bed and grabbed a kimono lying over the back of a chair. "Why should I be scared?" She couldn't keep her voice from catching slightly.

"But you'll be all alone there." Sue folded her sister's nightgown and searched her face. "I'm baking cheese rolls for breakfast. They should be about ready."

Tears sprang into Carolien's eyes. The soft buttery rolls stuffed with cheese and herbs were her favorite breakfast food. Carolien threw her arms around Sue's stout figure and whispered, "Thank you, *Chi-Chi*." Only at times like this did Carolien revert to the traditional way of calling Sue *older sister*, as she had when they were little girls.

After Sue left the room Carolien opened her closet. The shelves were almost bare. She had already moved her belongings to her future home with Po Han and his grandmother.

Carolien had visited Ocho only three times. The first time was to be introduced after she had accepted Po Han's proposal. "My grandmother is going to be so happy that I'm finally getting married," Po Han had told her. How excited she had been. Po Han was different from previous suitors. He was like the men in the romantic Dutch novels she borrowed from the library; he asked *her* to marry him, rather than asking her family.

Ocho's reaction had not been what she expected. The elderly woman had squinted at Carolien with glassy eyes. "Where did you pick her up?" she asked.

"Carolien lives uptown with her family," Po Han said, ignoring his grandmother's insinuation. "I don't think you're familiar with the neighborhood."

Carolien had felt uneasy around Ocho. Was it the Malay that Ocho spoke? In Nanna's house only the servants spoke Malay, everyone else in the family spoke Dutch. Thinking of their different backgrounds made Carolien feel uneasy. Accustomed to the order and formality of Nanna's household, she had a hard time with the casual manner in which Ocho ran hers.

Carolien quickly harnessed her thoughts. Today was her wedding day and she wasn't going let anyone spoil it. She finished dressing and walked to the dining room.

Breakfast was a meal everyone usually ate on their own, but today the whole family was sitting around the dining table. Carolien glanced around the room. "Good morning. What brings you all to breakfast at the same time?"

The three teenagers rose and, almost in unison, asked to be excused.

Carolien gripped the back of her chair and swallowed hard. She was particularly fond of Eddie and her niece, Els. "After today," she said, "I will no longer live here."

Ting shot Carolien a sharp glance. Chip put down his coffee cup without taking a sip, and Nanna sat rigid in her chair.

When Carolien looked at Emma, her oldest niece averted her eyes. Carolien took a deep breath. "I'm going to be married today, and when I come back from my honeymoon I will be living with my husband."

Silence followed her announcement. Then Eddie walked to her with an outstretched hand, ignoring the glances the adults threw him. "Congratulations, Auntie. Can we come to see you after you're back?"

"Yes, can we, Auntie?" Els' voice was hardly audible.

"Of course you can." Carolien took Eddie's hand and pulled Els against her.

"You're going to be late for school," Chip said, reaching for his coffee.

Emma glanced from the adults to Eddie and Els. "Let's go." Emma poked her sister in the back. Passing Carolien, she mumbled, "Congratulations, Aunt."

After the children left the room, Carolien took her seat at the table.

Sue's hand trembled as she lifted the napkin off the cheese rolls and placed the basket by Carolien.

"Thank you." Carolien didn't feel like eating but she didn't want to seem ungrateful.

Chip finished his breakfast and took leave from Nanna. On his way out he said, "If you aren't wise enough to figure what's best for you, I wish you'd given your family's reputation some consideration."

"I sure hope you know what you're doing." Ting followed his older brother out of the door.

Carolien pressed her lips together. She wanted to jump out of her chair and scream at her brothers, but Nanna's stern posture kept her quiet.

The women finished their breakfast in silence. Then Nanna rose and walked to the altar. She lit a bunch of incense sticks and, handing them to Carolien, said, "Here, pay your respects to your father. I'm sure he didn't have this in mind when he accepted the Dutch."

Despite her lack of religious beliefs, Carolien obeyed. Her offerings at the family altar were a ritual prompted by Nanna, but this time a prayer did spring from her heart. *Dear God, please make them understand.* Though she had addressed an unknown deity, she placed the incense sticks in the urn under her father's portrait. Turning to Nanna, she asked, "Can I send Mundi to find me a cab?"

"Sure." Nanna paused, looking at her youngest daughter dressed in white. "Remember, your family did not throw you out. It's you who decided to leave. We will always be here."

***

Ocho dragged herself out of bed with a sigh. She had spent the night tossing and her hair had become undone. She gathered the long silver strands and twisted them into a knot she fastened on top of her head. Roosters crowing and early vendors calling out their wares gave the morning familiarity, but this was not an ordinary day. Her awareness sharpened as the patterns of sunlight progressed along the wall. She glanced in her vanity mirror and massaged her face, but her drawn look remained. Po Han had decided to marry Carolien. What could he possibly see in her? No self-respecting Chinese family would allow a girl to work in a Dutch office. A girl like Carolien would never know how to run a household properly.

Ocho lit the two charcoal stoves in the kitchen and began preparing steamed pork buns and coffee. She had tried to prevent the marriage by refusing to ask for Carolien's hand on Po Han's behalf, but her plan had failed. In their striving to emulate the Dutch, Carolien's family had become shameless. How could they allow Carolien to leave the house and marry without permission? Even teahouse girls didn't just take off without the proper exchange of visits between the proprietress and the man's elders. Carolien's behavior was worse than that of a prostitute or concubine. When she heard Po Han in the dining room, Ocho brought him breakfast. Pouring his coffee with an unsteady hand, she spilled onto the saucer.

Po Han touched his grandmother's arm. "Please try to understand. Carolien makes me happy. I don't want a housekeeper, I want a wife."

Ocho pulled away from him. "You had a choice of many girls. Good families. But you have to choose some useless woman whose head is filled with Dutch nonsense." Her voice broke as she took two pork buns out of the bamboo steamer and placed them on Po Han's plate. "I just hope I'll stay around long enough to take care of you."

Po Han pushed his plate away. "If only you'd listen–"

At the short blast of a claxon in front of the house he rose. "That's Jaap. He's picking me up. He's my witness." Po Han grabbed the handle of a small leather suitcase sitting on the floor by his chair. He stood for a moment, the suitcase dangling against his side, then rushed out of the room.

Standing in the doorway, Ocho watched Po Han hurry toward the waiting car. Tears streamed down her wrinkled cheeks. "You'll regret this," she whispered. "You'll regret marrying a woman who doesn't know when rice turns to porridge."

***

Carolien spotted Po Han as soon as he entered the foyer of the courthouse. Dressed in her white linen two-piece suit, she stood between William Wachter and his wife. Her employer, after hearing about the situation with her family, had agreed to give her away.

Po Han took Carolien's hands. "You're much too beautiful to be the wife of a typewriter salesman," he said.

"This is just the beginning." Carolien smiled behind a short voile veil and puckered her lips to form a kiss, something she had never done before in public, but she felt bold and reckless. She knew the Dutch kissed each other like this.

After they completed their civil wedding vows, a Dutch judge declared Po Han and Carolien man and wife. As a token of his appreciation for the years of Carolien's service, William Wachter hosted a luncheon for the small party at the nearby Hotel Homan, one of two upscale hotels in Bandung's Dutch business district.

A handful of mutual friends showered the newlyweds with grains of rice. Carolien leaned over to Po Han and, smiling, flicked a few grains off his jacket. "There's one good thing about my mother not being here," she whispered. "She'd have a fit if she saw all the rice wasted on the ground."

***

After the wedding festivities Carolien and Po Han drove toward Lembang, a small resort town outside of Bandung, in a car loaned to them by Mr. Wachter. Carolien let out a deep sigh and rested her head against Po Han's shoulder as he steered the car.

"I think we've announced ourselves enough," Po Han said. Laughing, he pulled the Wolsley over to the curb and got out of the car to remove the string of empty cans their friends had tied to the rear bumper.

Carolien slid across the seat and swung her legs out of the car as Po Han took out his pocketknife. He was tall for a Chinese man. She hoped that if they had a son he would look like Po Han.

"There." Po Han threw the string of empty cans in the trunk and they resumed their drive.

They were not far from Nanna's house. Carolien pressed her head into the hollow of Po Han's shoulder and closed her eyes. She was on her honeymoon, with a husband she loved and who loved her in return. Their marriage was going to be different from the dutiful union of other Chinese couples. Po Han was right. There was no need to keep fretting about her family's misgivings. Carolien reached up and kissed him on the cheek.

The Lembang Mountain Resort lay nestled in a grove of pine trees close to the crater of Tangkuban Prahu. Po Han shifted gears several times as they passed vegetable and dairy farms tucked between stretches of rice paddies along the winding road. A light breeze carried a whiff of sulphur and Carolien wrinkled her nose.

They walked into the large lobby holding hands. Native waiters, gracefully balancing trays of cool drinks, moved barefoot across the shiny tile floor. Bamboo shades filtered the blazing light of the tropical afternoon sun. Several Dutch guests carried on lively conversations. Carolien met their curious glances without hesitation.

The Dutch clerk frowned when the couple stepped up to the marble counter. "Do you have reservations?"

"Oh yes." Carolien smiled. "We're Mr. and Mrs. Lee. Mr. Wachter made the reservation." At the mention of her employer's name the desk clerk's manner changed.

"Ah, of course. Here you are." He reached behind him for the room key.

A native porter clad in a forest green uniform showed Po Han and Carolien to their room. The Western décor gave the room a feeling of unfamiliar luxury.

Carolien walked over to a window overlooking the gardens. In passing, she ran a hand over the hibiscus print bedspread on the teak double bed. Tonight, she and Po Han would sleep in this bed. Blushing, she sat down in one of the plantation chairs by the window.

"Mr. and Mrs. Lee, how do you like the sound of that?" Po Han pulled Carolien into an embrace.

"I like it. I like it a lot." Carolien looked up into Po Han's beaming face. She brought her arms around his neck and sank into the intimacy of their first private moment. Unable to sort out the torrent of new emotions that Po Han's searching hands evoked, she followed the waves of her own impulses until she noticed that they were standing in front of the open window. "Oh, my God!" she cried. Jumping out of Po Han's arms, she pointed at the window.

"It's okay. We're married, you know," Po Han laughed.

Carolien smoothed the skirt of her suit. "Let's unpack. We might have time for a walk around the grounds before dinner."

Po Han opened their suitcases. Grinning, they hung their clothes in the same closet and put their toiletries on the vanity. Carolien's cheeks flushed when she touched the smooth silk of her nightgown and she quickly placed her undergarments and nightclothes into a separate drawer.

They spent the rest of the afternoon strolling through the manicured gardens. Po Han couldn't take enough photos of Carolien and agreed to anything she suggested they do. "As long as I have something worthwhile to photograph, I'll go anywhere you want to go." Later, standing in front of the open window of their room, he said, "I like sharing what I see. Colors, shapes, the way light moves across objects, filters through leaves. Would you be happy as the wife of a photographer?"

"I'd be your happy wife whatever you do." Carolien put an arm around Po Han's waist. She hesitated before adding, "But how do you find a job as a photographer? Will you be able to make enough money to support us?"

It didn't bother her when Po Han said, "I don't know."

After dinner, they took turns using the bathroom to change. Po Han went first. He returned to the bedroom wearing a smoking jacket over his pajamas.

"Your turn." Po Han tapped Carolien on the back in passing. She had taken off her shoes and stockings and stood barefoot by an open dresser drawer. She watched Po Han adjust the angle of the standing lamp and settle in one of the rattan chairs with a photography magazine before she eased into the bathroom.

Carolien took her time changing into the peach silk peignoir set she had bought for her honeymoon. Standing in front of the vanity mirror, she ran her hands down her sides and over her hips, luxuriating in the feel of the smooth silk. The saleslady was right, the color did make her complexion glow.

Po Han looked up when Carolien returned to the bedroom. Without taking his eyes off her, he put his magazine on the table.

Carolien's heartbeat quickend and her body tensed as he came toward her, his touch warm and firm. Their first lovemaking moved quickly from a gentle curiosity into a passionate release of the past year's unfulfilled needs.

***

On the last morning of their honeymoon, Po Han suggested a hike to the rim of the crater. Morning fog shrouded the path winding through thick verdurous growth to Tangkuban Prahu's peak. The vegetation thinned as they climbed higher and their footing changed from stamped dirt to rock. The scent of sulphur permeated the air. At the crater's rim, Carolien held onto Po Han's arm. The cracked earth of the crater's floor, far below them, gurgled and spit mud.

"Look! Isn't it beautiful how the light is working its way through and settling on the crater walls?" Po Han reached for his camera.

Carolien let go of him and walked a short distance away. She looked into the crater's mouth. Crags and sulphur deposits in the crater wall had formed skeleton-like faces and they reminded her of Ocho. Carolien shuddered. The thought of living with the old woman frightened her, but she knew there was no way around it. Ocho had raised Po Han after his parents died during a cholera outbreak and he was her only kin.

Perhaps their decision to have her quit work wasn't wise. Going to an office would have kept her away from Ocho for most of the day. Maybe that was more important than proving to her family that Po Han could support her, and proving to Ocho that she was a good housewife. They were up against so much, but she was determined to prove those who doubted them wrong.

The wind fanned a fresh whiff of sulphur across the terrain. Carolien walked back to Po Han who lay on the edge of the crater rim looking through his camera lens. She dropped a hand loosely on his shoulder. "Han, how's Ocho going to take the change?" Thus far Po Han had been able to ease her anxiety about the situation, telling her that everything would work out, but right now she wasn't so sure.

Po Han got on his feet. "Ocho will have to make some adjustments. It might be hard for her at first, but when she sees how happy you make me, she'll be okay." Po Han put an arm around Carolien and squeezed her shoulder. The sun broke through the fog and the day began to turn warm and clear.

"Do you mind having a Dutch meal mid-week and on Sundays?" Carolien searched Po Han's face.

"I'll eat what comes to the table," Po Han smiled. "Ocho usually cooks Chinese or Malay food. I don't think she's ever had a real Dutch meal." He paused and laughed. "She'll find out one is never too old for new experiences."

"You said I could change things around the house if I wanted to, and we don't have to keep the maid around on Sunday afternoons, right? It would be nice to have some time just to ourselves, without servants hovering all the time. Of course, I'd talk to Ocho first—and when the maid is gone, you and I will take care of dinner and the dishes."

"Do whatever you want. You're the queen and the house is your palace." Po Han soothed Carolien's apprehension.

"Thanks." Carolien picked up a rock embedded with sulphur and turned the bright yellow streaks toward the sun. "I'd like having Dutch food twice a week," she said. "It's good practice for when we go to Holland."

"Holland?" Po Han picked up the tripod. "Holland? Why would we go to Holland?"

"Oh, I don't know. I just assumed we'd go there someday, when you're a famous photographer." Carolien brushed some sand off her skirt. "Don't you want to go?"

"If the opportunity arises, sure."

That afternoon they went swimming. Jumping into the pool next to Carolien, Po Han declared, "I want children, lots of children. I grew up alone and don't want that for my child. Can you imagine how much fun it will be to watch a small you-and-me grow into herself?"

"Herself?" Carolien laughed. "Don't you want a son?"

"Not especially. Sons or daughters, they're welcome. All I want is for us to be a happy family."

Carolien smiled. She pushed off the wall and moved through the water on the cadence of Po Han's words. How many men would be happy with a girl child? Her family was wrong about Po Han, she was sure of it.

CHAPTER 3

As they turned into the narrow street, Carolien reached for Po Han's hand on the steering wheel. She noticed how closely together the houses were built, only a narrow yard separating them from the street. It wasn't like Nanna's neighborhood, with lush gardens and large homes.

"Here we are." Po Han brought the car to a halt in front of the house.

"Han?" Carolien moved closer to the window and looked for movement behind the sheer curtains.

"Don't worry." Po Han leaned over and kissed her. "Everything will be all right." He jumped out of the car and came to Carolien's side to help her. She slipped her hand into his as they walked to the front door.

Po Han gave the doorbell two short taps before unlocking the door. Even though it was afternoon, the windows of the living room were closed. Last week's unread papers lay scattered on the coffee table, the ashtrays were full.

A young native woman entered the living room and brought a waft of pungent spices with her. *"Tuan Muda!"* She shot Carolien a curious glance and smiled. *"Njonja Muda!"*

Carolien realized she would no longer be addressed as *Non*, the Malay word for miss. She now was *Njonja Muda*, young mistress. Ocho was *Njonja Besar*, grand mistress, like Nanna.

"Where is *Njonja Besar?*" Po Han asked the maid in Malay.

"Njonja Besar is in the kitchen." The maid stepped aside to let the couple pass.

Carolien followed Po Han to the kitchen.

"We're home!" Po Han gave Carolien an encouraging nudge in her back. "What are you cooking? It sure smells good in here!"

Carolien moved next to Po Han and raised her clasped hands to her face in Chinese greeting. "Ocho, you look busy. Can I help?" Her Malay was stilted and she felt awkward. Turning to Po Han she switched into Dutch. "Let me change into a housedress. I'd like to help."

Ocho, sitting on a footstool in front of two charcoal stoves, looked up from a sputtering pot and eyed Po Han. "You've been gone for a week," she said, wiping perspiration from her forehead. "I thought I'd better cook you a nice meal. God only knows what you ate." She glared at Carolien before returning her attention to the pots on the stoves.

"As a matter of fact, I ate quite well. They had an excellent chef at the hotel," Po Han said, and ushered Carolien out of the kitchen.

Carolien looked up at Po Han. "You said she'd be happy to have you married, but she has never said a kind word to me. Why does Ocho dislike me so much?"

"Don't worry." Po Han closed their bedroom door and swung a suitcase on the bed. "Give her some time. She's never been around someone like you. The Chinese girls she knows are the dull type–the kind that don't have an opinion and only talk about the amount of spices to put into a dish." He pulled Carolien into an embrace. "I'm sure glad you're not like that."

After they unpacked and changed, Po Han said, "Let's go into the livingroom. It might be better to leave Ocho to herself for a while."

Carolien opened the windows and fresh air swirled into the room. Looking across the narrow weed strewn green strip between the house and the sidewalk, she couldn't help think of Nanna's house where the livingroom windows looked over manicured lawns and flower beds and the street, at the end of a long driveway, was hidden behind a hedge of tall oleanders. The only color here came from an unwieldy blooming poinsettia growing in a corner near the gate. Carolien suppressed a sigh and, feeling guilty, turned away from the window.

Po Han was looking through stacks of mail and Carolien began to straighten up the room. She was just about finished when the maid came and announced that dinner was ready.

The center of the round dining room table was covered with several dishes. A large bowl of steaming rice sat on the side. Po Han pulled a chair for Carolien then sat down in the one next to her.

"Thank you." She looked at him, smiling. Would any other Chinese husband treat her like that?

"Han, hand me your plate." Ocho's voice jarred Carolien out of her dreamy mode. She watched Ocho serve Po Han and quietly took the plates that were passed in her direction. The food was much spicier than she was used to, each bite set her tongue on fire.

Po Han noticed her predicament. "I'm sorry, I should have told you, Ocho and I like hot food." Turning to Ocho he said, "The food is really good, but perhaps you can tone the heat down a bit until Carolien is used to it?"

"Please, don't bother," Carolien said. "I'll be fine." She lowered her eyes under Ocho's gaze.

"Huh! All the years I fed you, now you're telling me to change the way I cook?"

"No…" Po Han shifted uncomfortably in his chair.

"I'll be fine." Carolien put a hand on his arm. Turning to Ocho she said, "Please don't change anything. I don't mean to be a bother."

Ocho pushed her chair back, scraping the floor, and left the room.

That evening they turned in early. The light of a utility pole made patterns on a wall of the dark bedroom. Lying next to Po Han, Carolien listened to his even breathing. His cigarette breath tickled her nostrils. The first day in her new home hadn't gone the way she had hoped. Still, they'd make their future together, she'd see to that. Po Han reached for her in his sleep and she nestled against him.

The next day Carolien saw Po Han off to work at the front gate. He had to return the car. Leaning into the open window, Carolien said, "I'll try to save as much as I can, so one day we'll have our own car."

"Do we need one?" Po Han ran a hand across her cheek and smiled.

After Carolien waved a last goodbye she returned to the house. She went into the kitchen to discuss the meals and order of the day with Ocho.

Stooped in front of the charcoal stoves, Ocho stirred several simmering pots. A young maid chopped onions at the cluttered counter. Every so often she wiped her tearing eyes against a sleeve of her blouse.

"Ocho, you're already cooking? I just came to see if you'd like to plan dinner with me." Carolien lingered in the doorway staring at Ocho's narrow stiff back.

Ocho remained silent.

Carolien began to stack the dirty breakfast dishes strewn on the counter and tried again. "What are you making? Can I help?"

Ocho dropped the ladle against the side of the pan. "How can you expect meat to have flavor and be tender at dinnertime if you still have to figure what to cook while the sun is already high in the sky?"

Carolien bit her lower lip. She left the kitchen and wandered through the house. Po Han had told her that there were only two maids, one to do the laundry, and the other to clean the house and help Ocho in the kitchen. Still, the house wasn't that big. She couldn't find any reason for the messy state it was in.

Carolien collected pages of the morning paper Po Han had left scattered on different tables. An article about schools caught her attention. Private schools now required government permission to operate, and factions of the Volksraad–the native representation in the Dutch government– were protesting against the new ruling. Carolien frowned and put the papers away. It seemed that the native independence movement gained momentum every day. She wondered what Chip and Ting would have to say about the article. Thinking about her family was so painful that Carolien quickly shut down her thoughts. She gathered several ashtrays and took them to the kitchen.

"Why are you bringing ashtrays to the kitchen? Minnie is too busy to clean ashtrays." Rummaging through the spice drawer, Ocho snapped at the native woman, "Hurry up, I need those onions. When you're finished, I want you to string the beans." She slapped a lid on a simmering pot and finished under her breath, "Crazy Dutch nonsense. Who's ever heard of washing ashtrays?"

Carolien felt like screaming. Instead she washed the ashtrays herself and, when Po Han returned home later that day, she did not say anything about the incident. Despite Ocho's obvious dislike for her, Carolien was determined to win Ocho over, one way or another.

***

Since Ocho did not allow her to help with the meals, Carolien filled her mornings with sewing. She made drapes and curtains for the living room windows and new slipcovers for the pillows on the rattan couch. When they were ready, she hired a painter. The walls had turned a dingy yellow and gave off a stale odor from years of absorbing tobacco smoke.

Carolien stood by the furniture that had been moved into the center of the living room and covered with old sheets. A morning breeze came through the wide-open windows. She couldn't wait to clean the room, put everything in its place, and bring out her new window coverings and slipcovers. She tied a scarf around her hair and went into the back of the house looking for the maids.

Sari, the laundry maid, stood by the clotheslines. Carolien reached into the basket of wrung out laundry and, fastening a pillowcase to the line, she said, "When we're done here, I'd like you to help me clean up the livingroom."

A frown spread across Sari's face. "I've a lot of ironing to do. Yesterday, *Njonja Besar* changed her linens and I didn't get to *Tuan's* trousers." She adjusted a few clothespins on one of Ocho's sarongs.

"Don't worry about the master's trousers. I'll tell him I needed you to help me. He'll be happy to come home to a nice living room," Carolien said. She handed Sari the empty basket, and started back toward the house.

In the kitchen, Minnie was washing pots and pans. "Please come to the living room when you're done with those," Carolien said. "I'm doing a big cleaning in there and need your help." When the native woman looked skittishly at Ocho, Carolien added, "I want to have the room in order before *Tuan* comes home." Turning to Ocho, she asked, "What else, besides washing those pans, does Minnie have to do?"

"Nothing, I guess she can go help you now. I don't want my grandson to come home to the mess you made."

Carolien chuckled under her breath. For once, she and Ocho agreed.

That evening, while they ate their dessert fruit, Carolien presented her housekeeping calendar to Po Han and Ocho. Peeling a mango for Po

Han, she said, "I hope the menus I made up are acceptable."

"Ours will be the most efficiently run household in the archipel." Po Han gestured to Carolien's notes, "I bet not even Dutch households could hold up to this."

Carolien blushed but Ocho remained silent.

"Aren't you happy that you don't have to worry about planning meals anymore?" Po Han turned to his grandmother.

"Why?" Ocho's fork made a sharp clink on her plate. "There's nothing to it, especially now that you're earning a good salary. Even when I had to sell pastries and do laundry for the Dutch soldiers, I managed. Only girls with a useless Dutch upbringing need a piece of paper to bring food to the table."

Carolien placed the plate with mango slices by Po Han. "Here you are," she said stiffly.

"Thanks." Po Han pressed Carolien's hand and ate his fruit.

"My grandson is not used to meals that are a mere snack of tasteless potatoes and a sliver of meat." Ocho reached for the chewing pouch she carried in the folds of her cummerbund and began rolling a wad of betel leaves, tobacco and chalk. "If that's all you can prepare, I better continue to take care of his meals." She looked around the room. "Where on earth is my spittoon?" When she couldn't find the copper pot she stomped out of the room, slamming the door behind her.

"I put it out of sight." Carolien grimaced. "I really don't like to have a bowl of spit sitting around, especially not while we're eating." She reached across the table for the dirty dishes and stacked them. Scraping a serving platter, she said, "I thought you liked Dutch food."

"I do." Po Han took the serving spoon out of Carolien's hand and placed it in the bowl. "I'm sorry." He closed his arms around her rigid body. "It's going to be rough for a while. Ocho's not used to having another woman around, especially not someone with your energy and efficiency."

Carolien gave in to Po Han's calming touch. Relaxing against him she wondered how it had been for Sue. Her sister had never complained about her in-laws. She had most likely simply followed their established routines. Carolien sighed. "I'll try to stay out of Ocho's way," she said, stepping out of Po Han's embrace. "I'll just leave the meals to her, except for Sundays when she goes out to play mah yong."

Minnie came in and removed the dirty dishes. Carolien could hear the shuffle of Ocho's slippers through the open dining room door.

Po Han took Carolien's hand and ushered her toward the door. "Let's enjoy our sparkling living room. I can't believe that this is the same room and the same furniture." He walked around the room beaming.

Carolien forced a smile. Drawing the new curtains, she asked, "Han, when do you think we can move?"

"Move? Why would we move?"

Carolien sighed. She could not bring herself to tell Po Han that she wanted to move out of their drab neighborhood. Instead, she turned on the radio. "Never mind, it was just a thought. Let's see if Radio Hilversum has something good to listen to," she said settling on the couch.

***

On the wings of the winds that cross the Pacific, the World Depression drifted to the Dutch East Indies. As the calendar turned to 1933, most businesses were forced to shrink their operations. With money tight and rumors of an oncoming war, the demand for new typewriters dropped. The size of Po Han's paychecks continued to decrease. With mounting anxiety, Carolien anticipated the day they would cease completely.

On the last day of August Carolien's fears came true. Po Han entered the living room where she sat reading on the couch. "I've been laid off," he said.

Carolien placed her bookmark before closing her book. "What are we going to do?" She stared at Po Han, pressing her fingertips against her lips.

"It's okay." Po Han took Carolien's hands.

"How can you say that?" Carolien pulled out of Po Han's grip. It would be hard for Po Han to find another job. Many companies were letting people go. Would her family's predictions come true after all? She had managed to make do with the smaller paychecks, but now they'd have no income at all.

"They used my highest earnings of the last five years to calculate my severance check–that comes to roughly six months' pay, during the good times." Po Han dropped on his knees. "Don't you see?" He squeezed Carolien's hands. "This is my chance to try making it as a professional photographer." He pulled Carolien towards him and closed his arms around her. "Don't worry. Everything will be all right."

Swayed by Po Han's optimism and her own desire to prove her family wrong, Carolien agreed when he used his severance money to add to his collection of cameras and lenses. She overcame her inherent sense of order when he converted the pantry into a darkroom and set up an easel in the living room. During the next weeks, Carolien coaxed her insecurity into a trusting acceptance. With great anticipation she watched Po Han as he spent his days capturing images and his nights developing the rolls of film. Po Han's entries in the monthly contest sponsored by the local photographer's association often took first prize. When *The Java Bode*, a regional paper, featured him as a promising up-and-coming photographer, Carolien and Po Han pored over the article.

"You were right all along." Carolien smiled. "I'm going to start a folder of your reviews." She walked to her desk and came back with a pair of scissors. "You think you'll be selling any of these photographs soon?" Po Han was talented, even the Dutch critics said so. All he needed was a chance.

"I hope so. Jaap Vermeer and Ito Nakamura said I could hang work in their studios. They also promised to let me know if they need help in the darkroom or the store." Po Han lit a cigarette.

When the passing days turned into weeks, and then into months without notification of a sale, Carolien's doubts returned. The balance of their savings account continued to decrease. One night, after dinner, she suggested Po Han stop taking photographs for a while and try the job market again.

"I have to keep producing if I want to keep people's attention on my work." Po Han paced the floor of the living room. "People are getting to know me. After I was written up in the last national photography bulletin, you said yourself that I'm on my way."

He is right, Carolien thought. Not producing would move the spotlight away from him. There was a Dutch photographer who lived in

Nanna's neighborhood. People passed his house with a curious reverence. Once Po Han succeeded, he would be earning a lucrative living and her family would have to admit that they were wrong. She'd just have to stick it out. Life beckoned Po Han in a peculiar way and she watched him race toward it, capturing its shapes, shades, and substance on miles of film.

***

On a chilly November morning, a good three months after Po Han was laid off, Ocho rummaged through the kitchen. She blamed the bare shelves on Carolien's inability to run a household properly. Po Han had told her that he no longer worked for the typewriter store. Instead, he said, he was going to work as a freelance photographer.

Ocho didn't quite understand what that meant, but this new job seemed to make him happy and that was all she cared about.

She opened and closed a few empty containers. No flour to make snacks, no sweet sticky rice either. The can she usually kept raw shrimp chips in held only an odor. Frustrated, Ocho banged around a few pots and pans. She reached into her cummerbund and took out her money pouch. She didn't have enough to go to the market.

Ocho stomped into the living room and confronted Carolien. "Aside from a crock of rice and a half-empty can of sugar, there's nothing to prepare a meal with." Carolien continued sorting old magazines and Ocho took a seat on the rattan lounge. She watched Carolien tidy the room. Why did Carolien always think up ways to make life more difficult? Why did she have to make such a fuss over a bit of dust?

"There are leftovers from the meat stew you made yesterday. We could get some vegetables when the vendor comes by," Carolien said, starting to dust the small bureau.

Ocho smothered a cough. Clearing her throat, she started to leave. By the door, she said over her shoulder, "Since you got rid of the maid, you'd better mop the floors. One could stick to them!" She didn't care what the floors looked like, but she took pleasure in upsetting Carolien.

"If I wanted to be a household slave, I would have been one in my mother's house!" Carolien shouted and slammed the lid of the bureau shut.

"Perhaps that's where you should have stayed." Ocho walked out of the room. Unbeknownst to Po Han and Carolien, she had jewelry and several socks filled with guilders that she had saved and hidden in her mattress.

A few weeks later, when Carolien announced that the monthly budget only allowed for fried eggs over steamed rice, Ocho dipped into her reserves to buy the fixings for an elaborate dinner. She watched Po Han enjoy the meal. Serving him another portion of braised fish, she said, "All you need to know is how to shop. And, of course, you do need to know how to cook."

Ocho knew that Po Han never worried about money but that Carolien kept a close accounting of their funds. Carolien's raised eyebrows at the sight of the dinner had not escaped Ocho. She knew she'd better be careful lest she be found out. Yet she could not resist the temptation to deliver a sly stab. "But since there are no children," she said, "I guess being able to cook is not that important."

Carolien winced while Po Han took a sip of water. Ocho suppressed a smile. She knew that it was neither through Carolien's calculations nor Po Han's precautions that a baby had not been conceived.

While the couple was on their honeymoon Ocho had visited a *dukun*. "I need to prevent the useless woman who seduced my grandson from carrying his seed," she told the native sorceress. After Ocho had spoken the words, the smoke of the incense kettle billowed and the *dukun* burst into a clattering laugh that sounded like a stack of plates smashing on a tile floor. The *dukun's* price amounted to almost a full sock of silver guilders. Ocho had been reluctant to part with so much of her savings, but she didn't dare bargain with the black magic witch.

Ocho hurried home with a cloth doll that had a rock in its stomach, which she was to sew into the couple's mattress. The *dukun* had also given her the names of several fruits and vegetables that would prevent anything from lodging inside Carolien's womb.

During the months following her visit to the *dukun*, Ocho had listened with interest to Carolien's frequent complaints of stomach cramps. Ocho considered the money she paid the *dukun* well spent, when, after seeing the doctor, Carolien said she apparently had a hard time becoming pregnant.

"I warned you," Ocho said to Po Han, chewing her wad of tobacco and betel leaves. "She's useless. She won't be able to bear you sons."

"I don't care about having sons. It's Carolien's health I worry about," Po Han said.

"All I want for you is what every man deserves, a good woman and sons to bear his name. If you want to hold that against me, I'll just have to carry your wrath to my grave."

"It's okay," Po Han rubbed Ocho's shoulders. "I'm not interested in a son, but I should know that *you* want a great-grandson. I'll make sure that one day you'll have one."

***

Perched on top of one of the low brick gateposts, Ocho swung her legs and rocked back and forth. The afternoon breeze cooled her burning cheeks. She brought the half-empty bottle of beer to her lips and took a swig. The amber liquid was her only relief from the insecurity she always felt around Carolien.

Ocho rolled herself a chewing wad. The sharp juices of the betel leaves stung her sinuses and filled her mouth with saliva. For a moment the piercing sensation burned away her gnawing fear that the *dukun's* spell would wear off. She pursed her lips and squirted angry spurts of red spit onto the sidewalk.

A *delman* turned into the street. Ocho slipped off the pillar and stumbled into the house. The bamboo blinds that kept the afternoon sun out were still down. Her room was cool in the filtered light.

Ocho peeked through the slats of the blinds. The horse-drawn carriage was pulling away from the curb and Carolien walked up the driveway with several shopping bags hanging from her arms.

Ocho retreated farther into her room. She noticed that the tablet calendar on the wall displayed the number five. That's why Carolien had gone shopping. It was the fifth of December, the Dutch holiday that acknowledges the birth of St. Nick with presents and special food.

That evening, as they lingered at the table after dinner, Carolien passed a cookie tray filled with *speculaas*. The scent of the crisp spice cookies mingled with the rich steam of hot chocolate and filled the room with a cozy aroma.

"It's too bad Sinterklaas didn't have any reason to stop by this house." Ocho referred to the Dutch belief that during the night of December fourth, St. Nick leaves presents for children who set out a shoe filled with grass clippings and carrots, along with a bowl of water for his white stallion.

"What do you mean? Where do you think these delicious cookies came from?" Po Han joked, but shot Ocho a warning glance.

Carolien smoothed the tablecloth with a forced smile. "Who would like another cup of hot chocolate?"

Ocho dropped half a cookie on her saucer. "No more for me." She reached for the small pouch where she carried the fixings for her chews. "I need something more potent." She looked around the room. "Where did my spitting crock go?"

Carolien rose and left the room.

"Why, why do you always have to keep poking?" Po Han walked over to the window and lit a cigarette.

"I'm not poking at anything. Since you've been with that woman you've nothing good to say anymore." Ocho pouted. "Tell me what she's good for. She can't keep the shelves stocked. She can't cook. Her womb won't hold your seed. I wonder how much pleasure she gives you." Ocho peered at Po Han's rigid back. She wished he'd turn around so she could see his face and read his thoughts.

***

In the kitchen Carolien leaned into the counter, feeling dizzy. She had visited her gynecologist earlier that day. After the elderly Dutch physician examined her he said, "This time, you did it. You will have to be careful, but I'm confident that you'll be able to pull through. Congratulations!"

Recalling her doctor's visit, Carolien felt an almost choking excitement. If only she could just be happy. But there was Ocho and their financial situation. Carolien moved a hand over her stomach. It was still hard to believe that she was carrying a child. She had to make sure that he was well provided for. Carolien took a deep breath and returned to the dining room.

"Where's my spitting crock? Didn't you hear me ask for my spitting crock?" Ocho asked as soon as Carolien entered the room.

"I didn't bring it." Carolien walked to the middle of the room and, shifting her eyes from Ocho to Po Han, she continued. "I brought something else."

Po Han snuffed his cigarette in a nearby ashtray.

"I have another gift. One that could not be wrapped." Carolien had not felt so calm in a long time.

Po Han pulled her into his arms. "Holding you is a gift," he whispered in her hair.

Carolien placed a hand against his chest and moved away. She met Ocho's disapproving glare and said, "I am pregnant."

Po Han's face lit up like fireworks on Chinese New Year. "Are you sure?" He grabbed Carolien by the shoulders. "Did the doctor tell you?"

"Yes, I've had lab tests and the doctor examined me. He said it's certain." Carolien looked up at Po Han and saw the man she had fallen in love with two years ago. He had the same exuberance as back then, when he talked about their life together.

"But I'm scared. How are we going to take care of a child when we can barely hold our own heads above water?" Tears ran down her cheeks. "I'm sorry, I really meant for this to be a happy time." She wiped her face with the back of her hands.

"I can't believe it. You're carrying a life that came from us." Po Han squeezed Carolien in his arms before turning to Ocho. "Carolien is pregnant. Your great-grandchild is on its way." His voice was filled with excitement.

Ocho turned pale. She gave Carolien a hard glare and shuffled out of the room, slamming the door behind her.

Po Han's jaws tightened as his grandmother left the room, disappointment and pain filled his eyes. Carolien rested her head against his chest and said, "It doesn't matter what anyone else thinks, as long as you're happy about the baby."

That night, as Carolien fastened the flaps of the mosquito netting around their bed, Po Han lay back against the pillows. "I can't wait to show our child everything there is to see," he said. "All the colors and all the shapes that surround us."

"You'll have to find a job so we have an income we can count on." Carolien fastened the last tie and added, "Our son will have to go to Dutch schools and that will cost a lot of money." She pulled her legs to her chest and rested her chin on her knees while she searched Po Han's face.

Po Han pulled Carolien into the crook of his arm and stroked her hair. "What makes you so sure the baby will be a boy?" He chuckled and added, "I wouldn't mind if it's a girl. A happy little girl who smiles a lot; the way you used to smile in the park with the sun dancing on your face."

Carolien didn't answer. Was it only two years ago that she had been filled with such hope and trust in the future? Did Po Han remember that time and, like her, sometimes felt it was lost forever? Carolien pulled out of Po Han's embrace. "The baby will be a boy." She turned on her side clutching her roll pillow. "I will prove the old hag wrong."

Po Han stroked Carolien's cheek and caught a tear before it rolled down her face. "I will do anything I can to make sure our child is happy." Po Han leaned over Carolien's shoulder. "If needed, I will accept work in any trade." He tucked her hair behind an ear and eased Carolien onto her back. That night, their lovemaking was tender and hopeful.

If anything is going to make Po Han responsible, it will be the baby, Carolien thought before being carried away by sleep.

***

Nanna heard the gate creak and looked up from sorting a bag of mung beans. Her heart skipped a beat. That was Carolien walking slowly toward the house. During the long hours of picking through beans or rice, Nanna's thoughts drifted frequently to her youngest child. What could it be that brought her energetic impatient daughter home? Carolien would not be defeated by hardship. What was it that slowed her? She usually moved with a quick secure stride.

"Ma." Carolien came up the last porch step and raised her folded hands in greeting.

Nanna grasped an arm of the bench as she rose. Carolien was not alone. Now that she stood close to her daughter, Nanna felt the vibrations of new life. Carolien was pregnant.

"Come, sit down." Nanna was concerned about the unhappiness her daughter appeared to be wrapped in while new life grew inside her. "Is it being with child that brings you home?" A hint of surprise in Carolien's eyes was quickly replaced by the comforting calm of knowing.

"Yes. You have a new grandchild coming." Carolien rested a hand over her stomach.

The information lay like a yoke between them until Nanna lifted her end. "Go inside and tell your sister," she said. "Your brothers should be home soon." She cinched up the bag of beans and pushed it under the bench. Carolien was pregnant and, regardless of her past actions, the family now needed to stand by her.

Nanna straightened herself and rubbed her lower back, bending over was getting harder. Walking into the house, she anticipated the family's reaction. Sue wouldn't give her any problem, but she expected resistance from Chip and Ting. Her sons would regard their sister's pregnancy as unwise and would not be supportive. She didn't like going against their wishes.

At the altar, Nanna lit a bunch of incense sticks and wondered where the supposed progress of Western ways would lead them.

When her sons had moved the family into this house and provided her with all the amenities a Dutch family enjoyed, she had seen the Dutch lifestyle as a way to make life easier, better. She enjoyed the electric lighting, running water and flush toilets, refrigerator and gas stove. She had allowed Carolien and her grandchildren to attend a Dutch school. She had permitted Carolien to work in a Dutch office.

Nanna moved the incense sticks up and down in front of her face, then held the offering high over her head and gazed into the gray spirals. Was she being punished for allowing Dutch influences to penetrate her household? If so, what other misfortune would come to her and the family? Would the gods punish Carolien for thinking that a woman might be better off if she were not so dependent on her family or husband?

Nanna placed the burning incense in the urns. Voices came from the back of the house. Through the sheer curtains she saw Sue and Carolien coming toward the dining room. Carolien's slender figure, Western dress, and hairdo accentuated Sue's matronly figure and native dress. "Lien, greet your father and ask the spirits to bless your child," Nanna said when they entered.

Carolien lit a bundle of incense sticks. Nanna hoped Carolien would actually reach out for the spirits, but she knew her children didn't share her beliefs.

A little later, still apprehensive about her sons' reaction to Carolien's visit, Nanna took her place at the dinner table. Chip and Ting acknowledged their sister's presence with a brief hello, then carried on a conversation about the arrest of Sukarno, Hatta, and Shahrir, leaders of a radical native group that promoted Indonesian independence from the Dutch. The rest of the family listened quietly. Every so often one of the teenagers threw Carolien a curious glance. It was as if time had not moved.

"Does your husband know you're here?" Chip asked Carolien.

"I hadn't planned to come." Carolien speared a piece of pork with her fork. "But I will tell Po Han I went to tell my family about my pregnancy."

"Oh!" Sue brought her napkin to her mouth. Eddie, Emma, and Els gasped while Chip and Ting exchanged glances.

"I hope that being a father will motivate him to find stable employment," Chip said.

Ting reached for the rice bowl. Emma jumped up and served her uncle as Sue spooned another serving of stew onto his plate. "What has your husband been doing since his company closed down?" Ting asked.

Nanna caught the expression on Carolien's face. She leaned forward in her chair, and said, "It's a better use of time to think about your sister and her baby than to worry about what a stranger is doing." Chip and Ting busied themselves with their food and Carolien shot her mother a grateful look.

A few days later Nanna visited the Chinese temple. After making her offering of incense sticks she asked the priest to select a boy's and a girl's name. The priest in turn looked to the gods for advice. After burning more incense sticks and shuffling a stack of red papers with names written on it, he folded two pieces and handed them to Nanna. She kept the sacred information on her altar until the time came for Carolien to give birth.

***

Ocho watched grimly as the baby grew inside Carolien over the next few months. Once again, she decided to seek help from a *dukun*.

"Please, help me," she begged the old native woman seated on a woven bamboo mat in the middle of the small, dank room. "I need to prevent the birth of a child that will be a threat to my life." Ocho sank to her knees. She brought her palms together and, touching her forehead with her thumbs, she bowed her head. "The woman who bears this child seduced my grandson and will use the child to turn him against me." The dampness of the dirt floor crept through her sarong and touched her knees. Ocho shivered.

The *dukun* placed a piece of myrrh onto the smoldering coals in the small earthen incense burner. "You want to snuff out a candle even before it has been lit?" she asked, speaking into the wafting smoke screen. She took a pinch of tobacco and a few betel leaves from a pouch she carried around her waist and rolled a chewing wad. For a while the only sounds were the crushing of betel leaves between the witch's stained teeth. The *dukun* reached for a copper bowl near her and spat into it. "Bring me all the beer and gin you'd normally drink during the next seven days and seven nights."

"Will you take the equivalent in money?" Ocho reached inside her cummerbund. "I could give it to you now."

"No." The witch grinned. "I want the alcohol. And remember, it's the amount you usually *drink*." She moved her chewing wad to the other side of her mouth and flung the bottom part of her shawl across her shoulder. "If you want what you asked for bad enough, it won't be a problem." She laughed and left the room.

During the next week Ocho was often tempted to open and replace one of the bottles she kept hidden in a crate under her bed, but fearing the *dukun's* curse she restrained herself. The lack of alcohol made her feel jittery. She stayed mostly in her room and indulged in an excessive amount of chews. Now and then she pulled out the crate and ran her unsteady hands over the cool bottles.

Ocho returned to the *dukun* with three bottles of gin and seven six-packs of beer. "Now add seven silver guilders to that and I'll make double-sure that the child won't be a thorn in your side." The *dukun* put a block of incense on the burner and took a seat in an old wicker chair.

Ocho sighed but reached into her chemise for the money. The *dukun* tucked the silver coins into her cummerbund, grinning.

Ocho came home from her secret visit with two rag dolls. The bigger doll had pins stuck all around its head and tamarind seeds inside its stomach. Its arms and legs were pieces of string. The smaller doll's head was wrapped in a piece of gauze and didn't have eyes. It was tied between the legs of the bigger doll. The *dukun* had instructed Ocho to place these dolls under Carolien's birthing bed, along with something Carolien was deathly afraid of.

Ocho knew Carolien was afraid of frogs. She remembered the day she had come from the market with a basket of frogs to make frogmeat stew. Carolien, taken by surprise, had run screaming out of the kitchen.

During the last days of Carolien's pregnancy, Ocho prepared for Carolien to give birth. In the market, she found the frog vendor and ordered a large bullfrog. "Yes," she said to the surprised native, "I know they're not edible. I still want a bullfrog, the largest you can find. I will pay you well for it."

A few days later, when she brought home a basket with a bullfrog jumping wildly in it, Ocho was ready.

***

Carolien watched Po Han putting the finishing touches on his mural. During the past two months he had transformed an entire wall of the room they were going to use as a nursery into a woodland scene from a fairy tale. Elves danced with gnomes on wide mushroom caps while baby birds peeked out of their nests. A family of deer grazed in a meadow. Bumblebees sat on fully opened flowers and butterflies fluttered around. A large rainbow held everything under a colorful halo. Po Han had let all of his playfulness and tender fantasies about the baby flow through his brushes onto the wall.

Carolien leaned against the doorjamb. She watched Po Han's lithe body and followed the movements of his brush as he applied the paint. If only Po Han could meet their financial needs, he would truly make her happy. Absorbed in his work, he seemed unaware of her presence.

"It's beautiful," Carolien exclaimed when Po Han finally turned around. "And it can be used to teach the baby colors and the names of animals. How clever of you to think up a picture like that."

"You give me too much credit." Po Han put an arm around Carolien. "I didn't have any usefulness in mind. I just wanted to give her something happy."

They were silent for a moment. Po Han dropped his arm and took Carolien's hand. "What makes you so sure the baby will be a boy?" he teased, swinging her hand back and forth. "What if it turns out to be a girl?"

"You really wouldn't mind?" Carolien shot Po Han a sideways glance.

"How many times do I have to tell you, I'd love to have a little girl."

"Really?" Carolien walked to the baby's dresser. "Whatever it is, we have to make sure it will have everything it needs."

Po Han followed Carolien and closed his arms around her from behind. "We have to make sure that she's happy," he said, nuzzling her hair. They looked at the dresser drawers filled with neatly stacked linens and clothes. Carolien was at the end of her pregnancy. Everything was in order.

CHAPTER 4

Carolien let go of the roll pillow she held pressed against her stomach and turned onto her back. She stretched one leg, then the other, trying to get comfortable. The baby filled her to bursting. Cramps had kept her awake most of the night. The bedding felt warm from the night's use. Next to her, Po Han breathed evenly in a deep sleep. She ran her fingers through his hair and whispered, "The baby's coming." It was close to five o'clock in the morning on August 8, 1934, a little more than two weeks past their second wedding anniversary.

Po Han threw off the light cover-sheet and jerked up. He swung his legs out of the bed, eying Carolien. "Are you hurting badly?"

Carolien forced a smile. "It's normal." A new cramp pierced her stomach and she winced. "We've got to get the bed ready." She grabbed Po Han's arm.

Po Han changed the bedding. He laid a large rubber sheet over the fresh linens and stacked heavy towels on it. Carolien followed him as he hurried to the kitchen.

In the kitchen, Ocho took a boiling kettle off the stove. "What's all the rush so early in the morning?" She glared at Carolien and poured the hot water into her coffee mug.

"Carolien's in labor. I've got to get the midwife." Po Han filled two caldrons with water. The wet bottoms sizzled when he set the pots on the charcoal stove. "Please make sure the fire stays on," he said to Ocho as he added more charcoal.

Carolien walked to the living room, leaning heavily on Po Han's arm. "Please, be back soon."

"I'll be back as soon as I can." Po Han held Carolien tight before running out of the house. Through the open window she watched him disappear into the street, whistling for a *delman*.

Carolien tried to ignore Ocho who came into the room and stood staring at her. She paced the floor, holding a pillow pressed against her stomach. From time to time the cramps knocked her, gasping, against a wall.

"Why don't you lie down for a while?" Ocho took Carolien by the elbow and walked her to the couch. She fluffed a few pillows. "Just lie down. I'm going to see if the windows in your room are open and fill your water carafe."

Carolien lay writhing on the couch. It was as if someone were twisting a knife inside her stomach. She didn't like being alone with Ocho. How much longer would Po Han be gone?

***

Ocho reached under her bed and pulled out the basket where she had been keeping the bullfrog. She lifted the lid and reached into the container. The animal's back felt coarse and cold. Its soft belly pulsated anxiously against her palm.

Ocho retrieved the box she had stuck under the bed in Carolien and Po Han's room several weeks before. The dolls were still in place. Ocho wet a handtowel and wrapped the frog in it. She then placed him in the box with the dolls and pushed everything back under the bed. She closed the door and returned to the living room. "Po Han should be back soon," she said, walking across the room.

Carolien breathed heavily between groans.

Ocho chuckled. "I hope Po Han's son won't surprise him by being here when he walks in." Her chortle turned into a shallow cough. She cleared her throat and spit a mouthful of phlegm out of the open window.

Carolien closed her eyes and sighed.

The clip-clop of horse hooves accompanied by hurried voices drifted through the open window. Ocho hurried to open the front door for Po Han and the midwife.

"She's doing fine." Ocho said to Po Han, who rushed immediately to Carolien. Ocho scowled at the Chinese midwife. "What's the fuss? Birthing is a woman's normal task." When the midwife's eyes widened in surprise, Ocho became irritated. "I'm sure you agree," she grumbled, leaving the room.

***

"How are you?" Po Han stroked Carolien's forehead.

"I'm so glad you're back." Carolien took Po Han's hand and placed his palm against her cheek. She turned to the midwife, wincing. "Thank you for coming," she stammered and made her way to the bedroom, leaning on Po Han's arm.

The fresh bedding felt cool and, for a minute, Carolien relaxed. She wished Sue would show up for her daily visit. Most likely she'd bring Mundi. Nanna had begun sending Mundi to take care of the heavy house chores as Carolien's pregnancy advanced. But even if Sue came right now and sent Mundi back immediately to get Nanna, it still would take another hour before Nanna would arrive. Carolien folded her arms and doubled over. A new wave of labor pains crawled up her spine and exploded in her belly.

There was a short tap on the door and Sue walked into the room. "Hi," she said, stroking Carolien's arm. "Ocho told me that you were in labor. I sent Mundi back to get Mother."

"*Chi-Chi*." Carolien brought a hand to her head and whispered, "Ouch, my head. It hurts badly. My scalp feels like it's being punctured by needles."

"Is it normal for someone in labor to have a headache?" Po Han massaged Carolien's temples, looking from Sue to the midwife.

"Po Han–" Ocho's shrill voice came through the open bedroom door before either could answer.

"Go. I can't deal with her screaming." Carolien flinched. She moved Po Han's hand away and turned her head. "Please keep her quiet."

"I don't want to leave you." Po Han shot the midwife a desperate glance.

"There isn't anything you can do here. Maybe it's better you wait outside," the midwife said.

"Po Han–" Ocho's piercing voice insisted.

"Please, go," Carolien whispered, closing her eyes. All she wanted was for Nanna to arrive.

***

Sitting at the dining room table, Ocho spread chalk paste and tobacco over betel leaves to make a chewing wad. "Han, Po Han!" she hollered into the hallway.

"What do you want?" Po Han stormed into the dining room.

"What are you doing in there?" Ocho put the new wad into her mouth. "It's bad luck for a man to witness childbirth. If that woman had any pride, she wouldn't make such a display of her pain." Ocho crushed the betel leaves between her teeth. "She doesn't even care that there isn't anything to fix for lunch."

Ocho stiffened when screams drowned out Po Han's answer. As he ran back to the bedroom she shouted, "Stay out of there! It's bad luck. I'm telling you, it's bad luck." She followed him, yelling.

The midwife sat on her knees by Carolien, who lay unconscious on the floor, while Sue chased a jumping bullfrog around the room with the bedbroom.

"What on earth is happening?" Po Han lifted Carolien and carried her to the bed.

The midwife retrieved a vial of smelling salts from her instrument bag and held it by Carolien's quivering nostrils.

"I don't know," she said. "We heard a frog croak, and then it leaped into the room from under the bed." She felt for Carolien's pulse. "Your wife jumped out of the bed and fell. I hope the baby isn't hurt." The midwife glanced at her watch.

Ocho grabbed the doorjamb and tried to calm her rapid breathing. She never thought the frog would jump out of the box. Perspiration broke through her palms while she watched Po Han apply a cold compress to Carolien's head.

"Here." The midwife handed Po Han a bottle with eau de cologne. "Splash some on her wrists and ankles. It will help her regain consciousness."

"How did a frog get into the bedroom?" Po Han patted the liquid on Carolien's wrist.

Sue pinned the frog against a wall with the long needles of the bedbroom. Then she grabbed his legs and flung him out of the open window into the yard. "I don't know," she mumbled, keeping her eyes lowered.

Ocho sighed with relief but stiffened when Sue moved the broom back and forth under the bed. Any minute now, the broom would sweep out the box with the voodoo dolls. Ocho tried to calm her rapid breathing. What would happen when Sue swept the box into the room?

Ocho wanted to leave, but her legs felt as if they were filled with lead. Her feet seemed to be bolted to the ground as the open shoebox swished into the room.

"Oh my God!" Sue dropped the broom and brought a hand to her mouth.

"Watch Carolien." Po Han handed the compress to the midwife who, holding onto the headboard, stared at the box. Two steps brought Po Han next to Sue. His eyes traveled from the box to Ocho. She crumbled under his glare.

Unable to keep herself together any longer, Ocho burst into a coughing spell. "I–I better get a glass of water," she stammered and scurried out of the room.

***

When Nanna entered the dining room she took a step backward. The smell of beer crawled up her nostrils. She took a quick look around. Sue and Mundi had not exaggerated. She saw it herself now. Ocho, her face blotched red by the beer, scrambled to her feet. Nanna put her hands together and raised them in greeting.

Where was Po Han? Behind the closed bedroom door Carolien's whimpering was the undertone for different voices. Nanna stiffened when she heard a male voice. Men were not allowed in a delivery room. Had the doctor been called? Nanna turned the doorknob and entered the room.

Carolien lay on the bed. Sue and the midwife stood by her side. Po Han, standing in the middle of the room, whirled around. He brought his hands together in greeting. "Thank you for coming," he said awkwardly.

Nanna returned Po Han's greeting. Here he was in the middle of the birthing room, despite traditional beliefs and, most likely, his grandmother's scorn. Perhaps Carolien did have reasons for marrying him. Looking at the box on the floor, Nanna saw the voodoo dolls. "It's the old woman and her wicked ways," she said, looking at Po Han.

Po Han lowered his eyes. He comforted Carolien who had regained consciousness and groaned softly.

Nanna picked up the box. Dark powers were threatening Carolien's life, endangering the baby. Nanna had learned to follow her intuition. She looked out of the open window. A mango tree branch, heavy with fruit, filled a corner of the window opening. The plump ripening mangoes swayed with the light breeze and the scent of gardenia wafted into the room. Nanna closed her eyes until she came to peace and knew what to do. Salt was purifying, essential to life. "Sue," she said, "Please get me some kitchen salt."

Nanna rubbed the sea salt over both dolls. She took the pins out of the big doll's head and removed the tamarind seeds from its stomach. She told Sue to feed them to the flames of the kitchen stove. Then she cut the strings that tied the small doll between the legs of the larger one. Returning to Carolien's bedside she soothed her youngest child. "You should feel better soon."

Carolien moaned softly.

Nanna snipped off a piece of the cummerbund that held her sarong in place. She made new, larger arms and legs for the big doll out of the unbleached cotton and stuffed them with spices and grains of rice. Then she sewed them to the doll's body, replacing its string limbs.

"Sue, see if you can find me two clear glass buttons in your sister's

54

sewing kit." Nanna drew two circles in the face of the small doll and sewed the buttons on as eyes. She returned the dolls to the box and put the box under the bed.

Nanna placed her hands on each side of Carolien's stomach. "Rest," she told her daughter. "This child will take a lot of your strength." The life pulsing against her hands felt hot and anxious. Nanna closed her eyes. Thinking of the clear cold water running through the creek behind her house, she cooled her hands and soothed Carolien's writhing body until her breath became even.

Nanna moved to the foot of the bed. "Lean into your husband," she said, gently pushing Carolien's legs up. "Help her push," she said, looking at the midwife.

For a while, everyone supported Carolien through her contractions. Then, bracing her daughter's knees with one arm, Nanna pushed up.

Carolien gave birth with a piercing scream.

Nanna caught the red mass that slipped into her hands. The baby didn't cry. Its head was encased in membrane. Sue and the midwife exchanged nervous glances, only Carolien's heaving cut the thick silence. Nanna took a pair of scissors from the midwife's instrument tray. She cut into the red mass and folded back the film. Then she gave the baby a firm pat on its bottom.

The infant suddenly bellowed. The baby's cry dissolved the tension in the room. Nanna asked for fresh drawn water from the well to cool the boiling bathwater. She smiled when the infant bawled as she bathed it.

Nanna dressed the umbilical cord and folded a heavy gold coin into the baby's cummerbund to hold the cord stub in place. She swaddled the infant and handed the baby to Po Han. "Here's your daughter," she said, holding him with a steadfast gaze. "The priest at the temple said she should be named Siu Yin."

Po Han pressed the baby against his chest and whispered, "Thank you. Thank you very much."

Po Han seemed not at all bothered by the fact that the baby was a girl. Did Carolien realize how lucky she was? Nanna fluffed some pillows and propped Carolien up. "Now, let's see if your breast will quiet her." Nanna moved aside for Po Han. Later, she'd burn an extra offering of incense sticks to thank the gods.

Carolien sunk back into the pillows. She lowered her eyes and whispered, "Thanks, Ma."

Po Han lay the crying baby against Carolien's bared breast. The infant's lips closed around the nipple and the frantic cries subsided into sporadic whimpering sighs. Po Han traced his daughter's face with his index finger. Suddenly, he looked up. "I'm going to get my camera," he said, with a feverish urgency.

Nanna watched Po Han dash out of the room, an unfamiliar fondness filling her chest.

***

The baby was only a few days old when, standing with Po Han by the cradle, Carolien suggested, "Let's give Siu Yin a Dutch calling name."

Po Han stroked the baby's fist. "What would such a little girl do with so many names?"

"It will be easier for her when she goes to school, and it will be a name we chose for her."

"You think your mother would be okay with that?" Po Han walked to the open window. A breeze stirred the curtains and made the appliquéd yellow ducks on the border swim in the waves of material.

"Why not?" Carolien looked up. "Sue and I have Dutch names, so do my nieces and nephew." She smoothed the baby's blanket. "What do you think of calling her Jenny? It sounds feisty. Do you think she'll be a spirited child?"

"With a mother like you, what else can she be but lively?" Po Han laughed and returned to the cradle. The baby rubbed a fist against her own smooth cheek as she slept. "Okay," Po Han whispered. "That's what we'll call her, Jenny." He tapped the baby lightly on her short nose and murmured into the cradle, "Hi there, Jenny. Hello."

"Han," Carolien threw Po Han a sideway glance. "We have to send Jenny to the best schools." She put an arm around his waist, bending next to him over the crib. "I want her to have a good education, so she never has to bow her head for anyone."

"Sure," Po Han mumbled without taking his eyes off the baby.

As Carolien predicted, Nanna readily accepted the Dutch name they gave the baby and the child was soon known only as Jenny.

***

"Look at all that hair! It needs to be shaved to get rid of the bad luck she brought with her," Ocho said each time she saw Jenny. She subscribed to the native belief that the hair a child is born with represents its mother's evil and needs to be removed. True to custom, she insisted on calling a *dukun* to perform the cleansing ceremony when Jenny was seven days old.

"Why do you insist on conforming to some native superstition?" Carolien looked at Po Han for support.

"You live here, right?" Ocho said. "You better keep the spirits of the land appeased, or–"

"Forget it, we won't have it done. That's final." Po Han interrupted Ocho, giving her no other choice than to leave the room.

A few days later Ocho needed chalk for her chewing wads. She sat down on the back porch steps, her gnarled body hunched over the stone mortar she held between her thighs. The bony tip of her shoulder raised the light fabric of her *kebaja* each time her hand came up with the pestle. Neither time nor alcohol had treated Ocho kindly. At sixty-six, she had lost most of her once lush black hair. Now, a tiny knot of thin gray strands was secured on top of her head by a jeweled comb.

Ocho watched Po Han from the corner of her eye as he placed Jenny's bassinet in the shade of the mango tree. She heard him cooing to the baby. If a girl spun his head this much, imagine what a boy would have done.

Pounding the pestle onto the clumps of chalk, she noticed Po Han close the mosquito netting and go back into the house, leaving the baby unattended. Ocho dashed into the kitchen– this was her chance! She grabbed a sharp paring knife, scooped up a dab of lard with two fingers, and rushed to the mango tree.

Ocho smeared the lard over Jenny's head and began shaving her, moving the knife with quick strokes. Jenny began to cry when Ocho turned her to get to the back of her head. "Shh, shh. It's okay." Ocho rubbed the baby's back and pulled up the light blanket. She looked anxiously over her shoulder. A few more passes and she'd be rid of all the bad luck contained in Jenny's birth hair.

The knife was in midair when Ocho heard Carolien scream. "Don't touch my baby. Stop her!" Ocho dropped the knife and disappeared into the house as Po Han came running into the garden.

Carolien's screaming had more than startled Ocho. What was there to be so upset about? All she wanted to do was to get rid of bad luck. If she had only a few more minutes, she would have finished the job. But of course, the dumb woman had to make a fuss.

Ocho put a hand against her pounding chest as she peeked through her sheer bedroom curtains. On the sidewalk, Po Han lit a cigarette and looked up and down the street. Why was he standing there? Po Han threw his cigarette down and whistled. Ocho held her breath. He was calling a *delman*. Why? Who for? After a brief conversation with the buggy driver, Po Han hurried back into the house.

There were muffled voices in the hallway, the front door opened. Po Han helped Carolien, who was carrying the baby, into the carriage. Ocho sighed. Carolien probably wanted to complain to her family about the incident.

Ocho sucked in her cheeks. She moved her tongue around her mouth searching for a taste of betel leaves. Perhaps she should dig out some of the money she kept hidden in her mattress and prepare a nice meal. Ocho started to turn away from the window when she noticed Po Han still standing on the curb. His rigid posture frightened her. She took a seat on the edge of her bed.

After a short knock, Po Han walked into her room.

"That woman has bewitched you," Ocho shouted covering her face with her hands. "That's why you can't see how disrespectful and incompetent she is." Her fear turned into anger, Ocho reached for a pillow. She buried her face in it and wailed, "She even had trouble producing only a girl— and on top of that, she insists on keeping the child's bad luck around."

"That's enough!" Po Han's voice flicked like a whip. "Just imagine what could've happened if you had cut into Jenny's scalp."

Jenny, that's all he could think of! Only a few weeks old, the child already managed to capture all of his attention. "I might as well sit on the railroad tracks and have the train run over me," Ocho wailed. "It would hurt less than to have you side with that woman." She shot Po Han a miserable glance, but the hard look in his eyes didn't soften.

"I have a much better place for you to sit than on the railroad tracks." Po Han's cold voice sent a chill down Ocho's spine. "I think it's best that you live somewhere else for a while," he said.

"Wh-a-t?" Ocho gasped. "Where would I go? You're all I have." Her lips began to quiver. "You're putting me out on the street for a useless woman and a piece of bad luck?"

"For a long time, all we had was each other." Pacing the floor, Po Han rolled an unlit cigarette between his fingers. "Now I have a wife and a daughter. I would have been happy to share them with you, but you chose to be alone." He stopped. "I'm going to get you a room in Pension Waringin. They serve meals there. I'll give you pocket money to buy the fixings for your chews and things like that. I'll visit you every day–"

His voice faltered. "Why, for God's sake, did you have to keep pushing?"

Ocho blinked when the door slammed. There was nothing she could do to change the situation. Anything she did now would only make it worse.

Po Han was silent during the *delman* ride to Pension Waringin. Rocking along with the buggy's rhythm, Ocho recalled a train ride long ago. Po Han was two when she left with him after he lost his parents. Never, during the past thirty-some years, had she imagined life without him. "How can you forget how hard I worked raising you?" she asked. Ocho noticed Po Han cringe and shifted her attack. "Mark my words. That woman will give you more trouble than you can handle." She stopped when Po Han glared at her.

The foyer of the pension was small and dimly lit. Seated on the edge of a worn rattan chair, Ocho watched Po Han take out his wallet and slide a few bills across the counter. She moved her trembling hands over the canvas bag in her lap, feeling for the bottles of beer and gin she had slipped in when Po Han's back was turned. Pressing the bag against her stomach, Ocho remembered a time in a teahouse. She was only sixteen years old. Standing in the corner of the vestibule, she watched her father put away the coins the madam gave him for leaving her there. Being only a girl, she had been powerless then. But now it was a baby girl who caused her predicament. Ocho shook her head, clutching the canvas bag.

Nick de Graaf, the middle-aged Indo proprietor, showed them to Ocho's room. Ocho scanned the furnishings–a single bed and a closet with a mirror marred with spots at the edges. A small sink hung off the wall next to the closet. The aroma of spicy Malay food wafted into the room through the dark-brown curtains hung in the narrow window opening.

The room and shabby furniture reminded Ocho of the small house close to the military barracks where she had raised Po Han. She worked hard to move away from it. Did he remember the military uniforms she pushed across the wooden washboard? The hours she stood ironing? Did he remember those early mornings filled with the aroma of fresh baked pastry she carried in baskets to the platform of the train station? Ever since he was two years old, she had worked hard to provide him with an opportunity to have a better life. And now that it was his turn to provide for her, he was unable to do anything else but return her to a world she thought she had risen above.

"You're paid up for a week." Po Han's voice broke into Ocho's thoughts. "I saw people playing cards on the verandah." He placed the last items in the suitcase on a closet shelf. "Some of them might be mah yong players."

"You're talking as if I haven't lost enough."

Po Han winced. "They serve dinner between seven and nine." He started to leave. Halfway out of the door, he turned. "I'll be back tomorrow," he said and pulled the door closed.

Ocho hung on Po Han's words like a spider dangling from a loose web thread. The room was a gaping hole. Its empty silence dragged her back into the past, to a time when she had just given birth. The baby was only a girl, not good enough to fill a sugar king's dreams and make him want to marry his concubine. Ocho shuddered and reached for the canvas bag. Her fingers curled around the cool neck of a beer bottle. Po Han said he'd be back. He had not completely forsaken her, like his grandfather had.

Ocho took a few quick swigs. Heat spread through her chest and rushed to her head. Po Han was coming to see her, tomorrow. He was only silencing that woman's nasty nagging. Ocho poured some gin into the beer bottle. Her hands shook and she spilled. She wiped her hand on her sarong and took another gulp. "Tomorrow," she mumbled.

***

Carolien hurriedly paid the delman driver and burst into Nanna's house. "Ma! Sue!" She rushed into the dining room where Nanna and Sue were having lunch. "Look what she did to Jenny." Carolien folded the blanket back.

"Oh, look at Jenny! She looks like a real Chinese baby now." Sue took the baby from Carolien and fingered the little tufts of black hair Ocho had missed.

Nanna left the room and came back with Chip's shaving tools. "You need to be careful," she said. "That woman is capable of doing great harm." Using Chip's soft shaving brush, Nanna lathered soap on Jenny's head. She moved the knife with long smooth strokes and shaved Jenny completely bald.

Carolien held back her questions when Po Han came to take them home in the late afternoon. As soon as she walked through their front door she knew Ocho was gone. Nothing was misplaced, yet the rooms felt uncomfortably empty. The silence reproached her.

"I rented a room for her in the Pension Waringin." Po Han explained.

Carolien glanced at him. Had he moved Ocho out for good? How did he expect to pay for Ocho's rent?

Before the questions and comments could form in Carolien's mouth, Po Han said, "Can we not talk about it?"

Carolien noticed a shadow of pain slide across her husband's face. It must have been difficult for him to leave his grandmother in a simple boardinghouse. She took a step closer to Po Han and reached for his hand. Perhaps, she should just be happy that he had removed Ocho from their home to protect her and Jenny.

When Nanna came to visit the next day, Carolien told her mother that Po Han had moved Ocho out. Nanna carefully placed the food she brought on the kitchen table. "Ocho's a mean woman, but she's your husband's grandmother. She belongs in his household. It's only right that he takes care of her."

"But he is!" Carolien protested. "We don't have enough money to support ourselves, yet he's paying for her room and board and giving her spending money."

Nanna shook her head. "Money doesn't replace presence."

Carolien sighed. She would not admit it, but Ocho's moving out gave her an uneasy feeling. She felt guilty for her part in creating the situation.

CHAPTER 5

Carolien breathed easier when, shortly after he moved Ocho out, Po Han's sporadic attempts to secure employment were rewarded. A large Dutch accounting firm hired him part-time to maintain their typewriters and adding machines. He worked evenings, when the machines were not in use. But the job didn't pay enough to cover all of the couple's expenses.

At first Carolien enjoyed the responsibility and the challenge of making ends meet. She spent many evenings at the desk in the living room. Bent intently over papers, a pencil tapping against the desktop, she worked on ledgers that showed their insufficient income, increased spending, and rapidly dwindling savings.

Carolien decided to take in sewing to supplement their sparse income. She enjoyed preparing healthy yet affordable meals without Ocho's meddling. If it were not for their financial situation, she would have been happy.

One Sunday evening Carolien showed Po Han her rows of meticulously kept figures. "Here, see for yourself." She pushed the tablet closer under the desk lamp. "One way or another, you must bring home more money. What will we do when we have used up all of our savings?"

The column for Po Han's photography supplies showed the largest figure in the ledger. Carolien circled it with her pencil. "This is where most of the money goes. It's the only place we can cut back."

"But that's if I don't sell anything and no one gives me an assignment." Po Han glanced at the figures. He took the pencil out of Carolien's hand

and put his arms around her. "Be patient. Things will work out. You'll see. I'm pretty sure the shots I took of Braga Street will sell."

Carolien hoped that Po Han would look for a full-time job, but he remained focused on establishing a career as a photographer. Sporadic sales of his photographs and isolated assignments boosted his confidence. Jenny was his favorite subject. On countless rolls of film, the baby grew from a newborn into a toddler, and a preschooler.

Month by month their savings got smaller and Carolien began to resent Po Han's photography. "What did you waste your time on today?" she asked one day when he returned from a photo shoot. "I wish you'd stop fiddling around with cameras and look for a real job."

Later that evening, when he showed her prints, she barely glanced at the photographs. "It's time you stopped spending money on the production of worthless pictures," she said and forced herself to ignore the pain she saw in Po Han's eyes. She glared at him when he silently collected the prints spread over the dining room table. Didn't he love her enough to make the sacrifice?

Earlier that day, Carolien had taken her diamond pendant to a pawnshop. It was the only piece of jewelry she had ever bought for herself. It had taken her more than a year to save up for it. She hooked a finger around the now bare chain, wondering how long it would take before Po Han would notice.

Nanna dropped by often with large canvas bags filled with containers of basic household staples, several pots of prepared food, and a jar of cookies or a toy for Jenny.

Carolien emptied Nanna's bags with restrained reluctance. Having to accept her family's charity shamed her.

"Do my brothers know you're bringing me all of this?" Carolien asked Nanna once, while pouring sugar into her own empty container. The money from the red envelopes that Chip and Ting had sent at Jenny's birth had been used for household expenses, instead of being put away for Jenny's education fund.

"It isn't any child's business what a mother gives to another child," Nanna said. She raked the charcoal in the clay stove and placed a pot of beef stew on the blackened iron grill. "Where's your husband?" she asked, stirring the stew.

"I don't know." Carolien wiped her cheeks with the back of her hands and placed the filled containers on a cupboard shelf. "I hope he's looking for a better job."

"What are you going to do if he isn't?" Nanna placed the lid on the simmering pot.

Carolien was silent. It wasn't too long ago that she had been a self-assured young woman who moved with confidence in the Dutch business world. Now she was no different from any other Chinese housewife, subject to her husband's whims.

Jenny, playing at the kitchen table, started to fuss.

Nanna left the stove to hand the child a cookie and Carolien looked around the tidy kitchen as if she was taking inventory. Over the last four years she and Po Han had completely depleted their savings. She straightened and pulled back her shoulders. "If he doesn't get a job by the end of this month, I will," she said, looking Nanna straight in the eye.

"Is that what you married for, to support a man and a child?" Nanna gave Jenny another cookie and returned to stirring the beef stew.

"No." Carolien straightened her skirt. "Perhaps I should take Jenny and divorce him." An odd unsettling feeling filled her heart as she heard herself say the words.

"Is divorce the Dutch way of settling problems between husband and wife?" Nanna added a few briquettes of charcoal to the stove.

Carolien didn't answer.

"I hope you realize that the Dutch way you chose to get married was wrong," Nanna said. "Now, don't go making another Dutch mistake." With that statement, Nanna gathered her belongings and left.

Carolien checked the simmering stew. Their conversation echoed in her head. She was certain that Nanna disapproved of Po Han's attitude. Yet it seemed that her mother placed blame on her Dutch thinking, rather than on Po Han's irresponsibility.

"Mamma, cookie." Jenny tugged at Carolien's skirt.

"No more, you won't be able to eat dinner." A stubborn anger filled Carolien while she wiped Jenny's hands. No self-respecting woman would leave herself and her child to the whims of an unproductive man. She'd show Po Han that she could raise Jenny alone, that they were better off without him. And she'd show Nanna that there was nothing wrong with her Dutch thinking. Carolien stared at the calendar page on the wall. Po Han had twenty-five days to get a job or she'd make good on her word.

***

Each day as she tore a leaf from the calendar, Carolien felt as if she ripped off a layer of her own skin. She knew that each page brought her closer to the end of the month.

There were only twelve more days left when Po Han accepted an invitation to enter a photography contest put on by the Association of Dutch Photographers. Carolien watched while he enthusiastically pulled the literature from his briefcase. The first prize was money, and a yearlong internship in a well-known Dutch photography laboratory.

"It's an honor to even be invited," Po Han said. The pride and eagerness in his voice irritated Carolien. "I'm the only Chinese photographer invited. If I didn't have my work hanging in Jaap's gallery, the committee wouldn't have known about me."

"Han, you must find a job, a real paying job. We can't go on like this beyond the end of the month." Carolien drummed the coffee table with her fingernails.

"I know," Po Han mumbled, without looking up from the publication. But instead of combing the job market, he spent the next ten days collecting material for the contest.

"I'm getting quite a collection together," Po Han said, one morning during breakfast. "Today, I'm going to shoot another couple of rolls."

"Where do you think you'll get the money to pay for it?" Carolien asked. It was the last day of the month. She took a sip of her tea and put her cup brusquely on the saucer. "Jenny's outgrowing her shoes and there's no money to pay the utility bills."

They were seated across from each other with Jenny between them. The youngster tried to push her fork under the last bites of food, but instead pushed the food off her plate.

"Jenny, don't play with your food." Carolien wiped up the bits of scrambled egg from the tablecloth.

"What do you want me to do?" Po Han walked to the open window, lit a cigarette, and took a long drag.

"Don't you understand that you've got to stop playing around? You've a child to support. It takes money to buy food and clothes and to send Jenny to school. It takes money to *live.*"

"I'm giving you all the money I make. What else do you want me to do?"

The anguish in Po Han's voice startled Carolien, but she quickly gathered herself.

"I want you to give up photography," she said, tapping the tip of her knife against her plate. "You'll never make enough money to support us taking pictures."

"I can't." Po Han gripped the back of a chair until his knuckles turned white. He looked like he was trying to force the chair through the floor.

Carolien dropped the knife and pressed her napkin against her lips. After four years of trying to make a living as a photographer all he had to show for it was a scrapbook filled with newspaper articles and some blue ribbons, neither of which paid the bills. His hobby had led them into a desparate financial situation. Yet, like a child with a toy, he refused to stop playing. Did he understand what was at stake?

"I can't," Po Han repeated.

Something in Carolien broke. She ran to the pantry Po Han had converted into a darkroom. She flicked the light on and pulled equipment and paper off the shelves. The trays filled with photographic solution clattered onto the tile floor, the liquid sloshing out. Carolien ripped the thin wire lines with drying prints clipped to them. Dropped to the wet floor, the proofs stuck together.

"Stop it! What are you doing?" Po Han grabbed Carolien by the arms. She tore away and flung items off the shelves.

"What does it look like I'm doing?" Carolien stormed into the living room and, with a sweep of her arm, toppled the easel and tripod that were set up in a corner. She grabbed Po Han's camera bag from the coffee table and threw it out of the window, tears streaming down her face.

"My God, come to your senses!" Po Han ran out of the front door.

Through the open window Carolien saw him pick up the camera and check the lens. Back in the living room, he started to collect the brushes and tubes of paint strewn across the floor. Every so often, he glanced nervously at Carolien.

Carolien leaned against her bureau and stared at the mess. She felt as if she was in the middle of a nightmare. This wasn't the way it was supposed to turn out.

"Daddy! Mommy!" Jenny had climbed off her chair and stood in the doorway.

Po Han dropped a handful of paintbrushes back onto the floor. "It's okay. Shh. Shhh. It's okay." He navigated his way through the clutter of books, photographs, magazines, and canvasses. "Come here. Let's draw some pretty pictures." Po Han held his hand out but, before Jenny could reach him, Carolien grabbed the child's arm and pulled her back.

"Jenny doesn't need pictures. She needs food and clothes. She needs to go to a good school! Can't you get that through your head?" Carolien picked Jenny up and walked to the dining room, slamming the door behind her.

"Daddy," Jenny cried.

Po Han flung the door open. "Don't you take my child away from me."

"Daddy!" Jenny wrestled out of Carolien's arms and ran crying to Po Han.

"Shh, shh. Daddy's here." Po Han carried Jenny back to the living room.

"Where do you think you're going to take her?" Carolien shouted. "What are you going to feed her? Pretty pictures?" Carolien grabbed a bundle of unpaid bills off the desk and flung them at Po Han. "You can't even take care of those. How do you think you can take care of a child?"

"No! Mommy, no!" Jenny buried her face into Po Han's shoulder, crying.

Carolien pressed her hands against her mouth. "I'm sorry, Jenny," she said stiffly. "Mommy won't throw things anymore. Let's clean up this mess."

Jenny slipped down Po Han's chest onto the floor and ran to Carolien.

She wrapped her arms around Carolien's legs and pushed her head into her mother's skirt. "Mommy, Mommy," she whined.

"Shh, shh." Carolien rubbed Jenny's back. She pulled out a handkerchief from under her sleeve and wiped Jenny's face. The stark red numbers of a bill kept her eyes glued to the floor. She turned when she heard Po Han walk away.

Po Han headed for the storage room and grabbed a suitcase. In the bedroom he opened the closet and pulled shirts and pants off hangers. Standing in the doorway, holding Jenny tightly in her arms, Carolien watched. This was the beginning of a divorce. She had kept her word. Tears stung her eyes, but she felt strangely calm.

Po Han shot Carolien a desperate glance.

"Daddy!" Jenny pulled herself out of Carolien's arms.

Po Han caught Jenny. "I'm leaving," he said, holding the child tightly against his chest. "I need to figure out how to make a living without abandoning myself." Jenny put her head on Po Han's shoulder. "I can't give up photography," he said, running a hand down the youngster's back, "and I know I have to take care of her." His face twisted as he eased Jenny onto the floor. "But I can't think or work around you."

Carolien steadied herself against the doorjamb. A stream of words caught in her throat and wouldn't leave her mouth. She ran the tip of her tongue across her dry lips. "Jenny, come here," she said with a tight voice.

Jenny, standing on her father's shoes, wrapped her arms tightly around Po Han's legs. She pushed her face into his thigh. "Daddy, Daddy," she cried.

Carolien pulled the child loose. Dragging Jenny into the living room, she heard the suitcase close with a decisive click.

***

Ocho carried the basket with longbeans to a corner table on the large veranda of Pension Waringin. During the past four years she had established a routine of helping with the kitchen tasks. The early morning sun reflected off the white wrought-iron furniture. It was only ten o'clock, but the morning felt steamy already. Ocho sized up a few newcomers. Perhaps she'd cajole them into a game of dominoes a little later. Among the old-timers she had a reputation as a shrewd card player. People stayed away from her table unless they had some money to lose.

A *delman* stopped and Po Han climbed out of the buggy. Ocho's heart jumped in her throat. Why did he come so early? She leaned over the banister to get a better look. Po Han was carrying a suitcase. Had her exile come to an end, had he finally come to his senses and left that no-good woman? Triumph and joy rushed through her, but vanished quickly when she noticed Po Han's lumbering gait. She had never seen him so disheveled. "Han–" She stopped when she saw him stiffen.

"You can be happy now," Po Han said. "We'll be living under the same roof again–I'm getting a room."

Ocho pressed her quivering lips together. This was not the way she imagined Po Han leaving Carolien. He didn't look at all like a man who'd just put a woman into her place. Leaning across the counter on his elbows, his head in his hands, Po Han looked worse than a beaten dog. Nick de Graaf handed Po Han a key and they shook hands. Ocho started toward Po Han.

"Please–" His voice broke. "Please, leave me alone." Ocho followed him silently down the hallway. Po Han set down his suitcase by the door of his room and stuck the key into the lock. "I need to be alone for a while–" He choked up and went into his room, closing the door behind him.

Ocho fingered the doorknob. What had happened? What had that woman done to him?

***

Carolien took Jenny to see Nanna the next afternoon. After the four-year-old took off to play with the dogs, Carolien joined Nanna who sat sorting beans on the back porch. The dense growth of a chayote squash vine covered the pergola, creating cool shade. "Ma." Carolien ran a finger through the beans on the bamboo tray. "Yesterday, Po Han left."

Nanna swished the beans around with a smooth rotating motion. She picked up a few shriveled beans and dropped them in an empty can.

"What are you going to do now?" Flicking a finger through the beans on the tray, she seemed untouched by the news.

"I need to find a job." Carolien paused. She had been worried about her mother's reaction to the situation, but Nanna remained calm. "I need to earn a living for Jenny and me."

Nanna looked up. Their eyes locked for a moment. "It's best for Jenny if you moved back home," she said, pouring the sorted beans in a bag. "She needs someone to take care of her while you're at work. Tonight, at dinner, I'll tell your brothers."

***

Ocho shuffled behind Po Han up to the front door. Not much had changed during the four years of her absence. She tried to find a sign of disorder, some evidence of the fight she suspected Carolien and Po Han must have had. But everything was in its place. When Po Han opened the door to her room Ocho caught her step. "Where's my bed?" Her bed, her mattress, had Carolien thrown them out?

"This is your bed. Carolien just fixed it up to look like a couch. See?" Po Han pushed the bolsters and pillows aside. He pulled back the gingham cover, exposing a familiar mattress.

"Carolien did her sewing here while you were gone. I have to put up the frame for your mosquito net and find your regular bedding." Po Han opened the door of Ocho's closet and stared at the empty shelves before pulling out the large bottom drawer. "Here's the stuff for your bed."

Ocho noticed how flat his voice was. She tried to calm herself, plucking at the tip of her *kebaja*. "You can take care of my bed later. Just leave my suitcase."

As soon as Po Han left the room Ocho flipped the bedcover up. She ran a hand across the side of the mattress and, when she felt the heavy thread she had used to hand-stitch the material, she let out a sigh. For all of Carolien's Dutch education, she hadn't noticed the tight hand stitching on the side of the mattress. The three diamonds from her *kebaja* pin and the socks filled with silver guilder coins should still be buried in the *kapok*. They'd come in handy now.

Ocho caught a glimpse of herself in the mirror of her closet door. Unable to find a trace of the beautiful woman a sugar king had found worthy of adorning with gold and diamonds, she dropped the sheet. She might have lost her beauty, but she certainly still had her wits. Unlike Carolien, she'd run the household without complaints.

That night Ocho cooked for Po Han. "Don't worry about the house," she said as she spooned another piece of chicken onto his plate. "Just like before, I'll make do. I'm sure there'll be plenty of folks who'll like my pastries. The guests of Pension Waringin wouldn't do without them for their afternoon tea."

Po Han sent Ocho a wan smile. "I need some money for supplies, but I'll give you everything else." He hesitated before adding softly, "It isn't much."

"Don't worry," Ocho assured him. Even if Po Han didn't earn anything, one of her diamonds would sell for enough money to support them for a year.

***

After she and Jenny settled into Nanna's household, Carolien went to see her former employer, William Wachter. Due to the depression, the job market was tight. War rumors had begun to escalate. Hitler had started his march through Europe and Japan was moving in on China. Wachter said that, given the economical and political situation, she'd be better off with a government position.

Chip was assistant to the chief accountant of the Department of War and Welfare. Ting held a similar position in the Department of Communications. Backed by her brothers' support, and a glowing reference from her former employer, Carolien was soon hired as a private secretary to a department head in Chip's office.

Carolien loved being employed again. When she joined her brothers to leave for work in the morning, she left Jenny in Nanna's care. She earned a reasonable salary and contributed half of it to the household. After taking out some spending money, she saved the remainder. Her supervisor's lavish praise boosted Carolien's self-confidence and Sue was a patient listener to her animated office stories.

"How can you stand it, day after day, taking orders from Mother and catering to Chip and Ting's needs?" Carolien asked her sister one morning as they stood at the kitchen counter before Carolien left for work.

"I told you a long time ago, I'm happy I only have to get the food to the table and the clothes in the closet and don't have to worry about the money it takes to buy those things." Sue secured the lid of the last lunch box and wiped her hands on her apron.

"Thanks." Carolien grabbed the lunch boxes and rushed to her waiting brothers. Halfway out of the kitchen, she turned. "Money isn't a problem," she laughed. "A job's all you need."

CHAPTER 6

Jenny loved to follow Nanna around while Carolien was at work. The house was surrounded by two acres of gardens. Each day started with feeding the animals.

Going ahead of Nanna, Jenny ran between clumps of lemongrass along the creek that meandered through the backside of the property. Chickens, ducks, and geese prevented the watercress and swamp lettuce from taking over the creekbank and controlled the slug and snail population.

When the fowl crowded around them with loud clucking and quacking noises, Jenny clung to the tip of Nanna's *kebaja*. "All they want is their food," Nanna said. She took a handful of feed from the large enamel bowl she carried in the crook of her arm and scattered it on the ground. Then she handed the bowl to Jenny. "Here, now you feed them," she said.

Ting's dog kennel was behind the garage. Five rambunctious German Shepard pups easily reached Jenny's shoulders when they jumped, but she soon discovered that the dogs meant no harm.

The women in the household constantly reminded Jenny not to bother Ting and Chip, but one day Ting called her to him and handed her a ball. "Here, tell Claus to sit; then throw the ball and see if he'll get it for you when you tell him to fetch."

Jenny clutched the ball and pressed her lips together. The dog circled and nudged her, panting. "Claus, sit!" she said, her heart pounding. When the dog obeyed, Jenny smiled. She threw the ball as hard as she could and ordered, "Fetch!" For a moment, she forgot the rules about behavior and jumped up and down, clapping as the dog bolted to retrieve the ball.

"*Goede hond!*" the myna bird yelled from its cage hanging from a low branch of the mango tree. "Good dog!" she repeated, tripping around her cage.

Jenny stuck a finger between the bars of the cage and stroked the bird's shiny black feathers. "Beo is a good girl," she said. The bird cocked her head and Jenny ran her finger across the myna's bright yellow wattle.

"Good girl," the bird said.

Every so often, mostly around bedtime, Jenny missed Po Han. No one ever mentioned him. It was as if her father had never existed. He became someone she visited quietly in her imagination, just before she fell asleep.

***

As soon as she had established herself at the office, Carolien began to think of ways to hold Po Han accountable for fatherhood. He had tried several times to visit Jenny, but each time Mundi announced him Carolien instructed the houseboy to tell Po Han that there was no one to receive him. One day, however, she came out of the house to see him.

Po Han pleaded with her through the closed gate. "I'm almost there. I think I have a good chance of winning the photography contest. The prize money will get us back on our feet, and I'm sure that the internship will lead to something. Maybe, you and Jenny can join me in Holland. People have more of an appreciation for the arts there."

Carolien began to slip into Po Han's fantasy, but quickly got a hold of herself. She remembered the pile of unpaid bills, the empty bank account. Po Han had persuaded her to marry him with stories about happiness that were not based on financial security. She was not going to make the same mistake again.

"You always say that you want Jenny to be happy," Carolien said, leaning into the closed gate. "How happy do you think the child will be when she has nothing to eat? Please stay away until you can provide for her."

Po Han did not try to argue with Carolien. He left silently.

Carolien pressed her forehead against the iron bars and watched Po Han walk down the street until he turned the corner. She wiped the tears streaming down her cheeks and filled the void inside her with angry thoughts.

Carolien discussed the matter with Chip and Ting. Together they hired a Dutch lawyer and started legal proceedings against Po Han. It was agreed that Carolien should ask the court for custody of Jenny as well as child support.

One afternoon, after she came home from an appointment with her lawyer, Carolien joined Sue on the back porch in the shade of the chayote squash vine. "Maybe a court order will make him understand what I couldn't," she said, watching Jenny play with Claus on the lawn.

"Why don't you just leave it alone?" Sue looked up from her mending. "Working and all, you might meet another man and marry again."

"Do you think I'm stupid?" Carolien leaned back in her chair. "I'll never again depend on a man, especially not when it comes to taking care of Jenny and me. Once is more than enough."

Jenny came running onto the porch with the dog on her heels. "Look! I can make Claus jump over my stick."

Carolien caught Jenny by the shoulders. She smoothed Jenny's hair and wiped her daughter's face. "Jenny, what would you like to be when you're grown up?"

"I'm going to have many dogs." Jenny wiggled loose and threw her arms around the panting pup. "Down, Claus, down."

"What are you going to do with them, Jenny?" Sue collected her mending.

"Teach them tricks, like Youngest Uncle," Jenny answered with her face buried in the shepherd's fur.

Sue laughed, but Carolien shook her head. "Youngest Uncle is an accountant and, when you grow up, you'll be a lawyer." She grabbed Jenny's arm and pulled the child off the dog. "Go on, it's time to clean up for dinner."

Jenny and Claus ran off toward the kennel.

"She sure is different from Emma and Els when they were four," Sue said.

Carolien pursed her lips. She had no intentions of teaching her daughter subordinate behavior or the traditional reverence for males. "I'll make sure," she said, "that Jenny grows up to be independent."

***

Jenny's favorite man in Nanna's household was her cousin Eddie. Jenny idolized the tall handsome boy, fifteen years her senior. Sue's son was enlisted in the KNIL, the colonial Dutch army. Every morning Jenny watched as Eddie carefully placed the khaki military cap on his wavy hair before leaving for the Dutch Army Compound.

At bedtime, Eddie read Jenny stories. The family had adopted the Dutch habit of reading for pleasure. Over the years Chip and Ting had filled the shelves of the tall bookcases in the library.

Jenny looked up at Eddie as he turned the little brass key to open the glass doors of the bookcase and reached for an illustrated edition of the stories from the Grimm brothers. Only the uncles used the library; being there with Eddie gave her a sense of importance.

Sitting on Eddie's lap, Jenny traveled through the imaginary world of fairy tales. When thoughts of Po Han intruded into these moments, she rubbed her head against Eddie's chest to get rid of them. Jenny had learned that questions about her father were never answered.

***

One Sunday afternoon, Carolien joined Ting on the back porch as he sat drinking iced tea and watching Jenny play with the dogs. "Jenny's quite a kid." Ting chuckled. "Watch how she handles the pups. She doesn't let the dogs intimidate her."

Carolien didn't answer her brother. She wasn't particularly interested in Jenny's ability to handle the dogs. "Do you think we're going to have trouble enrolling Jenny in kindergarten at the Oranje School?" she asked. "She'll be five in August." Carolien wanted Jenny to have a prominent place in society, and a Dutch education was the first step. For a Chinese applicant to a Dutch school, a special dispensation was required.

"I don't think so." Ting moved the slice of lemon against the edge of his glass of iced tea. "Older Brother and I have responsible positions in government offices and Eddie is enlisted in the KNIL. That should be enough to give the petition a solid foundation. We'll also have several affidavits from important government officials." Ting leaned back, at ease with the family's position. "Don't worry about it." He finished his beverage and pushed his empty glass across the table toward Carolien.

Carolien reached for Ting's empty glass. "Would you like a refill?" If they hadn't been discussing Jenny's future she would have ignored her brother's gesture. She even might have told him to get the refill himself, but she didn't want to risk annoying him right now.

"No, I'm okay," Ting answered with a smile.

Carolien shot her brother a glance. At forty-five, he was still unmarried. Sometimes she wondered about Ting. Would he ever marry? What did he expect from a wife? Chinese girls brought up in traditional households bored him, but he didn't like her Western behavior either. Ting would be uncomfortable sharing his life with a woman who would defend her opinion and expect him to help with what were considered women's tasks. It was amazing how most Chinese men felt they were superior to women, yet were helpless without them. Po Han was the exception. She remembered him helping with the house-cleaning when their budget only allowed one maid. Carolien sighed. Po Han had been helpless in other ways.

***

Ocho pulled a chair at the dining room table to prepare a fresh chewing wad. She worried about Po Han. He kept to himself, spending hours in the darkroom. She knew that he missed Jenny, possibly even Carolien. Ocho was carefully smearing chalk paste on a couple of betel leaves when the door flung open. Startled, she dropped the pinch of tobacco she held between her fingers.

"Look! Look!" Po Han burst into the room, waving a letter. "Remember, the national photography contest? I won first prize!" Ocho stared at the certificate. She couldn't read, but sensed the importance of the blue ribbon fastened to the side. Po Han held up a check. "I'll send half of this to Carolien and Jenny–maybe it will prove to Carolien that my photography is not a waste of time."

"Why are you still worried about those two? First, she turns your life upside down with all her Dutch nonsense. Then she breaks your back with outrageous demands–" Ocho caught Po Han's glare and stopped mid-sentence.

"Jenny's my daughter." Po Han turned and walked out of the room.

Ocho sighed. She needed to learn not to vent her feelings about Carolien and Jenny. Hopefully Po Han wouldn't be so foolish to look them up now. The thought squeezed at her heart and Ocho pressed a hand against her chest. He was thirty-nine, in the prime of his life, and far too young to be without a woman.

Po Han appeared to be almost light-hearted during dinner that evening. Ocho enjoyed his appetite. "I went to see Jaap," Po Han said between bites. "He thinks I'd probably be able to leave early next year. But don't worry, I'll make sure someone looks after you."

"Where're you going?"

"To Holland. It's all part of the prize."

Ocho's eyes widened, as she caught her breath. "Holland? How long are you going to be gone?"

"I'll be gone for a year." Po Han put his utensils down. "But as I said, I'll make sure you'll be okay." He leaned toward Ocho. "This is my chance. I'll get an education in what I want to do. It'll help me make a living."

Ocho quickly calculated the possibilities of the cards life had just handed her. Being too far away for contact with Carolien and Jenny might not be such a bad idea. Coming back with a Dutch education would not only open up important positions for Po Han, it would also erase part of the stigma his failed marriage had created. While he was gone she could lay the groundwork for him to meet a few decent girls. After his experience with Carolien, he might be more receptive to her suggestions. Ocho looked up from her plate, smiling. "You go. I'm so proud. I can't wait to tell everyone at mah yong that my grandson is going to Holland."

Po Han returned her smile. "I'm going to ask Mr. de Graaf to keep an eye on you while I'm gone. I'll ask him to read my letters to you and help you cash the checks I'll send. I'll be getting paid for working in the photography lab, you know." Po Han's voice was filled with enthusiasm.

***

Jenny stretched and blinked as the early morning light slipped between the curtains and dropped across the bed. As usual, she was the last one to wake up. When they moved in with Nanna, Carolien returned to the room she used to share with Auntie Sue, and Jenny joined Emma and Els in sharing Nanna's room and sleeping in her bed.

Nanna's large solid mahogany bed easily took up one-third of the bedroom. When the mosquito netting was down it was like a small room. Her place was next to Nanna, who lay lengthwise on the outside. Emma and Els lay widthwise. There was plenty of room to turn—they never even touched one another.

In the center of each of the three side panels of the bed a lion's head was carved in the wood. Jenny looked at the lion straight across from her. A sunbeam fell across its golden mane and made it look like flames.

The door opened and Carolien walked into the room. Jenny sat up, rubbing her eyes. Her mother wore a two-piece suit and looked important. She carried a dress over her arm and motioned Jenny to get out of the bed.

"Here." Carolien wiped Jenny's face with a cold washcloth, then pulled the white organza dress over her head.

"Why do I have to wear this dress? Where are we going?" The ruffled neckline made her itch and Jenny scratched at her throat.

"I want you to look nice." Carolien handed Jenny her socks and took a pair of white patent leather shoes off the shoe rack. She helped Jenny with the buckles and gave her a pat on the bottom. "Okay, go get your breakfast."

Carolien still hadn't told her where they were going, but Jenny knew better than to insist on an answer when her mother was in a hurry. She slipped into her chair at the breakfast table and ate her oatmeal porridge.

Jenny was surprised to see Chip, Ting, and Sue waiting for them in the driveway by Chip's car. Sue wore a dress and shoes instead of the sarong, *kebaja*, and low open slippers she wore around the house. Her hair was braided and pinned around her head rather than knotted in the bun that usually lay in the nape of her neck.

Chip drove. Ting sat next to him. Jenny sat in the back seat, between her mother and aunt. She had never been in the car before. She had many questions, but each time she started to ask something Sue shook her head and tapped a finger against her lips. "Shh. Be quiet. Don't upset your mother and uncles," she whispered.

Jenny looked out of the window, but they passed houses and trees so fast she never saw anything clearly. She climbed on the hump in the middle of the car floor and peered between her uncles' shoulders. The scenery became blurry and her stomach twisted in a funny way. Where were they going? She hoped they'd get there soon.

***

The last time Carolien had seen Po Han was when she sent him away from Nanna's front gate, almost a year ago. She impatiently pushed away the lingering feeling that crept up with the memory of their early days together. She had been a fool to fall for his dreams. Life was based on essentials, such as jobs. They had freed themselves from the yoke of tradition to live a comfortable secure life, not to have to struggle from one day to the next for necessities.

"I wonder if he'll have anything to say for himself," Ting said.

"It really doesn't matter. The fact is that he has a responsibility to fulfill." Chip looked in the rearview mirror at Carolien. "You don't have any second thoughts, do you?"

"No, no. Of course not." Carolien looked away. She could not help wondering how Po Han would look. Why couldn't he have found himself a paying job like everyone else?

A food vendor pushed his cart across the street and Chip slammed on his brakes. Jenny swayed with the motion and Carolien caught her. "I want you to be a good girl when we're in court," she said, smoothing her daughter's dress.

"What's court?" Jenny wriggled in her seat.

"Look, that's the courthouse." Carolien pointed.

The courthouse was set back from the street and stood, with cool white importance, at the end of a walkway flanked by palm trees. Carolien was suddenly not sure if the lawyer's suggestion to bring Jenny was such a good idea.

Carolien and Sue, with Jenny between them, walked behind Chip and Ting up the wide steps to a spacious open verandah. Men carrying large briefcases mingled and engaged in muffled conversation. There were very few women and no children. A tall skinny Dutchman wearing round gold-rimmed glasses approached Chip and Ting and shook their hands.

"That's the lawyer." Carolien left to join the men. "Hello, Mr. van Buren." Carolien stepped into the circle.

"Hello, Mrs. Lee." Theo van Buren shook Carolien's hand. He nodded in Jenny's direction. "That must be Jenny. She's five, correct?"

"Yes." Carolien could not keep the nervous quiver out of her voice.

"Don't you worry," the lawyer soothed. "This is an easy case. We have plenty of proof that he never made enough money to support a family. We'll have no problem convincing the judge to rule for custody and child support."

"But how can you make him pay anything if he doesn't have the money?" Carolien pretended not to catch the warning glance Chip shot her.

"Don't you worry, that's his problem." Theo van Buren looked at his watch. "We better get to our seats," he said.

The courtroom was filled with Dutch people and hummed with hushed voices. "Remember, I told you to be a good girl," Carolien whispered. She lifted Jenny onto a wooden pew in one of the front rows and took a seat beside her.

Carolien smoothed her skirt, crossed her legs, and folded her hands in a prayer-like fashion on her lap. Despite the lawyer's reassurances, she couldn't help feeling anxious. Her thoughts drifted back to her struggles with Po Han. How could he have wasted time taking worthless pictures when they needed household money? He never even noticed she had taken her diamond pendant to the pawnshop. Carolien brought her hand to her throat and hooked a finger around the gold necklace where the pendant used to hang.

***

The bailiff announced the judge and the room fell silent. Jenny leaned forward to take a better look at the man behind the podium. His flowing black robe and headdress made him look like a magician.

Someone sneezed. Jenny looked to see who it was and caught sight of Po Han. She wasn't sure at first and scooted to the edge of the pew to get a better view.

Po Han sat across the aisle, dressed in a white suit. He scanned the rows of pews around him. When their eyes met, Jenny jumped off the bench.

"Jenny." Po Han lunged toward her. His familiar voice was hardly audible.

"Daddy!" she called, starting toward him.

"Be quiet!" Carolien grabbed Jenny by the arm and yanked her back into her seat.

"Daddy! Daddy!" Jenny pulled away from Carolien, kicking at Sue who tried to hold her.

"Please, take her outside," Carolien whispered.

Jenny thrashed her arms and legs while Sue carried her out of the courtroom into the adjacent hallway. "Shh, shh," Sue soothed. "Poor child, your mother will come soon." She tried to fold Jenny into her arms.

"Daddy! Daddy!" Jenny remembered the morning of Carolien and Po Han's fight. She had clung to his legs while Carolien was trying to pull her away. "Daddy!" Jenny screamed. Kicking and pushing against Sue, she tried to twist out of her aunt's grip.

"Jenny. Hush, be quiet." Neither the lollipops, miraculously appearing from Sue's handbag, nor her agitated whispers, could quieten Jenny.

The doors of the courtroom finally opened. Jenny spotted Po Han among the crowd. He strode down the long hallway.

"Daddy!" Jenny wrestled in Sue's arms. When Sue wouldn't let go, Jenny bit hard into Sue's hand and tore loose. She ran after Po Han, yelling, "Daddy! Daddy!"

***

Carolien moved quickly ahead of her brothers and the lawyer. Jenny's cries filled the hallway as she ran after Po Han. Carolien caught up with Jenny and shook her hard by the shoulders. "Stop it!" She hissed, scooping up the crying child.

Carolien stared at Po Han's disappearing back. She wanted to feel triumphant, energized, and powerful. The judgment was in her favor. She had succeeded. Yet she couldn't feel anything other than a sharp pain. Carolien brushed a hand across her face as she pushed her hair in place. Turning, she carried Jenny back to where the others were waiting.

Sue took Jenny from Carolien. "Sshh," she soothed. "When we get home, Auntie Sue is going to make you a batch of cookies." Sue held Jenny and rubbed her back.

"That wasn't too bad," Ting said on the drive home. He turned sideways to face the others.

"We're not done yet," Chip said, glancing in the rearview mirror. "Just because the judge ordered him to pay doesn't mean he will."

Carolien grabbed the back of Ting's seat and leaned forward. "Why do you say that?"

Chip raised his eyebrows. "Don't forget, he just won that national photo contest. I heard at the club that the winner has a year of internship in Holland. Po Han might soon be living too far away to find him." Chip maneuvered between taxis, bicycles, *delmans*, and pedestrians crossing the street. "Knowing him he'll go, in spite of the fact that war could break out in Europe at any time. Hitler keeps on moving and it won't be long before the Brits and the French get really fed up."

"But Holland isn't involved," said Carolien as she shifted back in her seat.

"We'll see about that," said Chip. "Don't forget that Holland is practically sandwiched between Germany, France, and England. How long do you think it will take before the Dutch will be forced into the mix?"

Chip's suggestion that Po Han might leave and be caught in a war in Europe made Carolien's heart jump into her throat. She swallowed a couple of times and ran the tip of her tongue across her lips.

"For that matter, it might get real messy right here," Ting said. "Radio Hilversum announced that Holland has rejected the native's petition for autonomy." He waved at a group of native food vendors, cigarette and paperboys as Chip drove by the town's square. "I hope the Dutch are not biting off more than they can chew. They have the Germans at home, Sukarno is constantly stirring things up here, and the Japanese are slithering in."

Chip's prediction proved to be true. After receiving several payments with Po Han's local address, Carolien received the check for March of 1940 in an envelope with Dutch stamps. Po Han had moved to Holland.

***

Ocho leaned over the banister of the front porch and spit into the bushes in the front yard, feeling an elated sense of freedom. The memory of Carolien's disgusted looks every time the woman had caught her spitting brought a hot flush of anger to Ocho's cheeks. Po Han had left in early February and told her not to expect a letter until mid-March. She had been waiting each day for the mailman ever since.

A few houses away a dog barked and, minutes later, the mailman approached on his bicycle. "You have mail from Holland." He handed Ocho a light-blue envelope with foreign stamps. Excited, she left the house immediately for Pension Warringin.

Nick de Graaf read Po Han's letter to Ocho, and she hung on every word.

Amsterdam, March 7, 1940.
Dearest Ocho,
    After a month on the boat, it feels good to walk on solid soil. It is very cold here. I don't think I'll ever

complain again about the heat of the tropics. I hope that you're doing well. Remember, Mr. de Graaf will help you whenever you need it.

Jaap's friends helped me to find an attic room. I have to climb three flights of very narrow stairs to get to it, but that is fine. Today I went to see the people at the photography lab. They were very nice. It seems that my portfolio made quite an impression on them. They told me that I'll have complete access to the lab as long as I put their name on anything I send out. I still can't believe that I can shoot as many rolls as I want without worrying about the cost. I'm starting on Monday. The amount of images just begging to be photographed is overwhelming. I have to go now. It just started snowing and I want to try to capture a falling snowflake so you can see it too.

Give Mr. de Graaf my best and tell him how grateful I am for his care of you. I'll write to him tonight. I have to go now. Take care.

Respectfully,
Po Han.

Nick folded the letter and returned it to the envelope. "It seems that things are going well," he said, handing it to Ocho.

"He didn't say anything about where he's getting his meals. Who's cleaning his room and doing his laundry?" Ocho stuck the letter into her cummerbund. The thought of being unable to care for Po Han brought a sharp pain. She wished Po Han had promised to send her pictures of his room and the Dutch people he lived with rather than the thing he called snowflakes. Ocho squinted at Nick. "The Dutch people liked Po Han's pictures, yes?"

"Yes, they did." Nick smiled.

"Po Han will be an important man when he comes back." Ocho moved a hand across the letter to disperse the pain of missing him.

"Better yet, Po Han will be a happy man when he comes back. The only thing that can mess things up is this war the newspapers are full of."

Ocho shrugged. She wasn't going to worry about something she didn't understand. She went to sleep that night with Po Han's letter safely tucked in her pillowcase.

CHAPTER 7

Nanna and Mundi were working in the vegetable garden when they heard a horn blare. Mundi ran to open the gate and Chip's car roared up the driveway. Sue and Emma came out of the house, drawn by the noise. Why was Chip home, only hours after he had left for the office?

Chip jumped out of the car. "The Germans have invaded Holland! They've taken Waalhaven and are trying to get to The Hague." He ran into the house and straight to the living room, where he turned on the radio. The family followed behind.

"At three o'clock this morning, the German Wehrmacht crossed our borders, violating Holland's neutrality," a Dutch reporter announced. Everyone huddled around the small speaker. "Waalhaven and several other airbases are under heavy attack by German bombers. This is Radio Hilversum with a special continuous broadcast."

"Emma–get Jenny. The schools will be closed." Chip turned to Nanna and Sue. "The Japanese have an alliance with Germany–we could be involved any time now. We've got to get ready. Fill up the water containers and make sure we have food in the house. Have a supply of candles, matches, and flashlights on hand. I've got to go back to my office. We have to remove some important documents." He looked at Nanna, "I've ordered Mundi to begin digging a bomb shelter." Chip rushed out of the room. "Batteries," he shouted over his shoulder. "Don't forget to get batteries!"

***

1941 marked the steady deterioration of Dutch and Japanese diplomatic relations. Nanna listened to the agitated dinner conversations between Chip, Ting, and Carolien about the war. The Japanese insisted on annexing the Netherlands Indies to their East Asia Co-Prosperity Sphere, which would give the colony the right to self-rule. The Dutch, naturally, opposed that idea. They also refused Japan's demands for oil, rubber, and aviation fuel.

Occasionally the siblings involved Eddie in their conversation. Until this point, being enlisted in the KNIL only meant Eddie wore a Dutch army uniform when he left for work in the morning. This changed in December when he was called to active duty. The Japanese had attacked Pearl Harbor and the Dutch, along with other Western nations, had declared war on Japan.

Nanna sat on Eddie's bed while he packed his duffle bag.

"How long will you be gone?" she asked her only grandson.

"I don't know. We were only told to get ready."

Sue came into the room with a stack of clothes for Eddie to pack. "Do you have everything you need? Can I get you anything?"

"I have everything. Thank you." Eddie looked from Nanna to his mother and said, "Please, try not to worry too much. Until the Japanese are actually here I'll most likely be downtown at the base."

"I'll be on the back porch if you need something." Sue left the room, wiping her cheeks.

Nanna watched Eddie finish packing. He cinched up his duffel bag and came to her. "I've got to go now," he said, falling to his knees.

Nanna placed her hands on Eddie's bowed head. "Get up," she said, lightly touching his shoulders. "Let's ask the spirits to keep you safe."

Nanna lit a large bundle of incense sticks at the altar in the dining room and handed half of them to Eddie. Standing next to him, she begged the spirits to keep her grandson safe.

Eddie held his offering high, the way Nanna had taught him. She noticed his clenched jaw, his shoulders and chest moving with rapid breathing. Nanna asked the gods to forgive Eddie for being so wrapped up in his worries that he was unable to receive their presence. She asked for a calm that would hold both of them. When Eddie's breathing became even, Nanna thanked the gods and placed her incense sticks in the urns on the altar. She wished her grandson would employ the gods as she did; she knew he only went through the motions to please her.

After Eddie left, Nanna followed the news closely. The radio and newspapers reported rapid advancements of Japanese military forces, but it wasn't until February of 1942 that the Japanese began air raids on Java. Bombs fell on cities as close as Batavia, everyone worried.

The Japanese takeover was swift. Fighting a hopeless battle in the rice paddies at Bandung's city limits, Eddie's unit was quickly overpowered. The KNIL surrendered to the Japanese Army on March 8th. After Chip broke the news to Nanna she took up a daily vigil on the front porch bench, hoping her grandson would return.

***

It was several days before a clink of the gate latch interrupted Jenny's game of hopscotch on the driveway and Eddie staggered toward the house. "Eddie!" Jenny ran to meet him. His military uniform was crumpled and muddy. One of his sleeves was torn and he had a wide bloody bandage wrapped around his shoulder. Dark stubble covered his cheeks and throat.

"Careful." Eddie caught Jenny. He held her briefly before pushing her out of the way and walking up the porch steps to greet Nanna.

"Come. Let me take care of you." Nanna walked ahead of Eddie into the house. Jenny started to follow, but Nanna told her to go play in the yard.

The door to Eddie's room remained closed for the rest of the day. Emma hovered nearby like a sentry. When Jenny ran down the hallway Emma scolded her. "Stop making so much noise. Those rotten Japs shot Eddie. He hasn't slept for three days."

Eddie remained in his room until the next day. Jenny was sitting at the dining room table doing homework when he appeared. Clean-shaven and cheerful, only his bandaged shoulder revealed that anything had happened to him. "How's my monkey doing?" he asked, ruffling Jenny's short hair.

"Eddie, why did the Japs shoot you? Do you have a big hole? Can I see it? Does it hurt?"

Eddie slowly lowered himself into a chair. "They told you in school that we were at war, right?"

"Yes. That's why we have the bomb shelter. When the sirens go off we have to bite into this rubber block," Jenny held up the piece of rubber dangling from a string around her neck. "So when the enemy throws bombs down, we won't bite off our tongues."

"That's right." Eddie rubbed his injured shoulder. "The Japanese are the enemy. We fought to keep them from coming here, but we lost and now they're here."

"What do they look like?"

"Japanese people look like us," Eddie said. "They're people, like you and me. It's just that they are at war against us."

"Are they scary?" Jenny recalled the mean faces and scary figures of enemies depicted in her storybooks.

"No, they're not scary," Eddie paused. "It's their guns and bombs that are scary." Jenny stared at the bulge at Eddie's shoulder and he unbuttoned his shirt. "See, it isn't that bad."

Jenny scrutinized the white cloth. It wasn't at all what she had imagined a bullet wound would look like, nothing was bloody. She fingered the bandage and thought suddenly of Po Han. Was he also fighting in the war and shot, like Eddie?

***

Carolien looked up from her book when Eddie joined her on the back porch. "How do you feel?" she asked him. He looked thin.

"I'm okay." Eddie leaned against one of the pergola posts. "It's interesting to hear what a child thinks about war."

"Has Jenny been pestering you?"

"No. Not at all."

Carolien laughed. "You'd be the last one to admit it if that child was bothering you."

Eddie smiled briefly.

"You're lucky you got out, Ed. How bad was it?" Carolien fixed her eyes on her nephew.

He remained quiet for a while before speaking. "God, Auntie, it was awful. To sit in that foxhole, just shooting and being shot at. And later, to pick up the guys who got wounded and the guys who died. It was a bloody mess." Eddie's voice trailed away.

Carolien glanced at Eddie's taut face. After a moment of silence she asked, "How did you manage to get away?"

"The Major summoned me after our last briefing before the encounter. He instructed me to detach from the unit as soon as I was sure the Japs were winning. I've been ordered to hook up with the Underground."

***

Jenny saw her first Japanese the day three soldiers rang the gate bell and asked for Chip. From her hiding place on a branch of the mango tree she watched him walk to the garage with three men in uniform. It was hard to hear them talk over the dogs' barking. They spoke broken Malay with an accent she had trouble understanding.

Jenny peered through the branches. Eddie was right, the Japanese looked like Chinese people. Their eyes were shaped similarly and they had the same skin color.

Chip opened the garage. "Where are you taking my car?" he asked. They all went inside and Jenny couldn't hear the answer. The car engine started and ran for a few moments before it was turned off. Chip and two of the soldiers walked out of the garage. One of them tried to hand Chip a piece of paper but Chip ignored him.

The other soldier took a cloth from his trouser pocket. He wiped the perspiration off his face and stuffed the cloth between the collar of his shirt and his neck.

"*Tekan!*" The soldier pointed where he wanted Chip to sign the document. The car started again and slowly rolled out of the garage. The third Japanese soldier sat behind the wheel. He stopped behind the three men in the driveway.

Jenny shifted on her tree branch. What were the Japs going to do with Oldest Uncle's car? She leaned over, trying to catch the conversation.

"*Tekan.*" The Japanese soldier shoved the document into Chip's hand.

"When will I get it back?"

"You won't." The soldier laughed. "You're donating it to the Japanese government."

"What?" Chip whirled around.

One of the soldiers shoved Chip toward the front fender of the Simca, the others reached for the clubs hanging from the wide belts around their waists. "Are you refusing to show the Emperor goodwill?"

Chip took out the fountain pen he always carried clipped in his shirt pocket. Using the car's hood as a table, he signed the document. As Chip screwed the top of the pen back on, a soldier pointed at the pen. "The pen," he said, "beautiful." Grinning, he held out his hand.

Chip looked at the man and slowly put his pen back into his pocket. The soldiers laughed, jumped into the car, and drove off.

Chip stood motionless in the middle of the driveway. Then he threw his arms up and yelled, "*Schoften, God verdomde Jappen*!" Bastards, Goddamn Japs!

The myna bird cheerfully repeated, "*Jappen, God verdomde Jappen.*"

CHAPTER 8

Nanna made a food offering to the spirits of her parents and her dead husband, on the fifteenth day of the Chinese month, when the moon comes to a full round. Performing the ritual one day in May, shortly after the Japanese invasion, she cooked each family member's favorite dish, as well as a large bowl of fluffy steamed rice. Fruits, tea, and sweets completed the meal. It took her all day to prepare the food. This time the sweets were native cakes instead of Dutch pastries. Imported items such as wheat flour had become unavailable since the war, and once the Japanese took over the Dutch dairy farms, milk and butter became unobtainable as well.

In the late afternoon Nanna took a shower and put on clean clothes. She ordered Jenny to do the same. She served the food onto platters and arranged it on the altar table just before sundown. When Jenny joined her, she lit a bundle of incense sticks and said, "Let's show the spirits the way." Together they opened all the doors leading to the front porch.

Holding the lighted incense sticks in her clasped hands, Nanna walked praying through the open doors. She faced west and lifted the burning incense high in prayer. The sweet fragrance wafting around her, Nanna invited the spirits to come to the table she had prepared for them and asked that they bless the house. This time, she also asked her late husband if he approved of his children's involvement in Dutch political matters. She asked him if she did well to support their sons.

Nanna placed half of the smoking incense sticks in a hanging holder by the door. She divided the other half amongst urns on the altar. Then she took Jenny's hand and walked to the front porch, leaving the food to the spirits.

Nanna sank into meditation on the porch bench. With each exhalation she expelled her thoughts and feelings. The concrete shapes around her shifted into shadows. Other images moved into their place. Hazy at first, then rising from the mist with an unmistakable clarity, Nanna saw her house shrouded in darkness. She remained still for a while, engulfed in its emptiness, but her vision did not change. There was death and mourning, a loss in the family. She felt a sharp pain in her chest as the image blurred and moved into the background.

Nanna gazed down the driveway and rested her eyes on the gate. She knew now that the tall wrought-iron enclosure would not be able to keep harm out. The soft scent of jasmine drifted on the early evening breeze. A pale full moon hung high above the top of the tamarind tree and traveled across a cloudless sky. Jenny sat quietly next to her. Nanna tapped Jenny on the arm and rose. The darkness over the house had remained throughout the vision; it was a warning.

***

"The Japs are cruel bastards," Chip said that night at dinner, "but I must give them credit for one thing—they certainly don't tolerate any thievery." The family looked up from their dinner plates. "Don't go by the old Dutch Catholic School for Boys. The Japs have an *inlander* strung up against a tree trunk in front of the building. The poor devil is wearing nothing but a loincloth. Apparently, they caught him stealing."

"Is that what it was?" Ting filled the silence that followed. "I noticed a crowd of Japs when I turned down the street on my way home. They were rowdy and I heard some native screaming. I decided to turn around and come home another way."

"Lucky you. I didn't notice anything until it was too late to turn around." Chip took a sip of water, perspiration beading on his forehead. "The Japs will make you slap the guy to demonstrate your disapproval of stealing. If you don't slap him hard enough, they'll slap you. That's their way of teaching how to punish a thief. Those cruel runts sure went overboard here." Jenny looked at Oldest Uncle. Had the Japs made him slap the man too?

That night, in the bedroom, Jenny watched Els prepare *bedak dingin*, a cooling powder Nanna made from rice-flour and rose extract. Els put a few balls of the dried powder in a glass bowl. She added enough water and a few drops of eau de cologne to make a runny paste and smeared a thin layer on Jenny's arms and legs. The powder would dry on her skin and keep her cool during the night.

Jenny loved the soothing feeling. She drew figures in the still wet chalky film on her thigh while Els cleaned the glass bowl in the bedroom sink.

An unusual sound drifted through the half-open shutters. Someone wailed. Faint at first, the crying grew louder and louder. Jenny swung her legs over the edge of the bed and walked to the window. She finally distinguished the anguished words. *"Ampun, ampun!"*

Jenny tried to peek through the half opened shutters. It was dark outside. The wind had picked up and brushed against house.

"Ampun... Ampu-u-n."

"Els, is that the guy on the tree asking for forgiveness?"

"I think so." Els finished drying the bowl and returned it to the vanity. She nudged Jenny toward the bed. "Go lie down now."

Nanna walked into the room while Jenny climbed back in bed. "Els," she said, "please close the shutters all the way." She propped her pillows against the end of the bed and patted the place next to her. "Come, Jenny, lie down. It's time to sleep."

Jenny turned on her side and moved her forehead against Nanna's arm. She took Nanna's hand and traced the blue veins that ran crisscross through the top of her grandmother's hand. Outside, the wind carried a man's cry for forgiveness through the sultry July night.

***

The back porch was the coolest place to play in the afternoon. Jenny peered through the sheer curtains of the library doors. Chip sat at his desk. Would she disturb him if she played here? She took a big marble out of her pocket and rolled it with a flick of her thumb across the tiled floor. She chased it with another one and when the two marbles collided with a sharp click, she looked at Chip. He remained bent over his papers. The sound must not have bothered him.

One of the marbles rolled under the table and Jenny crouched to retrieve it as the library door opened behind her. "Jenny!" Chip called.

"Yes, sir." Jenny crawled out, bumping her head. She stuck the marble into her pocket and slapped some dust off her knees. She had disturbed Oldest Uncle after all.

"Come here." Chip flicked a cigarette stub into the yard.

Jenny gathered the rest of the colorful glass balls and put them in her pockets before walking toward her uncle.

Chip lit another cigarette and took a long drag. "Would you like to do something very important?"

Jenny lowered her eyes, fingering the marbles. Oldest Uncle usually only spoke to her to say she was being too noisy.

"Come with me." Chip headed for the bike shed. "I'm taking Jenny with me on an errand," he called to Sue as they passed the kitchen.

Chip pulled his bike off the rack. "Get on," he ordered.

Jenny climbed on the buddy-seat. She wondered where Oldest Uncle was going to take her, but she was too afraid to ask.

"Hold on tight," Chip said when they went around the first corner. He turned his head, "Are you okay? You're awfully quiet there."

"I'm all right." Jenny leaned sideways, trying to figure out where they were going.

They rode in silence, until Chip stopped at a vacant field. Big clumps of pampas grass and wild mulberries grew freely around abandoned old shacks. Chip went into one of the huts. Wheeling the bike next to him, he motioned for Jenny to follow.

Chip leaned the bike against a crumbling wall and cleared his throat. "Jenny," he said, looking at her. "I need you to do something important. Do you want to?"

"Yes, sir."

"Listen and do exactly as I tell you–and for once don't ask any questions. I need you to take medicine into the camp." Chip's expression was sterner than ever, but his voice was scratchy.

Jenny swallowed. She knew her uncle was talking about the Japanese-run internment camp nearby. She ran the tip of her tongue across her lips, but didn't dare voice the questions that tumbled through her mind.

Following Chip through the tall clumps of pampas grass, Jenny peered into the dense growth. She could see the barbed-wire fence that marked the edge of the camp. The camp guards marched in fours from one end of the fence to the other.

Chip grabbed Jenny by the arm and pulled her back. He placed his index finger against his lips, shaking his head. After the guards walked away he took a claw hammer from a bag he carried and began clearing a layer of fallen leaves and underbrush. He unearthed a manhole cover and lifted it. A foul stench rose from the exposed main sewer line. Jenny wrinkled her nose.

Chip took a white box out of his trouser pocket. "Jenny, without this medicine, someone is going to die." He handed her the small container. "Put it in your pocket as deep as you can. Don't drop it."

After Jenny stuffed the little white box into her overall pocket, Chip strapped a flashlight to Jenny's waist and gave her detailed instructions about navigating the pipe. "Try not to fall," he said. "I'll be here, waiting for you."

Chip lowered Jenny into the dark hole. The sewage stench enveloped her as she sank deeper. She gasped when Chip dropped her onto a slippery surface. The smell turned her stomach.

"Listen for the guard's footsteps before you knock on the cover-plate," Chip whispered, before pushing the manhole cover back in place.

Jenny put one hand up against the slimy sewer wall and switched on the flashlight. Sewage fumes filled her nostrils. A wave of nausea went through her and she swayed. Crossing her arms against her stomach, she doubled over and retched.

Jenny reminded herself that she was not supposed to fall and started to slide her feet forward. She had just become accustomed to her footing when she heard footsteps right above her. She groped her way forward, making sure that the footsteps remained above her, until she reached a fork in the tunnel. Following Chip's instructions, she searched the top of the tunnel with her flashlight until the narrow light-beam hit a metal plate.

Jenny stood still and listened for the guards to pass. She searched the sewer wall with her light until she saw a stick stuck against the wall of the tunnel, just as Chip had told her she would.

Above ground, the Japanese guards came to the end of their stretch. Jenny heard the stomping of their about-turn before they resumed marching. Chip had instructed her to count to one-hundred-and-ten before tapping on the metal plate.

Jenny pulled the stick out of the metal clamp. She slid her hand across the smooth wood. It was as if she held a magic wand. She tapped against the metal manhole cover and the plate lifted instantly. A shaft of light tumbled into the hole. A hand filled the space.

Jenny took a deep breath of fresh air and reached into her pocket, trembling. She placed the small box in the open hand and watched the bony fingers close around it. The hand pulled back and the metal plate moved across the circle of light.

The stench in the sewer seemed to be stronger, the light from the flashlight weaker than when she first walked through the pipe. Jenny pressed her hands to her mouth, afraid that the guards might hear her if she vomited. What would they do to her if she were caught? She slipped a few times as she made her way back down the tunnel, scraping her face against the sludgy sewer wall.

When she returned to the place where she had entered, Jenny stood listening. Everything was quiet and she tapped on the metal plate above her. It moved immediately.

Chip leaned into the hole. "Grab my arms and hold on tight," he whispered, reaching for Jenny. He took hold of her elbows and pulled her out of the manhole.

"Thank God you're back," Chip murmured, steadying Jenny. He shoved the manhole cover back in place and pushed dry leaves and loose dirt over it. Then he took Jenny's hand and pulled her along through the brush.

Chip stopped in a small clearing, surrounded by dense growth. He wiped the perspiration off his forehead and looked down at Jenny. She stood before him, catching her breath. Chip brusquely pulled her into his arms. "You're a brave little girl," he mumbled.

Jenny trembled and Chip eased his grip. He stroked her head and picked off some of the sludge stuck to her hair. Jenny slowly relaxed in her uncle's arms, her heartbeat slowed but a deep sense of accomplishment remained. She and Oldest Uncle had outfoxed the Japs!

Chip moved a few steps back and gave Jenny a once over. "We'd better get you cleaned up before going home." He took a crisp white handkerchief out of a trouser pocket and wiped Jenny's face and arms. Then he dug a deep narrow hole with the claw hammer and buried his soiled handkerchief.

Jenny watched Chip tamp the soil with the heel of his shoe. Oldest Uncle must be happy with her–he had used his clean handkerchief to wipe poop off her face! The next time Emma or her mother said that she couldn't do anything right, she would tell them that they were wrong.

"Jenny, listen," Chip's normal voice was back and he grabbed Jenny by the arms.

"Yes, sir." Jenny looked up at Chip.

"Promise you won't tell anyone about what we just did. *No one*, not even Nanna. Promise?"

Nanna always said that making a promise was a very serious matter. One was never to make a promise lightly. Jenny swallowed hard. She was disappointed that she couldn't brag about her adventure to Emma, but even more, she wanted to preserve the esteem she had gained from Oldest Uncle.

"I promise," she said, looking straight at Chip. He let go of her, sighing.

"Will I get in trouble for getting my clothes so dirty?"

"I promise you won't," he assured her.

Neither of them spoke on the way home. Jenny leaned forward when they turned onto their street, her cheek almost brushing against Chip's arm. "What do I say when they ask why I smell so bad?"

"No one will ask you anything," Chip answered firmly. He helped Jenny off the bike by the front gate. She walked quietly behind him to the bike shed.

Nanna, Sue, Carolien, Emma, and Els sat around the table on the back porch as Chip and Jenny walked up from the bike shed.

"I took Jenny with me on an errand and she got dirty," Chip said, stepping into the archway of the chayote squash vine.

Nanna and Sue looked up from their beadwork, Carolien dropped her knitting into her lap, and the girls halted their mending. Chip held Jenny by her shoulders in front of him.

Jenny glanced around the circle of women. She tried to catch the look in Nanna's eyes, but her grandmother's gaze fastened on Chip. "Els, give Jenny hot water to take a *mandi*," she said.

Only important people were given boiling water to mix with the cold well water for their dip shower. A quiet pride filled Jenny as she followed Els to the bathroom. She was getting a hot shower, just like Nanna and the uncles.

Jenny watched Els mix the water. She didn't protest when Els handed her a sponge made from the fibers of a dried-up squash. "Here, scrub yourself well, okay?" The sponge was rough and it hurt to scrub with it, but it was what Nanna and the uncles used. Jenny dipped the *gajung* into the water and emptied several of the saucepan-like containers of water over her head. The warm water flowed around her. She rubbed the wet sponge across a bar of soap and covered her body with the rich lather.

***

Carolien folded her knitting and stuck the needles into the ball of yarn. Jenny had mud on her clothes and shoes and her oldest brother was avoiding their mother's scrutinizing look. There was a forced calmness in his voice when he said, "I'd like to take a *mandi* after Jenny is done. I'll be in the library."

Carolien jerked her chair back and followed Chip. "Where did you take Jenny?" she asked, closing the library door behind her.

"It's better you don't know." Chip looked away. "Jenny's a brave kid. You can be proud of her, Carolien. We all can be proud of her–and the Dutch better be damned grateful when this is all over."

Carolien knew that Chip was having trouble passing material across the fences with the heightened security around the internment camp. "Don't tell me you used Jenny as a courier."

"As I said, it's better you don't know."

"I won't have you risking Jenny's safety. I'm telling Mother. She won't let you–" Tears sprang into Carolien's eyes. It didn't matter what she did. In the end, she remained the youngest sister with no say over anything, not even the safety of her own child.

"You don't have to. Mother knows what's going on without being told, you know that as well as I do." Chip put his hands on Carolien's shoulders. "I'm sorry," he said, "It had to be done."

CHAPTER 9

Nanna covered the tender buds on the rosebushes with empty eggshells to protect them from insects and wished there were a way she could shield her family from harm just as easily. She knew the ancestors and gods would not be able to keep them safe until the war was over. Nanna had always considered war to be a man's affair, but this war not only involved Carolien, it had also found its way to Jenny.

The voices of Chip, Ting, and Mundi came from the kitchen area, interspersed with hammering and sawing. Chip had decided that he would use the kitchen cupboard as his hiding place should the Japanese come looking for him, and the dogs would serve as protection. Nanna had not asked for details. She was fully aware of the tension that hung in the air. It made the women nervous and irritable and the men more silent than usual. Nanna spent a lot of time on the front porch bench, looking down the street. When Jenny joined her she silently rubbed the girl's hand, her heart filled with a mother's fear for the safety of her children.

Almost a week went by before a Japanese jeep stopped in front of the house one afternoon. Four Japanese soldiers jumped out and walked up the driveway with their rifles slung loosely across their shoulders. Nanna grabbed Jenny's arm and drew her close.

The Japanese halted for a moment in the driveway before the sergeant walked with confident strides up the porch steps. He bowed to Nanna and flashed a big smile to Jenny. He then took a letter out of his shirt pocket and handed Nanna the document.

She shook her head. "I can't read."

"Who else is home?" The Japanese spoke in heavy accented Malay.

"My daughters and granddaughters."

One of the soldiers offered Jenny a piece of melted chocolate. When she shook her head and scooted closer to Nanna, he shrugged his shoulders.

"Do you know Ong Chip Hong?" the sergeant asked.

"Yes, he's my son."

"Where's he now?"

"Not home."

"When will he be home?"

"I don't know."

"Who's the head of the household?"

"I'm a widow. He's the oldest son living with me, so he is." Nanna held the Japanese in a steadfast gaze. "Who's the letter for?"

"The head of the household." The soldier replied, puzzled.

"Then I guess you have to come back when he is home."

The soldier who had offered Jenny the chocolate held his arms out for her. "Come." His broad smile showed a gold tooth. "At home I have a little girl, just like her." The soldier patted Jenny on the head, then abruptly turned around and joined the others walking down the driveway.

Nanna waited for the sound of the jeep to disappear into the empty street before taking Jenny inside the house. She knew it was only a matter of time before the Japanese would be back. Her children's Dutch involvement drew them, and it would not be possible to hold them off forever.

Two days later, Nanna and Jenny were dusting the altar tables while Carolien worked on a sewing pattern at the dining room table, when the dogs barged into the room barking furiously. Someone was at the gate.

Nanna put her dust rag down. "Lock up the dogs," she said, "and tell Chip and Ting the Japs are here." Nanna threw a quick glance at her late husband's portrait on the altar wall.

The same four Japanese soldiers who had come two days before stood on the porch. The one closest to the door asked, "Is Ong Chip Hong home?"

"No." Nanna put an arm around Jenny.

"We need to search the house," the soldier said.

Nanna pulled her shoulders back and looked at each soldier with a steady gaze. "I won't let you in," she said firmly.

Some of the soldiers shifted the guns slung across their shoulders.

The dogs' barking became faint. Nanna knew they would be locked up in the kitchen by now. She took a few deep breaths.

Ting opened the front door and spoke into her back. "Mother, please, let me help these gentlemen."

Nanna did not move. She had always given Ting the same preferential treatment reserved for Chip, even though he was only a second son, but now he was asking her to take direction from him. Was this the day that her vision would come true?

Nanna put a hand on Jenny's shoulder. She steered the girl past the soldiers. "Jenny, come," she said, "sit by me."

Jenny obeyed quietly.

The men entered the house as Nanna and Jenny took their seats on the porch bench. The dogs barked ferociously at the intruders, until a rapid rattling of gunshots rang out, followed by screams from Sue, Emma, and Els, mixed with agitated Japanese voices. Nanna felt her chest expand. She clamped one hand around the edge of her seat and grabbed Jenny's arm with the other. The dogs were quiet now. Nanna took a deep breath. Something hard and large dislodged itself inside her as she tried to breathe and stay calm. Had the time of mourning come already?

Els came running through the front door. "Nanna! Nanna! They shot the dogs! The Japs are going to kill us all!"

Jenny jumped up. "Is Claus dead? Did the Japs kill Claus?"

"Jenny, stay here!" Nanna pulled Jenny back into her seat. Making room for Els on the bench, Nanna reached for the sobbing girl.

Voices came closer. The Japanese soldiers came through the front door. Nanna spotted Chip in their midst. She saw Ting, Eddie, Sue, Carolien, and Emma following them and she breathed easier. It seemed the dogs had been the only victims of the gunshots.

Nanna stiffened when the men walked by. She closed a hand around Els' shoulder. Pulling Jenny closer, she cast a glance at Chip. He looked away but she caught a glimpse of his battered face and noticed the bright red spots on the handkerchief he held pressed against his mouth.

Nanna watched Chip climb into the Japanese jeep. He moved slowly, burdened by Dutch secrets. Nanna knew her son would not talk. His blood would be thick and silent.

***

Carolien sat on the floor of Ting's room with Claus' head in her lap. Ting, sitting next to her, wrapped one of the dog's front paws in a towel. Claus whimpered and she stroked the dog between his ears.

One of his pads is cut wide open." Ting looked up, his face ashen. "He might have stepped on broken glass."

"What are you going to do?" Carolien was irritated. She had never understood Ting's devotion for his dogs. She wanted to tell him to be happy the Japs had only shot the dogs, it could have been any of them, but she knew better.

"I've got to find the shard and take it out. Here, hold the towel against the wound. Try to stem the blood flow." Ting rose. "I've got to get a few things."

Once alone in the room, Carolien straightened. Her back hurt from sitting bent over for so long. A heap of bloody towels reminded her of the afternoon. The Japs storming into the house, waving their guns, screaming, "Ong Chip Hong! Come out!" The dogs barking and jumping against the closed kitchen door, the sudden gunfire, the dogs dropping to the floor, her standing there with shaking knees, afraid the bullets would hit the cupboard, penetrate the wood, and hit Chip. What would the Japs do to Chip? Although she was aloof with her brothers, she looked up at Chip and admired him greatly.

Ting returned, followed by Eddie and Jenny.

"Claus!" Jenny cried, dropping next to the dog. He lifted his head, whimpering.

"Here, if you hold his head in your lap, I can help Youngest Uncle check his leg." Carolien shifted the dog's head carefully into Jenny's lap.

"Oh, Claus. You'll be okay." Jenny scratched the dog's ears. Stroking his muzzle, she repeated, "You'll be okay. You'll see." Claus sighed and slapped the floor with his tail.

Jenny watched as Ting washed the dog's paw in a solution of water and iodine before pulling out the shard with a pair of tweezers. "I want to be a veterinarian when I grow up," she said.

Ting laughed and Eddie said, "I think you'll be a good one."

Carolien frowned. Jenny was picking up too much of Nanna's and Ting's ways. With all the decent occupations to choose from, why did she want to become a veterinarian?

Eddie helped Ting and Carolien pick up the room before taking a seat on the edge of Ting's bed.

"Where are all the other dogs?" Jenny stroked Claus between his ears.

"Dead." Eddie clenched his jaws.

"Caesar too?"

"No. He almost killed one of the Japs. You should've seen how that dog attacked." Eddie rose. "Fortunately, the Japs didn't shoot him, they only clubbed him. Youngest Uncle was able to get him away in the midst of the commotion and put him with Emma in the servant's bathroom. He might have gotten away with a broken shoulder."

"Why did the Japs take Oldest Uncle with them and why did they kill all the dogs?" Jenny asked, keeping her eyes on Claus.

"Before the war, Oldest Uncle worked for the Dutch government. As a matter of fact, he still does." Eddie stopped abruptly when Carolien glared at him.

"And?"

"The Japs wanted Oldest Uncle to tell them about his office. He hid in the big kitchen cupboard, we thought he would be safe there. No one expected the Japs to gun down the dogs."

"Are the Japs going to kill Oldest Uncle?"

"Let's hope not," Carolien said. "The Dutch will be back soon and I'm sure they'll set Oldest Uncle free." She tried to sound convincing, but she knew that no one, including herself, believed her.

***

Chip's capture by the Japanese moved slowly into the background of everyday life. Across the country families bound together to get through the war. With the Dutch government shut down and no salary coming in, Ting and Carolien began trading on the black market. The tobacco store that Chip and Ting had set up as a front for their undercover work now also carried clothing and foodstuffs. Carolien took in sewing. Along with Eddie and Ting, she was active in the Dutch Underground.

With the Dutch schools shut down Els took responsibility for Jenny's schooling, tutoring her every day so she wouldn't fall behind. Els had received her teaching credential just before the war broke out but had not worked in a school yet. The family disapproved of her teaching at a school for natives and there had been no openings yet at any of the Dutch schools.

By September, the mango blossoms had turned into plump, deep-yellow fruit but the war showed no signs of ending soon. Jenny was in the backyard, helping Nanna and Mundi prop up the laden mango branches, when a car stopped by the front gate and the bell rang. She ran to see who it was, but Nanna called her back and sent Mundi instead.

Jenny shot Nanna a sideways glance. The dogs lay near her, their ears perked, noses pointed toward the gate. An eerie stillness filled the moments before Mundi returned with a letter in his hand. He fell to his knees and bowed deeply before handing Nanna the brown envelope.

Nanna straightened herself. "Thank you," she said. Her voice was steady but her hand trembled as she took the item. "You and *Non* Jenny finish up while I take this inside."

Mundi remained on his knees as Nanna walked away. "It's all because of the Dutch, *Nonnie.*" Mundi sighed, rising when Nanna was out of sight.

"Why do you say that?" Jenny frowned. She wasn't used to servants talking without being spoken to first.

Mundi reached for the bamboo pole Nanna had left leaning against the tree trunk. "It's time for the Dutch to go back to their country, Young Miss," Mundi said and walked away.

Jenny watched Mundi disappear into the garden. Was Mundi against the Dutch? Did he side with the Japs? Maybe Mundi was traitor....

After dinner that night Nanna took a letter from the altar table and handed it to Ting. "The Japs delivered this earlier," she said.

Ting used his fruit knife to open the envelope. Jenny saw him blinking hard as he glanced at the page. He cleared his throat before reading aloud to the gathered family. "The Japanese Emperor and government regret that prisoner Ong Chip Hong's uncooperative attitude necessitated the use of more forceful methods than are customary. We further regret to have to inform you that during the course of interrogation, the above mentioned prisoner died on September 27, 1944. The Japanese authorities have disposed of his body." Ting's voice faltered.

Sue burst into tears. Els got up and walked to Nanna. Eddie pulled Jenny on his lap so Els could sit in the chair next to their grandmother. Carolien and Emma cried into their napkins.

Nanna walked to the altar. She lit a bundle of incense sticks and raised them high in prayer. "The Dutch are asking too much," she said without turning around.

Jenny stared at her grandmother's rigid back and chewed her knuckles. She noticed a new urn on the altar table. When did Nanna place it there? Was Nanna now asking the spirits why Oldest Uncle had to die? What would their answer be?

CHAPTER 10

On a hot day in August of 1945, Nanna and Jenny were sitting at the back porch table, picking debris out of rice. They looked up when Ting flung the garage doors wide open and the tones of the Dutch national anthem blared through the air. "Listen! Listen! Ting waved his arms wildly and ran back into the garage.

Jenny jumped up and ran after him.

Nanna placed the basket of beans on the table, frowning. What was happening? Why was Ting giving away the radio's hiding place? She followed Jenny to the garage. Sue, Emma and Els came running from different parts of the house.

In the garage, Ting stood by the soap crate he and Chip had used to camouflage the radio when the Japanese ordered all radios to be turned in. A Dutch voice boomed through the air. "As a result of the American bombings of Hioroshima on August 6 and Nagasaki on August 9, the Japanese have surrendered to Allied Forces. The British forces are now in charge of the Netherlands' Indies."

"Listen to the news!" Ting shouted. Turning to Nanna, he continued, calmer. "I think the POW camps will be opened. Can you have Mundi get the cots out of the bomb shelter and fix up Chip's room? Eddie and Carolien will be bringing home their camp liaisons." Nanna understood the news. The Americans had bombed Japan and the war was over. But did Ting really expect her to allow strangers in his brother's room?

"Mundi. Quick. Bring a ladder and get the flag pole." Ting ran into the house and returned with a folded piece of cloth, which he attached to the staff Mundi handed him. When Ting pulled the string, a big Dutch flag unfurled.

Nanna watched the red, white, and blue sweep over her roof with an ominous feeling of loss. She knew danger still lingered close.

The whole family gathered in a circle around the ladder while the servants watched from a small distance. Nanna overheard Rina, the old cook. "*Bendera Belanda!*" she whispered as the Dutch flag fluttered in the wind.

Her daughter Mia, the laundry maid, remained quiet, but Mundi murmured, "It won't be for long."

"Come." Nanna tugged at Jenny's hand and they walked into the house.

Chip's room had remained untouched since the day he had been taken prisoner. Nanna entered it every day by herself. She often asked the spirits why they had found it necessary to take Chip's life, but they had not answered her. Now Ting had asked her to make Chip's room available to Dutch strangers. The white god was apparently not finished yet. How much more would be demanded?

Nanna started to put Chip's desk-set into an empty box. The solid silver ink-blotter lay heavy in her hand. The set had been a gift from the head of the Dutch Department of War and Welfare when Chip was promoted to Chief Accountant. Nanna fingered the silver rim around the desk pad. The Dutch gave useless gifts while asking for great sacrifice.

"*Njonja Besar* needs something?" Mundi's voice broke into Nanna's thoughts. He stood in the doorway, his dark eyes filled with curiosity and concern.

"Please get the cots out of the bomb shelter." Nanna placed the blotter into the box. "We need to rearrange Oldest Master's room. We're going to have Dutch houseguests. Tell Miss Jenny I need to see her, then come back to help me."

Alone again, Nanna pulled the sheets and a gray and white striped blanket off Chip's bed. The faint scent of Chip's pomade made her nostrils flare when she shook the pillow out of the case. Nanna pressed the bulk of soft kapok hard against her chest. Chip would have asked her to house the camp people, yet she felt reluctant to care for the strangers Chip had died for.

"Nanna, Mundi said you called me?" Jenny came into the room, Mundi behind her.

Nanna gathered the linens and handed Jenny the bundle. "Here, take these to Mia and get Emma." She looked around the room and took a deep breath. Then she turned to Mundi. "Move the bed into that corner and place two cots against that wall." Nanna grabbed Chip's pillows and took them to her bedroom.

In the cool and quiet of her spacious room, Nanna lifted the heavy brass latch on an ornately carved wooden chest. She fingered the *cheong sam* she had worn on her wedding day, and a Western suit her late husband used to wear at official Dutch functions. She buried her face into Chip's pillows before putting everything away.

***

The gate bell rang and the dogs barked at the intrusion. The myna bird responded cheerfully. "*Dag mevrouw, hoe gaat het er mee?*" Hello, Madam, how are you?

Jenny ran to the gate. A *delman* was parked in the street. Her mother sat in the carriage, a Dutch woman leaning against her. "Hurry, get Emma and Els," Carolien shouted, but Jenny didn't need to do anything, the whole household came rushing out the front door.

"Help me carry Mrs. van Houten," Carolien said. "She's too weak to walk."

Jenny leaned into Nanna while Emma, Els, and Carolien carried the woman into the house.

"*Dank U wel mevrouw, dank U wel.*" The woman thanked Nanna with a barely audible voice as they passed. Jenny had never seen anyone so skinny or so pale.

"Shhh, Greet, don't talk now." Jenny noticed that her mother's voice, although still authoritative, was strangely soothing. She slipped a hand around Nanna's arm and pushed the side of her face against her grandmother.

112

Nanna handed Jenny some change from the coin pouch she always carried around her waist. "Here, go pay the *delman* driver."

Jenny ran out to the waiting native. She usually asked to pet or feed the horse, or clank the foot-bell, but not this time. Instead, she quickly returned to join the others going inside the house.

"It's a good thing that woman didn't have to stay in the Jap camp one day longer," Emma said, as she and Els came back into the room.

"She has dysentery and her legs are all swollen. I better get the kettle going for bathing water," Els said.

"She also has lice." Emma followed Els to the kitchen.

Jenny was surprised. Natives had lice because they were dirty, but Mrs. van Houten was Dutch. Perhaps the Japanese were as dirty as the natives–the Dutch lady had caught lice in their camp.

The dogs began barking furiously while Mundi announced Ting's arrival with another Dutch guest. The myna bird tried to calm the dogs. "*Af* Caesar, *af* Claus," she shouted.

But the German shepherds didn't stop barking until Ting firmly said, *"Goed volk!"*

The "good folk" was a tall skinny Dutchman. His crumpled and torn clothes hung loosely around his emaciated body. His face was framed by uneven strands of blond hair and an unkempt beard. Ting introduced him as Mr. Bouwman.

Everyone stood in the shade of the mango tree where the myna bird's cage hung. The bird sat on her perch. She cocked her head and observed the stranger. Her bright orange temples pulsed as she cleared her throat.

Jan Bouwman approached Nanna and bowed. "Thank you so much for your hospitality. I'm sorry to be so dirty," he apologized, wiping bony fingers against torn trousers.

The myna bird recognized the word dirty. "Bring the bath-water! Bring the bath-water," she cheered.

"I think that there's a caldron of boiling water ready," Nanna said.

Ting showed Mr. Bouwman to the bathroom and Jenny followed Nanna into the house.

Greet van Houten did not come to the table at dinnertime. Jan Bouwman was now clean-shaven and wearing a shirt Jenny recognized as one of Chip's. He ate heartily from the steaming soup and meat pie Sue had prepared.

"This feels like a dream–I never thought I'd eat a decent meal again." Jan put his utensils down and leaned back. "It's hard to believe that the war is really over."

He spoke with a lisp and Jenny noticed that his front teeth were missing.

Carolien dabbed her mouth with her napkin. "How soon do you think everything will be back to normal? When will the schools reopen?"

"Your guess is as good as mine." Jan took another bite.

"How did you know the Japs had capitulated?" Ting asked.

"The radio. It was my turn to listen to the news." Jan put his fork down and leaned slightly into the table. "When the news broke over the wire, I turned the volume up full blast. Everyone began to run and break down the camp barriers. The guards were caught by surprise. One of them tried to shoot at us, but the mass overpowered him. They broke his gun and threw him onto a pile of his own barbed wire barricades."

Jan took a sip of water and continued. "The Commander came running out of the compound. He shouted something in Japanese and all the guards marched into their barracks. We never saw any of them after that."

"According to the peace treaty, the Japs will be held responsible for the way they treated their prisoners," Ting said.

"Greet told me that in the women's camp, they heard of the Japanese capitulation from *gedek* messengers," Carolien said. "They shouted the news through bullhorns and thrashed the bamboo-mat fencing. Greet said the Japs never tried to stop the women from leaving the camp."

"I heard that the Kempei Tai Commander committed *hara kiri*." Ting reached for his water glass.

"Suicide is one way to avoid a war trial," Jan Bouwman said. "The bastard knew he'd be held accountable for the way he mistreated prisoners. He used the end of his gun to hammer my teeth out."

The conversation reminded Jenny of the day Eddie had come home wounded. In the excitement of the camp people arriving, she hadn't noticed that Eddie had not returned home for dinner. Was he okay? Why hadn't he come home? Perhaps the Japs had shot him again.

"Where's Eddie?" Jenny shoved her plate to the center of the table and jumped off her chair. Neither Nanna nor Emma was quick enough to grab her. "I want Eddie!" Jenny ran out of the room, crying.

"Jenny, sit down," Carolien yelled.

"Calm down," Ting ordered.

"Jenny!" Nanna called.

Jenny ignored everyone. She ran out of the dining room. Slamming the door behind her, she headed for the bike shed. Agitated voices and crunching gravel told her the adults had caught up with her. The dogs barked at Jan Bouwman, who led the expedition of adults. Jenny grabbed her bike and pushed it out of the shed.

"Where do you think you're going?" Carolien stepped forward and reached for her.

Jenny ducked. She pushed her bike into her mother and ran toward the front gate.

Jan Bouwman caught Jenny around the waist and folded her into his long arms. His grip immobilized her but she struggled to get loose. The Dutchman's hairy arm lay across her chest and she bit hard into it.

"Ouch!" Jan Bouwman let go and Jenny ran off again. "I'll tell you where Eddie is," Jan called after her.

The closed gate stopped Jenny from running further. Jan Bouwman leaned against the garage door, his arm pressed against his back. "Please, go finish dinner," he said to the other adults. "Jenny and I will be in soon."

Jenny noticed the authority in Jan's voice. She glared at him, wondering why everyone listened to him. Was it because he was *Dutch*?

"I'll tell you where Eddie is and why he isn't home if you sit with me on the porch." Jan held his hand out. "Deal?"

Jenny eased toward him. "How do you know Eddie?" she asked.

"You have a very brave family, Jenny." Jan Bouwman's blue eyes under the heavy blond eyebrows were kind. "Your family was faithful to the Queen and the government through the war. They helped the people in the camps survive. Your uncles and Eddie visited us many times, in secret." Jan took a seat on the porch bench. "Your mother often smuggled food and carried messages into the camps."

"How did they get in?"

"Oh, they'd crawl through holes in the fence. Or, they'd throw things over as they passed by."

Jenny thought of her sewer experience. The image of Chip's face suddenly appeared and she heard him whisper, "Promise, Jenny. Promise, not even Nanna."

"Is Eddie in the camp now?" Jenny blinked.

"No, Jenny, there are no more camps. The war is over. But Eddie has to make sure the people from the camps are safe and the Japanese soldiers stay in their compound."

"Are the Japs going to hurt Eddie?"

Jan Bouwman put an arm around Jenny's shoulders and pulled her closer. "I don't think Eddie is going to get hurt. I think he'll be home soon."

"Promise?"

Jan slowly shook his head. "I can't promise, but we can both wish it. We'll wish it so hard, it just has to happen."

The next days went by slowly. Jenny ran to the front gate several times a day to look down the street, hoping she'd see Eddie come biking up the hill. The khaki military clothing Jan Bouwman wore reminded her sharply of Eddie.

A week went by. Jenny was picking jasmine blossoms with Nanna when she heard Eddie calling her, "Jen, Jenny!"

Eddie and a Dutchman jumped off their bikes by the front gate. Jenny dropped her flower basket and ran into Eddie's arms. He smelled dusty and sweaty as his unshaven cheek scraped against hers, but Jenny didn't care. She squeezed her arms tightly around Eddie's neck.

"You're choking me, Monkey." Eddie set Jenny down. "Say hello to Mr. van Houten." He pointed to the stranger and walked to Nanna. Eddie moved his clasped hands in front of his face, greeting his grandmother the Chinese way. "I brought Mr. van Houten. Is his wife okay?"

Nanna nodded. "You're thin," she said with a strangled voice, touching Eddie's shoulder briefly.

Peter van Houten leaned both bikes against the porch wall and walked to Nanna. "Thank you, Mrs. Ong. Thank you so much for all that you're doing for us."

Nanna extended her hand to the tall scrawny Dutchman. Peter van Houten's eyes were like big blue marbles lying on the bottom of a deep box. He wore a torn shirt and faded khaki pants. Most of his face was covered with a wad of reddish curly hair. A rope running through the belt loops kept the pants from falling off his waist.

"I'm glad everyone is safe. Now Greet will get better," Nanna said.

Peter van Houten took Nanna's hand in both of his and bowed.

"C'mon, Peter," Eddie opened the front door. "Let's see where we can find Greet."

Jenny ran ahead of the others into the house. "Eddie's home. Eddie's home and he brought another camp man," she shouted.

Sue, Emma, and Els appeared from different parts of the house. Soon there was a cacophony of voices. Even the myna bird participated in the excitement. *"Wel heb je ooit! Kunt U dat nagaan?"* The bird flapped its wings. "I'll be darned! Can you imagine?"

Then, in the midst of it all, cutting through all the talking and quieting everyone, including the myna bird, Greet van Houten cried out, "Peter! Peter!"

She rose from the porch bench. The white sheet covering her legs fell in folds around her ankles. The bun in the back of her head came undone and her long blonde hair covered her shoulders. She reminded Jenny of a picture of an angel walking on the clouds.

Peter van Houten reached his wife with a few steps. Jenny had never seen two grown-ups embrace before. Wide-eyed, she watched their bodies cling to each other. Then Peter van Houten lifted his wife into his arms and carried her like a baby into the house. The door to Greet's room closed behind them and stayed that way for the rest of the day.

CHAPTER 11

Nanna picked up the open newspapers from the coffee table. A large picture of Sukarno appeared on one of the pages. She couldn't read the article, but from listening to the radio and conversations around the dinner table, she knew that while the war with Japan was over, the Dutch were now fighting the native uprising. The natives, under leadership of Sukarno, had denounced the colonial Dutch government and proclaimed The Netherlands' Indies to be the Republic of Indonesia. Nanna shook her head. How would peasants and servants be able to manage a government? She placed the papers in the teak wood rack and walked to the back of the house.

Ting had gone back to work as chief accountant as soon as the Department of Telecommunications reopened. The KNIL had re-assembled and Peter van Houten, Jan Bouwman, and Eddie reported for military duty. Peter placed Carolien as a private secretary to one of the administrative officers. The schedule of the Red Cross transport ships carrying ex-internees to Holland and bringing Dutch professionals to the Indies was often the topic of dinner conversation and always piqued Nanna's interest. She wondered how much longer she would be expected to house and feed the Dutch strangers.

On the back porch Greet van Houten sat reading. Nanna suppressed the irritation she felt around the Dutch woman. If Greet could sit and read for hours, she was surely strong enough to sort beans, pick debris out of rice, or do some mending. "Have you seen Jenny?"

Greet looked up from her book. "She just left to put her schoolbooks away."

Nanna reached under the table for the beanbag and bamboo mat she kept there and poured a small amount of soybeans onto the mat for sorting. She glanced at Greet but the Dutch woman had returned her attention to her book. Nanna flipped the beans impatiently.

"Nanna! Nanna! Can we see if the eggs have hatched?" Jenny came bounding out of the house.

"Sure. Go on. I'll be right there." Nanna put the beans away and headed for the chicken coop, smiling.

"We have twelve chicks!" Jenny called. She sat on her haunches by a hen and her yellow downy brood. "Look, Nanna, look. They're already eating." Jenny picked up one of the chicks and cupped her hands around it. Rubbing her cheek against the chick's back, she whispered, "It's so soft."

Nanna smiled. The girl had such a love for animals. "Would you like to have that chick?" she asked.

"Oh, can I?" Jenny's eyes widened and a broad smile spread across her face. "Thank you, Nanna." Jenny held the chick close to her chest and repeated, "Thank you."

Nanna pulled Jenny against her. Maybe nature's simple things would keep this child from harm.

***

Carolien carefully filled out the application to enroll Jenny at the Christelijk Lyceum, an all-Dutch private high school not far from Nanna's house. The instruction sheet stated that Jenny would have to take a placement exam and, because she was Chinese, she also needed a dispensation before she'd be accepted. Carolien wasn't worried about either requirement. Els and Greet, who had been a schoolteacher before the war, had assured her that Jenny would have no trouble passing the exam for the freshmen entry. She might even make it in as a sophomore. Ting would take care of the dispensation. The family's work for the underground assured their preferential status. Jenny's education was one of the reasons

Carolien had joined her brothers in working for the resistance.

At the dinner table, a few days before Jenny had to take her exam, Ting took an envelope out of his breast pocket. He proudly handed the letter to Carolien. "I received the dispensation today. If she passes the exam, Jenny can go to the Christelijk Lyceum."

"Let me see." Carolien grabbed the document. She unfolded the paper and scanned through it. "Jenny, you better use the next days to study hard and put your best foot forward when you take the test," Carolien said. "You won't get another chance like this. Just think, with your Lyceum diploma, you'll be able to enroll at the university in Leiden and study law. You can be one of the first woman lawyers in the Indies—"

"I thought that Jenny wanted to become a veterinarian." Greet interrupted.

"Oh, Greet, don't pay attention to the child's nonsense." Carolien barely paused to breathe. "Isn't it true that Leiden has the best law school?" she asked and leaned toward Greet imagining Jenny graduating from the Lyceum and preparing to leave for Holland.

***

At bedtime that night, Jenny asked Els about the school and dispensation. "They made an exception and accepted you in this all-Dutch high school because of Youngest Uncle's position in the Dutch government and all that our family did during the war. You're fortunate," Els said. "All-Dutch schools have much higher standards than the schools for the natives or Chinese."

"You think I'll do okay with math?" Jenny asked while changing into her nightgown.

"Don't worry," Els smiled. "The tests will be geared toward the children who were in the camps and unable to get books to study."

Jenny sighed and climbed in bed. "Els, why does Mom say that I have to be a lawyer?" she asked arranging her pillows. "I just want to take care of animals."

"I wouldn't think about that now." Els began tucking the bottom of the mosquito curtain under the mattress. "You might change your mind over the next five years."

"No I won't." Jenny jutted her chin.

"Okay," Els laughed. "But for now, we're just going to make sure you know how to solve your math problems and know important history dates by heart."

"Hmmm." Jenny crawled under the sheet.

"Goodnight." Els turned off the lights and left the room.

Jenny put her arms around her roll pillow. What would it be like to go to school with other children? She vaguely remembered being in a classroom, sitting in a big circle playing games.

***

On the morning of Jenny's placement exam, Carolien hurried Els and Jenny into a *delman*. She wanted to make a good impression, and being late for their appointment with the rector of the Lyceum definitely wouldn't do.

"Come in," a voice responded to Carolien's knock on the door. The Dutch rector rose from his high-backed swivel chair and extended his hand. "Hans Overbeek. It's a pleasure meeting you. Please, have a seat." He waved at the two chairs in front of his massive mahogany desk and walked across the room to pull up another.

Carolien handed the rector the dispensation document. He verified the information then smiled at Jenny. "So, you'll take the freshman entry test. Are you looking forward to going to school, Jenny?"

"Yes, sir. I think so."

"Good, I'm sure you'll do well." Hans Overbeek turned to Els. "It's encouraging to come across a child who is applying for placing in the appropriate level. So many students fell behind during the war. I understand you tutored her?" He glanced at Jenny's birth certificate. "Still eleven, she's even slightly ahead. Good work, Miss Ong."

"Thank you, sir." Els smiled shyly.

Hans Overbeek looked at his pocket watch. "We better head for the testing room." He walked around his desk and ushered them out of the room, tapping Els on the shoulder in passing. "Have you found an appointment yet, Miss Ong? I hope you're not going to let your teaching abilities fall by the wayside."

"I have applied for a position at the new Communal Grade School." Els lowered her eyes as she mentioned the first school to have no specific racial reference in its name.

Carolien whirled around. She had assumed that Els had applied for teaching positions at the re-opening Dutch schools. Why bother with a public school where the students would be a mixture of *inlanders* and low-class Chinese?

"Judging by what you did with Jenny, I think you could've done better," Hans Overbeek said.

"Well, I thought I'd be of more help to the Chinese and native children." Els avoided Carolien's gaze. She knew her family wouldn't approve, so she hadn't yet told anyone of her decision.

"Hmmm," the rector rubbed his knuckles against his jaw. "In the long run, your choice might turn out to be the best."

Jenny was the smallest and the youngest in the group of about twenty boys and girls taking the entry exam. As they shuffled through the classroom door she disappeared between the taller, bigger bodies of the other children.

Standing on her toes, Carolien saw through the window that the teacher who was supervising the test gave Jenny a seat in the first row.

The exam took the whole morning. Carolien, Els, and Jenny spent the afternoon in the school lobby, along with other students and their parents, waiting anxiously for the results. At the end of the day, Jenny's exam number was called out as passing with honorable grades.

"Congratulations!" Els pulled Jenny into an exuberant embrace.

"Oh, Jenny, you made it! You even passed with honors." Carolien grabbed Els and Jenny by the arm. She turned to Els, smiling. "Thanks for helping Jenny. You did a marvelous job. Overbeek was right. You should apply for a position at a Dutch school. I'm sure you'll get accepted."

"Maybe." Els smiled quietly.

"You got off to a good start, Jenny," Carolien said during the *delman* ride home. "Be sure to stay on this path." She frowned when Jenny simply nodded. Ting and Greet should stop encouraging Jenny's fascination with becoming a veterinarian. Perhaps Eddie and Els would talk some sense into Jenny's head. Carolien knew, Nanna would be of no help. She glanced proudly at Jenny. Po Han's absence had not prevented her from sending her daughter to the very best school.

***

School agreed with Jenny and her teachers liked her. Recess was the only period of the day she disliked. Most of her classmates had spent the war years in the internment camps without schooling and now had to catch up, many of them in grades lower than they should be. The fifteen and sixteen-year-old girls in Jenny's class were no longer interested in playing games, and eleven-year-old Jenny was bored by their girl talk. She spent most of recess watching the boys play tackle ball on the lawn. One day she caught one of their stray balls in mid-air.

"Here, here," the boys shouted waving their arms. Jenny kicked the ball dead center into their middle.

"C'mon, why aren't you playing?" Tim de Vries yelled. From that day on Jenny joined their daily tackle-ball games and after school track practice. It was much more fun than watching from the sidelines.

The self-proclaimed Indonesian Republic continued to strive for recognition as an independent nation. It founded the TNI, the Indonesian Armed Forces, and supported guerrilla movements against the Dutch govenment. Not a day went by without a confrontation between the Indonesian and Dutch authorities. Jenny read newspaper articles about these military confrontations in class. The casualties sometimes ran into the thousands on either side. The articles reminded her of the time Eddie came home after being shot by the Japanese. She wondered about the possibility of him getting shot again, by Indonesians this time, and resented them instantly.

Around Nanna's dinner table, talk of war was replaced with talk of revolution. Instead of talking about the Japs, the adults now spoke about Sukarno, the leader of the Indonesian Revolution. His demands to the Dutch and his revolutionary speeches to the natives made the daily headlines in every newspaper and were on all the radio broadcasts.

***

Sukarno's feverish orations reached Nanna's servants' quarters as well. One afternoon Nanna was sitting on the front porch picking debris from a bag of mung beans when Mundi approached. He crouched to his haunches a respectable distance away and asked, "Grand Madam, may I please leave for a couple of hours after dinner? I'd like to attend the Progressive Meetings in the nearby native village."

Nanna gave Mundi a once over. "Why do you have to do that?"

Mundi bowed deeper and said, "Grand Madam has been good to my family and me, but the population is suffering. You allowed me to go to school. I can read and write, but most of the people are kept in ignorance."

Nanna reluctantly granted Mundi's request. "Stay out of trouble and keep safe," she warned.

"I will." Mundi raised his head slightly. "And I'll also try to keep harm from coming to Grand Madam's household," he said, and left as quietly as he came.

Nanna wondered what Mundi meant. The young native had spoken with a strength she hadn't felt before and she had seen a faint glow around his head while he talked to her. From her seat she could hear low voices coming from the side of the house. She rose to see what was going on.

Mundi and Rina were engaged in a whispered conversation in the shade of a flaming poinsettia. As soon as he saw Nanna, Mundi walked off.

"Grand Madam, please forgive my son." Rina fell to her knees. "He's young and foolish. He doesn't realize his own good fortune. Please keep him away from harm."

The sound of Mundi's garden broom scratching the path with rhythmic drags as he raked the dry leaves of the tamarind tree cut through the afternoon. Nanna thought of Chip and felt a strange closeness to the native woman who had served her for so many years. "Sometimes, Rina, we can't keep our sons from moving forward on the path they choose," she said." All we can do is support them."

During the next weeks Nanna paid extra attention to the news. The

KNIL expected native riots and a major uprising. Eddie's unit was on alert, the entire city felt like it was on edge.

One afternoon, picking over rice on the front porch bench, she noticed that Mundi kept sweeping along the frontage of her property, back and forth over the same section of dirt. Every so often, he paused to peer over the hedge of oleanders. She stiffened when Mundi threw his broom down and ran toward the gate.

Eddie pedaled through the gate and Mundi grabbed the bike to stop him. Eddie planted both feet on the ground. They were close enough for her to hear their conversation.

"Young Master, please…" The two young men had grown up together. Mundi, four years older than Eddie, had taught the boy how to climb trees and ride bikes. As a youngster, Eddie had shared his snacks with the native.

"What's the matter?"

Mundi took off his *petji* and ran a hand over his bared head before replacing the black cloth cap. He dropped a hand on the bike's back fender. "I think it would be good to make sure people can't climb over the back wall."

Eddie leaned into his handlebars.

"I don't want harm to come to Grand Madam's household." Mundi picked up his broom and went back to sweeping the garden with no further explanation.

When Eddie came to greet her, Nanna did not question him about his conversation with Mundi. But that evening, she took Eddie aside and suggested he talk to Ting about securing the back wall with glass chips and barbed wire.

***

A few weeks later, on a cool April morning in 1946, Prawira, the Lyceum's custodian, interrupted the freshmen history period. He handed the teacher a clipboard and looked solemnly at the class while Kees de Jong read the message from the rector's office.

Kees cleared his throat a couple of times before he addressed the class.

"Mr. Overbeek has just received orders from the Security Council to close the school immediately. The Indonesians are expected to launch a major revolutionary attack on the Dutch."

Jenny clutched her ruler so hard that the edges hurt her palm. Her classmates responded to the announcement with alarmed whispers.

"You are to go straight home." Kees tapped the wooden pointer against the blackboard. "The school will be closed until further notice."

Jenny raced her bike up Nanna's driveway. She came to a screeching halt when Emma crossed her path with an armful of blankets.

"Good, you're home," Emma said. "Put your schoolbag away and come help me in the bomb shelter after you greet Nanna and Aunt Sue. They're in the kitchen," she called over her shoulder and rushed off.

"Hi, Nanna. Hi, Auntie." Jenny went to each adult and raised her clasped hands in greeting. She noticed the stack of banana leaves, the big basket with steaming rice, and the bowl of salted fish on the kitchen table. Why were Nanna and Aunt Sue making rolls of war rice?

"Be a good girl. Help Emma and Els get the bomb shelter ready." Nanna turned Jenny toward the doorway.

Emma walked by carrying a stack of pillows. "Here," she said, shoving the pillows in Jenny's arms. "Take these to the shelter."

"Are the rebels coming?" Jenny asked, helping Emma and Els prepare the cots as the sun began to go down and darkness fell.

"Hurry, we still have to fill up bottles with drinking water." Emma fluffed the last pillow.

"C'mon, Jenny, let's load the flashlights." Els tugged on Jenny's elbow. In the dining room, she took the flashlights out of a buffet drawer.

"What's going to happen to us when the *inlanders* come? Are the natives going to kill us like the Japs did to the dogs and Oldest Uncle?"

"I don't know. Hopefully they won't get here." Els lined up the contact points on the batteries before screwing on the bottom.

"Do you think they're going to close the schools like the Japs did?"

"They're not closing the schools. They just won't allow teaching in Dutch anymore." Els loaded the last flashlight.

Jenny frowned. Dutch was the only language the family used. How was she going to learn anything if she couldn't speak Dutch?

"*Bersiap!*" Distant shouts filtered into the room through the open windows. "*Merdeka! Bunuh Belanda asu!*"

Jenny grabbed Els' arm. "The rebels! They're coming." The rioters continued their chanting, telling people to get ready, proclaiming freedom and yelling, "Death to the Dutch dogs!"

"Hurry. Lock all the doors!" Els gave Jenny a shove and yanked the windows closed. Through the living room window Jenny saw Ting running toward the gate. Clattering gunfire accompanied the shouts demanding freedom. The noise became louder as the crowd came closer.

Everyone ran to the bomb shelter where they huddled together. Ting stood in the open entryway. Jenny noticed that her mother, the camp men, and Eddie were missing. In the servant's corner, Rina and Mia shared a cot, but where was Mundi?

The shouts proclaiming freedom and the firing of artillery intensified rapidly over the next few minutes. After a series of explosions, Ting exclaimed, "Oh my God, they're setting fire to everything!"

Everyone joined Ting in the entryway. Squashed between the adults, Jenny saw a dark sky filled with smoke and the occasional flare of fire. "Nanna." Jenny tugged on her grandmother's arm. "All the animals are still out. What if the rebels come and set fire to them?"

"I wonder where the rebels are. They sound close," Ting interrupted, easing out of the shelter's entrance. "It's a good thing we put all that broken glass on the back wall." He stared at the blackened sky. Then he looked at Jenny, "Do you think you can climb the mango tree in the dark?"

"Jenny is not going to climb anything in the dark." Nanna put her hands on Jenny's shoulders.

Jenny didn't answer Ting. She had never seen anyone oppose Nanna or her uncle, now they opposed each other. She moved closer into Nanna arms, pressing her back against her grandmother's chest.

"We have to know if they are in the village behind us, Mother," Ting whispered. "Jenny can climb like a monkey. I'll go with her."

Still worried about the animals, Jenny stared at the smoke columns in the sky. The air was filled with clapping noise of gunfire. Light beams streaked through the smoky sky.

"War is a man's affair." Nanna folded her arms across Jenny's chest.

"Bersiap!" The hoarse Malay voices were frightfully close.

"Mother, it's important that we know where the rebels are." Ting started to leave the shelter.

Nanna shoved Jenny toward Ting. "Go, quickly! Be sure to listen to Youngest Uncle." Jenny ran after her uncle into the darkness of the yard.

"Climb as high as you can and tell me what you see." Ting leaned into the trunk of the old mango tree. "Don't yell it out from up there, wait to tell me until you're on the ground," he said, looking up into the tree.

Jenny worked herself quickly up the short trunk base and then swung onto the first branch. She moved sure-footed onto the higher branches. It was a moonless night and the foliage closed like a tent around her. For a moment, she enjoyed the mystery of being high among the thin branches.

"Jenny, this is no time to fool around. Get up there, take a look, and then come back down. Hurry!" Ting's tense whispers crawled between the leaves.

"Yes, sir." Jenny parted some foliage to get a better look at the sea of flames. It seemed that the southern part of town had been turned into a bonfire, with smaller fires scattered throughout the city. A big explosion nearby startled her. She looked into the direction of the noise. Flames shot up from houses at the end of their street, where Dutch families lived.

Jenny clutched a branch. The nearby village was alive with a shouting crowd. A mob of natives carried kerosene lanterns and bamboo poles with knives securely fastened at the ends. The men wore red strips of cloth tied around their head and yelled, *"Bunuh Belanda asu!"* The steel blades of the knives gleamed in the light of the swaying lanterns. Those who did not carry knives swung sickles. "Kill the Dutch dogs! Burn out the rats!" The chanting mob moved toward downtown.

Jenny climbed down, trembling. What would happen if the rebels found out that there were Dutch people staying with them? A few times she missed stepping on a branch and slipped. "They're going downtown," she whispered. She slid down the last part of the trunk, skinning her arms and legs.

"Are you sure?" Ting grabbed Jenny's arms, steadying her.

"Yeah, they went that way." Jenny pointed south.

Ting reported Jenny's sighting to the family.

Nanna took Jenny's hand and sat down at the end of the first cot. "Lie down," she said.

Ting positioned himself at the shelter entrance with a gun. Jenny did not ask where the gun came from. There was some rustling by the shelter opening. Mundi appeared out of the darkness and approached Ting.

"They're gone," the servant said. "It looks like they're headed downtown."

"How many were there?" Ting asked awkwardly, he was not accustomed to being reliant on a servant in this way.

"It's the people, Master. The voice of the people is numerous." Mundi's words had an unusual firmness to them, something none of the family had heard before.

The next morning everyone returned to the house. Ting immediately turned on the radio. The early-news broadcast announced that the revolutionaries had burned down the business districts in the southern part of Bandung. The city had been divided into north and south. The railroad tracks served as the dividing borderline while the government was in negotiation with the rebels. The Allied Forces held jurisdiction over the northern part. All businesses were to resume as normal in this sector.

After listening to the news and reading the morning paper, Ting joined Nanna and Jenny for breakfast. "Everything seems to be under control," he said, pulling out his chair. "The schools are reopened. Tomorrow you're off to school, Jenny."

CHAPTER 12

The fire that burned down half of Bandung became an event of the past and the Dutch and Indonesian revolutionaries entered into lengthy negotiations. The Dutch planned to reinstate the colonial government in the Southern part of Bandung and needed to know if the Chinese population was supportive. The Underground approached Carolien for an assignment. She was to move into the home of an Indo family who had recently repatriated to Holland and turned over their belongings to the Dutch government. The house was located less than five miles south of the railroad tracks, a neighborhood of middle class Chinese and Indo families that had not been affected by the April revolutionary fires. Carolien was to be on the lookout for any hints of brewing unrest among the natives. Her house would serve as a radio transmitting station, but she was to present the façade of a normal neighborhood resident.

The authorities had assured Carolien that the job had little to no risk. Still, she was apprehensive about Jenny's safety. She accepted the assignment in the hope of earning privileges that would help secure Jenny's future. Her work for the Dutch government would make Jenny eligible for financial aid and scholarships for schooling in Holland.

***

Carolien and Greet van Houten were in the midst of packing when Jenny walked into the dining room.

"What are you doing?" Jenny dropped her schoolbag on the floor.

Various household items and clothes lay scattered on the chairs and table. Several suitcases and wooden crates lay on the floor.

"We're going to move into our own house," said Carolien as she wrapped a glass in a sheet of newspaper.

"With Nanna?" Jenny couldn't imagine living anywhere without her grandmother.

"Didn't you hear? I said we're moving into our own house," Carolien said. Jenny bit her lip and Carolien continued in a softer tone, "Wouldn't you like to have your own room?"

"You should be happy! You no longer have to sleep in one bed with so many people." Greet placed a wrapped item in a box.

Jenny was speechless. Where was this house? Did Nanna know? How would she be able to sleep all by herself without snuggling up to Nanna?

Carolien handed Jenny a suitcase. "Put your clothes in here. The moving *gerobak* will be here soon. It will take the man a while to pull the cart, but we should be moved in before dark."

Jenny pictured the suitcase piled onto a cart along with the boxes that lay scattered on the floor.

Carolien shifted some boxes and sent Jenny a piercing look. "C'mon, get going."

Jenny dragged the piece of luggage into Nanna's bedroom. She placed the empty suitcase on the floor and looked around the room where she had slept for the last seven years.

The big solid mahogany bed she shared with Nanna, Emma, and Els took up one third of the room. She had grown a lot since she first came to Nanna's, yet the bed was still big enough to hold everyone comfortably. Nanna's vanity stood along a wall. Next to it stood the big wooden commode she was allowed to use if she had to go to the bathroom in the middle of the night.

"Let me help you pack your clothes neatly, so you won't look all wrinkled going to school tomorrow." She hadn't heard Nanna enter the room.

Nanna packed the three shelves of Jenny's clothes. She emptied Jenny's vanity drawer and took a small, blue, cut-glass bowl from her vanity shelf. The bowl had a silver lid with an angelic boy on top. Jenny had always liked the bowl. Held up to the light, the glass was radiant with different colors.

"I'll put this in your suitcase. Now you have your own cool powder bowl," Nanna said.

Jenny flung herself across the bed. She grabbed Nanna's pillow and pushed her face deep into its cool softness. "I don't want to go. I don't want to have my own cool powder bowl. I want to share yours. Nanna, please, don't make me go." Jenny burrowed deeper into the bed.

"Stop crying. You're going to get the bed dirty with your shoes." Nanna tapped Jenny's thrashing leg. "If your mother finds you like this, she'll get angry with you." Nanna sat down and rubbed Jenny's back. "You can come to visit me every day, and maybe sleep over on holidays," she said.

Jenny moved her face into Nanna's lap. Nanna's sarong felt cool against her hot cheeks. She closed her eyes and pushed her head against Nanna's stomach. This is just a nightmare, she thought. When I open my eyes, everything will be different.

"Are you about done?" Carolien's impatient voice brought reality.

Jenny pushed her face deeper into Nanna's lap and squeezed her arms around her grandmother.

"There's Jenny's suitcase. Why don't you take it with you?" Nanna stroked Jenny's head and tried to loosen her fingers. When Carolien remained silent Nanna said, "Maybe it's better to leave Jenny here tonight. That'll give you time to get settled. You can pick her up tomorrow, after school."

"Don't you want to see the new house and your own room?"

Nanna pulled Jenny up. "Answer your mother, Jenny."

Keeping her eyes on her suitcase, Jenny shook her head. "I'd like to stay with Nanna, if that's okay."

"Very well then." Carolien grabbed the suitcase. "Your grandmother's right," she said brusquely. "You'll only be in my way while I have to get things in order."

The sight of Jenny sobbing in Nanna's lap had unsettled Carolien. She hadn't given much thought to how close the child had grown to her grandmother.

"Is Jenny not coming?" Greet van Houten asked when Carolien

walked back into the dining room alone.

Carolien shook her head. "She didn't want to and Mother decided it was best to leave her here while we're getting settled." Her voice broke and she couldn't hold back tears.

"The way your mother spoils Jenny, it's normal that the child rather stay here than come with us." Greet put an arm around Carolien. "Don't worry, she'll change her mind once sees her own room." Greet grabbed her purse and handed Carolien hers. "Let's go, the *delman* is waiting."

***

Nanna had a hard time imagining not having Jenny around. She enjoyed the child's rambunctious spontaneity. She was worried about Carolien's involvement in Dutch affairs and the danger that might bring to her daughter and granddaughter. At least they were taking the camp people with them. Nanna had grown weary of caring for the Dutch guests. Why didn't they just go back to Holland?

Nanna went to the front porch and called Mundi. He dropped on his heels some distance away from her, a position servants were to take when interacting with their masters. "*Njonja Muda* Lien is moving somewhere across the railroad tracks with the camp people. I'd like to send Mia with Young Mistress Lien. Do you want to bring your wife here to take Mia's place as the laundry maid?"

"Yes, Sari will be happy to come." Mundi quickly looked up before continuing with downcast eyes. "If *Njonja Muda* needs a houseboy, Mia could bring her husband. Amin used to work as a houseboy for some Dutch people. He's working for a Chinese family right now, but he doesn't like it."

"That would be good. I'll tell Young Mistress." Nanna looked at the young native who had grown up in her household. Mundi would not bring harm to any member of the family. "Go to the *kampong* tonight. Meanwhile, help *Njonja Muda* Lien at her house. Here." Nanna reached in the money pouch she carried in her cummerbund and handed Mundi a few bills. "Use this to cover whatever expenses."

"Thank you. I'll try not to come back too late from the village." Mundi

133

slipped the money into a pocket. "Is that all *Njonja Besar* needs?"

"Yes, thank you."

Nanna was relieved that the Dutch people were leaving. Before the war any Dutch contact had brought pride, now she felt burdened by it. The Dutch no longer provided shelter; instead, they brought harm.

***

Jenny rode her bike out of the schoolyard. She smiled when she saw Eddie waiting for her. "I'm going to show you the way to your new house," Eddie said as they pedaled down the street. "It's not far into the southern part of town."

"Aren't we going to Nanna's first?" Jenny asked. Eddie knew she didn't want to live at her mother's house. Why was he taking her there? When her cousin calmly pedaled on, Jenny added, "I have to feed Big Red and clean the chicken coop. Big Red has chicks, you know."

"I told Nanna I'd take you to your new house," Eddie said, looking straight ahead.

Jenny was glad Eddie didn't say *home*, because home was Nanna's.

For a while they coasted down the hills in silence. The houses and yards became smaller as they reached the flat part of town. "This is your street," Eddie turned into a street lined with palm trees. "Look, that's the house." He pointed to a whitewashed house somewhere in the middle of a row of houses to his right.

The house was much smaller than Nanna's. Unlike Nanna's front yard with trees, a large lawn, and numerous flowerbeds, her mother's front yard was a narrow strip of lawn with a yellow alamanda hedge running along each side. The canopy of an avocado tree partially shaded the red tiled roof.

Eddie rested his foot on the low brick wall that defined the driveway. Jenny pushed each pedal slowly until she was next to him. "I have a surprise for you," Eddie said as they walked their bikes up the graveled path. Coming around the house he called, "Aunt Carolien! Hello!"

"Oh, there you are," Carolien opened the door. "Well, do you think you can find your way to school and back?" she asked Jenny.

Jenny looked up at Eddie.

"I'll go with her for a few days," Eddie ran his fingers through Jenny's short hair. "Come, let's see what you think of my surprise."

Jenny followed Eddie. The living room and dining room were smaller than at Nanna's, but there were four bedrooms. "This is Mr. Bouwman's room, Mr. and Mrs. van Houten sleep here." Eddie pointed to the closed doors, "This is your mother's room, with yours right next to it." He opened the door. "I was here last night and helped your mother put things in order." Eddie ushered Jenny into the room. "Do you like the way I set things up for you? We can rearrange it, you know."

Jenny looked around. The only familiar item was the cool-powder jar Nanna had given her. It sat under a lamp on a corner of a small desk. "Why can't you live here too?" she asked, tracing the angel's wings with a finger.

"Well, first of all, there are no more rooms left–"

"I don't mind sharing mine," Jenny interrupted. "We could put your bed right there." She pointed to empty wall space. "I promise, I won't make a mess on the desk."

Eddie opened the big window. "C'mere." He patted the wide sill. "Jen, trust me. It's going to be okay."

Jenny kicked her heels hard against the wall and stared at a big avocado tree. Heavy ropes hung from a thick branch. At a second look, she saw rings and a swing. She slipped off the windowsill into the yard and ran to the tree. "Did you put them up, did you?" She jumped, grabbing one of the rings.

"I told you I had a surprise," Eddie laughed. "I almost didn't bring the swing. I thought you were getting too old for that."

Jenny ignored Eddie's comment. She swung her legs into the other ring. "Watch me," she let go with her hands and waved her arms. Then she swung up, grabbed the ring, and dropped lightly onto the ground. She ran around the tree and jumped on the swing. "Will you push me?"

"Sure." Eddie grabbed the wide plank and pushed with the full length of his long arms.

Jenny pumped her legs and caught Eddie's push until the swing went so high her pointed toes almost hit the fringe of the tree's canopy.

After the swing came to a swaying halt, Jenny slid off the seat and ran to a small chicken coop in a corner of the yard. "Eddie. You brought Big Red and her chicks." She pushed the gate open and scooped Big Red up in her arms. She brushed her cheek against the hen's soft shiny feathers.

"I told you it was going to be okay," Eddie ruffled Jenny's hair.

Back in Jenny's room, Eddie put up the frame for the mosquito netting. "Why don't you try out your new desk and do your homework while I talk to the camp people?"

"And then?" Jenny didn't dare to ask Eddie to stay, but couldn't bear the thought of him leaving.

"And then it will be dinner time. I bet your mother will have one of your favorite dishes. I'll stay until you go to bed."

When Amin, the houseboy, called her for dinner, Jenny shuffled toward the dining room.

Carolien, her Dutch houseguests, and Eddie stood talking around the table. Carolien pulled out a chair and patted the seat next to her. "Come, Jenny, why don't you sit here?"

Jenny glanced at the food on the table. The large serving bowl held a steaming heap of *hutspot*.

"Hmmm, that's what I call a lucky girl." Eddie took the seat on Jenny's other side and served her. "Isn't this one of your favorite dishes?" He broke off a big piece of wurst and placed it on top of the potatoes and vegetables on her plate.

Jenny nodded. Els had told her that Dutch knights used to eat this dish when they fought their feudal wars. The potatoes, carrots, green beans, and cabbage were boiled with a side of salted pork. The dish was finished with a plump ring of wurst.

After dinner Carolien said, "Jenny, get yourself cleaned up for bed." Jenny hesitated and Carolien added, "Els isn't here to help you, but you're now big enough to do it yourself."

"Just think, tonight you'll get to sleep all by yourself in your very own bed." Greet van Houten's comment made Jenny hang her head.

"Go on, Jenny. If you hurry, there'll still be enough time to read together." Eddie nudged her.

In the bathroom, Jenny took off her street clothes and stepped into her pajamas. Her chest felt strangely tight. What would Els be doing, now that she did not have to help her? Jenny cleaned up and walked back to the dining room. She didn't feel good at all.

The adults were still gathered around the table. "It's going to be interesting to see where the talks held at the Hoge Veluwe will take us." Peter van Houten said, stirring his coffee.

"Probably nowhere." Jan Bouwman leaned back into his chair. "The Hague refuses to understand that it's time for us to pull out of here."

Eddie poured himself another cup of coffee. "These people don't want a democratic partnership, they want independence."

Amin cleared the used plates and dishes and placed a big bowl of fruit in the center of the table.

Jenny stood quietly in the doorway. She was afraid to say anything.

Carolien, reaching for the coffee pot, looked up. "Did you brush your teeth? Did you go to the bathroom?"

Jenny nodded.

Eddie rose. "Let's go," he said. "There's still time to read." In Jenny's room he took the Dutch translation of *Uncle Tom's Cabin* from the bookshelf.

Jenny climbed in bed and moved her pillows around. The bed was much smaller than Nanna's. Her stomach began to hurt. She pulled up her legs and wrapped her arms around them. Her eyes caught the glass jar with the silver boy angel top. Tonight was the first time she had gone to bed without using Nanna's cool powder.

"Here." Eddie touched her shoulder. "Lie down."

Jenny slipped under the covers and clutched her rollpillow, tears breaking.

Eddie rubbed her back and started to read. Listening to Eddie's deep voice she became sleepy.

Jenny woke up the next morning with a jarring sense of unfamiliarity. Even the air wafting through the shutter slats smelled different. Rubbing her eyes she looked for Nanna's jar. There was a damp spot under her and her pajama bottoms clung to her behind. She had wet her bed.

Carolien walked in and Jenny pulled her blanket around her. "Good, you're up already." Carolien walked toward the window, but stopped midway, sniffing the air. "Oh, my God. I don't believe it." Carolien grabbed Jenny's arm and yanked her out of bed. "All you needed to do was to get up and go to the bathroom. How can you be so lazy?" Carolien ripped the sheet off the bed.

Jenny stared at the large dark spot on the mattress. She had never wet her bed before. "But I was asleep. I didn't feel I had to go," she said miserably.

"What nonsense is that, you're twelve years old. How can you stand to lie in urine?" Carolien pushed Jenny out of the room. "Hurry up. Take your *mandi*. Next thing you'll be late for school."

In the bathroom, Jenny stepped out of her soiled clothes. Why had she wet her bed? Only babies did that. She was definitely not a baby. Jenny scooped a full dipper of cold water out of the water container and threw it over herself. She scrubbed her thighs, trying to ignore her feelings of shame.

Over the next few weeks, Jenny continued to wet her bed regularly. She became scared to fall asleep. Despite going to the bathroom several times during the night, she still woke up wet. Only when she spent the weekend at Nanna's did she sleep through the night without having an accident.

One Sunday Nanna asked Jenny why she wet her bed at her mother's house. "I don't do it on purpose. It just happens" she answered, her face flushing hotly. "Maybe I should just sleep here, so I won't wet the bed over there."

Nanna shook her head. "That isn't going to solve the problem."

Carolien began to shake Jenny out of bed in the middle of the night to march her to the bathroom. She became frustrated when Jenny still managed to wet her bed. More than once, she spanked Jenny with a bedbroom. The palm-leaf ribs left red streaks that turned into welts.

Eddie noticed Jenny's bruised legs when he pushed her on the swing. He grabbed the seat mid-air and walked the swing to a halt. "What happened to your legs?"

"I got a spanking with the bedbroom 'cause I wet the bed." Jenny looked away. "I never do it when I sleep with Nanna. Why can't I sleep there? Why do I have to sleep here and get in trouble all the time?" Jenny kicked the bottom of the swing seat with her heels.

"You have to sleep here because you live here, Jenny," Eddie said. "You live here because you belong here. Aunt Carolien is your mother. Children belong with their parents."

"But I like it much better at Nanna's." Jenny kicked so hard that her heels hurt.

"It doesn't matter what you like better. You can't always change things just because you like something else better."

"Why?" She looked at Eddie, but he looked away. Perhaps he didn't know why either and just said it because it was somehow supposed to be that way.

CHAPTER 13

On a muggy afternoon in July of 1947, a Red Cross transport truck stopped in front of Carolien's house. On the sidewalk, Jenny watched the van Houtens say goodbye to her mother. Jan Bouwman stood next to her.

"We'll write as soon as we have an address." Greet hugged Carolien, crying.

"Shh, Greet, don't get yourself all worked up." Carolien patted the Dutch woman on the back. She took Greet's arm and walked her to the waiting truck. "You'll need your strength to travel."

"Jenny, your mother is the bravest, most generous woman we've ever met. Do your best to grow up just like her," Peter van Houten took Jenny into his arms and squeezed her so tight she could hardly breathe.

"Yes, sir." The Dutchman's statement gave Jenny an odd sense of pride.

"Thanks, Carolien, thanks for everything." Peter held Carolien's hand in both of his. "Don't ever hesitate to call on us when you need to," he said.

"Have a good trip, take care of Greet." Carolien pushed Peter toward his wife.

"So long, keep in touch," Jan Bouwman and Peter van Houten exchanged handshakes and shoulder slaps. Then Peter climbed into the truck and Jan secured the tailgate.

Jenny went to stand next to Carolien. Peter's words still echoed in her mind. Jenny observed her mother while the engine rumbled and the truck moved away. Carolien was in her mid-forties now, about five feet tall. She wore her hair, black with strands of white, pulled back and pinned in little rolls on the back of her head. Her feet were planted firmly on the ground in sturdy, black, laced shoes. One hand in an apron pocket, the other waved at the moving vehicle.

Jenny wondered if her mother would miss Greet. The two of them had spent a lot of time together. Jenny scanned Carolien's face. The black eyes following the disappearing transport were clear and dry. Her mother wasted no emotion on the departure of people she had housed and fed for nearly two years.

"I'm glad Greet is so much stronger now." The truck drove out of sight and Carolien started walking back toward the house. "They'll be able to make the journey easily and, hopefully, it will still be warm when they arrive in Holland."

Jan Bouwman and Jenny followed a few steps behind her. Jan stuck his hands into his pockets. "It's a good thing they're able to leave now. God knows you'll have enough on your hands."

Carolien turned sharply and Jan walked to her side. Walking close behind them Jenny heard him whisper, "Hopefully, everything will go as planned. We should be able to regain control of the whole city quickly."

***

"Jen, Jenny! Wake up!" Carolien shook Jenny by the shoulder and pulled her out of bed. The cold tiles sent shivers up her body. Jenny ran her hands across her bottom and the inside of her thighs, nothing was wet.

"Hurry up, get dressed. We've got to get out of here." Carolien reached for shoes under the bed. It was three weeks since the van Houtens had left for Holland.

Still half asleep, Jenny obeyed her mother's orders. "What's going on? Where are we going?" she muttered, buckling her shoes.

"The Dutch are trying to keep the Indonesians from taking over." The whistling of hand grenades and the rattling of gunfire accompanied Carolien's answer. "Hurry!" Carolien pulled Jenny's coat off the hanger.

Jenny stuck her arms in the sleeves and followed her mother to the living room. Jan Bouwman stood by the front door. He was dressed in a military uniform and carried a gun.

Mia picked up a suitcase and hurried toward the door. She handed Carolien the luggage and said anxiously, "Here. You go."

"Be careful. Take care of the house. I'll be back as soon as I can." Carolien glanced around the room. "Lock up. Help yourself to the food in the pantry."

"Don't worry, ma'am. Please, go now and be safe." Mia put a hand on Jenny's back. "Amin and I will watch the house. Don't worry, we'll be okay." She leaned over Jenny and threw Jan a skittish look before whispering, "Remember, Amin and Mundi are members of the nationalist movement."

Carolien nodded and grabbed Jenny's hand.

Jenny followed in a daze. Mia made it sound like the servants were going to protect them against the rebels. But Amin and Mundi were members of the nationalist movement, which made them rebels. Was Jan Bouwman going to use his gun on Amin and Mundi? Would they hurt Jan? Everything was so confusing.

Jan Bouwman took the suitcase from Carolien. "Hurry. I'd like you to be on the other side before the Indonesians close the roads."

It was dark outside and a cold mountain wind whipped their faces when Carolien opened the front door. They were almost into the street when Jenny thought of Big Red and stopped in her tracks. "When are we coming back? I need to feed Big Red."

"There's no time for that. Hurry." Carolien grabbed Jenny's arm and tried to pull her along. Jenny yanked her arm loose and ran past Jan Bouwman into the backyard where, out of nowhere, Amin suddenly appeared.

"Where are you going, *Nonnie?*" the native whispered. He scurried after Jenny toward the chicken coop. "Little Miss, where are you going?"

Jenny unlatched the gate and Big Red got off her nest, pulling up her wings. The chicks started to putter around. Jenny grabbed Big Red and put the hen inside her coat. She looked at the chicks, but there was no way she could take them too.

Jan Bouwman put a hand on Jenny's shoulder and pushed her toward the house. Carolien stood in the driveway with Mia. She grabbed Jenny by the ear.

Jenny pressed Big Red tightly against her chest and moved as fast as she could between her mother and Jan Bouwman. It was the only way to lessen the pain of Carolien's grip. They ran through the dark deserted streets. When Carolien let go of Jenny's ear, Jenny wanted to rub the stinging spot but didn't dare to let go of Big Red. Sometimes they took shortcuts by going through alleys between rows of houses. Suddenly, like a burst of fireworks on New Year's Day, the sky lit up from several directions.

The streets filled with running and shouting people. "Hold my hand and don't let go," Carolien yelled over the noise of artillery fire. She reached for Jenny's hand, but Jenny held on to Big Red with both hands.

"I've got her, Carolien." Jan Bouwman grabbed Jenny at the nape of her neck and pushed her ahead.

Jenny wished she were at Nanna's house where she could climb the mango tree and see what was burning. What if Nanna's house was on fire? Her heart pounded so hard it felt as if her chest would burst.

She couldn't make sense of the yelling and crying voices. The only clear words came from a distance. "*Merdeka! Merdeka!*" a mob shouted, declaring freedom.

Two bright headlights came their way. People moved to the sides of the street to let the military jeep through. Jan Bouwman pushed Jenny toward it. Carolien, running ahead of them, waved her arms wildly above her head and screamed, "Eddie, Eddie. This way! We're here."

The jeep came to a screeching halt and, before Jenny knew it, she was lifted inside. Carolien jumped in behind her. The door slammed shut while the jeep picked up speed with a roar. Jenny stumbled and almost let go of Big Red.

"C'mere, girl." Eddie let go of the steering wheel with one hand and, reaching back, pulled Jenny onto a little bench between the two front seats. "What have you got there?" Eddie shot a quick glance at the big bulge under Jenny's coat.

"We almost didn't get out because she went back to the chicken coop.

Can you imagine fussing with a chicken at a time like this?" Carolien shifted in her seat.

"But you did make it, Auntie." Eddie looked in the rearview mirror. "Everything is going to be okay."

"Mr. Bouwman. We left Mr. Bouwman." Jenny jumped out of her seat, allowing Big Red to slip on the jeep's floor.

"It's okay, Jenny. Mr. Bouwman had to go back to work." Eddie moved the gearshift. "Get back into your seat."

"Is Mr. Bouwman coming later?" Jenny grabbed the hen and settled back into her seat.

"No, Mr. Bouwman will have to stay at the barracks," Carolien said.

"Even when we go back to our house?" Jenny turned in her seat.

"Yes." Carolien's clipped voice kept Jenny from insisting on a more elaborate explanation.

They drove for a while in silence while dawn spread across Bandung's northern hills. Mundi opened Nanna's front gate before Eddie could tap the horn. Eddie brought the jeep to a halt at the end of the driveway and jumped out of the vehicle. "C'mon, Jenny! I'm sure Aunt Sue is cooking breakfast for you."

Jenny jumped down into Eddie's outstretched arms, holding on tightly to Big Red. The front door opened as they walked up the porch steps. Nanna and Els appeared in the doorway.

"Nanna. Nanna!" Jenny ran to Nanna and the safety of a quiet orderly house steeped in the aroma of chicken rice porridge.

"Let's take Big Red to the chicken coop." Els took the hen from Jenny. When they returned to the house, Nanna, Sue, and Emma were sitting around the breakfast table.

"Where's Eddie? Did Mom go back to her house? Are the Indonesians winning?" Jenny took off her coat.

"Eddie and your mother had to go to work. They'll be back later." Els' answer satisfied Jenny. She was back at Nanna's house. As long as the fighting lasted, she was most likely going to stay.

Els served Jenny a bowl of porridge. Jenny scooted into her seat next to Nanna and took a spoonful of the hot rice gruel topped with pieces of crusty golden fried bread, toasted shallots, green slivers of scallions, and celery leaves. She wrinkled her nose when Els poured her a tall glass of milk. The canned milk from the Red Cross rations had a metallic taste. The Japanese had slaughtered the dairy cows during the war, fresh milk was almost impossible to get.

"Here, let me fix it for you." Nanna put two big scoops of sugar in Jenny's glass. Then she took a spoonful of her coffee and drizzled it into the milk.

"Thank you, Nanna." The coffee erased some of the chalky taste and the sugar made the drink more palatable.

"As long as school is closed, I'll give you assignments in the morning," Els said as they finished breakfast.

Eddie was on active duty and Carolien was working in the administrative office of the KNIL. Ting wasn't around very much either. From listening to snippets of adult conversation, Jenny gathered that the Dutch had tried to suppress the Indonesians' rebellion with military force. The news broadcasts referred to the military confrontations as the Dutch First Political Action.

There was a break in fighting while the Dutch and Indonesian governments conducted another phase of negotiations. Schools reopened and life returned to normal. On August 3, 1947, Jenny was sitting at Nanna's dining room table, trying to solve a math problem, when Carolien entered the room. She greeted Nanna who sat stringing green beans in one of the big rosewood armchairs that flanked the altar table and said to Jenny, "It's okay to go home now. Get your bike."

"I'm not done with my math problems." Jenny clutched her pencil, glancing at Nanna.

"Jenny, you heard what your mother said." Nanna kept her eyes on the tray of green beans. Her hands never stopped the routine of stringing each bean on both sides, then dropping them in a bowl.

Jenny pushed her chair back, scraping the floor harder than was necessary. She wanted Nanna to look up and see how miserable she was. But Nanna's head remained bowed, her eyes focused on the beans.

***

Carolien rode her bike ahead of Jenny. She had chosen the shortest route home, through the Chinese business district.

The sharp smell of smoldering wood and smoke climbed up her nostrils and stung her eyes. Crumbling walls were all that was left of most of the shops. The doors and windows of still standing buildings had been boarded up. There were barricades of barbed wire in the driveways. Pieces of broken glass lay on the pavement.

The words *Bersiap* and *Merdeka*, written in big red letters, jumped at her from once whitewashed walls. The Indonesian revolutionaries were calling for freedom. A calico cat scurried by. It disappeared into a broken cabinet, carrying something in its mouth, and a soft mewling cut through the silence.

"Did you hear that?" Carolien squeezed her brakes and stepped off her bike.

"Yeah, maybe the cat has kittens somewhere. If we find them, can I take one home?" Jenny leaned over her handlebars and looked around.

Carolien shook her head. It was typical for Jenny to be interested in kittens.

The yowling persisted and they moved toward it. "It isn't a kitten. It sounds like a baby," Carolien muttered, walking her bike through burned wood and destroyed merchandise, broken glass crunching under her shoes.

They continued to walk through the rubble until they stood in what once had been a bedroom of the living area behind a shop. The fire had consumed the kapok mattress and gauze mosquito netting, but the metal bed-frame still held part of the bed's wooden base. A breeze fluffed a thin blanket of ashes.

"Wait here." Carolien leaned her bike against a half burned down doorjamb and made her way between burned pieces of furniture and household items. She bent and pulled out a galvanized washtub from under a metal table. Cries filled the air with rhythmic bawls. A strong odor of urine rose from the tub. "Oh, my God." Carolien reached for the crying Chinese baby. "Shhh." Carolien whispered, her heart racing.

Jenny lay her bike down and walked to Carolien. "Why–" She leaned

146

over, curiously, "Who would leave a baby here?" she asked, touching the baby's cheek.

"I don't know." Carolien rocked the baby in her arms and tried to cover the kicking legs with the cloth the baby was wrapped in. The infant's black hair was drenched in perspiration. "Hush, little baby, don't you cry," Carolien crooned, holding one of the wildly waving little hands. The infant whimpered and began to suck on one of Carolien's knuckles. "Poor baby, when was it that you last ate?" she muttered.

Overcome with concern Carolien placed the infant on half of a tabletop and began to unsnap the diaper pins. "My God, you couldn't be all but three months old." Folding the soaked diaper away she exclaimed, "No wonder they left you. You're only a girl."

Carolien scanned the area and pinned the wet diaper back in place. "Here," she said to Jenny, "Watch her. Be careful that she doesn't roll off the table."

Carolien walked away in a trance. She stumbled around the rubble, awkwardly shifting some half-burned drawers and kicking around the ashes. Who had left the baby? Why did they leave her? Where did they go? Judging by the metal flag pole, flying a red and white flag, she must be standing in the ruins of the district's police station. The rebels must have brought down the Dutch flag and, after tearing off its royal blue, hoisted its remainder.

Carolien looked at the Indonesian flag, flapping in the wind. She picked up the strip of blue cloth lying in the debris and made her way back to Jenny and the baby.

***

Alone with the baby, Jenny put her hands awkwardly on each side of the infant. Would she have been left if she were a boy? It was hard to believe that if it wasn't for her mother's Dutch way of thinking, she could have been left somewhere like this baby just because she was a girl.

The baby began to cry again and Jenny stroked the infant's head. Her tiny arms and legs moved spasmodically with each bawl.

They'd most likely take the baby home. Would she be as much fun to play with as the chicks, ducklings, and puppies at Nanna's?

Listening to the crackling sounds of Carolien's footsteps, Jenny waited for her mother to call her. But Carolien never did. Every so often the wind stirred through the ruins, gently rustling the mounds of ash.

Carolien looked harried when she finally returned, holding a long strip of blue material in her hands. "We need to get home," she said. She fastened the cloth with a flat knot behind her neck and placed the whimpering baby into the sling. "Come." She beckoned Jenny and reached for her bike. "Let's go. This baby is hungry."

***

When they arrived at Carolien's house, Jenny was relieved to find things in good order. Mia and Amin came running out of the house when Carolien called for them. Jenny wandered off into the backyard while the three of them poured over the baby. She broke a deep-red tomato off the vine and wiped it against her skirt. She set her teeth into the fruit and the juices filled her mouth. The avocados had doubled in size during her absence.

The chicken coop was open. There was no sign of Big Red's chicks. Jenny looked around the yard, making a clucking sound, until the aroma of cooking food lured her to the kitchen.

Mia stood in front of the charcoal stove. Something sizzled in a large wok. "Would you like to try the corn fritters?" The cook held out a spatula with a golden fritter.

"Thanks." Jenny held the hot morsel between her thumb and index finger, blowing on it. "What happened to Big Red's chicks?" she asked between puffs.

"I don't know." Mia kept her eyes on the corn fritters.

Jenny leaned against the doorjamb and tried to tune out the baby's crying. She glanced at Mia stirring the remaining batter. Could it be that the chicks had found their way to Mia's frying pan? Jenny flushed with anger, then became sad.

"You won't need chickens to play with any more," Mia said as Jenny started to leave. The cook lifted a batch of fritters out of the hot oil and dumped them on a tray lined with old newspapers. "Now, you have a baby sister," she laughed.

Jenny flung the fritter into the kitchen. It landed with a yellow splat on the white counter tile. "I don't need a sister! What did you do to my chicks?" Jenny ran toward the bike stand, grabbed her bike, and pedaled off which such force that her bike tires left large skid marks in the gravel.

The late afternoon wind had come up. The way to Nanna's house was almost all uphill but Jenny drove her pedals down hard, standing up as she rode the bike.

"Nanna!" Jenny bumped into Emma as she ran into the house.

"Nanna's in the living room." Emma put a stack of freshly ironed napkins and tablecloths in a buffet drawer as Jenny passed her. "What are you doing here? Where's your mother?" she called after Jenny.

"Nanna!" Jenny burst into the living room.

Nanna looked up and put the darned sock in the mending basket by her feet.

Jenny ran across the room and buried her face into her grandmother's lap. She told the story of the afternoon in agitated broken sentences, ending, "And now there's a baby who screams all the time!"

Nanna took Jenny's elbow and helped her up. Then she called Emma. "Em, go to your aunt's house and find out what's happening there. Jenny told me your aunt found a baby and took it home."

It was almost dark when Emma came back. "You're going to get it," she said as soon as she saw Jenny playing fetch with the dogs on the lawn. "You took off without telling anyone where you were going. You know your mother couldn't leave the baby to look for you all over the place. Wait 'till I tell Nanna." Emma walked briskly into the house with Jenny on her heels.

Nanna was in the dining room. Jenny quickly stepped behind her grandmother and took her hand. Nanna put an arm around Jenny. "What do I need to know about this baby?"

Sue and Els came into the room.

Emma looked at Jenny. "It looks like Jenny is going to have a little sister and Nanna another baby grandchild."

Sue and Els exchanged glances.

"Sisters," Nanna said, "are two girls who have the same father and mother." She gave Jenny's shoulder a squeeze and pulled her closer. "And I know nothing of new grandchildren."

Jenny felt Nanna's soft body grow rigid as she leaned into her. She scanned her grandmother's face. Nanna's lips were pressed together into a thin line. Her eyes had the same expression Jenny often saw in her mother's eyes when Carolien was displeased.

"Aunt Carolien said that Jenny should spend the night here," Emma said.

Jenny let go of Nanna's hand and ran back outside. She picked up a ball and threw it hard across the lawn. Was the baby still crying? She wished Eddie would come home soon so she could tell him what had happened.

CHAPTER 14

The Dutch authorities were far too busy keeping abreast of the Indonesian uprising to spend time worrying about a Chinese baby found in the ruins of a revolutionary fire. Carolien was given temporary custody of her foundling and ordered to keep looking for the child's parents. Ignoring the current political climate, Carolien named the baby Juliana after the Dutch crown princess. She converted the van Houten's room into a nursery and spent a great deal of time rocking the baby or playing with her on a large floor-pad. Jenny's old blocks and cloth books captured Carolien's interest as they never had before.

When a week went by without any visits from Sue with inquiries from Nanna, Carolien decided to take Juliana to Nanna's house. It was a Sunday morning and Carolien figured that everyone should be home. Jenny, who spent most weekend nights at Nanna's, was already there.

Carolien stepped carefully out of the *delman*. "We'll show Nanna and Auntie Sue and everyone else what a pretty girl you are," she crooned. She adjusted the blanket around the baby's face and rang the gate bell, peering impatiently between the iron bars.

Mundi came running down the driveway. He looked curiously at the baby while unlatching the gate.

"This is *Nonnie* Juliana." Carolien held the baby up and partially uncovered her. "*Non* Jenny now has a baby sister. Where is *Njonja Besar*?"

"Grand Madam is in the back yard. I'll tell her you're here." Mundi threw another uncertain glance at Juliana.

"Look who I brought!" Carolien laughed nervously when Sue, Emma, and Els gathered around her.

"Oh, you brought the baby!" Els gasped, fingering Juliana's face. "She's so tiny."

Sue tucked the blanket around the baby's shoulders. "Does Mother know that you're bringing her?"

"No. I figured if Mohammed doesn't come to the mountain, then the mountain must come to Mohammed." Carolien grimaced, rocking Juliana in her arms. She noticed Nanna coming toward the house. "I'm calling her Juliana," she said, fighting off another pang of anxiety.

"Juliana? After the crown princess?" Emma looked surprised.

"Yes. Don't you think she's as pretty as a little princess? She certainly deserves some royal treatment after all she's been through."

Nanna came up the porch steps and Carolien awkwardly turned to her. "Ma." She slightly tilted the baby.

"Mundi said you were here." Nanna glanced at the bundle in Carolien's arms. "You brought a baby with you?"

"I thought you'd like to see Juliana." Carolien plucked at the baby's blanket. She knew her mother nurtured fledgling sparrows that fell from the nest during monsoon season, why was she making her feel as if she'd done something wrong? She surely couldn't expect her to leave a baby in the rubble of a fire. "Can I put Juliana down somewhere?"

"Put her on the bench or on the table." Nanna started to leave. Halfway down the steps, she turned. "Don't you think you have enough on your hands?" Without waiting for Carolien's answer, Nanna went back to the garden.

Emma and Els went back into the house.

Carolien recalled visiting while Jenny was an infant. Nanna always lay Jenny in the middle of her bed and put roll pillows all around her.

Juliana started to whimper.

"Shhh," Carolien whispered. "It's okay. No one wants you, but I'll take care of you. Shhh." Rocking the baby in her arms, she blinked hard to keep back her tears.

"You can put the baby on my bed. I think she'll be okay there." Sue put a hand on Carolien's shoulder.

ONLY A GIRL

"Thanks, *Chi-chi.*" Carolien rubbed her arm across her face. "I think I better take Juliana home." She kissed Juliana's waving fist. "I just don't understand, Sue. Why does she have to be that way?" Carolien started toward the steps.

"Shhh!" Sue rubbed Carolien's back. "Don't make it worse by leaving. Stay at least till teatime. Come." Sue took Carolien by the elbow and ushered her into the house.

"Where is Jenny? And where are Ting and Eddie?" Carolien asked walking to Sue's room.

"Eddie took Jenny out. I think they went to the zoo. Ting said he had some work to do at the store. He'll be back for tea." Sue arranged the pillows along the edge of the bed. "There, put her down. She'll be all right." For a moment they looked silently at the sleeping baby. Then Sue said, "You know, it doesn't help that Jenny seems really upset."

"Jenny, upset? Why should she be upset?" Carolien frowned.

"Oh... I don't know." Sue shrugged and started to leave the room. "Are you coming?"

"Yes. Sure." Carolien threw a last glance at Juliana and followed her sister to the kitchen.

During teatime, Carolien tried several times to steer the conversation toward Juliana but no one showed any interest in the baby. "I'm going to adopt Juliana if her parents can't be found," she finally blurted out.

"Why do you always have to look for trouble?" Ting broke the tense silence. Frowning, he brought his napkin to his mouth.

"You only adopt a child to open the door for children who can't leave your womb." Nanna placed her fork on her plate and looked sternly at Carolien. "You have a child. If you want more, you should first get a good husband."

Carolien lowered her eyes. She knew better than to oppose Nanna. "I better be going. Eddie might take Jenny straight home," she said and started to leave the room.

"Wait, let me tell Mundi to find you a *delman.*" Sue followed Carolien.

On her way home, Carolien brooded. Why should she care about her family's disapproval? She really couldn't see anything wrong with what she was doing this time. Carolien looked down on the baby in her arms.

153

"Why can't they understand that I can take care of Jenny and you as well?" she whispered.

***

"Hello, Auntie, where are you?"

"Hi, Mom."

Eddie and Jenny walked into the back door.

Carolien rushed to meet them. "Shhh." She tapped a finger against her lips. "Juliana is asleep," she whispered. "Come, look how precious she is." She turned to Jenny and said, "You look like you had a good time. Go on now, clean up and get ready for dinner."

"Eddie said we might have time to try my new kite." Jenny looked up at her cousin.

"We still might. Go on now, listen to your mother." Eddie shoved Jenny toward her room.

Carolien waited for Eddie by the nursery door. As soon as he joined her she tiptoed to the crib and parted the tulle curtains. "Don't you think she's precious?"

A light flannel blanket covered most of Juliana. She lay with her head turned to one side breathing evenly. Every so often, her tiny fist rubbed across her round pink cheek. Carolien stroked Juliana's head before stepping aside to give Eddie a full view of the baby.

"This reminds me of the first time I visited Jenny," Eddie said, looking into the crib. "She's a pretty little girl," he added and carefully closed the curtains.

"Can you imagine her parents leaving her in the rubble?" Carolien asked as they walked out of the room.

Eddie pulled out a chair at the dining room table. "What are your plans, Auntie? How are you going to find her parents?" Carolien didn't answer and he continued. "You know that you've got to do that. There should be a search for the parents."

Carolien took a seat across from Eddie and smoothed the table runner. "Do you think they'll let me keep her if they can't be found?"

"Well, the alternative would be an orphanage." Eddie reached for an orange from the fruit-bowl in the center of the table. He threw the fruit up in the air and caught it with one hand. "And she'd be better off with you."

"Oh, definitely!" Carolien looked up at Eddie. "You know I would take good care of her."

"I know, Aunt Carolien, I know. It isn't me you have to convince." Eddie returned the orange to the bowl. "Just remember, Auntie, the possibility of finding her parents is definitely there. Be prepared to give her up."

Carolien sighed. If she couldn't win Eddie over to Juliana's side, she definitely would never be able to make the rest of her family change their minds.

***

No one responded to the announcements the authorities posted regarding the baby girl abandoned in the ruins and Carolien kept the baby.

She marked the day she found Juliana as the baby's birthday. One afternoon in August of 1948, a year later, she waited impatiently for the toddler to wake from her midday nap.

It had taken Carolien several trips to the fabric store to decide on the material for Juliana's birthday dress which took the seamstress almost a week to sew.

The white silk bodice of Juliana's dress was smocked with salmon pink thread. A white tulle skirt draped over a pink taffeta petticoat and a wide silk sash tied into a big bow at the back. Pink silk roses were attached to the hem at regular intervals.

At the first sound of Juliana's whimpering, Carolien grabbed the dress and rushed into the nursery.

"I'm coming, I'm coming. See, here I am. Come, my little angel, let's get dressed." Carolien put the dress on Juliana's dressing table and took the child out of her crib. Juliana, still rosy and warm from sleep, put her arms around Carolien's neck and snuggled against her shoulder.

Carolien put Juliana on the dressing table and slipped the dress over her head. She tied the sash into a fluffy bow and undid the soft cloth curlers she had put into Juliana's hair before putting the baby down for her nap. Carolien set Juliana on the floor and backed up a few steps to take a look at her. The puffy tulle sleeves looked like cropped angel wings. Dressed up in her birthday dress, her ringlets bouncing on her shoulders, Juliana looked like a life-sized baby doll.

"Mama!" Juliana toddled toward Carolien with outstretched arms.

"Oh, come here, my angel." Carolien caught the toddler. Juliana grabbed Carolien's index finger, gurgling and laughing. They walked into the dining room, where the pink frosted cake with red sugar rosebuds that Carolien and Mia had made earlier was waiting.

The back-porch door slammed. "Hi, Mom!" Jenny called out.

"Hi!" Carolien picked Juliana up and swung her into the highchair. "Isn't she pretty?"

"Yeah. Hi, Julie. Boy, you're all dressed up." Jenny slipped the saddlebag off her shoulder. It hit the floor with thud. Carolien frowned, but she quickly suppressed her irritation when Jenny walked over to Juliana and bounced the string of rattling balls attached to the high-chair tray.

"Are we having a whole cake for our tea snack?" Jenny stared at the cake. "Why is there a candle on the cake?"

"Her name is Juliana, not Julie." Carolien noticed Jenny flinch and continued in a softer tone. "Today is Juliana's birthday. Here, let me light the candle." Carolien reached for the box of matches next to the cake-platter. "Let's sing *Lang zal zij leven.*" After they sang the Dutch happy birthday song, Carolien attempted to make Juliana blow out her candle but finally snuffed the flame herself.

Juliana cheered and plopped both hands on top of the cake, barely missing the still smoldering candle. She looked at her hands, which were covered with pink frosting. Giggling, she grabbed a handful of her black ringlets.

"Oh, no! You're making yourself all messy." Carolien laughed. She tried to hold Juliana still, but the baby managed to wiggle a hand free and splashed pink frosting all over Carolien's face.

"Yikes." Jenny brought up both arms and covered her face.

"Don't just stand there! Can't you see I could use a wet washcloth?"

156

Carolien moved the cake out of Juliana's reach. Jenny always needed prompting. She was always belligerent. Yet no one at Nanna's seemed to have these problems with her.

"Ta-ta-ta!" Juliana banged the highchair tray with both hands.

"Here, Mom." Jenny handed Carolien a wet washcloth.

"Thanks." Carolien wiped Juliana clean. Jenny looked small, clad in overalls and her hair in a pageboy cut. What would it be like to have a real birthday party? The Dutch celebrated birthdays with friends and family, but when she envisioned her family's presence she realized that they had never celebrated Jenny's birthday. True to Chinese tradition, Jenny became a year older on Chinese New Year. Carolien bit her lip. Perhaps Nanna was right, maybe she did slight Jenny.

***

Sue took Jenny shopping in Bandung's Chinatown on the Sunday after Juliana's birthday.

"Look, Aunt Sue, they fixed everything." Jenny jumped out of the *betja* after it came to a squeaking halt at the curbside.

There were no signs of the fire. The street bustled with shoppers and traffic. A cacophony of clanking cyclo bells, honking taxicabs, and a steady stream of people speaking loudly in Chinese and Malay filled the streets. The odors of salted fish, curing meats, and trays of drying shrimp paste permeated the air. It was as if there never had been a time of smoky, smoldering quiet. Jenny tried to locate the place where she and Carolien had found Juliana but she couldn't.

"Now remember, Jenny, don't wander off. Stay close to me." Sue paid the cyclo driver.

Chinatown was a confusing place. The merchants spoke Chinese amongst each other, and heavily accented Malay to outsiders. Dutch was the only language Jenny knew, besides the little Malay she spoke to the servants. She followed Sue into different stores and wondered if the merchants who occupied the stores were the same ones as those before the fire.

Sue chatted with the storekeepers as she made her purchases. She spent a long time talking with two tofu vendors. When she was done she hailed a cyclo and gave the driver Carolien's address.

"Why are we going to my house?" Jenny asked.

"I have to talk to your mother." Sue rummaged in the shopping bag and handed Jenny a piece of sugar cane. "Here, you can have this."

At Carolien's house, Sue paid the cyclo driver and Jenny helped her carry the heavy basket into the house. She wondered why Sue was in such a rush.

"Carolien!" Sue called as soon as they entered the house.

Carolien came out of her workroom. She held a pair of scissors in her hand and had a pincushion strapped to her arm. "I didn't know you were coming back here." She tucked a few loose strands of hair behind her ear. "I just started cutting out a dress for Juliana. It's amazing how fast she's growing."

"Jenny, go look for the box of candied tamarind in the shopping bag and have some. I need to talk to your mother. Be a good girl and go play." Sue whispered something to Carolien and the two of them disappeared into Carolien's bedroom.

Jenny dug through the shopping bag and helped herself to a plump pod of sugared tamarind. On her way to her room, she licked the sugar crystals off the dark tamarind flesh. Sitting on the cool tiled floor, she leaned against the separation wall.

Jenny mostly heard Sue's agitated voice. Sue said, "I'm sure it's them." Jenny pressed her ear harder against the wall and heard Sue say, "Here, I wrote down the address. Gosh, Lien, what are you going to do?"

"Look them up, of course! They need to know that their child is okay."

"What if they want her back?" Sue sounded worried.

It was quiet for a while and Jenny wondered if it was Carolien or Juliana whom Sue was worried about.

"I doubt it. After all, they left her. They'll realize she's better off with me," Carolien said confidently.

"What if you're wrong?"

Jenny couldn't hear Carolien's answer.

"You might be right," Sue said.

Their footsteps moved toward the door. Jenny quickly walked to her desk and began to do her homework, but her mind kept wandering off to the conversation she had overheard.

***

The next afternoon, Carolien handed Juliana's parents' address to Amin and told him to fetch a *betja*. "Make sure the driver knows where to take me and is willing to wait." She ignored the quizzical look Amin gave her and placed Mia in charge of Juliana.

While the cyclo driver drove through unfamiliar streets, Carolien tried to imagine her meeting with Juliana's parents. She had decided that if Juliana's parents didn't want her back, she would keep the child. And if they did want her, well, she had no other choice than to return the girl to her parents. The thought of losing Juliana brought on a nauseating pain.

They were now driving through the outskirts of Bandung's downtown area. The cyclo driver panted as he peddled through the late morning heat. The broken pavement forced him through potholes. The vehicle bounced and Carolien clamped her hand around the frame of the cyclo's canopy to keep herself steady. The houses were shanties now, the front yards small, weed-ridden dirt patches with laundry lines strung across them. Every so often a light breeze carried a whiff of cooking aromas and smoke. It would be hard for people who lived here to feed another mouth.

Carolien was appalled by the living conditions, yet she was almost glad to see the rundown neighborhood; the situation might increase her chance of keeping Juliana. The cyclo driver turned into a small side street. "This is the street," he said. He wiped perspiration from his face and neck with a grimy hand-towel and pointed to one of the hovels. "That might be the house."

"Wait here for me." Carolien stepped slowly out of the *betja*. A thin column of smoke crawled out from under the thatched roof at the back of the house. Several pairs of Chinese pajamas hung on the laundry lines, along with a few tattered trousers and shirts. A worn gray and white striped military blanket, like the one Juliana had been wrapped in when Carolien found her, took up a line by itself. A bamboo incense holder hung off the wall by the front door. Carolien inhaled the familiar scent before she knocked.

A Chinese woman in her late thirties answered the door.

"I'm looking for Fong Hok Ma," Carolien said in Malay.

The woman's eyes widened and she took a hesitant step backward.

Carolien peeked past the woman into the dimly lit room. She was taken aback by the mixed odors of smoke, clove cigarettes and tofu wastewater.

The woman yelled something in Chinese over her shoulder. Loud voices called answers from the back of the house and a couple appeared in the doorway. The three of them carried on a conversation in Chinese while giving Carolien the once over.

Carolien wished she could speak Chinese. In their zeal to adapt to Dutch ways, her family had abandoned the Chinese language and she had not needed it until now. Carolien scrutinized the threesome in the doorway. She was obviously the subject of their conversation. They eyed her curiously and Carolien began to feel uncomfortable.

The man stepped forward. "Who are you looking for?" he asked in heavy accented Malay.

"Fong Hok Ma. Are you Fong Hok Ma?" Carolien glanced at the older-looking of the two women and pointed. "Your wife?"

Carolien's questions started a new round of dialogue between the three others. Was this Juliana's family? Which of the two women was her mother? Carolien sighed, frowning. Finally, she blurted, "Kosambi, did you live in Kosambi?" At the mention of the Chinese business district where she had found Juliana, the three others quieted instantly. Suddenly guarded, they exchanged silent glances. The older woman plucked at the edge of her blouse. She leaned toward the man and murmured a few words. He glared at Carolien. "Are you Fong Hok Ma? Is that your wife? I need to speak with you," Carolien repeated.

This time, the man nodded and his wife said, "Come in."

Everyone stepped away from the doorway and Carolien entered the shabby room. She took a seat in one of the worn rattan chairs. The wife whispered something to the other woman who then left the room. "Is she your sister?" Carolien asked.

"Yes, my younger sister." The wife nodded.

Carolien was unable to take her eyes off the older woman–this was Juliana's mother. Under the man's uncomfortable gaze, perspiration slicked her palms. She wet her lips and was about to speak when the younger woman returned with a wooden tea tray.

Juliana's mother poured steaming green tea into the cups. Carolien noticed that the woman's hand trembled. Juliana's mother handed Carolien a cup of tea. For a moment their eyes met and Carolien saw a resemblance between mother and daughter.

"You left your baby," Carolien said. "When the rebels burned down Kosambi, you left your baby girl." The man's face turned ashen and Juliana's mother began to cry. Her sister started to say something but stopped mid-sentence. Carolien moved her teacup aside. "She is okay. I found her and took her home."

"Is she with you now?" Juliana's mother wiped her face with the tip of her blouse. The eagerness in her voice speared through Carolien's heart. The woman turned to her husband who lit a clove cigarette. They exchanged a few clipped words.

"It's all right." Carolien interrupted their conversation. "Don't worry. The police didn't send me. I just want you to know that your baby is okay. She's healthy and she's happy. She just learned to walk and can say quite a few words." Carolien glanced at the faces around her. She tried to guess what they were thinking. Were they relieved? What did they want?

"I have to go back to work." Juliana's father said a few words to his wife and left the room.

"Will you keep her?" Juliana's mother lowered her eyes. "You won't take her to an orphanage?" she asked, smoothing her pant-leg.

"Don't worry. I would never take her to an orphanage. I love her as if she were my own daughter." Carolien leaned across the table. Her heart began to race; would they let her keep Juliana?

When she rose, Juliana's mother remained seated. Her sister spoke softly to her. "Here." Carolien took a notepad out of her purse, wrote her name and address, and folded the paper into Juliana's mother's hand. "If you like, you can visit and see for yourself how well she's doing." Carolien tried to control her rapid heart-beat and averted her eyes when Juliana's mother looked up at her, miserably. Her happiness about most likely to be able to keep Juliana overshadowed her empathy for Juliana's mother.

"Please…" Juliana's mother grabbed Carolien's arm. "Take care of my baby. Maybe, some day–" she said, breaking into sobs.

***

One day, the following week, Jenny and Eddie walked into the dining room where Amin was setting the table for dinner. "Where's my aunt?" Eddie asked.

"In her room, with Little Miss." Amin placed the utensils meticulously.

Jenny went to her room while Eddie knocked on Carolien's bedroom door. Jenny listened to the voices coming from her mother's room as she rummaged around her desk. Carolien spoke with a high pitch. She sounded excited, but not angry. Eddie's voice was deep and soothing.

When dinnertime came, Eddie was the only one at the table.

"Where's Mom?" Jenny asked anxiously.

"She's in her room, but I'll have dinner with you." Eddie pulled out Jenny's chair.

"Thanks." Jenny was happy with Eddie's company but felt uneasy about Carolien's absence. "Why isn't Mom having dinner?"

"Let me cut you a leg off that grilled chicken." Eddie filled Jenny's plate. Serving himself, he asked, "How's your homework coming along?"

"I'm done."

Eddie seemed preoccupied. Why wouldn't he answer her question?

"Go to your mother's room to say goodnight," Eddie said after they finished dinner. He tousled Jenny's hair and gave her an encouraging nudge. "Your mother isn't feeling very well, so be nice to her, okay?"

The night-light was on in Carolien's bedroom. Carolien sat up in bed, leaning against a stack of pillows. Juliana lay asleep next to her.

"Hi, Mom." Jenny took a few steps into the room. She searched for her mother's face in the dim light.

Carolien's eyes were red and swollen. She blew her nose and gave Jenny a vague wave. "Hi." She sighed. "Did you have dinner?"

"Yes, it was good." Jenny shifted her weight, rubbing her hands against her skirt.

Carolien began to cry. Juliana whimpered in her sleep and moved an arm aimlessly in the air. Juliana's movement tempered Carolien's tears.

Jenny stood motionless. It felt as if great danger lurked in the dark corners of the room. She didn't know what to do to stop Carolien's crying, so she eased toward the door, reaching for the knob.

Eddie looked up from reading the paper when Jenny tumbled through the door. "There you are. Now, let's–"

"Eddie, Mom's crying!"

"Shhh, Jen, shhh. Look at me." Eddie rose and shook Jenny's shoulders. "Your mother is very sad. Aunt Sue met someone at the Chinese market who knew Juliana's parents. Your mother went to visit them last week. They're very poor Chinese. They lost what little they had in the fire. Now they live among the natives in a village all the way across town. They make tofu to sell at a market close to their house."

Jenny thought of the time Mia took her to buy tofu from the Chinese tofu maker. She remembered the sour stench and the slimy green fluid that flowed alongside the *gedek* walls.

"They have two other small children, both boys. They couldn't carry the boys, the baby, and their belongings. Something had to be left behind. The baby was a girl, so she wasn't important to them and they left her." Eddie's voice trailed off.

Jenny tried to slump against Eddie's chest but he pushed her back. "Straighten up. Listen. You need to be a big girl, okay?" Eddie gave Jenny's hands a squeeze. "At first, they agreed to let your mother keep the baby. They were happy that the child was alive and cared for. But then someone told them that if an abandoned child was found by someone like your mother, this child, even though it was a girl, was born with an extraordinary amount of luck." Eddie took a deep breath. "They changed their minds, Jenny. They think that the baby's luck will rub off on them. They came today to tell your mother that they want Juliana back."

Jenny squeezed Eddie's hands so hard her fingernails dug into his palms. How could Juliana, always pink and fluffy, live in the damp slippery filth of a Chinese tofu maker's place?

"What are you thinking, Jenny? Are you happy Juliana is going back

163

to her parents?" Eddie looked straight at her.

Jenny frowned. Since Juliana's arrival Carolien was not always on the lookout for something to be angry about. But the baby's presence caused a lonely blurry sadness deep inside her, the kind of sadness one feels when missing or losing something. There was just too much to sort out.

"I don't care!" Jenny blurted and pushed two fists into Eddie's chest. All she wanted was for this surge of conflicting feelings to stop. "When does she have to leave?"

"I don't know." Eddie looked puzzled. "Your mother wants to try to change their minds."

"Do you think they will?" Jenny carved lines into the polished tabletop with her thumbnail.

"I don't know. I'm afraid not." They were quiet for a while. Then Eddie said, "Jenny, after the baby leaves, your mother will need your company. You have to be a big girl. Be nice to your mother and try to help her."

Jenny nodded and hung her head. What new chores would her mother dream up when she no longer had Juliana to play with? Would she go back to waiting for her on the front porch with questions and tasks?

***

A few days later, Jenny came home to find two *betjas* parked in her mother's driveway. Voices, similar to those she had heard in Chinatown, drifted through the open windows of the dining room. When she walked into the room Juliana sat in her high chair. A strange woman sat on each side of her and two little boys were playing on the floor. Carolien, standing behind the high chair, waved at her. "This is my daughter," she said in Malay.

The two women turned to Jenny and said something in Chinese to each other and then to the boys.

Carolien asked the woman who was sitting next to Juliana where the boys went to school. The woman answered with a strong Chinese accent that Jenny couldn't understand.

Jenny clasped her hands and swung them slowly back and forth.

Should she shake hands with everyone? Perhaps, since the visitors were Chinese, she should greet them the Chinese way, but they spoke Malay. She forced her mouth into a sort of smile instead.

Juliana laughed and stuck her arms out.

"Do you want to see Jenny?" Carolien lifted Juliana out of the highchair and put her on the floor. "These ladies are Juliana's mother and her aunt, and those are her brothers. They came to visit Juliana." Carolien sounded tired.

Jenny crouched and opened her arms. "C'mon, Julie."

Juliana had almost reached Jenny when she staggered and dropped to the floor. Jenny reached for the toddler and so did Carolien and Juliana's mother. The women got to Juliana first. Each of them grabbed one of the child's hands and, together, they pulled her back on her feet.

"Ma-m-ma." Juliana pulled toward Carolien staring at the stranger who held one of her hands. She started crying when she could not pull her hand loose.

"Please, let go," Carolien begged.

Jenny had never heard her mother plead.

Carolien picked up the crying child and Juliana's mother lost her grip.

Juliana wound her arms immediately around Carolien's neck and buried her face into Carolien's shoulder.

"Shhh, shhh." Carolien rocked Juliana in her arms. "Juliana, sweetheart, it's all right."

"Hong, Hong, *li-li*." Juliana's mother clapped her hands and held her arms out. When Juliana buried her face deeper into Carolien's neck, the woman patted Juliana on her bottom, making her cry even more. The boys clung to their aunt who addressed her sister in Chinese with agitated statements.

"What's she saying? Why is she making Julie cry?" Jenny wanted to run to the back yard, jump on her swing, and swing hard and high.

"Hong is Juliana's real name. *Li-li* is Chinese for come here," Carolien explained with a shaky voice.

Meanwhile, the boys clung to their aunt who was still speaking loudly to her sister.

Jenny could no longer bear to be in the same room with Juliana's

165

family. "I have to do my homework," she said and left.

During dinner Jenny asked, "Mom, why were those people here?"

Carolien put her utensils down and was silent for a moment. "They wanted to take Juliana–" her voice broke and she had to stop. After a short pause she continued. "I was able to talk them out of it. They agreed to let her stay till the first Saturday of next month–another seventeen days."

Jenny threw Carolien a sideways glance. What would her mother do once she returned Juliana to her family? Eddie had told her to be good and helpful, but Jenny couldn't think of anything else to do other than to stay out of Carolien's way. Something she tried to do most of the time anyway.

During the next seventeen days, Jenny watched a collection of boxes grow against the walls of the dining room. Some boxes were packed with miscellaneous food items such as cans of milk and tea biscuits. Other boxes contained dresses and shoes that Juliana would need to grow into, and still others were filled with blankets and sheets.

What was going to happen when these clothes were too small and the food was gone? Frowning, Jenny ran a finger across the lids of a row of boxes.

***

Carolien sat in the narrow *betja* seat with Juliana in her lap. Every so often she pulled the child close against her and nuzzled the top of Juliana's head. Inhaling Juliana's familiar scent, Carolien fought back tears. She shot Jenny, who sat stiffly next to them, a sideways glance. Thank God the child wasn't bombarding her with questions. They rode in the first of three cyclos headed toward Juliana's parents' house. The second cyclo was loaded with boxes of food, clothing and linens. The third vehicle carried Juliana's crib and folded highchair. Carolien remembered the run down neighborhoods from her first visit to Juliana's parents. Each time the cyclo bounced through a large pothole in the pavement, Juliana clapped her hands and shouted, "Boom-boom, boom-boom." Jenny started to laugh, but stopped when Carolien shot her a weary look.

A hen and her chicks scattered off the road as they passed. Someone threw a rock at a mongrel. The mutt yelped and ran off with his tail tucked between his legs. They had passed through several alleys when Carolien told the driver to slow down. Two boys dashed into the road and yelled, "*Meme! Meme!* They are here!"

As soon as Carolien ordered the driver to stop, Jenny jumped out of the vehicle. Carolien handed Juliana to her and followed. Juliana's mother, her aunt, and the two boys crowded around them, speaking to each other in animated Chinese. Every so often the two women spoke to Carolien in Malay. Juliana's mother held out her arms and said in Chinese, "Come, little girl, come here." But Juliana clung to Carolien.

"Where would you like Juliana's things?" Carolien picked up the toddler and motioned the cyclo drivers to follow with the boxes and furniture.

Juliana's mother turned to her sister and, while engaging in a lively Chinese conversation, they showed everyone into the house.

Carolien pressed Juliana against her when they entered the small living room. She remembered the ragged furnishings, the scuffed wooden table and worn rattan chairs, the makeshift altar in the far corner. Today, incense sticks burned in the holders flanking the small statue of Buddha. A thin line of smoke wafted over a bowl of oranges.

Juliana's mother clapped her hands. She opened her arms, smiling, but the toddler buried her face into Carolien's neck.

After the cyclo drivers unloaded the boxes, Carolien paid two of the drivers and asked the third to wait for her.

Juliana's father appeared from behind a doorway curtain. He seemed overwhelmed by the stacks of boxes and furniture. Maneuvering his way around them, he spoke to his wife in Chinese.

When Juliana's mother reached for her again, the youngster wound her arms tightly around Carolien's neck and began to cry.

"Look, darling, there are your mamma and your papa." Carolien's voice faltered and tears streamed down her cheeks. She tried to loosen Juliana's grip with trembling fingers. When she fumbled for a handkerchief, Jenny offered hers.

Juliana's father pinched the girl's cheek, but quickly pulled his hand back when she turned away from him, hollering.

Carolien rocked Juliana in her arms and wished she understood Chinese. Juliana's father seemed upset. His eyes flashed angrily in his gaunt face as he spoke rapidly to his wife. She tried to interrupt him, but her words dissolved in his speech. He scowled at Carolien and returned to his troughs of tofu. Was he the reason Juliana had been left to fate?

"Shhh, shhh, it's okay." Carolien rubbed Juliana's back. "Sshh, please, don't cry."

Juliana's mother stroked the child's back and spoke softly to her in Chinese. Each time her mother tried to lift her out of Carolien's arms, Juliana cried louder and buried her face deeper into Carolien's neck. Meanwhile, Juliana's aunt kept talking in Chinese to her sister and the smaller of the two boys tugged on his mother's blouse.

"I'll take her now." Juliana's mother said finally. Ignoring the child's crying, she pulled Juliana out of Carolien's arms.

Carolien let go. She swayed and tried to steady herself.

"Mom, let's go." Jenny put a hand on her mother's arm.

Carolien numbly moved her feet. It felt strangely comforting to have Jenny guide her.

"Thank you, for all you've done." Juliana's aunt patted Carolien on the shoulder. Moving toward the door, she repeated, "Thank you."

Jenny took Carolien's hand and walked her to the waiting *betja*.

"Mam-ma-a-a-a!" Juliana's cries filled the narrow street between the shanties. Carolien stared ahead. She moved a hand against her chest, shivering despite the murky heat. The wind blew wisps of her hair, pulled loose by Juliana's clutching hands, across her face, but Carolien did not attempt to fasten the strands. She clutched her hands in her lap while thoughts tumbled through her head.

Ten years ago she had argued in a court of law that a child was always best cared for by its mother. Why did she now feel that it was better for Juliana to stay with her? Carolien glanced sideways at Jenny sitting straight in her corner. Her set jaw was a replica of Po Han's, but Carolien claimed the girl's strength. Satisfaction surged through her pain. Jenny was growing into the independent woman she wanted her to be. So what if the child preferred to be with Nanna, Eddie, and Els?

Carolien didn't say a word during the entire *betja* ride home. She shook and swayed in her seat as they drove through the potholes. Every so often, she squeezed her interlaced fingers together until the knuckles came up white.

***

At home, Carolien walked straight to her bedroom. Something sharp churned inside her chest. The pain was the only substance that supported her body. She felt weightless. Passing the familiar objects in the room she moved toward her bed.

Carolien stayed in bed for many days. At times, she tossed and turned, but she mostly lay still while tears rolled down onto her pillow.

One day, when Jenny came to see her, Carolien said, "If I die, you will stay with Nanna. Or maybe you can live with Eddie when he gets married."

Jenny stood stiffly by the foot of the bed, her hands clamped around the frame.

"Would you like to stay with Nanna?"

Jenny kicked a couple of times hard against a leg of Carolien's bed. "Yes!" she said loudly. "I always want to stay with Nanna." Running out of the room, she shouted over her shoulder, "I wish I could live there now!"

Carolien burst into tears as the door slammed. Regardless of how hard she worked, she never seemed to achieve anything. She had tried to break out of the subservient position of women in a Chinese family. She had even bucked tradition and gotten a divorce. But after Po Han left, her life had turned into a series of duties and obligation and she felt anything but free and powerful. Her hopes had let her down.

Juliana had brought some lightness back into her life. With the little girl riding on her knees Carolien hadn't worried about the future. Juliana had filled the lonely hours when Jenny was at Nanna's with spontaneous laughter and baby jabbering. Carolien had given to Juliana the light-hearted tenderness she kept away from her own daughter, for fear that it would make Jenny weak and dependent. Now even that was gone. Carolien turned on her side and smothered her sobs with her pillow.

***

A few days later the bedroom door opened. Nanna stood in the dim light.

"Ma?" Carolien brought a hand to her disheveled hair and tried to smooth it away from her face. "Ma, you came."

"You didn't think I would come when I'm told that my daughter has lost the will to live while she still has a child to raise?" Nanna walked to the window. She pulled the drapes open and reached for the shutter handle.

"Please," Carolien mumbled. "Don't open the shutters. I've a very bad headache, the light bothers me." She propped her pillows up and lay back against them.

Nanna turned away from the window. She took a seat on the side of Carolien's bed. "Anyone who doesn't eat and doesn't get fresh air will get a headache."

Carolien lowered her eyes and glanced sideways at Nanna's erect figure. She remembered how, thirteen years ago, Nanna had come to her bedside to ease Jenny into the world and saved her life. Carolien wished that she could bury her head into Nanna's lap the way she often saw Jenny do.

Nanna smoothed the bed sheet. "You took on a burden," she said. "You carried it with joy and you carried it well." Carolien looked up and Nanna patted her arm. "But you've come to the end of that road and now you need to put that burden down." Carolien tried to look away but her mother's gaze firmly held hers. "The days of your responsibilities have not yet been counted. You still have a long way to go."

Nanna went back to the window and opened the shutters. Sunlight poured into the room and a fresh breeze slapped the sheer curtains. "I came with Sue. Let me see what food we can prepare." Nanna walked toward the door.

"It's okay, don't bother. I'm not hungry." Carolien protested, but she knew she would eat the food Nanna prepared.

That night Carolien slept well. She woke to the call of early morning food vendors and the sloshing sound of Amin's mop against the pail in the next room. For a minute she listened with a sharp longing for Juliana's whimpering sounds, but then she willed herself to focus on the new day. Like Nanna said, the episode with Juliana was behind her and she needed to move ahead. She pulled her drapes and pushed the windows open. The morning sun flooded the room with light.

Carolien ignored the surprised looks from Jenny and the servants when she came to the breakfast table. Her voice had its normal strength when she asked, "Are you having any tests today?"

"No." Jenny finished buttering her toast, and volunteered, "But next week I have a big geometry one."

After Jenny left for school Carolien busied herself with household chores. By the end of the morning she had decided to clear out the nursery. It was best to put the room to good use. Perhaps she should take in sewing again. She could use the room as a consultation and fitting room and there was enough space in the garage for four seamstresses. Carolien poked the cobweb cleaner into one of the ceiling corners and gave the long handle a firm twist.

CHAPTER 15

For parenting advice, Carolien turned to a series of Dutch pedagogy books. The books said that when a girl was twelve her mother should discuss the ovulation process with her to prepare the girl for her first period. Carolien glanced at the wall calendar. It was October of 1948 and Jenny was fourteen. How could she have let so much time pass without taking care of such an important issue? Carolien closed the book feeling guilty. Her focus the last year and a half had been on Julianna. She tried to formulate her dialogue with Jenny but could not come up with the words. She dreaded having to answer the string of questions Jenny would undoubtedly respond with.

That afternoon Carolien went to visit Nanna.

"But of course, you need to get ready–you don't need the Dutch to tell you that." Nanna set down the basket of beans she was sorting and took out two empty containers from the buffet. She filled one with a strong scented herbal tea and the other with pink rose-flavored rock candy. "Here, be sure to give Jenny her moon tea during her rag days."

Carolien remembered the tea being so bitter that it made her tongue curl. Nanna claimed that the herbs used in the brew had a cleansing and tightening affect on the female organs. Carolien never quite subscribed to that belief, but she didn't think it was worth the trouble to oppose Nanna.

"What do I tell Jenny? I mean… should I tell her everything, like the book says?" Carolien stacked and unstacked the containers.

Nanna shrugged. "Why worry a child with life? Life will burden her with worry soon enough." She began rummaging through the buffet. "And while you're at it, you should go over Jenny's wardrobe. It's about time she steps out of those overalls."

"Oh, Ma. Just look at the Dutch fashion magazines. Women are starting to wear slacks more and more," Carolien laughed.

"Dutch this and Dutch that," Nanna muttered. "When will you see that not all the Dutch people preach is gospel?"

Carolien was filled with thoughts while preparing Jenny's mooncloths. As she tapped the pedal of her electric Singer, she shaped Jenny's future. She'd take the van Houtens up on their offer to house Jenny in Holland. She'd write letters to the authorities and petition for any dispensations needed to further Jenny's education. She'd send Jenny to study law in Leiden. Jenny was going to be a careerwoman, perhaps even the first female lawyer in the country.

Carolien tossed the last cloth into a small enamel pail with the others. She couldn't remember anyone telling her anything about her first period, but she did remember catching Sue doing her moonwash. When she asked where the bloody rags came from, Sue said, "It's what happens to every woman. It will happen to you too. You'll see."

Carolien folded the cloths into little pillows and placed them in a big blue cardboard box, along with the two cloth belts she had made, new safety pins, and a small new notebook. She closed the box, grabbed the bucket, and walked to Jenny's room. It was hard to think of Jenny as a young woman, rather than a rambunctious child.

Jenny sat at her desk doing homework.

"Here are your mooncloths." Carolien set the box on the bed. She hesitated before adding, "Pretty soon, you'll need them."

Jenny stared at the box, frowning.

"Soon, you'll have your period. Every month you'll bleed for a week or so. You need to wear your mooncloth then. It'll keep the blood from spotting your clothes." Carolien shook out a little white pillow and showed Jenny how to form it by folding the cloth strip back into the pouch. "Use this pail to do your moonwash." She picked up the notebook next and said, "Don't forget to write the date down each time it happens."

Jenny fingered the box quietly.

Carolien looked at Jenny's bowed head. There must be more she needed to say. She hesitated, then started to leave the room. She turned by the door and said, "Tell me when it happens, so I can show you how to use everything."

Jenny nodded, holding the pail between her knees.

"You better stop horsing around with the boys once you're using your mooncloths." Carolien turned the doorknob back and forth. "Don't let any of them touch you. Be especially careful with the Dutch boys, they'll take a lot more liberties than the Chinese."

Carolien avoided meeting Jenny's eyes. She quickly left the room and closed the door behind her.

***

During the next week Jenny ran frequently to the bathroom to check on her panties. She was relieved each time she didn't find any blood. Several months passed during which nothing happened. She began to forget about the mooncloths in her closet until one day, during track practice with the boys, something warm and wet seeped between her legs. She ran a hand down her inner thigh and stared at the red smear on her palm. Horrified, she ran off the field and headed home.

The next morning at breakfast Jenny noticed a small cup with a lid on it by her plate. She lifted the cover and a bitter steam wafted up her nostrils. "That stinks." She wrinkled her nose. "What is it? Why's this sitting by my plate?"

"I noticed your moonpail in the bathroom. Are you getting along all right?" Carolien buttered her toast and reached for the marmalade.

Jenny nodded.

"Nanna wants you to drink a cup of this herb tea every morning while you're using your mooncloths, and three more days after you're finished."

Jenny stared at the small cup. It looked the same as the ones that sometimes appeared by Els and Emma's breakfast plates. She remembered her cousins taking a deep breath and emptying the cup in almost one big gulp.

"There's a piece of rock candy on the saucer. You might like to suck on it afterward." Carolien took a bite of her toast.

Jenny stared at the dark liquid. "Did Nanna say I've to drink all of it?"

"If you drink half of it, we'll dump the rest and won't tell Nanna." Carolien's voice had a strange tightness to it. She took a sip of her coffee, blinking. "You better hurry or you'll be late for school."

When Jenny went to visit Nanna that afternoon, her grandmother was working on the bougainvillea vine. "Were you a good girl and did you drink all of your moon tea?" Nanna asked after they had exchanged greetings.

Jenny looked away, feeling guilty. "Nanna, why do I have to drink that awful stuff?"

Nanna fastened a loose wisp of flaming bougainvillea against the trellis. "For a girl's first moon tea, she gets pink rock candy that is scented with rose oil. It's to make her understand that if she drinks her bitter moon tea, she'll have sweet things to look forward to." Nanna brushed Jenny's cheek with her index finger. "A girl has to drink her moon tea if she wants to be a good woman and have her husband take pleasure in her."

Husband? Jenny had never thought of having a husband. She petted Claus who nuzzled her hand and followed Nanna to the jasmine hedge.

"The flower saucers need fresh flowers." Nanna handed Jenny a small, cloth-lined rattan basket. They picked the swollen but still closed jasmine buds. "Now that you've started using your mooncloths, you should try behaving more like a girl and stop playing with boys so much. Especially Dutch boys." Nanna gave Jenny a scrutinizing look. "Perhaps you should wear dresses more often and let your hair grow."

Jenny crushed the bud she had picked into a fragrant mush. "Nanna, I've got to go to the bathroom. I'll be right back." She placed the flower basket on the path and ran toward the house with Claus on her heels. Why was Nanna sounding just like her mother?

CHAPTER 16

Ocho filled the last tray of a three-tiered bamboo basket with savory pastries. She glanced at the kitchen clock, it was nearly ten-thirty. The vendors should start arriving soon to pick up their baskets. Each of the ten bamboo stacking baskets held sixty pastries. If she wanted to, she could probably sell at least two or three more, maybe even five, but she was already starting the day at four-thirty. Ocho sighed. It was getting harder and harder to get out of bed that early. Through the open window she heard gravel crackle under hurried footsteps on the path alongside the house. Ocho caught her breath and grabbed the kitchen counter– none of the vendors walked that fast.

Nick de Graaf had told her that Po Han would be home soon. When nothing happened during the weeks following Nick's announcement, Ocho had given up. Now she leaned trembling against the counter as the door flung open. Unable to move, she stared speechless at the tall unshaven man standing in the doorway.

Po Han dropped a suitcase to the floor. "Ocho! It's me, I'm home!" He crossed the room with a few strides.

"Ha-an! Po Han!" Ocho put a shaking hand against his chest and grabbed the soiled lapel of his white cotton jacket. "Han!" She reached for his face with the other hand. The stubble on his cheek scratched her palm and she could smell the travel, dust, perspiration, and cigarette smoke on his skin. She wasn't hallucinating. After being gone for a good seven years, Po Han had returned. Blood surged to, then drained from her head. Suddenly dizzy, Ocho fell against Po Han. "Ohh… thank God… you're back… you're back!"

"Yes, I'm back." Po Han's voice was thick with emotion. He rubbed Ocho's shoulders and walked her to the kitchen table. "Here, sit down," he said, pulling a chair.

Po Han walked across the room and poured a glass of water from an earthen carafe on the kitchen counter. He was thin and disheveled. How long had he been on the road, Ocho wondered. When was the last time he had a decent meal? She dried her tears with the tip of her *kebaja* and took a few sips of water. Then she put water to boil on the charcoal stove for coffee and took half a dozen of pastries out of one of the baskets. Opening the door into the dining room, she yelled at the maid, "Ni, *Tuan* is home! Come, get his luggage." When Po Han reached for his suitcase, she pushed him back into his chair. "Leave it, leave it. Let the maid take care of it."

The vendors arrived and shot curious glances at Po Han.

"This is my grandson, he just came back from Holland." Ocho proudly introduced Po Han. She ordered the maid to boil a caldron of water for Po Han's bath while she served him a cup of strong coffee and a couple of savory pastries. Meanwhile, a nagging thought filled the back of her head. Would he go see Carolien and Jenny? What would Carolien do when she heard that he had come back? Ocho felt her mouth go dry.

Po Han pressed the tines of his fork into the pastry flakes left on his plate. "Would you like another one?" Ocho held out the serving plate.

"No, thank you." Po Han laughed and finished his coffee. "It was delicious. God, I didn't realize how much I missed you, your food, and not being so cold all the time." He lit a cigarette and leaned back into his chair.

"Are you going to tell Carolien that you're back?" Ocho shot Po Han a sharp sideways glance.

"Yes, I will. But first, I have to find a steady job. I want to have something to offer Jenny when I see her." Po Han slowly exhaled a long stream of smoke.

Ocho noticed the pain in Po Han's eyes as he looked away. She bit hard into her chewing wad. After all these years, nothing had changed.

She needed to keep Carolien and Jenny away if she wanted to have some good years with Po Han before she died.

***

Carolien was reading the morning paper when she heard steps on the front porch. It was Sue, on her way home from a mah yong game, and full of gossip to share.

"Po Han has come back from Holland. One of the women in my mah yong group lives in his neighborhood. She told us he has joined the group that just opened the new textile factory. Apparently he learned how to produce textiles while he was in Holland." Sue fluffed the pillows and arranged them against the back of the couch. "He still lives with his grandmother in the same old house."

"Are you sure she was talking about Po Han?" Carolien gave Sue a piercing look. The textile factory at the edge of Bandung's Chinese business district was owned by a few affluent Chinese businessmen and managed by an Indonesian figurehead. The new enterprise was the talk of the town.

"Do you know of any other Chinese man who went to Holland to be a photographer?" Sue grabbed her bag and prepared to go. "What will you do when he comes to see you?"

"I don't know." Carolien accompanied her sister to the sidewalk to wait for a *betja*. "When did he come back?" she asked, looking down the street.

Sue hailed an empty cyclo. "She didn't say."

***

Carolien mulled over the information. During the next weeks she imagined many different scenarios in which Po Han would show up on her doorstep. Almost ten years had gone by since she last saw him in the courthouse. How would it feel to come face to face with him? Po Han must have changed if he had used the time in Holland to learn a trade. Perhaps, with this change, they'd be able to work out their differences. But then Ocho came to mind and Carolien quickly dismissed the notion.

Still, tending the flowerbeds in her small front yard she caught herself staring down the street as if expecting someone. When the doorbell rang she ran to answer it, pushing her hair in place and straightening her dress.

Carolien lived in this state of anticipation for months, and when Po Han never showed up she began to feel bitter. After all, even Jenny didn't mean enough to Po Han to come see her.

Once, while mending Jenny's clothes, Carolien suddenly had a dreadful thought. What if Po Han came and persuaded Jenny to live with him? He would undoubtedly be more lenient with the child than she was, Jenny would probably like him better. Carolien thought of her encounters with Jenny. Maybe she should pull back a bit? In her zeal to raise her daughter properly, she might have become overly demanding. The child was too young to understand that her nagging and criticisms were all for her sake.

The next morning, during breakfast, Carolien said to Jenny, "I made arrangements for you to skip your first class today, it's only PE."

"But, Mom–"

Carolien quickly squelched Jenny's protest. "I heard that your father came back from Holland. I want to show you where he lives and what he looks like so you can stay away from him. As unpredictable as he is, he might decide to contact you on the street and try to persuade you to live with him."

"Why can't I see my father? When do you think he will come? Do you really think he'd ask me to live with him?" Jenny pushed her plate away and jumped out of her chair. "Are we going now?"

Carolien had not expected this reaction from Jenny. Would her plan backfire?

A twenty-minute *betja* ride took them to the southeastern part of Bandung where Po Han lived. Carolien held on tightly to the *betja* frame. She had not been back since she left, some ten years ago, but the neighborhood had not changed much. When they turned into Po Han's street, Carolien scanned the houses and pointed to a house with a blooming poinsettia in the corner of a narrow yard. "That's where he lives." Carolien instructed the cyclo driver to park the vehicle a few houses away, with the frontshade down.

The grass under the poinsettia was tall. The small lawn had large brown spots and was mowed unevenly. Weeds had taken over the flowerbed where she once grew dahlias. Would the living room be a mess, just as she had found it when they came home from their honeymoon? Did Po Han still sleep in the room they had shared? What did he use Jenny's room for?

Carolien tensed when Po Han pushed his bike around a corner of the house. She moved closer to the cyclo's side, straining to get a glimpse at his face. "Look. That's your father." Carolien pulled Jenny in front of her. "Can you see? Remember what he looks like."

Jenny tried to move the shade aside. "He looks nice, Mom."

"Shh." Carolien pulled Jenny back and peeked anxiously through a slit in the cyclo's shade while Po Han rode his bike down the street. When he was a safe distance away, Carolien ordered the cyclo driver to take them to the Lyceum.

Po Han seemed to have gained some weight. She wished she could have seen his face. What would happen if they came face to face with each other? Carolien tried to calm her fluttering emotions.

"Well, now you know what your father looks like." Carolien glanced at Jenny who sat slumped into her corner. "I told you, he has no sense of responsibility. Here he's back after disappearing for several years. You'd think he'd at least try to see you. But no, he happily settles down with his grandmother without a worry about you."

Jenny sucked in her cheeks and banged her heels against the betja seat. The sound got the better of Carolien. "Stop it! You're scuffing your shoes. They don't grow on trees, you know."

Jenny stopped abruptly. For a moment their eyes met and Carolien said in a softer tone, "Walk to Nanna's after school. I'll have Amin take your bike up. I'll stop by the Dutch bakery on my way home and get us some creampuffs for tonight's dessert."

Jenny shot her a grateful smile.

Tears sprang into Carolien's eyes and she quickly turned away.

CHAPTER 17

On the first day of the 1949-1950 school year Jenny made her way to the assembly hall through the crowd of students. The air was charged with energy and expectation. Greetings were exchanged and the halls buzzed with mixed conversations. "Hey! Wait up!" Tim and a few other boys joined her.

As Els had predicted, the Indonesian Revolution had brought some drastic changes to the Lyceum. Hans Overbeek, the rector, announced in his opening address that the school had added Indonesian language and history to its curriculum. "After all, it's only normal that the citizens of a country should know that country's language and history." Hans gazed over his quiet audience and proceeded to introduce the two new Indonesian faculty members who were to teach these subjects. He also welcomed a handful of new Indonesian and Chinese students, who stood huddled together in a corner of the assembly hall.

"We are headed for a difficult, yet enlightening and progressive time." Hans paused to clean his glasses with his handkerchief. "It's been the decision of our government and the leaders of the Indonesian Revolution that there'll be a period of adjustment. During this time, the Indonesians will be given a chance to gradually take over the government of their country. Here at the Lyceum, we will do everything in our ability to make that transition smooth." The words resounded through the auditorium. "In the interest of a brighter future for all of us, I expect the cooperation of everyone to achieve our government's objective."

Jenny threw a curious glance at the two new teachers, Sardjono and Ko Ping Hwat. She checked her roster. She would have Sardjono for two classes. She had never had an *inlander* as a teacher and was doubtful that he had anything to teach her.

Jenny spotted two new students in the fifth year section, Grace Tan and Theresa Wong. She knew they both lived near Nanna. Grace and Theresa came from the Catholic Dutch-Chinese school downtown, a good school but not as prestigious as the Lyceum. Mr. Tan was a licensed public notary with his own office in Bandung's Dutch business district. Mr. Wong was a well-established dentist.

Jenny remembered Ting referring to the Tans and Wongs as "guilder-and-a-half Dutch." Before the war, the Dutch government issued equalization certificates to Chinese for a fee of one-and-a-half guilders. The certificate gave the holder access to Dutch schools, clubs, and establishments. No one in Nanna's family was an equalized Dutch citizen. Their status came from the patronage of the former mayor of Bandung and the positions that family members held in the Dutch government. There was no need for them to purchase what had already been earned.

In the classroom, Jenny dropped her schoolbag onto a seat in the front row. She arranged her books in the drawer while joking with Frans, the Dutch boy who took the desk next to hers.

Grace and Theresa chose adjacent seats a few rows behind Jenny. Through the rustle and shuffles of students settling into their seats, Jenny overheard the girls' whispers. They spoke Malay with each other, but she could make out what they were saying.

"She's got a boy's haircut." Theresa giggled.

"Isn't her dress weird?" Grace whispered into her notebook.

"It isn't a dress, she's wearing pants. Her mother probably doesn't know how to sew dresses."

"She might as well be a boy."

Jenny put her thumbs behind her denim overall straps and straightened them, then she made sure the collar of her blouse lay flat. For a moment she wished she'd paid more attention to Nanna's lectures about dressing.

When the bell for recess rang, a ball landed with a thud on Jenny's desk. "Hey, forgot how to catch?" Tim yelled out.

Jenny grabbed the ball and jumped out of her seat. "Just wait till I get you." She was running towards the lawn when she remembered her first miserable days at school. She stopped and, tapping the ball with alternate hands to keep it bouncing, shouted in Grace and Theresa's direction, "Want to come?" The girls shook their heads, giggling, and Jenny ran off.

***

Though Carolien didn't bring Po Han up in any of her conversations with Jenny, she often wondered how much impact the morning she took her to his house had on the girl. How did she handle herself when her classmates talked about their parents? It was Sue who brought her the answer.

One morning, when Carolien was in the midst of an explanation to the seamstress, the garage door flung open and Sue barreled into the room. She grabbed Carolien by the arm and pulled her out the door. "Do you know Jenny told the Tan and Wong girls that Po Han is dead?" she whispered as soon as they were alone.

"What?"

"I ran into Mrs. Tan at the market. She told me how sorry she was to hear Po Han had died. I was so shocked I thought I'd drop dead myself." Sue smoothed her hair.

"Hmm, I wonder what's going on?"

"You tell me. All I know is that Tan woman grabs every opportunity to make snide remarks about your divorce. But I put her in her place. I told her that Po Han is the operation manager and fabric designer of the new textile factory." Sue straightened her skirt.

"Why would Jenny tell those girls that her father is dead?" Carolien frowned.

"Yes, I'm curious too. I got so upset I came straight here," Sue said. "I better get home now, I kept the *betja* waiting." She grabbed her purse and walked ahead of Carolien to the waiting cyclo.

Carolien spent the rest of the morning brooding over the incident. When she heard Jenny come up the gravel path on the side of the house, she rushed to the open window. "Jenny!"

"Yeah?" Jenny parked her bike and came into the dining room, perspiration still dripping off her forehead from her bike ride in the tropical afternoon sun.

"Why on God's earth did you send a story around that your father is dead?"

Jenny looked away, quiet for a moment. "Well," she finally said, "he's never around and no one ever talks about him. He might as well be dead!"

"But you know where he lives. You saw him! Why did you lie?" Carolien searched Jenny's face.

Jenny rocked her chair back and forth. The gesture was something that would normally annoy Carolien, but this time she didn't respond to her daughter's challenge. She said, "Your father is the most irresponsible person on the face of this earth. He left me without a cent to care for you. I had to go to work and leave you with Nanna."

Jenny shrugged her shoulders. "So, what's so bad about that?" She leaned forward and the chair hit the floor with a bang. "I like it at Nanna's."

Carolien pressed her lips together. She had to admit, in spite of the war, Jenny seemed happy when they lived at Nanna's. Would she prefer to be with Po Han if they met? She gasped at the thought of losing Jenny and tried to overcome. "Don't you care that your father never bothered to worry whether or not you had food in your mouth or clothes on your back? Does it ever enter your mind how hard it is for me to make enough money to pay for your school, see to it you have decent clothes, keep you in shoes that fit, pay for the house and servants and buy all the food we need? Fortunately, Youngest Uncle and Eddie are helping me out." Carolien ended her rant, but the gnawing pain in her chest remained.

Jenny looked out of the window. She shrugged her shoulders again and rocked the chair hard back and forth. Each time the front legs hit the tile floor, they made a dull thud.

"Stop rocking that chair, I'm talking to you! Are you listening at all?"

Jenny dropped her arms on the table and buried her head.

Carolien rose. Resting both hands on the tabletop she leaned over Jenny. "Hopefully you'll understand one day how much I did for you while your father played around with his camera. Right now, instead of taking care of you he's probably involved with some money-wasting paint or photography project."

"Is my father a photographer?" Jenny looked up.

"Neither his pictures nor his ideals paid the bills or stocked the pantry. He was never able to hold a job." Carolien had exhausted her reasons. She glared at Jenny. Frustrated by the far-away look in her daughter's eyes, Carolien said, "Why don't you think about what you can do to bring your father to his senses rather than declaring him dead?"

***

A few days later, while rummaging through old files, Carolien stumbled upon the court papers from almost ten years ago that required Po Han to pay child support as well as alimony. With his unexpected move to Holland, and the war that kept him there, the payments had stopped arriving.

Carolien leaned against the file cabinet and tapped the side of the document against her mouth. The paper's sharp edge stung her pursed lips. She had caught herself wandering back into the past more often.

Now, she remembered standing with Po Han in Jenny's nursery. He had just added the image of a little girl to the sunlit woodland path of the fairy tale world he had painted. "I just want her to be happy," he had said in response to her dreams for Jenny's future.

Carolien sighed. Po Han's dreams had not been able to provide any security. He had not tried to get in touch with her since he had returned from Holland. If Po Han were at all responsible, he would have contacted her after settling into his job and at least offered support for Jenny's education. Instead, he went on with his life as if he didn't have to care about anyone other than his wicked old grandmother.

Carolien put the document away in the top drawer. There was no reason why she should carry the financial burden of Jenny's upbringing by herself any longer. It was time to remind Po Han of his responsibilities.

Over the next few weeks Carolien collected facts about Po Han. She enlisted Sue as a scout to gather information about Po Han's social life in

Bandung's Chinese circles. Before too long Carolien had clear evidence that Po Han held an important position at the new textile business, Tekstil Permai. He should be perfectly able to pay the financial support the court had ordered.

"Why do you want to build a house with rotten lumber?" Nanna asked when Carolien shared her thoughts with her family. Ting shrugged his shoulders and declared her intentions a waste of good time, while Eddie reminded her of the pain that opening an old wound could cause. Sue, Emma, and Els did not voice opinions but Carolien sensed their apprehension about the success of her undertaking.

***

Carolien sat on the front porch waiting for the mailman. He arrived at the same time that Jenny swerved her bike into the driveway. "Hi, Mom!" she called, squeezing her brakes.

"Hi, please bring me the mail." Carolien set her mending basket aside.

Jenny stuffed the handful of envelopes the mailman handed her behind the bib of her overalls and continued to pedal up the driveway. She got off her bike at the porch and handed Carolien the mail.

"Thanks. Ask Amin to bring us some orange juice and come tell me how school went today." Lately Carolien felt a need for Jenny's company. She often watched her daughter behind the sheer curtains of a closed window and wished Jenny would include her in some of her games the way she did Eddie. She opened an envelope with the Lyceum's address on it and frowned.

Jenny returned to the porch and glanced at the letter. "It's only November. Did they already send out the schedule of next year's classes?"

"No, it's a notice of a tuition increase for next year." Carolien lowered the paper onto her lap. Perhaps she could work this to her advantage.

Amin carried in a tray with two tall glasses of iced orange juice and Jenny reached eagerly for one of them.

Carolien put the unopened mail in a neat stack and smoothed the school's letter out on the porch table. She waited for Jenny to put the glass down. "We need to talk," she said.

Jenny took a seat on the low wall surrounding the porch.

Carolien fingered the letter. "I don't know if you'll be able to go to the Lyceum next year. It's been hard enough to come up with the tuition, but with this increase, I'm afraid I may not be able to afford it."

"What?" Jenny sat up. "You mean I won't be able to go to school anymore?" She stared at Carolien, wide-eyed.

Jenny's panic struck Carolien. Perhaps her idea wasn't so good after all. Jenny was doing well in school, she had no intention to jeopardize the child's studies.

"Mom?"

"I'm sorry." Carolien sighed. "Unless your father pitches in, I'm afraid you won't be able to go to the Lyceum next year."

"My father? What's he got to do with it?"

"You must try to understand, Jenny. You do have a father and he is supposed to take care of you." Carolien observed Jenny. She leaned forward pushing her feet against the porch wall. Would she catch on to the idea? After a long pause, Carolien said, "If you really want to stay in the Lyceum, you might have to remind your father of his responsibilities."

"How am I supposed to do that?" Jenny jumped off the low wall and ran across the yard to the bike shed without waiting for an answer.

Carolien picked up the half-empty juice glasses and the stack of mail. Jenny was most likely headed for Nanna's. Hopefully Nanna would agree that Po Han should shoulder at least part of Jenny's expenses. What would Nanna say if–through Jenny–she and Po Han managed to get back together?

***

The next day, Jenny went straight home from school. Preoccupied with her plans she had a hard time studying for her history test. As the hands of the small alarm clock on her desk moved into the next hour she tried to concentrate on the political turmoil of Indonesia. The test would only cover the past two years, but the political developments between the Dutch government and self- proclaimed Indonesian Republic were intricate. In December of 1947, under the Renville Agreement, the

Dutch had acknowledged the Republic of Indonesia as a governing authority and both parties agreed to a ceasefire while they prepared for Indonesian independence. Three months later, the *Dutch East Indies* became *Indonesia* in the Dutch constitution. Batavia, the capitol, became Jakarta. Political reverence in the colony shifted from Queen Wilhelmina to President Sukarno. The Indonesian Communist Party opposed the agreement, while the Indonesian Islamic Party fought the socialistic Indonesian government under Sukarno as well as the Dutch. "They're just making a big mess," Jenny yawned.

It was almost five o'clock and she slapped her books closed. Rising, she took a deep breath and walked to the bike shed.

Carolien was on the front porch. "Where are you going?" she called when Jenny rode passed her.

"Where you sent me," Jenny yelled and pedaled away quickly.

Po Han lived a good twenty-minute ride away, in the eastern part of town. Hopefully she'd be able to find the house. The route was flat but her heart pounded as hard as it did when she rode her bike fast up the hills to Nanna's.

Jenny left her bike in Po Han's driveway and placed her thumb firmly on the doorbell. She pressed the shiny brass knob long and repeatedly until the door swung open.

"My God, is there a fire?" An old woman stood in the doorway. Her labored breathing sent off a pungent odor.

Jenny took a step back from the short gnarled figure. So this was Ocho, the drunk. Jenny couldn't help staring at the large black mole at the base of Ocho's left nostril. Ocho's knobby hand, still clutching the door handle, reminded her of a big rooster's scaly toes. A shiver went up her spine but Jenny pulled her shoulders back and met Ocho's inquisitive gaze with a brazen glare.

"Who are you?" Ocho asked in Malay. "Who are you looking for?" She grabbed the doorjamb and peered at Jenny. "We don't need anything, go away." Ocho started to close the door.

Jenny moved quickly forward and pushed hard against the closing door. "*You* might not need anything, but *I* do. I need my father." Her voice wasn't as firm as she would have liked. She had not expected that

Ocho would speak Malay.

Startled, Ocho took her hand off the doorknob. The door swung open behind her and she lost her balance. Ocho steadied herself and gave Jenny another scrutinizing look. "Who are you?"

Jenny took a few steps into the room and glanced around. Open newspapers lay scattered over the glass-top coffee table. The faded pillows on the couch were in disarray, and filled ashtrays sat next to stacks of books and magazines on the endtables.

Jenny sized up Ocho's quivering jaw, her hunched back, and the small knot of gray hair on the top of her head. "I'm Jenny Lee," she said calmly. "My father lives here." She took pleasure in the bewildered look that spread across Ocho's face. Jenny stuck her hands into the pockets of her overalls. An unfamiliar sense of power made her stand tall. "Where's my father?" she asked, "Your grandson."

Ocho wobbled across the room and closed the door leading to the rest of the house. "Why did she send you here?" she asked, stumbling toward the couch. "What do you want?" She moved a few pillows out of the way and sat down. "Close the door."

Jenny turned and started toward the front door but stopped midway. What if she couldn't get out and the witch held her captive?

"Come, sit down." Ocho smiled and patted the seat next to her.

"No," Jenny said firmly. "I didn't come to chat with you. I came to see my father. Go get him." She was surprised by her rudeness but didn't feel any remorse. Nor did she worry about repercussions. She looked at Ocho with open hostility.

"He isn't home yet. Sit down. It may be a while before he comes home. He will be so surprised." Ocho placed a small pillow on her lap and stroked the silky fabric.

Tears burned behind Jenny's eyes. Surprised he will be, she thought. Ocho's presence was overwhelming. It took Jenny all she had to say, "Okay, I'll wait for him. Go away."

Ocho stumbled out of the room, saying over her shoulder, "She sure didn't teach you any manners. Or does rudeness come with pretending to be Dutch?"

After Ocho left, Jenny closed the door and wandered around the small room. She straightened a stack of newspapers on a side table and drew a few lines in the dust on the glass top.

***

Ocho pulled herself a chair at the table in the dining room. She could use another beer but Po Han was due home any time and she needed to be able to think clearly. Ocho had learned that she could easily drown any kind of trouble in the bottles of dark beer, but that the liquid wasn't of any help when she needed to be alert. The wind had blown Bad Luck onto her doorstep. It was no use to move against a windstorm, but still, she needed to clean her stoop.

Ocho knew she had to be careful. Even as an infant this child had the power to turn Po Han away from her. Ocho grimly remembered the years she spent in the pensione due to Po Han siding with Carolien and this child. The girl had her mother's expressive eyes and her father's strong jaw. Ocho blinked and, biting hard into her chewing wad, she let the sharp juices burn another likeness from her mind. Jenny had inherited Ing Hwa's oval forehead and delicate cheekbones. Ing Hwa had not been much older than Jenny when she gave birth to Po Han. Ocho gritted her teeth and banished the image of her long dead daughter.

If only she had been able to interest Po Han in any of the young women she had found after his return from Holland. But every time she insisted that he at least take a look, Po Han had laughed. "Haven't you learned that I can only take care of *one* woman at a time, and that woman happens to be you?"

"But I'm old and soon I will die. Who will take care of you then?" Ocho griped, despite the great sense of satisfaction Po Han's answer had given her.

Ocho moved her chewing wad to the other side of her mouth and walked to the kitchen. Po Han always used the front door when coming home from work, she wouldn't be able to prepare him. The only thing she could do was make it appear as if she had taken care of the child the way he'd expect her to. Ocho prepared a tea tray and ordered the maid to carry it to the living room.

***

Jenny listened for sounds from other parts of the house. Her father's sitting room was a lot smaller than Nanna's and Carolien's. In a corner, close to the door leading to the rest of the house, a large grandfather clock ticked gravely away. The leather of the recliner showed worn patches at the armrests. She took a magazine off the stack on the coffee table. The cover of the Dutch periodical showed a big weave loom beneath the title, *Textiles Today*. She was thumbing through the magazine when she heard a key turn in the front door lock. She stiffened and quickly returned the magazine.

The door opened and a man walked in. For a moment they stared at each other. *It's him, this is my father.* The words pushed against her temples then dropped into her stiff knees and made her feel as if she was on the brink of collapsing. She stuck her hands deep into her pockets and gave Po Han a hard glare.

She had seen only a glimpse of his face on the morning Carolien pointed out the house to her. Now she noticed that it was fuller than in the photographs she had seen. It gave her satisfaction to see Po Han's Adam's apple move quickly as he swallowed. But her nervousness returned when she watched his jaw set.

Po Han flicked on the lights. "What can I do for you?" he asked, hanging his hat and coat on a wooden stand by the front door.

"You can send me to school, like you're supposed to," Jenny said to his back.

Po Han faced her slowly.

Jenny held his searching gaze and tried to stare him down. She became uncomfortable when the tension left Po Han's face.

"Please, sit down." Po Han waved at a chair. He lit a cigarette and took a seat himself.

"No."

Po Han winced then took a long drag, calmly eying Jenny. Leaning forward, his forearms pressing into his thighs, he held the burning cigarette between two fingers. "Didn't you just turn fifteen? Which school are you going to? What's your favorite subject?"

"What does it matter what my favorite subject is? Shouldn't you first wonder how I can even go to school? You just took off and never bothered–"

"Jenny!" Po Han rose. "Please don't pass judgment over something you don't have any idea–"

"But I do. I've got a very good idea. I still remember running after you that morning in the courthouse, and all you did was walk away." Tears sprung in her eyes and she brusquely wiped them away.

"If only I could–" Po Han began to pace.

"What? Explain why you walked out? I know. Taking photographs was more important than taking care of me."

"No, Jenny, no." Po Han's face turned red under Jenny's accusation. "I wanted to be with you, but I realized that your mother was right. I had no business being in your life while not being able to take care of you."

"But why couldn't you just get a job instead of taking photographs all day?"

Po Han sighed. "Capturing what life offers and sharing those images is what I have to do to stay alive, Jenny." *If I had to give that up, there wouldn't be anything to give you.*

Jenny frowned. She didn't understand what Po Han meant, yet she no longer felt angry.

"Here." Po Han waved at an armchair. "It's been so long. There's so much to catch up on. I really want to know everything about you."

Jenny told Po Han about school. At first the words came slow and measured, but under Po Han's intense attention she soon took down her guard. She told him how much she loved school; that her Dutch language teacher was nice and lent her books outside of the class library. "I love to read," she said. "I always get good grades on my essays."

With some hesitation, she then told him that sometimes she had trouble with math and science. When Po Han didn't comment or interrupt her with questions, Jenny spoke proudly about sports. She told Po Han that she could hit the ball harder than any girl in the class, and did not rate badly against the boys either.

Po Han did not take his eyes off Jenny. The cigarette between his fingers burned into a long, curved stick of ashes. Part of it broke off and scattered tiny gray flakes on the floor when he moved toward an ashtray.

"How's Nanna?" Po Han snuffed out his cigarette without bothering to clean up.

"She's well," Jenny responded quickly. "I see her almost every day and help her in the garden. I'm the only one she allows to get the ripe mangos off the tree." She scooted to the edge of her seat. "I can climb all the way to the top without breaking any branches or getting scared."

Po Han laughed, a deep warm laugh. They sat quietly for a while, each occupied with their own thoughts. Then Po Han said, "I'm so glad that you've come to visit. I hope that you'll come to see me often." He paused, looking at the window. "It's dark and your mother might be getting worried" Po Han rose. "I should get you home."

"My bike's outside." Jenny walked toward the front door when she realized she still didn't know if Po Han was going to pay her school tuition. "What about my school? Will you pay for my school?" She anxiously scanned Po Han's face and held onto the back of her chair so hard that her knuckles turned white.

"Jenny, I will try to meet your needs, but let's talk about that at another time. I'd like to get to know you. I'd like you to know me." Po Han put his hands on Jenny's shoulders. When she dropped her head he lifted her chin and searched her face. "Please, Jenny," he said quietly, "Come back soon."

He let go of her and walked brusquely toward the door. "Wait here while I get my bike," he said. "I'll go part of the way with you."

With Jenny leading the way, they pedaled through the poorly lit streets to Carolien's house. Jenny noticed the lights in the houses they passed. She wondered about the families who lived in them, families like Grace and Theresa's, with a father as the head of the household. They turned into her street. "That's where we live." Jenny pointed.

"You can go the rest of the way by yourself. I'll watch you from here until you get into the driveway." Po Han squeezed his brakes.

Jenny stopped next to him and leaned into her handlebars. She wished he'd come with her. "Why didn't you come to see me?" Jenny peered through the dim light at Po Han's face. His jaws tightened and his Adam's apple moved when he swallowed.

"I wanted to…."

"Why didn't you?" Jenny caught herself. She sounded like her mother.

"I guess I wanted to be sure I was able to resume my financial responsibilities before telling your mother I could."

Jenny could relate to Po Han's statement. No one told Carolien something without knowing he could be true to his words.

"You can't imagine how many times I fantasized this afternoon. But even in my wildest dreams, I never would have believed your mother would allow you to come see me…." Po Han's voice trailed away.

Jenny shot Po Han a sideway glance. "She told me to." Would Carolien allow her to visit him again? What would she do if Carolien told her she couldn't?

"I'll see you soon?" Po Han cut into Jenny's thoughts.

"Okay," she said awkwardly and tightened the grip on her handlebars before riding off. Midway, she looked back. Po Han sat on his bike, feet on the ground, halfway into the street. She saw the flame of his lighter flicker as he lit a cigarette before lifting his arm to wave.

The front porch was lit and so were the rest of the outside house lights. Jenny put her bike away and walked reluctantly up the back porch steps. She knew Carolien would be waiting for her.

"Well, have you been able to bring your father to his senses?" Carolien asked as soon as Jenny came into the door.

"I'm going to stay in the Dutch school." Jenny said and quickly left the room.

***

Ocho pulled a bucket out from under the kitchen counter. It was a good thing that she had brought home a live carp from the market earlier. Ocho grabbed the orange fish and carried him to the kitchen sink. She wanted to make sure the enticing aroma of his favorite dish greeted Po Han when he returned from taking Jenny home.

Ocho ordered the maid to make a fresh pot of steamed rice and set the table while she prepared the fish. She wasn't strong enough to remove Jenny. She had to come up with a plan that would make Jenny remove herself. Meanwhile, she needed to keep her feelings hidden.

Forty-five minutes later Po Han stepped into the kitchen and she looked up smiling. He eyed the wok on the stove, sniffing the aroma. "Hmm. I'm hungry."

Ocho slipped the whole fish, glistening in sweet and sour sauce, onto a waiting platter with a skilled tilt of the wok handle. "There!" She spooned some sauce over the fish and garnished the dish. "You're just in time to enjoy your favorite fish!" She ignored the maid, who reached for the platter, and carried the food into the dining room herself. Serving Po Han she said, "Well, you must be excited. Isn't that something? After all these years, poof! You suddenly have a daughter again."

"That's enough, thank you." Po Han put up a hand.

"You work hard. You need to eat." Ocho rearranged the food on the platters. "Don't you think Jenny looked skinny?" She served herself a small piece of the fish. "I wonder what they feed her. *She* probably still only boils potatoes."

Po Han put down his utensils. "I thought Jenny looked healthy," he said. When Ocho looked up he held her eyes and she saw how happy he looked. "Today is my lucky day. I hope it will last for the rest of my life."

Ocho returned her attention to the food on her plate. She was being warned. She had to be extremely careful.

They ate the rest of their dinner in silence. After Po Han took his last bite Ocho called in the maid to clear the table. "Would you like some fruit?" she asked before the maid left the room.

"No, thank you." Po Han pushed his chair back. "I'm going to work in my study."

Ocho did not understand what enthralled Po Han when he painted in his study or worked in the darkroom. All she knew was that it made Po Han happy, and that was enough for her.

CHAPTER 18

As soon as school was out, Jenny biked to Nanna's house. Nanna was picking beans in the vegetable garden.

"Oh, there you are." Nanna handed Jenny a trowel. "You're just in time to help me dig up some sweet potatoes for our afternoon snack."

Jenny squatted between two rows of sweet potatoes. The earth was loose and moist. She looked for a thickening in the stem of the crawling vine before pushing the trowel into the cool earth. Next to the black soil the yellowish orange skin of the vegetable appeared bright. Jenny worked the row until she filled a basket with plump sweet potatoes.

"I heard that you went to visit your father," Nanna said when Jenny stood up and stretched. Nanna's voice came from behind the green bean trellis. Her fingers poked through the wire squares as she fastened some loose shoots. There was an unusual tightness in her voice and, although Jenny wanted to talk about her visit, she felt suddenly uneasy.

"Yes, Nanna. I did." Jenny carried the basket of sweet potatoes over.

"I want you to remember that it was your mother who raised you since you were four and that it will be your mother who will take care of you for as long as you need." Nanna cut a piece of twine.

"He's nice, Nanna," Jenny said timidly.

Nanna shot Jenny a look and secured another bean shoot.

Jenny hung her head and kicked a dent into the ground with the point of her shoe. Would Nanna be angry if she went back to see her father? She had never defied Nanna.

Nanna picked up her gardening basket. "Let's take our harvest to the kitchen and clean up," she said and started toward the house.

Jenny followed carrying her basket with sweet potatoes. They passed the laundry area where Emma stood starching and Jenny asked, "Where's Els?"

"A pot of gold comes with the answer to that question." Emma flapped a wet pillowcase in the air. "But if I were you, I wouldn't go digging for it," she said, dipping the pillowcase into the starch bucket. "Go on, take those sweet potatoes to Aunt Sue."

Jenny placed the basket on the kitchen counter. She washed her hands and joined Nanna, who sat on the front porch with a sack of dry mung beans.

"Nanna, are Eddie and Els coming home soon?" Jenny took a handful of beans and let them slip through her fingers onto the tray.

"I doubt it." Nanna swirled the beans across the bamboo tray and said, "Why don't you do some homework while Aunt Sue prepares our snack? You came straight from school, didn't you?"

The secrecy around her cousins made Jenny uncomfortable. "I'd better be going home, Nanna. Jenny moved her folded hands up and down in Chinese greeting. "I'll see you tomorrow," she said and brooded about Eddie and Els' whereabouts all the way home. She couldn't remember the last time Eddie had come to visit her at her mother's house, and she hadn't seen Els in a long while either. Where was everyone?

***

When Jenny told Carolien she wanted to go see Po Han, all she said was "That's fine." Relieved, Jenny went to get her bike.

A maid answered the door. Po Han was home. The maid asked Jenny to be seated and left to get him.

"I'm glad you didn't take too long to come back!" Po Han said, entering the room. "Let's go to my study, it's more comfortable there." He led Jenny into another room across the corridor. Although the windows were open and a soft breeze moved the curtains, it reeked of cigarette smoke.

Books, magazines, and newspapers lay scattered on the large mahogany desk and coffee table. Gray specks drifted from half-filled ashtrays onto the tile floor and across the tabletops. A brown knitted vest lay askew across the arm of a high-backed easy chair.

Jenny had never been in such a messy room. The worst part was the corner where the easel stood. The floor under the easel had dried paint spots of different colors and sizes. Unevenly squeezed tubes of paint and jars filled with brushes lay on a table without a tablecloth.

Jenny glanced at the enormous sunflower on the canvas. Deep gold petals surrounding a warm brown heart brightened the whole corner.

"Here, sit down." Po Han moved a stack of papers off an easy chair. Jenny scooted deep into the chair.

"Well, what do you think?" Po Han reached inside his shirt pocket for a pack of cigarettes and took a seat on the couch.

"What do you mean?" Jenny frowned. No adult had ever bothered to ask her what she thought before.

Po Han put a cigarette between his lips. Well, are you comfortable? Would you like to spend some of your time here?" Po Han pulled on his cigarette. He searched Jenny's face before turning slightly sideways to exhale.

"Yeah, I think so." Jenny looked at the painting. She got up and walked to the easel. "Did you paint that?"

"I'm still working on it. Do you like it?" Po Han turned on a light.

Jenny looked at the deep yellow petals of the sunflower. The raised paint gave them an almost meaty texture. She discovered a face in the dark round center of the flower, a laughing face. "Nanna doesn't like to grow sunflowers. She says that if you grow them, you soon will have to move."

"That's an old superstition. Do you believe it?" Po Han laughed.

Jenny had never questioned anything Nanna said. She felt uncomfortable being called upon to judge Nanna's beliefs and chose to ignore the question. "I don't know how to draw and I've never painted," she paused before continuing. "We've art once a week. When the teacher makes us draw, I'm never able to do it."

Po Han slowly blew a thin long line of smoke toward the canvas. "Drawing and painting is nothing other than telling your hand to put on paper or canvas what your eyes see and your heart feels." He walked across the room and pulled a large sketchbook out of a drawer. "Here. Why don't you try?" Po Han cleared a space on his desk and pulled back the black leather swivel chair.

"What do you want me to do?" Jenny sat at the edge of her seat. The sudden task of having to fill the large white piece of paper with a drawing was intimidating.

"I don't want you to do anything. Didn't you say that you wanted to draw?" Po Han said, standing behind her.

"Yeah, but I told you, I don't know how."

Jenny bowed her head and dog-eared her paper. She wanted to try, but even more, she wanted to please her father.

"What would you like to draw? Look around, pick anything you like."

Jenny hesitated. "I like your painting best." It was true that she liked the painting best, but she felt like a copycat.

"What do you like about it?"

"The face, the laughing face in the center. It makes the whole flower laugh into the room and it makes me feel happy."

"Then that's what you should draw, a happy, laughing face. The way you feel and see it right now." Po Han held out a pencil.

For a moment she held the pencil loosely, but then her fingers tightened and a triumphant circle filled most of the paper.

"That's the outline of a face! Now place the parts in it," Po Han coached. "What do you want to do next? The eyes or the nose or maybe the mouth?"

Guided by Po Han's encouragement Jenny continued to draw. When she finished Po Han took a thumbtack and fastened Jenny's drawing onto the easel next to his painting. "Now, we have two faces laughing into this room," he said, smiling.

Jenny looked at her drawing with disbelief. It really was a face, a man's happy laughing face. It wasn't the same face as the one in her father's sunflower, but that didn't matter.

In an alcove, across the room, stood a chess table like the one in her uncles' library. Jenny walked toward it and picked up a rook. She pensively rolled the piece between her palms. She had often wondered what the game was like, but she was only allowed to touch the pieces when she helped Nanna with the dusting.

"Do you know how to play?" Po Han pulled the chair closest to Jenny before seating himself in the one opposite from it.

"No, but I would like to learn."

Po Han explained the functions of each piece. When he finally asked, "You want to play?" Jenny was so thrilled she could only nod. She gingerly advanced her pieces, blushing each time Po Han praised her for moving a piece correctly.

Jenny began to spend most of her afternoons with Po Han in his study. They read her literature assignments together and when Jenny struggled with math or science problems, Po Han explained and simplified what appeared to her an insurmountable problem.

One day, after taking a geometry test, Jenny said, "It was hard. I might not be getting more than a six." Since ten represented the highest grade, six was barely passing. Carolien demanded that she not score lower than a seven, and punished her if she failed to meet that standard.

"Do you feel you could've done any better?" Po Han cleaned his glasses with his handkerchief.

"What do you mean?" Keeping her eyes lowered, Jenny scuffed the point of her shoe against the floor tile.

"Could you've done better by studying longer or doing more exercise problems?"

"I don't think so. I did all the exercise problems. I know all the rules by heart. I just can't see the problem, that's why I can't solve it." Jenny slipped off the windowsill.

Po Han caught her and pulled her close to him. "So then, what's wrong with a six? You did the best you could." Po Han squeezed Jenny's shoulder. "Remember what you just said. You can't find any solutions unless you first see the problem. Life is like that, Jenny. You need to know what you're up against before you can do something about it."

Jenny smiled, nobody made more sense than her father.

CHAPTER 19

Ocho sat on the edge of her bed and ran her hand along the side of her mattress. Years of financing her drinking and supplementing Po Han's income had exhausted her hidden savings. She no longer had the resources needed to visit a strong *dukun,* she had to get rid of Bad Luck on her own. Better yet, she had to make Bad Luck get rid of herself.

That night Ocho made only a bowl of pork stew and steamed rice for dinner. "I'm sorry there's only one dish," she said spooning the food onto Po Han's plate. "Lately I've been very tired."

Po Han seemed indifferent to the proportions of dinner. "Thank you," he said picking up his utensils.

Ocho served herself, but kept her eyes on Po Han.

"The pork stew is delicious," he said between bites. "You don't need to make more than one dish."

Ocho lowered her gaze, relieved. Po Han apparently didn't suspect the real reason for the simple meal–she had fallen back into using the grocery money to buy her beer and gin.

"Any man who works as hard as you do deserves a good meal." Ocho mumbled into her plate. It was time to execute her second plan.

After that night Ocho made sure to answer the doorbell herself each time Jenny came. She wanted to use small talk as a preamble of the speech she had rehearsed numerous times but couldn't seem to find the courage to deliver.

Jenny met Ocho's ramblings with a stubborn silence that, time and again, sent the old woman back to her hidden bottles.

On a dreary afternoon in mid-December, a little over a month after Jenny's first visit, Ocho took a seat on the couch after she let Jenny in. "Come, sit here. There's something I need to tell you." Ocho patted the cushion next to her and adjusted her *kebaja* pins. Pulling down the corners of her blouse, she cast her bait. "I think you should know how much your father loves you," she said.

Jenny dropped her schoolbag on the floor, but remained standing by an easy chair.

"If it weren't for you, your father could have been a famous photographer. Because of you, he gave up the artistic career he loved so much for a menial job. Still, that wasn't enough. Your mother kept nagging and nagging. Every day, she wanted more things for you. They had horrible fights, because of you." Ocho saw the panic spread across Jenny's face. "If you were not born, they probably would still be together and my poor grandson would have a woman to take care of him when I'm dead," Ocho sighed.

"He could have been a big man in Holland, but he came back just in case you wanted to see him." Ocho had to catch her wheezing breath. She brought up phlegm when she cleared her throat and stumbled across the room to fetch her spittoon. "If it were not for you, your father would have a much better life. Why can't you leave him alone?"

Jenny gripped the back of the chair. She looked pale and her usual confidence was gone.

"Don't you want your father to have a good life?" Ocho peered at Jenny. "It would be so much better for him if you never came back. What do you want from him anyway?"

As Ocho delivered her final stab, the door behind her opened.

"Dad! Daddy!" Jenny ran across the room, crying.

Ocho's eyes widened. A chill ran through her spine and froze her on the couch.

Po Han held Jenny until her sobs subsided.

Ocho couldn't bear the look in Po Han's eyes when he turned to her and said, "Wait here," before leading Jenny out of the room.

How long had Po Han been standing by the door? How much had he heard? With trembling fingers, Ocho rolled a new chewing wad.

***

Tears streaming down her face, Jenny grabbed a pillow from one of the chairs and curled up in a corner of the sofa in Po Han's study. Was it true that she was the cause of her parents' divorce? During the short time she'd known Po Han he always made her feel wanted, while Carolien often told her that she was a lot of trouble. She was happy when she visited Po Han, but Ocho just said that she made him miserable. Jenny buried her face into the pillow, crying.

"Can you sit up? I need you to look at me." Po Han smoothed Jenny's bangs away from her forehead and offered her his handkerchief. Pacing the room he said, "Ten years is a long time to be away from someone you love with all your heart. I don't know if I'll ever be able to catch up on all that time, if I'll ever be able to bridge all of the distance my absence has created between us. All I can tell you now is that I'll never leave you again and I don't know what I'd do if you left me." Po Han took a seat at the edge of the coffee table.

"If I wasn't born, Mom wouldn't have needed so much money," Jenny cried.

"Jenny, the day you were born was the happiest day of my life." Po Han took Jenny's hands. "The day you came back to me is right behind it. I promise that Ocho won't bother you again." Po Han kissed Jenny on top of her bowed head and walked out of the room.

***

Alone in the living room, Ocho recalled her exile to Pension Waringin. When Po Han entered the room, she hollered, "I am not going to a pensione. I'll kill myself if you send me away." She banged her head against the side of the armchair, wailing. "You don't care about me. All you care about is that piece of Bad Luck." The tiny gray knot of hair could not hold the heavy gold pin in place under the jostling of her head. Ocho caught the pin as it slipped off her shoulder. She wiped her face with the tip of her *kebaja* and gathered her hair to twist it back into a knot.

"Why can't you leave things alone? Why do you have to keep prodding?" Po Han's voice was heavy with resentment.

"I didn't mean anything bad. I just don't want to see you hurt again." Ocho started to cry.

"Good. Then from now on, you will stay away from Jenny." Po Han folded his arms across his chest.

"Are you telling me that I'm no longer allowed to move around freely in my own house?" Ocho's voice quivered.

"From now on, you'll have the maid answer the door and let Jenny into my study. She will not be in your way there. I see no reason why the two of you should ever cross each other's path again," Po Han said.

"She's my only great-grandchild and you're keeping her away from me?" Ocho cried.

"Don't forget what I said," Po Han warned over his shoulder as he walked out of the room.

CHAPTER 20

When Jenny returned to school after Christmas break, she noticed quite a few new Chinese and Indonesian students. The posted faculty slate listed the addition of more Chinese and Indonesian teachers. The changes were the result of the Dutch having granted independence to The United States of Indonesia.

The Indonesian independence was a hot topic of conversation between the adults. Carolien and Ting were convinced that the new government wouldn't last long. "How can you expect a bunch of ignorant *inlanders* to rule?" Ting was fond of saying. Carolien said that instead of trying to rule, the natives should first learn to be more ambitious. Eddie agreed that the natives had a lot to learn, but said he understood why they wanted to be independent.

Walking to class with Tim and Frans, Jenny saw Grace and Theresa chatting with a group of Chinese teenagers she had never seen before. Daily Dutch class had been reduced to once a week. Bahasa Indonesia replaced all of the periods previously allocated to Dutch. The Lyceum was preparing to turn over its administration to the Indonesians.

"My father thinks that this will be our last year here," said Frans, whose father taught biology.

The third period that day was Current Events. The Indonesian teacher, Sardjono, was much shorter than his Dutch colleagues. He had to stand on a stepstool to reach the top half of the board. That day's lecture was *The Assimilation Process.*

"What does the word *assimilation* mean?" Sardjono drew a box around the word. Jenny, in her first row seat, looked over her shoulder to see which of her classmates were raising their hands.

"Muchtar?" Sardjono pointed with a piece of chalk at a new Indonesian student.

"Assimilation means becoming one, melting together."

"Very good." Sardjono walked to Jenny's desk. "Jenny, why is it important for the citizens of the Republic of Indonesia to participate in an assimilation process?"

Jenny studied the creases in Sardjono's heavily starched white denim jacket and counted the buttons on his coat. She knew what she was expected to say, but she did not believe in it. No one in her family supported the new Indonesian government or their plans to unify the various ethnic groups in the country. What was so wrong with the old system?

"Jenny, are you going to answer my question?" Sardjono tapped on her desk with the chalk. When she remained silent, he persisted, "How would you support the process, Jenny?"

Students shifted in their seats. Paper rustled. Out of the corner of her eye, Jenny saw a few hands go up. She scowled at the classmates with hands in the air. "I won't," she said.

The class gasped.

"And what exactly do you mean by that?" Sardjono crumbled the piece of chalk between his fingers.

Jenny shrugged her shoulders. Expecting to be expelled from class for either rudeness or insubordination, she closed her notebook and started to pack her schoolbag. However, nothing happened.

Sardjono turned to the blackboard and said, "Class, copy these questions and bring the answers to the next class."

What are the differences between the ethnic groups that compose the Republic of Indonesia?

Which applies to you personally?

What does Bung Karno mean when he speaks of the *gotong rojong* policy?

How could you participate?

Name some of Bung Karno's suggestions to promote assimilation and describe how you would apply them to your own life.

Jenny copied the questions. At the words *Bung Karno*, she hesitated. She resented the term used to refer affectionately to President Sukarno. He's not my brother, she thought angrily, and he won't recruit me to help accomplish any of his stupid endeavors.

The next day Sardjono reviewed the students' answers. When he called her name, Jenny read the question from her notebook, "Name some of Bung Karno's suggestions to promote assimilation and describe how you would apply them to your own life."

"Yes?" Even though he stood on a stepstool, Sardjono was still barely visible behind the podium.

"In his recent speech, the president suggested that fifty percent of the executive board of any private company should consist of individuals who are *warganegara asli*, natives. He suggested that in those enterprises where authentic citizens did not fill this quota, native employees should be promoted to positions that would enable them to be on the board. The president also insists that the Indonesian language be used for all matters of importance." Jenny paused. She had recited the passages from her textbook almost word for word.

"Yes, and…?" Sardjono drummed on the podium with his fingers.

Muchtar leaned over his desktop as if he did not want to miss a word of Jenny's answer. She sent him a dirty look and cleared her throat before continuing. "The president suggested that in order to prevent any kind of racial discrimination, all of those who have non-Indonesian names should take on Indonesian ones. He also suggested interracial marriages."

"And what do you think of those suggestions? Which ones would you apply in your own life?"

"I don't think it's right to promote anyone just because he's Indonesian." Jenny hesitated.

"Go on." Sardjono moved a pencil back and forth over the top of his right ear.

"And why should I change the name my parents gave me when I was born?" Jenny blurted out. "It's *my* name and I will never change it to suit any cause." She looked around the quiet classroom. The stares of her classmates cornered her. "And I don't want to get married to anyone!" she shouted, slapping her notebook closed.

Some girls started to giggle. Sardjono put his hands on Jenny's desk. Leaning over her, he asked, "Don't you realize, Jenny, that your name has already been changed?"

Jenny looked up into Sardjono's white starched chest. "What do you mean?" She shifted in her seat, trying to see his face. "Who changed my name?"

Sardjono straightened himself and looked over Jenny's head into the classroom. "Who of you has ever seen your birth certificate?"

Two Dutch girls raised their hands. "This won't apply to you," Sardjono said. "I want those of you who are Chinese or Indonesian to ask your parents if you can take a look at your birth certificate." Sardjono scanned the students' curious faces before he continued. "Most of you will notice that the name which appears on the document is different from the one you are using. To accommodate the Dutch, parents often changed the name they chose for their child to a Dutch call-name." Sardjono raised his voice to override the whispers his comments started. "If they didn't and it took too much effort for a Dutchman to pronounce or remember the authentic name, he would change it randomly. This is just another way the Dutch exercised colonialism."

The bell rang before Jenny could ask questions or utter a protest. She grabbed her books and pushed them into her bag.

Jenny biked home as fast as she could. Carolien was in the livingroom, reading. "Hi, Mom. Can I please see my birth certificate?" Jenny dropped her school bag on the floor.

"Why?" Carolien looked up from her book.

"Mr. Sardjono said that all Chinese and Indonesian children have a different name on their birth certificate than the one they go by. He said that the Dutch made people change names for their convenience. Did you change mine?" Jenny grabbed the back of an easy chair.

"What's the stupid *inlander* talking about?" Carolien inserted her bookmarker before closing her book. "These natives are really losing their minds," she muttered.

"He was explaining the assimilation process the president mentioned in his last speech." Jenny made a face.

"Don't pay any attention to it." Carolien began to stack some scattered newspapers and magazines. "Those natives don't know anything. Can you imagine, expecting us to change our names into Indonesian names and marry *inlanders*!"

"Mom, can I please see my birth certificate? It's homework." Jenny insisted.

Carolien took a flat box from the bottom drawer of her desk. She sorted through some papers and pulled out a yellowed document.

The birth certificate had been issued by the City Hall of Bandung with the specification *Chinese Registry.* The document stated that the daughter who was born to Lee Po Han and his wife Ong Kway Lyn was named Siu Yin. The only name Jenny recognized was Po Han's. She knew her mother as *Carolien Lee-Ong*, and she had never thought of herself as anyone other than Jenny Lee.

"Why am I called Jenny if you named me Siu Yin? If you wanted to call me Jenny, why didn't you name me that?"

Carolien grabbed the document out of Jenny's hands and returned it to the box. "Why should you, or anyone else for that matter, take issue with your name and what you are called?"

Jenny tried to get the answer from Po Han when she visited him later that afternoon. "Dad, why did you name me Siu Yin and then call me Jenny?" she asked, bent over homework at Po Han's desk.

Po Han looked up from his newspaper. Her question had obviously startled him.

"Mr. Sardjono had the Chinese and Indonesian children verify their names on their birth certificates and said that since we changed our names for the Dutch, we shouldn't mind now taking on an Indonesian name." Jenny hoped that her father would find a way out of her predicament.

"Your mother and I picked the name Jenny because we liked it. The name seemed to fit you. No one put us up to it. Now, why were you named Siu Yin?" Po Han ran his fingers through his hair, then pensively rubbed his knuckles across a cheek. "When you were on your way, Nanna went to the Chinese temple and asked a priest to pick a name for you. After you were born she told us that the priest said to call you Siu Yin."

"I feel so weird." Jenny tapped the desk with the end of her pencil. "It's like all this time I wasn't me. If it wasn't for Mr. Sardjono, I still wouldn't know that my real name is Lee Siu Yin. And if something happened where I had to prove that I was Jenny Lee, I couldn't, 'cause that name isn't even on my birth certificate." Jenny rose. "And now you're telling me that a stranger named me. Why didn't anybody ever tell me that I have two names?"

***

The next day Jenny dreaded the history period. After Sardjono wrote the Dutch names of the Chinese students on the blackboard, he turned to the class. "Those of you who have another name on your birth certificate, raise your hands."

Jenny was relieved when most of the Chinese students raised their hands with her.

Sardjono wrote everyone's Chinese name behind their Dutch name on the blackboard. "Well, then. Here you can see to what extent the Dutch manipulated the population." Sardjono tapped the board with his chalk. "Some individuals were so taken by the colonial power that they were willing to call their children by a different name." He paused and rested his gaze on Jenny. "They were motivated by political power. Therefore, another change that acknowledges a long overdue shift in power is in order."

Frowning, Jenny shifted the books on her desk.

***

Carolien spent Jenny's Easter break planning her daughter's wardrobe. The flaring skirts and ruffled bodices that were in style would look flattering on Jenny's slight figure. If only the girl would show more interest in her attire. It would be fun, Carolien thought, to pick out material and dress styles together. Would wearing dresses change Jenny's tomboyish behavior and draw attention to her as a girl? What if one of the Indonesian boys approached Jenny? From Jenny's stories, she gathered that two thirds of her classmates were now Chinese and Indonesian. She always could send Jenny to Holland if things got out of hand. In her last letter, Greet van Houten had suggested that she and Jenny both come.

There was a time that Carolien would have seriously considered the offer. She could surely make a living for herself and Jenny in Holland by taking in sewing or cooking. Perhaps she even could get a secretarial job. Maybe, away from Nanna and Po Han, Jenny would allow her to get closer. Carolien sighed. There was no need to waste time daydreaming. Chip's death had removed the possibility of her ever moving to Holland. Her responsibilities toward her family simply did not allow it.

***

Jenny swung around the doorjamb of Nanna's laundry room. "Where's Els? Why isn't she ever home anymore?"

"'Cause she isn't." Emma did not look up from ironing one of Ting's dress shirts.

"What do you mean, she isn't? Where is she?"

"I don't know." Emma concentrated on one of the cuffs.

Jenny glanced at Emma. She clearly wasn't going to give her any information. Jenny decided to turn to the source of all information, Nanna.

Her grandmother sat on the front porch with a large basket of spent roses next to her. "Can I help?" Jenny liked plucking petals. Nanna made oil and potpourri from the petals of roses, jasmine, lavender, honeysuckle, and lilac.

"Sure." Nanna moved over.

Jenny reached for a full deep-red rose. "Nanna, where's Els?" she asked, pulling off the fragrant petals.

"She's gone." Nanna shook the basket and the petals tumbled in a colorful fluff.

Jenny's eyes widened as she glanced at her grandmother, but Nanna kept her eyes on the petals. "Where did she go?" Jenny stammered, after a moment of silence.

"She went to marry that Dutchman." Nanna put the basket back on her lap and reached for another rose.

"What Dutchman?" Jenny stared at Nanna. The barely audible pop of the petal detaching from the seed-head was the only sound that broke the silence.

"He came to ask your uncle and me for her hand," Nanna said, finally, with a tight voice. The furrows above her thin eyebrows seemed to deepen as she continued. "When he needed help we took him in, and now he returns the favor by bringing shame to our house." Nanna's lips pressed together into a thin line. Her shoulders curved inward. "When your uncle told him that he could no longer see Els, he told her to come with him to get married–" Nanna's voice broke.

"Who's *he*, Nanna? Where did he take Els? Why did he bring shame to us by wanting to marry Els?"

"Jenny, we are Chinese." Nanna sounded tired. She clutched the sides of the flower basket and took a deep breath. "Our family doesn't have any other blood and that's the way it's going to stay." Nanna picked up another flower. "We don't mix blood."

There were hardly any flowers left in the big basket. Jenny had a hard time remaining seated. She knew socializing with natives was not allowed. However, this person was *Dutch* and he had come to ask for Els's hand properly. So what was wrong? "Nanna, is Els gone forever?"

"He said they were going to Holland as soon as possible. Youngest Uncle thinks that with his military record, he probably could arrange for that easily." Nanna placed the last handful of petals in the small basket. She rose with difficulty. "Isn't it time for you to go home?"

Jenny knew their conversation was over. She would have to get the rest of her information elsewhere.

Riding her bike home, Jenny recalled the contempt in Nanna's voice when she said Els had left to marry *that Dutchman*. If Els went to Holland, it meant she would not see her again. A deep sadness began to set in.

That evening Jenny decided to do her homework at the dining room table instead of in her room. When Carolien joined her with a mending basket, Jenny stood up the large geography textbook. Peering over the top, she said, "Mom, Nanna said Els is going to marry a Dutchman and live in Holland."

Carolien adjusted her glasses and made another stitch in a loose hem of one of Jenny's skirts.

"Do you know him?" Jenny persisted.

"Didn't Nanna tell you who he is?" Carolien's needle took two quick dips into the fabric.

"No. Nanna only said that it was bad to marry a Dutchman. She also said that it was bad to mix different blood. Why?" Jenny dropped her book onto the table. Carolien's reluctance to answer her questions piqued her anxiety. "Why's Nanna so upset?"

"Do you remember Mr. Bouwman?" Carolien snipped the thread.

"Yes, he was the camp man. He helped me save Big Red when we had to run from the natives during the big fire. Is Els getting married to him? Why's that bad? He's nice. Why do they have to go to Holland?"

"When the family found out Mr. Bouwman was in love with Els, I had to ask him to move." Carolien dropped her sewing into her lap. "We hoped that would take care of matters. We didn't know that he kept visiting Els at her school. Els never told anyone about these visits."

Jenny remembered wondering why Jan Bouwman had gone to live at the barracks after the second Dutch political action.

"I don't think it's so bad that Els and Mr. Bouwman get married," Carolien said. "They've been seeing each other secretly now for over a year. God knows, all sorts of things could've happened." Carolien paused and, frowning, folded Jenny's skirt. "I think it's best they get married soon. But no one agrees with me."

Jenny stared at her mother. Carolien was disagreeing with Nanna and Youngest Uncle, and it sounded as if she had told them so as well.

"I think the way things are now, really, is inviting trouble." Carolien rummaged in the mending basket for another garment.

"Do you know where Els is now? What trouble is she getting into?" Jenny rocked her chair.

"Els is boarding with one of her married Dutch teacher friends until she and Mr. Bouwman get their dispensation papers." Carolien threaded her needle.

"Why do they need dispensation papers? Mr. Bouwman is Dutch."

"Els is twenty-nine. She needs to be thirty-one to get married without parental consent." Carolien held up one of Jenny's blouses with a torn sleeve. "They have to petition the court and get a judge to grant them permission to marry."

Jenny glanced at Carolien and remembered that she needed dispensation papers before being admitted to the Lyceum. Why was it that dispensation papers were needed any time one became involved with the Dutch? "Are we going to Els' wedding?" she asked.

"Yes, we will," Carolien answered and Jenny smiled.

***

Nanna adjusted the roll pillow to fit in the hollow of her knees. She had difficulty falling asleep, lately. Often now, the night brought her turmoil instead of rest. The shadows sliding across her bedroom walls and ceiling had voices and carried thoughts.

Nanna moved a hand across the empty space next to her. She still missed Jenny. From the corner, at the foot end of the bed, Emma's soft snoring filled the room with a monotone buzz. Nanna sighed. There was a time she had been worried that Emma's sourness at being only a girl as the oldest child from the oldest son would turn into rebellion. But other than her shortness with Jenny and sometimes with Els, Emma seemed to accept her place in the household. Hopefully some day someone would be able to see past her chubby figure and appreciate her less than elegant but strong and capable hands. If Emma were to marry, it would be in the traditional fashion.

Nanna glanced at the large empty space next to Emma and a stabbing pain filled her chest. Chip, Ting, and Carolien, with their Western ways, had insisted that the girls, after passing middle school, were given the choice to either stay home or continue schooling to become a teacher. Nanna recalled the afternoon when Els surprised her by saying softly, "I would like to become a teacher."

Nanna abruptly rolled onto her side, turning her back to the empty spaces. She had been proud of her sons' accomplishments, of the way Carolien and Els and even Jenny were able to hold their own amongst the Dutch, but did her pride measure against this throbbing pain in her chest? Everything the Dutch gave, they took back doublefold.

"To-k-e-h-h." And again, "To-k-e-h-h." A gecko's call cut through Nanna's thoughts. The full, throaty voice of the big lizard echoed through the quiet house and faded into the night. Nanna clutched her rollpillow and closed her eyes but she could not sleep. She knew the choices her granddaughter made were leading her into dangerous waters.

***

On a mild May morning in 1950, Els and Jan Bouwman were married in the Dutch Reformed Church near Bandung's town's square. Jenny sat next to Carolien in the front pew. Eddie, dressed in his Dutch military uniform, sat on Carolien's other side. Jenny wanted to sit next to him, but her aisle seat had a better view. She scooted to the edge of the pew and craned her neck. Els was dressed in a simple, white, floor-length dress. A veil draped over her face and she wore a crown of white stephanotis, the same flowers that grew in Nanna's garden. Thinking of Nanna made Jenny feel uneasy and she moved her attention to Jan. He looked happy and handsome in his crisp military uniform.

The Dutch minister was a heavy-set, balding man. His stern voice carried the announcement of Els' marriage to Jan Bouwman to the far dark corners of the church. "And now, you may kiss the bride," the minister's voice boomed.

Jan Bouwman lifted the veil from Els' face and kissed Els on her lips in front of everyone in church. Jenny was dumbstruck. Chinese people never showed physical affection in public, Jenny had never seen a man and a woman kiss before. She had only read about it in the books she snuck out of her mother's bookcase when she ran out of reading material.

The organ belted out the wedding march while Els and Jan Bouwman walked down the aisle. They paused to exchange hugs and kisses with Jenny, Carolien, and Eddie. Els cried when she hugged them. Jenny heard Carolien whisper, but she was too busy trying to get Eddie's attention to hear what was said.

Eddie stood talking to an Indo lady who had sat next to him during the ceremony. When he ignored Jenny's gentle tugs on his coat sleeve, she tried to interrupt him. Eddie's companion was one of Carolien and Sue's visitors from when they still lived at Nanna's. Once, as her aunt and mother discussed the woman, Jenny had caught the words *divorce* and *promiscuous*. She still didn't know the meaning of the last word.

Eddie finally turned to her. "Jenny, you remember Mrs. Rose, don't you?" He put a hand in the tall woman's back and moved her forward.

"How tall you've grown," Peggy Rose said in a throaty voice. She reached for Jenny with a manicured hand. Her bright-red nail polish contrasted against her olive colored skin. "When I saw you last, you were barely this big." Peggy Rose pointed somewhere at her own knee level, smiling.

Jenny glared at Peggy. She disliked her for hogging Eddie's attention.

One of the guests passed around a small basket of uncooked rice. The newlyweds walked to the waiting jeep under a shower of rice as their cheering friends crowded around them.

Laughing, Els and Jan threw up their arms to ward off the pelting grain. Jan pulled Els protectively against him and Jenny heard her whisper, "I'm glad Nanna can't see all the rice on the ground."

Nanna had taught them to always treat rice with the utmost care. It was never to be wasted in any form and never, ever, to be stepped on. Nanna always said, "You will shed a tear for every grain you waste. Treating rice with disrespect is inviting bad luck." Jenny glanced at Els. Hopefully all the trampled rice would not cause her cousin any misfortune.

"You haven't showered any luck on the bridal couple." Peggy Rose offered Jenny the almost empty basket. "Here, take the basket and empty it on them."

Jenny shook her head and put a hand on Eddie's arm. "Nanna says it's bad luck to waste rice, and it's very bad to step on it."

"Oh, Jenny, don't believe old wives' tales!" Peggy Rose laughed and pushed the basket into Jenny's hands. "Ed, please tell this child not to worry about your grandmother's superstitions."

"Nanna would not like to see us throw around rice," Jenny jutted her chin and looked up at her cousin.

"Jenny's right." Eddie turned to Peggy Rose. "In my grandmother's house, it's a big no-no to waste rice. You can call it whatever you want, but that's a fact. Anyway, to believe that throwing rice will bring luck is just as superstitious."

For a moment, Peggy Rose seemed to be uncertain. Then she took the rice basket out of Jenny's hands. "Oh well, I'll just do it myself," she said and walked briskly toward the small laughing crowd gathered around Els and Jan on the church steps.

"Auntie, I was able to get a jeep from work. Why don't you and Jenny come with us?" Eddie said after they caught up with Peggy Rose. Carolien and Jenny had come to the church in a *betja*.

"Yes, there's plenty of room. As a matter of fact, we could take along two more people." Peggy Rose took Eddie's hand, smiling.

Jenny glowered at Peggy Rose. What gave the woman the right to determine how many people could ride in Eddie's jeep? Why was she holding Eddie's hand?

***

Shortly after the wedding Jan Bouwman received his relocation papers. Carolien asked the couple to come for dinner on their last evening in Bandung. In spite of the special dishes Carolien had the cook prepare, no one ate much. They finished dessert and Carolien said to Els, "You better go with Jenny to her room. It will be a long time before you two see each other again."

Els started to cry.

Jan Bouwman pushed his chair back and patted Els on the back. "Jenny, you know that you can come live with us as soon as you finish high school," he said.

"Why do you have to go? Why can't you stay here?"

"My work here is finished. In Holland I will have another job." Jan ran a hand across his buzz-cut. "Els and I want to have a family. I need a job to support them. I—"

"Why can't you work here? Why do you have to go to Holland?" Jenny forced the tines of her dessert fork into the tablecloth.

"You know that the Indonesians are trying to become totally independent from the Dutch," Jan's jaw tightened. "Soon, they won't allow any Dutch people to work or live here."

"Have you said goodbye to Nanna?" Jenny stabbed the table with her fork.

"We tried." Jan put an arm around Els who, sobbing, buried her head into her folded arms. "They didn't want to see us." Jan rubbed his wife's shaking shoulders. "They can't understand that although I'm Dutch and Els is Chinese, we love each other very much."

Jenny chewed her bottom lip. If falling in love meant having to leave Nanna and everyone else, she hoped she would never fall in love. "And what about Eddie? Did you say goodbye to him?"

"Eddie's a fine chap–"

"Jenny, you better be going to bed." Carolien interrupted nervously.

Els followed Jenny to her room. Fingering the blue glass jar with the silver boy-angel top, she asked, "You don't use cold-powder anymore, do you?"

"No, Nanna gave me that jar when Mom and I moved, but I never use it." Jenny reached for her pajamas.

"Let me make up some cold-powder while you finish getting ready." Els added some water to the riceballs and made a runny paste. She smoothed the substance on Jenny's arms and legs. The refreshing scent of mint wrapped the girls in a blanket of memories.

"Will you read to me until I fall asleep?" Jenny nestled herself against her cousin. For a moment, she felt childish. But bringing back old rituals seemed to be the only way to hold on to a time that was rapidly and inevitably passing. She tried listening to Els reading from *The Yearling*, but all she could hear was the echo of her own thoughts. After tonight, Els will be gone. She blinked hard but couldn't stop the steady flow of tears.

CHAPTER 21

The next morning, the first subject at school was history. Kees de Jong wrote *colonialism* on the blackboard. "No nation should exploit another," Kees lectured. "My government's colonial policy was inhumane. The Indonesian revolution is a natural result of more than three hundred years of oppression."

Jenny frowned. Mr. de Jong was one of the teachers who had recently arrived from Holland. Did he side with the natives? Did he know about the slogan rebels had painted on fences and walls? *Bunuh Belanda Asu.* In bright red letters the revolutionists had called the Dutch *dogs* and called for their murder. Did Mr. de Jong know that the Indonesians had burned half of the city? Jenny thought of the night Ting had sent her up into Nanna's mango tree and she saw most of the southern part of Bandung in flames. The rioting mob marching toward Nanna's street had carried bamboo poles with gleaming toad knives fastened to them. Did Mr. de Jong know that because the natives thought they could be independent, Jan Bouwman had to go back to Holland and Els had to leave too?

Muchtar raised his hand.

"Yes?" Kees pointed at the youth with a piece of chalk.

"The Dutch," the Indonesian boy spoke haltingly and with a heavy native accent, "are also not trustworthy."

"Can you clarify your statement?" Kees leaned on the podium.

"Just look at what happened last year. In January, the Dutch told us that they are willing to work out our independence under a ceasefire. In

December, they attacked us without warning or provocation. Even the Americans are on our side!"

A hush fell over the classroom and Jenny glanced around. The Dutch students stiffly straightened themselves. The three other Indonesian youths threw Muchtar admiring glances, then looked skittishly at the Dutch teacher. The handful of Chinese teens leaned across their desk and curiously observed everyone's reaction.

Jenny fastened her gaze on the large portrait of Queen Wilhelmina of the Netherlands hanging above the blackboard. The Dutch had always stood for everything right, honest, and admirable. She didn't particularly like Muchtar, but she knew his facts were correct.

"You are quite right." Kees called Jenny's attention back to the lecture. "Our recent political fiascoes have led to the Indonesians' demand for the immediate replacement of all Dutch entities by native compatriots." The bell rang and Kees ended his lecture. "I don't think I will be here for the next school year," he said collecting his books.

The next period was *Bahasa Indonesia*.

"Class, please turn to chapter eight. Jenny, read the first section." Sardjono settled behind the podium.

Jenny loved reading aloud during the Dutch, English, French, and German classes, but she hated having to read in Indonesian. When she stumbled over unfamiliar words some of the Indonesian and Chinese students exchanged glances and suppressed giggles in cupped hands.

"Why are you having so much trouble reading in the language you were born with, while you score very high in foreign languages?" Sardjono looked at Jenny. "I can understand the Dutch kids having trouble with this class. But *you?*"

Jenny blushed. It was the first time she was being reprimanded for poor scholastic performance, but then she remembered her mother's reaction to the changed curriculum. "Why would anyone want to spend time learning Malay?" Carolien had exclaimed after she read the announcement of the curriculum change.

Jenny pushed her book away and, groping for words, she said, "*Saja–ngak–ngerti–*" Her "I don't understand" in Malay, caused some laughter in the classroom.

"*Tidak mengerti.*" Sardjono corrected her. Writing the words on the blackboard, he said, "Remember, Bahasa Indonesia is not the same as Malay. Bahasa Indonesia is the Indonesian language, our *official* language." He turned to face the class. "Malay is the dialect the Dutch used to speak to Indonesians, mainly their servants." He scanned the classroom before he returned to Jenny. "Now, why can't you read fluently?"

"*Saja tidak mengerti....*" Jenny started to answer in halting Indonesian before, frustrated, she switched to Dutch. "How can I read fluently if I don't understand most of it?"

"And why don't you?" Sardjono asked in Indonesian. "We are reading a sixth grade grammar school text."

"But I never had Bahasa Indonesia. I never went to an Indonesian grammar school. I–"

"*Bicara Bahasa Indonesia*, Jenny, speak Indonesian!" Sardjono interrupted.

Jenny slammed her book shut. "Why do you always pick on me? I can speak Dutch whenever I want," she shouted. "This is still a Dutch school!"

The tension in the classroom was thick.

Sardjono reached for the stack of dismissal slips in a corner of the podium. "You're dismissed," he said, placing the red note on Jenny's desk.

***

Carolien looked at the clock. It was close to four and Jenny hadn't told her that she was going to see her father after school. She had most likely gone to see Nanna. The seamstress had enough work for the rest of the afternoon and there were no fittings scheduled. Perhaps she should head to Nanna's herself. Although Nanna seemed resilient, Carolien knew that her mother still grieved Chip's death, and that Els' choice to marry Jan Bouwman had hurt her deeply.

Carolien started to call Amin to hail a *betja* for her, but then decided to ride her bike so that she and Jenny could ride home together. Carolien stopped in the kitchen on her way out. "I'm going to *Njonja Besar*," she said to Mia. "We might stay for dinner."

221

"Very well, ma'am." The cook saw Carolien out.

Carolien was surprised when Jenny's bike was not in Nanna's bike shed. Where was the child? Jenny always told her if she planned to go to Po Han's after school. Carolien hurried to the house. Sue and Emma were on the back porch. After they exchanged greetings, Carolien asked, "Where's Ma? Was Jenny here?"

"Ma's somewhere in the garden. Haven't seen Jenny." Sue leaned sideways to look at the dining room clock. "She should have been home."

"I know, I thought she had come here." Carolien hesitated before adding in a lowered voice, "She was pretty shook up by Els' leaving. I can't believe neither of you said goodbye to her."

"Did you see Els?" Sue dropped her embroidery hoop into her lap.

"They came over and had dinner with me–"

"Shh, Nanna's coming." Emma interrupted Carolien.

Nanna walked toward the house, carrying an egg basket on her arm and Carolien went to greet her.

Nanna returned Carolien's greeting and asked, "Where's Jenny?"

"I thought she was here." Carolien bit her lip when Nanna, frowning, took stock of her.

"Doesn't Jenny tell you where she's going after school?" Nanna eyed the driveway.

"She tells me when she goes to see her father, not when she comes here–which used to be most of the time." Carolien could not keep the trace of bitterness out of her voice.

"If I were you, I'd keep better tabs on Jenny. Next thing you know the girl will be off on a Dutch tangent, too."

Carolien took a deep breath. "Ma, Els came to say goodbye. She's not on a Dutch tangent. She got married and left to live with her husband in Holland."

"I hope she doesn't live to regret it." Nanna passed Carolien on the garden path and walked with quick strides to the back porch where she handed Sue the egg basket. "The ducks are laying well," she said. "Let's salt the eggs."

Nanna turned to Carolien. "Maybe, someday, you'll stop promoting all these Dutch ideas. This isn't all of it. They're not done. Just watch–"

Her voice broke and she abruptly walked away.

"Well, you didn't get very far, did you?" Sue said, after the dining room door closed behind Nanna.

Emma fixed the rubber band around the end of one of her braids. "Is Nanna sad or is she angry?"

"Maybe some of each." Carolien recalled her family's reaction at the time of her own marriage. She disagreed with her mother and brother and didn't understand Sue and Emma's resignation to the situation. "But whatever it is, she better get a handle on it, each of us has our life to live." Neither Sue nor Emma responded and Carolien sighed. "Well, I better go back home and find out what Jenny's up to. Please send her home immediately if she shows up here."

"Sure," Sue and Emma said in unison.

Jenny's bike was in the bike shed when Carolien got home. In the kitchen, Mia was preparing dinner. "When *Non* Jenny came home, I figured you'd eat here." The cook smiled. "I asked the little miss if she saw you at Grand Madam's house, but she said she wasn't there."

"Thank you." Carolien started to leave but stopped. "When did *Non* Jenny come home?"

"Oh, about fifteen minutes ago."

"Thank you." Carolien rushed out of the kitchen. "Jenny!"

"In here," Jenny answered from her bedroom.

"Where were you? I thought you went to Nanna's and I went there thinking we could bike home together. Did you go to your father's? I want you to tell me when you go any place other than Nanna's after school." Standing in the doorway, Carolien gave Jenny a once over.

"I didn't go to Dad's." Jenny looked down on her notebook and kicked at a leg of her desk.

"Where were you?" If Jenny had not gone to see her father and she wasn't at Nanna's, where had the child spent the afternoon? "Jenny?"

"I had to stay after school and then I went for a bike ride." Jenny rummaged in her schoolbag. "Here." She handed Carolien her detention slip.

"What happened?" Carolien slowly unfolded the note.

"Mr. Sardjono picked on me. I sassed him and he threw me out."

Jenny slumped into her chair and kicked harder at the table leg.

"You shouldn't let a stupid *inlander* get under your skin." Carolien crumpled the letter and was ready to toss it into the wastepaper basket when Jenny said, "You have to sign it, Mom."

Carolien smoothed the wrinkles out on Jenny's desk and signed the detention notice. "There." She shoved the paper across the desk. "Don't worry about it."

"Thanks, Mom." Jenny folded the letter.

Carolien stood awkwardly by Jenny's desk. The girl wasn't just defying her teacher, she blamed the system for losing her cousin. If it weren't for the current politics, Jan and Els could stay and start their family in Indonesia. Carolien reached for Jenny's bowed head but something rigid in the girl's posture made her draw her hand back and smooth her skirt instead. "Well, I guess you better do your homework," Carolien said and walked out of the room.

CHAPTER 22

The next day, Jenny went to visit Po Han. When she rang the bell, an agitated maid answered the door and handed her a note.

> *Ocho fell. I'm taking her to the emergency room at St. Matthews. Can you please meet me there? Dad.*

"What happened?" Jenny folded the note into small squares.

"I was ironing," the maid began apologetically, "*Njonja Besar* was sitting on the back porch steps." She paused and looked away. "Suddenly, I heard Grand Madam scream. I ran out of the house and saw her lying on the ground. Your father was with her. He must have come home just as it happened." The maid plucked nervously at the corners of her *kebaja,* and added, "She probably rolled down the steps."

"Why would she roll down the steps?" Jenny asked, flabbergasted.

"Oh, well, you know..." The maid looked away.

"What are you saying?" Jenny frowned.

"After the Grand Madam drinks her beer and gin, she isn't steady on her feet."

"Are you telling me she was *drunk?*" Jenny searched the maid's face but the woman kept her eyes lowered. Jenny realized she could not continue her conversation with the maid. One never discussed the shortcomings of family members with servants.

***

225

At the hospital, Jenny hurried through the crowded halls of the emergency section. She spotted Po Han standing among several nurses and a doctor. Ocho lay wedged between pillows on a hospital bed near them.

"Dad!" Jenny flung her arms around Po Han. "What happened?"

"Ocho fell. Dr. Lim thinks that she broke her leg and maybe fractured her hip." He paused and ran his fingers through his hair. "At eighty-two, that can be pretty bad."

"Ha-a-an." Ocho called with a weak, screechy voice. Her bony hand groped through the air. "Ha-a-an, where are you?"

Po Han turned to his grandmother's bedside. He took Ocho's hand and rubbed her arm. "I'm here. You're going to be okay."

Dr. Lim, a short, middle-aged Chinese man, leaned over the bedrail. "Yes, don't worry, you'll be fine." The doctor turned to Po Han, "We'll get back to you as soon as we have the x-ray results."

"Thank you."

"Why don't you take a seat in the waiting area by the nursing station," one of the nurses said. "We have to work on her. I'll let you know when we're done."

"C'mon, Dad, let's go." Jenny took Po Han's hand. Glancing sideways at her father and holding his hand tightly, she felt protective of him.

Po Han sank in one of the wooden chairs against the wall of the small waiting area. With his elbows digging into his thighs, he buried his face into his hands.

Jenny sat down next to him. She was grateful that they were the only ones there.

Po Han lit a cigarette, and inhaled deeply. "She always took care of me, Jen," he said. "I used to wake up to the smell of freshly baked pastries–she spent half the night baking so she could sell them on a street corner at six in the morning. During the day she did laundry for the Dutch soldiers. All of this, just so I could go to school." He looked at Jenny. "And never, ever did she complain." Po Han crushed the stub of his cigarette in a nearby ashtray. He rose and began to pace the area. Every so often, he shot an anxious glance in the direction of Ocho's bed. Jenny didn't know what to say.

The screen moved and a nurse approached Po Han. "You can go back now," she said.

Po Han hastened to Ocho's bed and Jenny followed him. She had never thought of Ocho as anything other than a mean witch. She had never heard her father's side of the story, but it made no difference. Ocho had still been cruel to her and her mother. She wasn't to be forgiven so easily.

By Ocho's screen Po Han took Jenny's hand and whispered, "Please, Jenny, please, go see her and tell her hello. I think it might make her feel better."

Jenny stiffened. Po Han had never asked her to do anything before, but how could he ask this of her? To forgive the witch who had driven her parents apart, who had tried to kill her when she was a baby?

"I can't," she said, and walked slowly out of the ward.

***

Carolien noticed that Jenny's visits to Po Han had become brief and the girl seemed troubled when she returned. Carolien considered asking Nanna if she knew what was going on, but Jenny spared her the trouble. One night, during dinner, she asked, "Mom, can someone die from broken bones?"

Surprised, Carolien put her utensils down. "Not normally. Why do you ask?"

Jenny played with the carrots and potatoes on her plate.

"Jenny?" Tears rolled down Jenny's cheeks and Carolien put a hand on Jenny's arm. "Will you please tell me what's going on?"

"Ocho... she... fell." Jenny put her fork down. "She's been in the hospital for almost two months. Now she needs a machine to breathe."

Carolien dabbed her mouth with her napkin. So this was it. How was Po Han handling his grandmother's illness?

"Dad said she wants me to come see her." Jenny pushed her plate away and dropped her head into her arms. "I don't want to go."

Carolien turned her waterglass on its coaster. "Did your father say you have to?" Jenny shook her head and Carolien sighed with relief. "Then why are you so upset?" Carolien rubbed Jenny's back. "Your father must be beside himself."

"That's just it, he is–he looks awful and seems so sad." Jenny looked up. "But I don't want to go see her. You and Nanna said she was mean and–"

"Sshh," Carolien interrupted. "Here, have some water," she said, blinking to make sure Jenny did not see her tears. She had never suspected such fierce loyalty from her daughter.

Jenny held the glass in her shaking hands and took a few sips. "Do you think I should go?"

"If Ocho has been laid up for that long with a broken leg and she's getting oxygen, she may have developed pneumonia. At her age, she could die from it."

"That's what Dad said." Jenny carved lines in the tablecloth with her thumbnail.

"She must be in her eighties now. I think you need to go, Jen." Carolien ignored her daughter's raised eyebrows. "Everyone has the right to die in peace. If nothing else, she should be allowed to say what she has to say. After she dies, you won't be able to change your mind." Carolien patted Jenny on the shoulder. "Go on, do your homework now, I'll tell Nanna."

Carolien finished clearing the table and settled down with a book on the couch in the living room, but her thoughts kept drifting to Po Han. How would Ocho's death impact his relationship with Jenny? For a split second Carolien wondered what could happen between Po Han and herself once Ocho was out of the way, but she quickly harnessed her thoughts. There was no need to be looking for pain.

***

The next day, at the hospital, Jenny followed Po Han when he stepped behind the screen around Ocho's bed. Ocho lay wheezing against her pillows. She opened her eyes when Po Han bent over her.

"Look, I brought you a surprise." Po Han took Ocho's hand.

"Ha-a-an." A coughing spell kept Ocho from saying more.

"Shhh. I'm here and so is Jenny." Po Han motioned Jenny closer to the bed and put an arm around her. "See, she's here. I told her you wanted to see her."

"Jen-ny." Ocho's voice was raspier than ever. She pulled her hand out of Po Han's and beckoned her great granddaughter. Jenny slipped in front of Po Han. She clamped her fingers around the bedrail. Ocho looked even more shriveled than before. It seemed that she had no energy left. She even had trouble breathing.

After Ocho cleared her throat a couple of times she said, "I love my grandson. I shouldn't have caused your mother to leave." She rubbed her chest with the heel of her hand and sighed. "If I hadn't, he would have had someone..." Her voice trailed off. She began to cough again and Po Han took a few gauze pads from a jar on the nightstand and wiped away the phlegm at the side of Ocho's mouth. Her breathing was rapid as she strained to control the coughing spasm. Once she was calm again, Ocho turned to Jenny with piercing eyes. "Now, *you* take care of him. Tell me you'll take care of him!"

Po Han moved Jenny aside before she could answer. He bent close over his grandmother and whispered, "No, don't do that. Don't let a bird fly with one hand and catch it with the other. I can take care of myself, and of you, and of Jenny." His voice broke. "Just get better, okay?"

***

Po Han was not home when Jenny came by to see him the following day. The maid told her that he had come home mid-morning, but immediately left again to go to back to the hospital. Ocho had died during the night.

"The master told me to ask you to come back tomorrow afternoon." The maid sighed. "Poor *Njonja Besar*. If only she could leave the beer and gin alone, she'd have been a nice person."

Jenny's chest felt so tight, it hurt. She contemplated going to the hospital, but decided against it. Her father had left specific orders to come back tomorrow. "Please tell my father I came today and I'll be back tomorrow afternoon," she said before leaving.

229

Biking home, it occurred to Jenny that Po Han must feel worse than she felt when Els left to go to Holland. Ocho was dead. There was no hope for him to ever be with Ocho again.

CHAPTER 23

Eddie's work jeep was parked in Nanna's driveway when Jenny came biking up. It was a weekday and too early in the afternoon for him to be home. What was going on? She ran into the house.

"Hi! Why's Eddie home? Where's–?" Jenny stood breathless in the doorway of the laundry room. Emma looked up from the ironing board. She brought an arm up and, sniffling, wiped a sleeve across a cheek.

"Eddie's in his room with Aunt Sue. Don't go in there. They're talking."

"Why? What are they talking about? Where's Nanna?"

"In her room."

Jenny rushed to Nanna's room. Nanna was never in her room during the day. Jenny put her ear against the closed door. She called softly and when there was no answer she tried the door handle. The door was locked.

The only other time Jenny remembered her grandmother locking herself in her bedroom was when the Japanese soldiers brought the news of Chip's death.

Sue came walking out of Eddie's room and Jenny could tell she had been crying. "Oh, Jenny, please, try to bring him to his senses!"

Emma came out of the laundry room and put an arm around Sue's shaking shoulders. "Shhh, shhh, Auntie, you know that there isn't anything we can do." She turned to Jenny. "You try. Maybe he'll listen to you."

Eddie's bedroom door swung open. "Jenny!" he called with a tight voice when he caught sight of her.

231

"What's going on? Why has Nanna locked herself in her room? Why's everyone crying?" Jenny stared at Eddie's room.

Clothes were strewn on the bed, stacks of books piled on the desk and chairs. Exercising equipment, a camera, his military canteen, and other odds and ends lay scattered on the floor.

"Here. Sit down." Eddie moved a stack of books from his desk chair.

Jenny looked up into her cousin's face. Eddie's jaws tightened. "I have to leave," he said and swallowed hard. "You remember Mrs. Rose, don't you?"

Jenny nodded. She remembered Peggy Rose's red fingernails clutching Eddie's coat sleeve.

"I'm going to move to her house," Eddie said in a choked voice. "I'm sure you won't be allowed to come there, and I don't know if your mother will let me visit. I told Nanna that I'm going to marry Mrs. Rose."

"You what–?" Jenny grabbed the arms of her chair. Her eyes widened.

"I can't talk about it now. You won't understand. Even adults can't." Eddie slipped off the table. "Please, help me pack–"

"Wait!" Jenny jumped up. "You're just going to leave–"

"Jen, please, don't make it harder." Eddie's usually sunburned face was pale. When he took a step toward her, Jenny moved the chair between them.

"I can't believe you're making this mess to be with that–"

"Jenny, don't. Please don't say it." Eddie's voice broke. He made an awkward gesture with his hands, then dropped his arms by his side.

"Eddie, please, please don't go." Jenny pushed the chair aside and flung her arms around Eddie.

"She's–old–she's–Indo–and a divorcee!" Jenny stuttered against Eddie's chest.

"I know, Jen. I know." Eddie squeezed her shoulders so hard it hurt.

"Then why, Eddie?"

"I love her, Jen." Eddie loosened Jenny's arms around his waist. He picked up a stack of shirts. "Please, pack this. Maybe, afterward, you can go visit your father." He jingled the keys in his trouser pocket and added wearily, "Talk to him, Jenny. He might be able to explain what I can't."

Jenny watched as Eddie filled boxes and suitcases. Eddie would soon be like Els and her father, someone who was not talked about, whose place was no longer set around Nanna's large dining table. She and Eddie were Nanna's favorites. She had often imagined that she and Eddie were two parts of a jar–Eddie the lid and she the bottom. How useful would a jar be if it didn't have a lid?

Jenny followed Eddie while he loaded the suitcases and boxes into the jeep. When he bent to pick up the last box she grabbed him by his shirt. They stood silently by the loaded vehicle. Nanna's bedroom windows were open. A soft breeze rippled the curtains. The mosquito net canopy of Nanna's large bed filled the top half of the window frame.

"Jenny, be good, okay?" Eddie pulled Jenny into his arms. Jenny stared at the jeep and nodded. She pressed her forehead hard into Eddie's collarbone. "Take care of yourself," he said against the side of her head. "Listen to Nanna and your parents–" He broke abruptly out of their embrace and jumped into the jeep.

After the vehicle rumbled away, Jenny walked to the bike shed and, without saying goodbye to anyone, left for her father's house. She remembered how often, in recent days, she had looked for Eddie or waited for him in vain. She recalled Carolien, Sue, and Emma's evasive answers when she had asked about Eddie. She also had a clear vision of Nanna's pressed lips when she tried to get information from her. The late afternoon breeze dried Jenny's wet cheeks.

Po Han answered the door. "What's wrong?" He put an arm around Jenny and steered her to his study.

"Eddie's getting married and everyone's mad at him. He's moving out from Nanna's and he can't see me anymore!" Jenny flopped into a chair. "Why's he doing this?"

"Here." Po Han offered Jenny his handkerchief.

"Dad, she's Indo and divorced and she's old and ugly."

"What does being Indo and divorced and old have to do with being ugly?" Po Han lit a cigarette and looked at Jenny over the flame of his lighter. "Does being divorced make your mother and me ugly?"

Po Han's question threw Jenny off. She didn't think of her parents as ugly, but Eddie and Mrs. Rose was something different. Jenny brushed the back of her hands across her wet cheeks. "I hate her!" she shouted.

Po Han put an arm around Jenny. "Eddie must love this woman," he said. "He must love this woman so much that he's leaving all that *was* behind to go on with what *is*." Po Han lifted Jenny's chin. "Ugly. What is ugly? And right now, *who* is ugly, Jen?"

Jenny began to cry.

Po Han rubbed Jenny's back until she stopped shaking and dried her downturned face.

"Dad, what am I gonna do without him?"

"What you do should not depend on whether or not someone is around." Po Han brushed strands of hair from Jenny's damp forehead. "You'll miss Eddie, of course, but just like he has to live his life, you have to live yours."

Dusk began to fall. Jenny turned the lights on. The churning pain inside her chest was settling into a dull ache. She said, "It's getting late, I better be going now."

"I'll ride with you." Po Han put a hand on Jenny's shoulder.

They rode silently through the balmy evening. Jenny noticed the large moving shadows they created on the pavement as they passed under the yellow light of the street lanterns. A soft breeze carried the ripe scent of blooming tuberoses. Every so often, the call of a distant food vendor broke the rhythmic back and forth of chirping crickets.

"Dad?"

"Yes?"

"I don't get it. Why did you say that Eddie's leaving what *was*? Everyone loves him. We don't want him to leave." Jenny stopped her bike and leaned heavily into her handlebars.

"I know, Jen," Po Han said quietly. "I know and I'm sure Eddie knows—"

"Then why?" Jenny turned toward him.

"There are times when, in order to do what you feel you must do, you have to hurt those you love. And while you will hurt during the process, you still need to do it. Sometimes, it's worth it in the end. And sometimes, it isn't." Po Han's voice trailed away.

Jenny shot Po Han a sideways glance. Nothing he had said made sense to her.

234

"When your mother and I got married, we hurt a lot of people. In the end, we hurt ourselves the most. But through it all, I learned a few things and I'm sure your mother did too."

They rode the rest of the way in silence.

***

Eddie's wedding seemed more like a regular party. The doors and windows of Peggy Rose's house were wide open when Carolien and Jenny arrived. People stood in small circles, talking and laughing.

"Oh, I'm so glad you came!" Peggy walked up to hug Carolien. She wore a beige two-piece suit. A large white cyclamen was pinned to a lapel of her jacket and bobbed in the hollow of her collarbone as she breathed. Being Indo, she was taller and bigger boned than the average Chinese woman. "Ed, Eddie! Carolien and Jenny are here!" Peggy grabbed Jenny's hand and pulled her through the crowd.

"Jenny! Hi, Auntie." Eddie, dressed in a dark blue suit, appeared from one of the rooms.

Jenny pulled out of Peggy's grip and ran to him.

"I'm so glad you're here," Eddie said. "This is a big day for me."

Jenny noticed the shine on Eddie's black shoes. He must have used his military shoeshine kit.

"Is Nanna okay?"

Eddie's question jerked Jenny's head up, but she looked away from him. "Yeah, guess so," she said, staring at Carolien and Peggy who were engaged in a lively conversation. There was a moment of awkward silence, then Jenny asked, "Are you also going to Holland?"

Eddie looked around and automatically returned smiles that were thrown his way. "Jenny," he pleaded and reached for her shoulder.

"Are you?" Jenny shrugged off Eddie's hand.

Eddie sighed. "Yes. As a KNIL veteran, it will be easy to find a job. People won't give Peggy and me such a hard time in Holland. You can come as soon as you pass your high school exam. You can live with either Els or me, depending on which university you choose to go to."

"When will you leave?"

"We're on a waiting list and can be called any time." Eddie's words were monotone and definite.

***

A fresh pine scent laced the air when Nanna opened her bedroom door. Mundi sloshed the mop through the pail. The floor tile shimmered in the early morning sun. A cool morning breeze carried the heady perfume of blooming lilacs through the open windows into the diningroom.

Nanna walked to the altar and lit a pack of incense. She held her offering close to her forehead and sank into silent prayer. She asked the spirits of her ancestors and the god she worshipped to keep Eddie safe. She asked forgiveness for her weakness to love him in spite of his betrayal of the family, and she begged the spirits to bless his marriage. She asked to turn their displeasure toward her instead, since she had failed to prevent her family from straying.

Nanna held her arms up until the incense sticks burned down to the wooden handles. But as she wiped the ashes off the altar table and the floor with a damp rag, she knew her prayers were unable to change things. Carolien had told her that she and Jenny were going to Eddie's wedding today. Nanna brushed some ash flakes from her cheeks. She pressed the side of her hand against her tight chest and leaned against the altar table, closing her eyes. In the darkness, her visions waited. Her grandchildren were battling the elements.

Nanna felt herself swept up by waves that engulfed Els. The girl was drowning in a deep sea and she struggled to keep her head above water. Next, Nanna was thrown between the hoofs of a rearing stallion that carried Eddie. He tried to control the wild horse but it bucked and fought the reins. Trembling, Nanna waited. But she remained untouched by the whipping winds of a hurricane that Jenny fought, standing alone, high on a barren rock. She could see her youngest granddaughter struggle but the winds did not reach her, they were Jenny's alone. Did this vision mean that she was excused from experiencing the ordeal that awaited the girl?

"Nanna, are you ready for breakfast?" Emma stood in the doorway.

"Yes, thank you." A wan smile curved Nanna's lips as she pulled her chair up to the dining table. She was ninety-four. Perhaps the gods were merciful after all and would not require her to endure Jenny's storm as well. She gazed around the large table. Once, all the seats had been filled. Now, there were only four places set. She sighed, wearily. She had failed her family.

The aroma of fresh brewed coffee wafted around Sue, who came in with a breakfast tray. Emma placed the morning paper by Ting's plate before taking her seat. Sue served the *sago* porridge. Her swollen red eyes showed that she had spent the night crying over her son.

"Good morning." Ting walked in and took his seat.

"Good morning." The women returned Ting's greeting in unison. Emma poured his coffee and Sue filled his bowl. For a while, the only sounds were spoons clinking against the china bowls and the ticking of the grandfather clock.

Ting opened the newspaper.

"How much longer before all the Dutch have to leave?" Nanna folded her napkin. "How much more will they take?"

"It seems that the repatriation is happening pretty fast. Most likely they'll be done before the end of the year." Ting hesitated for a moment. "Ma, you can't blame the Dutch for our family troubles–"

Nanna glared at Ting and he stopped mid-sentence. Ting had still not figured out how much damage the Dutch had done to their family. Nanna stared across the table at Chip's empty chair. "If it weren't for the Dutch, your brother would be sitting right there," she said, squeezing her napkin into a tight roll. "Els wouldn't be off amongst strangers, and Eddie would have married a girl from a decent family."

"We have no control over world politics, Ma." Ting folded the paper.

"I'm not worried about the world, I'm worried about my own family." Nanna walked out of the room. Long ago, her husband had realized the devastating affects of opium and removed that evil from their community. The Dutch had rewarded her family with physical comfort and security, but Nanna knew now that the Dutch never gave anything without taking something in return. They had extracted a steep price for their gifts.

***

During the months immediately following Els and Eddie's departures, Jenny often cried for her cousins. Airmail was a luxury and it wasn't until after Eddie left in late June that Els' first letters began arriving in Carolien's mailbox.

Els wrote on June 20, 1950:

> *While we're waiting for our own place, we live with Jan's parents in their flat. It's very small and often feels crowded, but we're grateful for their hospitality and doing the best we can to not be a nuisance.*
>
> *Mother Bouwman tries to be nice, but I know she is disappointed that Jan married a Chinese girl. Hopefully, she will be able to love our children when we have them.*
>
> *I applied for a teaching position at several schools, but I'm afraid that I won't get a job soon. There seems to be a reluctance to assign such a position to someone with an Indonesian background. I also signed up as a volunteer to tutor children who have fallen behind during the war.*

When Eddie arrived in Holland in early August, he wrote:

> *We share a flat with two other couples also recently arrived from Indie. It's not too far from Jan and Els.*
>
> *Besides a tremendous housing shortage, there is a high unemployment rate here. Holland is a small country with a dense population to begin with. The current influx of immigrants is not helping the situation at all.*
>
> *Because of our military record, Jan and I are on a priority list for individual housing. We also submitted a request for shared housing for our families. Hopefully, something will break loose soon.*

Seated on her windowsill, Jenny absorbed her cousins' letters. Holland didn't seem like such a wonderful place, why did everyone have to go there?

CHAPTER 24

When Jenny returned to school, after the summer break of 1950, the Indonesian flag fluttered from the flagpole in the center of the school's front lawn and the lettering on the building's facade had been changed from Christelijk Lyceum to *Sekolah Menengah Atas,* Indonesian for "high school." On December 27, 1949, the Dutch had finally granted the Republic of Indonesia its independence.

Most of the students arriving, checking rosters, and looking for classrooms were either Chinese or Indonesian. None of her old Dutch classmates were there and Jenny began to feel as if she was a stranger in what used to be her own environment.

She knew that Sardjono had replaced Hans Overbeek as the head of the school. What would the rest of the faculty slate look like? The posted roster listed Sardjono as teaching Bahasa Indonesia and History to the seniors. That meant she'd have him every day for Indonesian language and twice a week for history. Jenny made a face.

There were new names. Warner Ford–English; Wilhelm Gross–German. Lisa Sung, who used to teach only music, was now teaching French as well.

The school bell gathered everyone into the assembly hall. Queen Wilhelmina's portrait had been replaced by President Sukarno's, and the lion of the Dutch royal emblem by the Indonesian eagle of the *Pancasila* crest. Apparently no one had thought to shorten the podium height for Sardjono. When the short Indonesian climbed on a stool and grappled for balance, Jenny snickered.

Sardjono welcomed everyone into the new school year. He introduced the new faculty members and emphasized the important role of the sixth year class. "Keep in mind," he accentuated his words by tapping the end of his pipe on the podium, "you will be the first high school graduates of the Indonesian Republic." Sardjono delivered his speech in rapid Indonesian and Jenny had trouble following him. She was grateful that her first period was English, taught by the new teacher, Warner Ford.

***

A couple of weeks into the first semester, Carolien received a note from Principal Sardjono. He wanted to discuss Jenny's grades. Annoyed, Carolien came to the appointment.

Sardjono told Carolien that Jenny needed tutoring in Indonesian in order to keep up with her studies.

"I find it strange that, after placing in the top five of her class during previous years, Jenny suddenly needs tutoring," Carolien said. "It must be that along with all the changes, the quality of teaching has declined."

"Perhaps you'd like to see Mr. Ford. He is Jenny's class counselor." Sardjono calmly stuffed his pipe. After he took a few puffs, he added, "He's *American*."

When Carolien rose brusquely, Sardjono remained seated. "Please, let me know your decision," he said, while shuffling some papers on his desk.

"I will," Carolien snapped and left the room.

Down the hall, Carolien peeked through the glass panel in Warner Ford's office door. The American was working at his desk.

"Come in." Warner responded in Indonesian to Carolien's knock.

Flustered, Carolien opened the door.

"Good morning, what can I do for you?" Warner spoke Indonesian with an American accent.

Carolien introduced herself and Warner pulled her a chair. Warner pointed out that since the Indonesian government had taken charge, all lectures, except those in the foreign languages, were now given in

Indonesian. Carolien shifted in her seat while Warner explained Jenny's learning problems. He used words she had never heard before. Carolien was having a hard time keeping up and was soon lost in the conversation. Is this what Jenny experienced during a school day? No wonder the girl was doing poorly.

Carolien reluctantly agreed that it was best for Jenny to be tutored in Indonesian and Warner offered to make the arrangements with Sardjono.

"Couldn't you tutor Jenny?" Carolien asked. "Why does she have to see Sardjono?" It was one thing that Jenny now had to learn some kind of fancy Malay they called Indonesian, but it was another thing to have her daughter tutored by an *inlander*.

"I'm sorry." Warner smiled apologetically. "I'm not qualified to teach Indonesian, and Mr. Sardjono wants to see to it personally that all seniors graduate with excellent grades."

Carolien lowered her eyes. She wasn't happy with the situation, but she didn't consider arguing with an American.

Carolien tried to hide her feelings when Jenny came home. "Until you bring your grades up, you have to go to Mr. Sardjono's office for tutoring after school. It shouldn't take you too long to catch on," she said sternly.

"Bahasa Indonesia is different from Malay." Jenny protested. "There are many words I've never heard. I don't understand anything anymore."

Carolien thought of her own experience earlier that day. She now understood that there was indeed a difference between the Malay spoken to the servants and the Indonesian taught and used in the schools. "Jenny," she said, putting down her mending, "I wish that I could send you to a different school. But there are no more Dutch schools and your school is still the best high school around. If you want to graduate, you must get your grades up. And the only way to do that is to learn Indonesian so you can understand the lectures."

"I wonder if Dad would've sent me to a Dutch school."

"If he didn't, it wouldn't have been because of his wisdom. It would have been because he couldn't afford it. You're forgetting that all he ever did was take useless pictures."

"Dad's paying for my tuition now," Jenny said with a stubborn edge in her voice.

"It's easy for him to jump in when it's convenient. Where was he when we needed him?" Carolien noticed Jenny's jutted chin.

"You know that he went to Holland to study and the prize he won for his photography made that possible." Jenny took a few books out of her bag and dropped them on the table. "Really, Mom, how bad would it've been if I hadn't gone to Dutch schools? I definitely wouldn't be having a language problem and–"

"Jenny, get used to it. Getting ahead takes work."

"You don't understand–I don't mind *work*, Mom, but it doesn't feel good to being laughed at behind my back. Do you know the other students call me *the abandoned Dutch dog*?" Jenny ran out of the room, banging the door closed.

CHAPTER 25

Jenny took a bite out of her sandwhich and stared across the lawn. Grace and Theresa sat with a group of girls on one of the benches in the shade of the old tamarind tree. Lam Ching stood in their middle.

During the Dutch times, popularity had been based on athletic or scholastic achievements, now the economic status of one's family was the deciding factor. Lam's father owned the only car dealership in town. Lam always dressed in a starched button-down shirt and sharply creased linen slacks and was often driven to school in a shiny black Cadillac. Under the new order, Lam Ching was winning the popularity competition.

"Why are you sitting here by yourself, *Nonnie?*" Prawira walked up from behind her and crushed the butt of a clove cigarette against the sole of his shoe. A pair of brazen sparrows pecked at someone's unattended sandwich.

Jenny shrugged. It struck her that the custodian always spoke Dutch to her and still addressed her as *little miss*, instead of using her name the way she heard him do with other students. "There isn't much else to do. I really don't want to be a part of those buzzing bees." She nodded toward the circle of giggling girls.

Prawira followed Jenny's gaze and shook his head. "You're right there. Someone in that bunch is going to be in trouble." He paused. "Deep trouble."

Jenny threw Prawira a scrutinizing look. What did he mean? The group of Chinese students didn't have any trouble getting along with

Sardjono, they always had good grades and nothing seemed to bother them. But before she could ask any questions, Prawira checked his pocket watch and said, "I better get ready to ring the bell. Recess is almost over."

Jenny was walking through the hallway toward her classroom when she saw Lam coming toward her. Tall for a Chinese boy, he towered over the crowd. "Where were you hiding during recess?" he asked, shuffling behind her into the classroom.

Jenny shrugged. "Obviously not where you could find me."

She took her seat ignoring Lam, who lingered by her desk until he bluntly asked, "How about seeing *Three Coins in the Fountain* on Saturday?"

"Wha-a-t?" Jenny caught Grace looking their way and watched her lean toward Theresa, whispering behind her hand. She had seen how the two girls flirted with Lam, how all the girls flirted with Lam. Jenny wasn't particularly interested in going on a date with Lam, but she knew how jealous it would make the other girls. She smiled at the girls and turned to Lam. "Why not?"

The teacher walked in and a hush fell over the classroom. Jenny felt Grace and Theresa staring at her back. She suddenly realized that she had accepted Lam's invitation without asking her mother. Hopefully Carolien wouldn't keep her from going.

CHAPTER 26

When Lam came to pick Jenny up on Saturday night he wore a white stiffly starched dress shirt and navy gabardine slacks. His tie was held in place with a diamond studded gold clip. He reminded Jenny of a strutting rooster and it made her uncomfortable.

"Sorry," Lam helped Jenny into the waiting *betja*. "My father needed the car, but we have real good seats."

"How did you get tickets when we haven't even gotten to the theater?"

"I had our houseboy get them earlier." Lam laughed. He lay an arm across the back of the *betja* bench. "I told him to get loge seats."

Jenny scooted toward the edge of the seat. This was nothing like the few times she and Frans had gone to the movies together. They had ridden their bikes and had a good time joking and talking about the movie.

"You're going to fall out, sitting like that." Lam grinned and crossed his legs.

"No, I'm okay." Jenny laughed nervously and grabbed the side of the cyclo's canopy.

The cyclo driver dodged several cars as they drove down Braga Street. Once an exclusive upscale Dutch business center, most of the stores were now owned by Chinese merchants.

At the theater Lam took Jenny's elbow and steered her through the crowd into the lobby. Jenny headed for the center entrance, but Lam lead her to the side doors. "Remember, we have loge seats," he whispered into her neck.

Jenny had never sat in the loge section before.

"Is this okay?" Lam ushered her into the private loge compartment. She could look down on the main floor seats below them.

"Oh, yes." Jenny settled into her seat and smoothed her skirt. Several couples entered the loge, but no one claimed the other seats in their compartment. Lam hailed a candy vendor and bought Jenny a large box of Chicklets and several candy bars.

"It seems that we are going to have this compartment all to ourselves," Jenny said when the lights went off and still no one had joined them.

"Of course we will." Lam paused before he leaned over. "I bought tickets for all four seats so we won't be bothered."

"Why did you buy four tickets when there's only two of us?" Jenny forgot to whisper.

"Shhh!" Lam chuckled softly.

The introductory scenes of *Three Coins in the Fountain* filled the screen and Jenny tried to relax. In the dim light she measured the space between them. Lam's starched shirtsleeve scraped her arm when he ran his fingers lightly over her hand. "Relax," he whispered, giving Jenny's stiff hand a gentle tug. She did not budge and Lam let go.

Jenny glanced sideways. Lam's attention was on the screen. He had crossed his legs and rested his elbows on the arms of the chair. His hands lay loosely in his lap. Jenny smelled the Brylcream he had used to slick back his hair.

The movie ended and, as the credits rolled up the screen, the lights came on, and the theme song filled the theater. Lam got up and moved in front of Jenny. He looked down and held his hand out, his knees touching hers. She let him pull her out of her chair and against his chest but tensed when Lam put an arm around her waist. As they shuffled their way out of the theater amidst the crowd, she felt his fingers move across her side, his thumb tracing the crease at the bottom of her bra. Gathering Lam's fingers in a tight grip, Jenny moved his hand away.

As soon as the thinning crowd permitted, Jenny stepped out of Lam's arm. But Lam held on to her hand while he hailed a *betja*.

In the cyclo, Lam pulled Jenny's hand across his lap and put an arm around her. "You've been a scared mouse all evening," he said, cradling

Jenny's shoulder. "What are you nervous about? You're not exactly acting like a liberated Western woman."

"What are you talking about?" Jenny pulled away. "I'm not scared. I just don't like you pawing at me like you've been all evening. I've tried to be nice about it, but if you think that I'm scared of you, you've got another think coming."

"Ho-o-oh!" Lam laughed. "That sounds like the Jenny I know." He pinched Jenny's cheek softly. She jerked away, and Lam, chuckling, slapped his own hand. "Okay, okay. No more touching."

Their conversation was sparse during the rest of the ride home. Jenny was glad that Lam did not make another pass at her that evening.

***

The next Monday, during recess, Lam followed Jenny around with idle conversation. Every so often he returned the waves of bypassers.

Grace and Theresa sat with a group of girls on one of the benches in the shade of the old tamarind tree. A small group of Lam's friends stopped in passing.

"We're going to grab some lunch," one of the boys said. "Want to come along and see what the vendors have today?" Since the Lyceum had turned into an Indonesian high school, food vendors were allowed on the school grounds.

"Want some?" Lam put a hand on Jenny's arm.

Jenny shook her head. "No, thanks, I have my lunch." She was not allowed to purchase food from a street vendor. Carolien was concerned with the risk of getting dysentery or tuberculosis from eating such food.

"Sorry, forgot eating off a banana leaf does not suit our mighty colonialist," one of the boys mocked.

"Hey, watch your mouth!" Lam took a step toward the speaker, but others came between them and, jostling and joking, the group moved on.

"You didn't have to stick up for me." Jenny planted her elbows on a banister and looked away from Lam.

"Don't let those morons bother you." Lam put an arm around Jenny's shoulders. "Wanna eat lunch over there?" he nodded toward an empty bench.

Jenny caught Grace looking their way and watched her lean into Theresa's side. They waved and beckoned her to an empty spot they made by moving over. They had never before invited her to join them and it was obvious that having Lam's attention was causing the change. Jenny gritted her teeth. She waved back at the girls and turned to Lam. "Okay, let's."

Jenny tossed her head as they walked toward the garden bench. She couldn't help feeling a sense of triumph as she took a bite out of her sandwhich.

***

Standing behind the sheer curtains of her living room window, Carolien watched the Ching's black Cadillac come to a smooth stop in her driveway. "Jenny! Lam's here. He came with a car." Carolien rushed to Jenny's room and gave Jenny the once-over. "Let me see, do you have a hanky in your handbag? Your slip isn't showing, is it?"

"Gosh, Mom, you're acting like Big Red clucking around her chicks." Jenny shook Carolien's hand off her arm.

Carolien bit her lip. Why was Jenny not more enthusiastic about her date? Lam Ching was polite and came from a well-to-do family. Judging by the flowers he sent after their first date, and now picking her up with his father's car, Carolien figured that Lam must have more than a fleeting interest in her daughter.

"What's the big deal about the car?" Jenny tied the sash around her waist. "It's his father's."

"But of course. You don't expect an eighteen-year-old–" Carolien was interrupted by a knock on the door.

"*Non*, Mr. Lam is waiting for you," Amin said.

"I'll be right out. Have him seated in the living room." Jenny smoothed a curled petal of her tulip sleeve.

Lam rose as soon as they entered the living room. He bowed to Carolien. "Good afternoon, Mrs. Lee, thank you for allowing me to take Jenny out." He picked up a package from the coffee table and offered it to Carolien. "I brought you some chocolates. I hope you like them."

"Oh, thank you so much." Smiling, Carolien took notice of the fancy foiled box. "My goodness. You took the trouble to go all the way into town to get them from the Dutch bakery?"

"It wasn't any trouble at all. I'm so glad you like them." Lam beamed. He reached for another small package on the table and turned to Jenny. "Here, I brought you a little something, too."

"Thanks." Jenny fumbled with the satin ribbon around the small box.

Carolien clasped her hands when Jenny held out a delicate silver replica of the Eiffel Tower. "How pretty." At the base, a small cobalt blue oval bottle was secured in a white velvet well.

"*Soir de Paris* is a very nice fragrance," Carolien said. "I'm sure that if Jenny had not already put on some cologne, she'd use it right now." She glanced at Jenny and wished her daughter would show a bit more gratitude or enthusiasm. Did the girl realize what was happening?

"Thank you." Jenny awkwardly balanced the keepsake on the palm of her hand before putting the perfume on the coffee table. "We'd better go or we'll be late," she said crumpling the wrapping paper.

"Lam, it was very thoughtful of you to bring us gifts. I know that Jenny's going to have a good time." Carolien ignored Jenny's glare and ushered Lam and Jenny to the front door. Smiling, she watched Lam help Jenny into the car. "Enjoy yourselves!" Carolien waved when Lam bowed to her before stepping into the vehicle himself.

The Chings were a prominent Chinese family. Carolien knew from Sue's mah yong stories that, despite Ching senior's reputation of sowing wild seed wherever he found fertile soil, many mothers considered Lam a good catch. Carolien chuckled. Who would have predicted that Jenny Lee, the wild unruly daughter of a divorcee, would bring home the day's catch. The only problem was that Jenny didn't seem to be interested at all.

***

While Lam instructed the driver to take them to the theater, Jenny wondered what had gotten into Carolien to display such enthusiasm about her date. True, Frans had never sent flowers, picked her up with a car, or brought her presents. But still, there was no reason for all that fuss. "I'm sorry, my mother has a way of being overbearing," she said, smoothing her skirt.

"What are you talking about? Your mother is very nice." Lam pulled his cuffs down with a short tug. After they drove for a while in silence he asked, "What's the matter, didn't you like my present?"

"Oh, I like it. It's very nice. The statue is so elegant. I've never tried *Soir de Paris* before." Jenny tried to sound convincing, but she heard the words echo in their own hollowness. "And picking me up with the car, that's special too," she added.

"Is it?" Lam raised his eyebrows and Jenny noticed how dark and thick they were. "It actually wasn't the perfume that I wanted you to have," Lam said. "It was the Eiffel Tower. I wanted you to have the Eiffel Tower."

"Why?"

"I just did." Lam took Jenny's hand and interlaced his fingers with hers. She didn't pull back and they rode the rest of the way holding hands.

At the theater Lam handed the driver a few bills. "Have a good time, but be here when the show is over," he said, helping Jenny out of the car.

Lam had bought loge seats again. He leaned back into his chair and put an arm around Jenny's shoulders. She tensed when Lam's hand traveled to the base of her neck and jerked away when his fingers eased under the neckline of her dress. "Okay, relax, I'm sorry," Lam whispered, softly squeezing her shoulder.

During intermission Jenny aksed, "Aren't you tired from sitting propped up like that?"

Lam chuckled, but didn't remove his arm.

The Ching's car was parked right by the entrance when they walked out of the theater. The driver waved at them.

"I'm hungry," Lam said, helping Jenny into the car. "Let's get some noodles, okay?"

Jenny hesitated. "Won't it get too late?"

"Afraid you'll turn into a mouse with a long tail?" Lam leaned laughing into the front seat and told the driver to take them to Tenfu, one of

Bandung's finest Chinese restaurants.

The host welcomed Lam and Jenny with a big smile and ushered them, ahead of other waiting customers, to one of the private compartments along the side of the large dining room. "Enjoy yourselves. I'll send the waiter right in." The host bowed himself out and the pleats of the red brocade curtains settled with soft shimmering waves.

"I hope you'll like the food. I think it's very good." Lam moved the small lazy Susan with bottles of different sauces to the side of the table.

The waiter came and Jenny was impressed with the ease Lam ordered. He asked Jenny what she wanted to drink and ordered himself a bottle of Chinese beer.

The aroma of the large platter of fried noodles made Jenny salivate. Crisp chunks of Chinese cabbage glistened next to slices of moist chicken and pork tucked into a heap of fat noodles.

"The shrimp is so moist!" Jenny held up a pink shrimp with her chopsticks. "Shrimp is usually tough and dry in restaurant noodles."

"I never pay attention to those details. I just know if a dish tastes good or not." Lam picked out pieces of shrimp and spooned them onto Jenny's plate.

"Thanks." Jenny smiled. "Have some yourself."

Lam emptied the beer bottle in his glass. "I'm so glad you like the food. It's about time I found something you like," he said pouring Jenny more hot tea. "I've never known a girl who appreciates food the way you do."

"Really?" Jenny shifted in her seat. She had enjoyed herself during the meal, but now the tone of Lam's voice made her uncomfortable.

Jenny let Lam hold her hand during the ride home. When the driver made an unexpected sharp turn she fell sideways against him and did not straighten up. Leaning her head against Lam's arm a warm contented feeling spread through her. She was almost sorry when the driver pulled up in her mother's driveway.

"Is that you, Jenny?" Carolien called from her bedroom when Jenny opened the back door.

"Yes, Mom." Jenny wished Carolien would come out of her room. She wet her lips and tried to slow her rapid breathing by swallowing.

Lam turned the lights off and began to pull Jenny back outside. She stiffened and held on to the doorjamb.

"Hi, little mouse." Lam took Jenny's hands and held them against his chest. "Have you ever kissed? Have you?" he asked with a low thick voice and rested his forehead against hers.

Jenny managed to pull her head sideways. She didn't like the smell of Lam's breath. "Of course I have," she lied. "But that doesn't mean I am going to do it with you!"

"Well, tell me how I can persuade you," Lam whispered. Closing his arms tightly around her, he pressed Jenny against the doorjamb.

Jenny quickly brought up a leg and, kicking Lam in the shins, she pushed two fists hard into his stomach.

Lam let go and tumbled backward. After he regained his balance, he rubbed his shins.

Jenny stared at Lam's bent back. She hadn't meant to really hurt him. She imagined the girls giggling when Lam took someone else to the movies next week. Jenny put her hands behind her back and held loosely on to the doorjamb. "I'm sorry," she said when Lam straightened up. She expected him to walk away without giving her another glance, but he simply looked at her with a quizzical amused gaze.

"Sorry if I hurt you, but you scared me," Jenny stammered.

"It's okay." Lam stepped closer, heat radiating from his body.

Jenny stood motionless while Lam moved his hands up her arms to her shoulders. When his fingers slipped between the leaves of her tulip sleeves, Jenny thought of the other girls and hoped there would be some truth to all that the movies and books said about kissing being pleasurable. She leaned her forehead against Lam's shoulder.

"Will you let me kiss you, just once?" Lam lifted Jenny's face.

Jenny caught her breath. The same reckless excitement she felt when she took her hands off the handlebars while racing down a steep hill on her bike took over. She closed her eyes and brought her arms up around Lam's neck like she had seen the girls in the movies do.

With the lightness of butterfly wings, Lam's lips first touched her forehead, then her eyes, her cheekbones, and her chin, until they finally closed fully over her mouth.

Jenny gasped and pulled back. Lam tightened his embrace and she relaxed gradually in his arms. The night air turned chilly and she shivered. "I better go in. It must be getting very late," she whispered, easing Lam away when he started kissing her again.

"Okay, little mouse, get into your warm nest." Lam's lips brushed her forehead before he skipped down the porch steps.

The sound of the slamming car door cut through the quiet night and Jenny closed the door. She leaned for a moment against the solid wood. When she ran a finger across her lips she felt the tingling sensation of Lam's kisses. Part of her wanted the moment to last, but another part told her she was about to get into great trouble.

***

Carolien often worried about her daughter's future. Indonesia had recently been admitted to the UN and the new Indonesian government had begun to focus on internal problems. The Chinese had used the political turmoil to gain control over the economy and, as a result, the government began programs that supported the native, non-Chinese businesses. What would happen if the anti-Chinese sentiment grew and the Indonesians pushed the name-changing issue as well as that of intermarriage? While she often thought about Jenny's future career, Carolien had not spent any time considering possibilities of her daughter's marriage. After all, Jenny was only in high school and, before anything else, she was going to make sure her daughter would have an education that would allow her to be independent.

Carolien glanced at the clock on her nightstand. It had been just past ten when Jenny came home. It was almost eleven now and she had not heard the Ching's car leave. She put her book down, listening for noises. Jenny and Lam must be on the back porch.

Carolien parted the curtains and peeked through the slats of the shutters. The back porch light was off. Sue's stories about Ching Senior buzzed through Carolien's mind as she leaned forward.

It was easy to imagine the intermingling of Chinese and Indonesian youth in the immediate future, intermarriage was being promoted as a way of strengthening the new Indonesian nation. Perhaps it would be best for Jenny's future if she didn't interfere. The Chings were a prominent Chinese family, Nanna would be pleased if Jenny and Lam got together. At least she would have one grandchild whose marriage she approved of.

Carolien returned to bed and picked up her book, but kept glancing at the clock until she heard the back door close and the Ching's car start. "Jenny, what took you so long to come in? Are you okay?" Carolien called when Jenny passed her door. "Jenny. Come in here." Carolien gave her daughter a scrutinizing look when Jenny entered the room. "What were you doing out there? Are you okay?"

"Yeah, I'm fine. We were just talking." Jenny fiddled with the doorknob.

"Was the movie good?" Carolien had not missed the nervous twitch in Jenny's voice. She wished Jenny would confide in her. Carolien was certain Jenny would have trusted in Eddie or Els if they had been around. How much would Jenny tell Po Han?

"It was very nice. We saw *The Greatest Show on Earth*. Boy, they were good on the trapeze." Jenny sounded like herself again.

"I'm glad that you had a good time." Carolien reached for the table lamp. "You better turn in now. It's plenty late." Carolien turned off the light and tried to get comfortable. Would the Chings send Lam to Holland after high school? They undoubtedly could afford it. In their last letter, the van Houtens urged her again to come to Holland with Jenny. Carolien sighed.

Ting had resigned from the Department of Telecommunications when the new Indonesian government demoted him from Chief Accountant to assistant to a newly appointed Indonesian department head. He now devoted all of his time to the smoke shop on Braga Street that he and Chip had opened during the war as a cover for their underground activities. Carolien helped her brother run the store when work in her own sewing business was slow. In spite of their Dutch background and loyalties, neither would emigrate to Holland. Concern for Nanna, Sue, and Emma was a silent responsibility the siblings shared.

CHAPTER 27

Jenny went out with Lam almost every Saturday evening during the remainder of her senior year. They fell into a ritual of going to the movies, eating out, and spending time on Carolien's back-porch steps. Coming home on a Saturday night in October, they were caught in an early monsoon storm. A strong wind turned Lam's umbrella inside out while they walked to the back of the house. By the time they stood in Carolien's dining room Jenny was soaked. "I need to change," she said with clattering teeth.

"Okay." Lam set the broken umbrella in a corner. He pulled out a handkerchief and dried his face and hair as Jenny left the room.

Jenny knocked and stuck her head around the door when she passed Carolien's bedroom. "Hi, Mom, I'm home."

"You're drenched! Get dry before you catch pneumonia." Carolien called from her bed.

In her bedroom, Jenny kicked off her shoes and took off her wet dress. She was standing in her slip when the door quietly opened and Lam walked in. Startled, Jenny folded her arms across her chest.

"Sshh." Lam quickly crossed the room.

Jenny put both hands against his chest and tried pushing him away.

"Relax, little mouse, relax." Lam took Jenny's hands and, moving himself against her, he backed Jenny toward the bed.

A curious tingling sensation came over Jenny when Lam moved down the straps of her slip and lifted her onto the bed. He lay down beside her and guided her hand inside his unzipped slacks.

Jenny held Lam with a timid curiosity. Her heartbeat quickened when she felt his penis pulse against her palm. Voices buzzed in her head and carried a blur of memories. *Don't let boys touch you.* The giggling whispers of the girls at school when they talked about boys. And now she wanted to hold on to Lam's pulsing penis, but she felt she was doing something wrong and was scared. Looking down to where her hand disappeared into Lam's pants she noticed his shoes on the bed. The shiny black shoes on her white sheets brought reality into the dizzy moment. "Please." She awkwardly moved an arm, trying to move the straps of her slip up. "Please, take your shoes off my bed."

Lam rolled onto his side. He propped himself up, resting on an elbow. He looked at Jenny with a velvet gleam in his eyes and chuckled. "Okay." He sat up and loosened his laces. "I'll take off my shoes."

After removing his shoes Lam unbuckled his belt and dropped his pants. Jenny noticed the hair in his armpits when he took off his shirt. She shifted her gaze downward when Lam pulled down his shorts. But when he put a knee on the bed, fear got the better of her and she shot up, her head colliding with Lam's chest.

Jenny pushed hard against Lam's shoulders. When he didn't budge, anger replaced Jenny's fear. She drove her nails in Lam's flesh and frantically moved her head to escape his roving mouth. "No!" she cried. "Get away!"

"Shhh! You don't want your mother to hear us." Lam skewered Jenny's arms and shifted himself on top of her. Though she tried to twist free, Jenny was unable to move. The skirt of her slip gathered in a roll around her waist. Lam held her in a suffocating grip, pinned to the bed with his body while his hand tore her panties down her thighs. She felt his penis rubbing her groin as he forced her legs open. Filled with rage, Jenny lunged and sunk her teeth into the tip of Lam's shoulder. He winced and, for a split second, pulled back. But when she tried to get up Lam dropped himself hard on top of her.

"Stop! Please stop!" Jenny pushed Lam back as hard as she could, but he continued to drive himself inside her. She felt a sharp pain as things inside her ripped apart.

"Oh…please…just a little longer." Panting, Lam moved with a great urgency until, out of breath, he fell back.

Jenny felt something warm and sticky seep between her thighs. She used Lam's sudden limpness to shove him away. "Am I going to get pregnant?" she cried, pulling up her panties.

Lam stroked Jenny's back with trembling fingers and pulled her against him. "Sshhh," he said softly. "Shhh, you won't."

"How do you know? What am I going to tell Nanna and my parents?" Jenny pulled out of Lam's embrace. She tried to sit up, but felt so sore she couldn't get comfortable.

Lam put his arms around Jenny and gently stroked her hair. "I'm sure I got out in time."

She looked up, not understanding.

Lam cleared his throat. "Do you know when you'll get your next period?"

Jenny looked away and shifted uncomfortably across the wet sticky spots under her. She had never discussed her period with anyone.

"You need to tell me, so we can figure things out." Lam swung his legs out of bed and held his hand out.

Jenny stared at the red stains on the sheets as she stood on the floor. Panicking, she reached between her legs, but didn't feel any wound. She slipped her pajama top over her head and retrieved her moon datebook from the blue box on the bottom shelf of her closet. Seated on the cold tile floor, Jenny figured out she only had two days to go before she would need the cloths. "This Tuesday," she said and put the little notebook back.

Lam smiled. "Trust me," he said, grabbing his shorts. "Nothing's going to happen and you don't have to tell anyone."

"But they will know," Jenny answered miserably.

"How? Nobody will know anything unless you tell them." Lam reached for his shirt.

"How am I going to explain *that?*" Jenny pointed to the red smears on her sheet. "Mia's going to tell Mom there was blood on my sheet!" She carefully sat down on the edge of the bed.

"Hmmm." Lam buttoned his shirt slowly. "What happens when you get your period at night?" He put his slacks on and fastened his belt.

"What?" Jenny looked at Lam, puzzled.

"What do you do when your period comes at night?" Lam picked up his shoes and sat down in Jenny's desk chair. "Sometimes, it comes at night, doesn't it?"

"Oh–yeah–I–take my sheet off and rinse it out." Jenny's cheeks flushed and she looked away.

"There's your answer," Lam said cheerfully. "You just say that your period came."

"But–it didn't."

"You know that and I know that. But no one else does, nor do they need to." Lam finished tying his shoelaces and jumped to his feet. "Tonight, little mouse, is *our* secret." Lam took a pocket comb out of his wallet and ran it through his hair. He handed Jenny her pajama bottoms. "Here, put these on. You'll get cold."

Outside the wind had stopped howling, but a soft ticking against the windows told Jenny that it was still raining. When she stumbled into the legs of her pajamas, Lam steadied her. He gently moved a lock of hair that fell across her face. "So, this is what my little mouse looks like at bedtime." Lam took Jenny's chin between his thumb and index finger and lifted her face.

"Oh, Lam, what's going to happen?" Jenny knew the events of the night were irreversible.

Lam took her in his arms. "Nothing bad is going to happen. Now you are my very own little mouse and I will make sure you always have plenty of cheese," Lam said lightly.

Jenny leaned silently against Lam. He looked at his watch and said, "I better get going or the driver will think I'm spending the night here!" He lifted Jenny and carried her to bed, laughing. "Goodnight, little mouse, my own frightened little mouse. Sleep well and have sweet dreams." Lam's lips brushed lightly across Jenny's forehead, her bedroom light turned off, and he was gone.

Jenny lay motionless, listening to the soft thud of the back door, footsteps on the gravel path, the car door slamming, and the engine coming to life. After a while, she moved her hands along her thighs and reached around her sore back. She wanted to take a shower, but her mother might get up and question her. She got onto her knees and pulled the mosquito netting closed. If only Eddie and Els still lived at Nanna's. They might have had answers to her questions. For once, Jenny didn't feel Po Han would be able to help solve her problems.

***

On Monday morning the doorbell rang just as Jenny was leaving for school. Startled, she listened to Amin and Lam's voices in the living room.

"Do I hear Lam?" Carolien rose from the breakfast table and followed Jenny into the living room.

"Good morning, Mrs. Lee." Lam bowed in Carolien's direction then turned to Jenny. "Oh, good. You're ready. Let's go."

"Why are you picking me up?" Jenny followed Lam to the waiting car.

"Didn't I tell you that my little mouse would always have plenty of cheese?" Lam handed Jenny's bag to the driver and ushered her into the car.

She glanced akwardly at Lam and he reached for her hand, smiling.

During the next three days, Jenny often went to the bathroom to check her panties. She struggled through Tuesday without her period arriving. Finally, on Wednesday, she felt moisture between her thighs during the last class. She almost cried in relief when a quick trip to the bathroom confirmed that her period had arrived. But as she was cleaning herself, the fear and shame that had cloaked her since that rainy Saturday wrapped tightly around her again.

Later, riding home from school in the Ching's car, Lam asked, "Did it come?" Jenny merely nodded and Lam reached across the seat to pat her knee. "See, I told you, there's nothing to worry about."

"I guess." Jenny plucked her skirt as she forced back tears. When the driver pulled up in Carolien's driveway, Jenny hopped out.

Lam started to follow her. "Do you want to do homework together? I can keep the car."

Jenny shook her head and pushed the door shut. "No, I'm going to see my father."

"Okay. I'll pick you up tomorrow morning." Lam said, a twinge of disappointment in his voice.

Jenny watched the Ching's car drive off then walked into the house. The past few days had established her and Lam as a couple. In school, Lam carried her books and sharpened her pencils. She shared the chocolates Lam placed in her desk drawer with the envious girls and, while she began to enjoy her new popularity, she also dreaded Saturday night when, after seeing a movie and going out to dinner, Lam would expect to revisit her bed. Could she deny him? And if she did, would he tell everyone at school what they had done? Jenny's feet dragged on the walkway as she realized she was trapped. She could never run the risk of her family discovering the truth.

One night, after they eased into her room, Jenny asked Lam what they would do if Carolien caught them. He ran a finger across the bridge of her nose, and soothed, "Don't worry. I'll take care of it. When will you learn to trust me?"

Jenny shuddered at the thought of Carolien, Nanna, and Po Han's reaction when they discovered that she had brought shame upon them. What if they all turned their backs on her? If anyone in school found out she would be ostracized. "What if I get pregnant?" she blurted.

"Don't worry, you won't." Lam put his arms around Jenny, chuckling softly. "We'll watch the calendar and I'll be careful." Kissing her, he murmured, "Don't worry, little mouse. I'll take care of you."

***

Carolien credited Lam with having a calming influence on Jenny. The girl no longer changed into shorts as soon as she came home. Nor did she go on wild bike rides or spend hours in the garden, climbing trees or hanging from her exercise rings. Carolien rewarded Lam by making him feel welcome when he came to do homework with Jenny. This relationship could put an end to Jenny being a misfit in Chinese society.

"Why do you think Lam's hanging around so much?" Carolien asked one evening while Jenny finished up homework at the dining room table. She continued her knitting, trying to appear only casually interested.

"Beats me." Jenny yawned. "I'm going to finish reading this stuff in bed," she said, and quickly gathered her books.

"Nanna's happy you're dating a Chinese boy from a good family." Carolien tried again. Jenny clearly did not want to have a conversation about her relationship with Lam.

"Gosh, Mom, don't you guys have anything more important to talk about than Lam?" Jenny grabbed the stack of books and notebooks. "G'night." she said over her shoulder, leaving the room.

"Goodnight." Carolien shook her head. She could never figure Jenny out. The girl didn't seem to be at all impressed with the attention Lam lavished on her. Carolien stuck her needles into the ball of yarn. She needed to be careful. She still wanted Jenny to go to Holland to study law. A degree from Leiden would give Jenny the education needed to be an independent woman. It also might turn her into a good catch, despite the fact that her parents were divorced and her family was not as wealthy as the Chings.

Carolien sighed. There had been a time when economic status came secondary to a Dutch education, but that time was gone now.

***

Nanna looked up from picking debris out of the rice on her bamboo tray when the gate creaked. Jenny came racing up the driveway on her bike. Someone was following behind her. Nanna squinted. A Chinese boy got slowly off his bike. Had Jenny brought Lam?

Jenny parked her bike and, without waiting for Lam, ran up the porch steps. On the top step, she stood still and raised her folded hands in greeting. "Hi, Nanna."

"Hello, Jenny!" Nanna smiled and looked past Jenny at Lam who calmly walked up the steps.

"Nanna, this is Lam." Jenny turned and stepped aside.

Lam bowed, then greeted Nanna the Chinese way.

Pleased, Nanna returned his greeting and invited Lam and Jenny into the living room. "How are your parents, Lam?" Nanna took a seat and folded her hands in her lap.

"They're fine, thank you."

Mundi carried in a tea tray and Nanna poured the tea. "Do you have any brothers and sisters?" she asked, handing Lam his cup.

"No, ma'am, I'm the only child." Lam placed his teacup carefully on the table.

"Nanna, don't you need me to pick mangos? Can we check on the chickens now?" Jenny started to get up.

"Even as a toddler, Jenny always helped me in the garden." Nanna smiled.

"If there's anything you need done, I'll be glad to help," Lam offered quickly and rose.

"There's nothing I need right now. It's nice to visit with you. Please, don't let your tea get cold." Nanna held out the cookie platter. Jenny's jutted chin did not escape her. Why was Jenny upset? The boy seemed to be nice enough. He was definitely well mannered and hadn't done anything to offend her.

Jenny flopped on her chair and ate all the cookies on the plate without offering any to Lam. Dismayed, Nanna rose. Considering the way Jenny was acting, it was best to cut the visit short. "Well," Nanna said stiffly, "it was nice meeting you, Lam. I'm sure you and Jenny have other things to do besides keeping an old woman company." Walking Jenny and Lam out, she asked, "Will I see you tomorrow, Jenny?"

After a short hesitation, Jenny said, "Sure, Nanna."

Nanna watched Jenny and Lam bike away. There was something wrong with the way Jenny had behaved. No amount of Western influence could change a woman's ways around a man she desired. Nanna remembered how Carolien had been around Po Han. Lam could be the ticket to Jenny's acceptance into Chinese society, but nothing would happen unless Jenny was willing to invest in that ticket.

Walking into the house Nanna heard Emma laughing at something Sue said. Emma was in her early thirties now. Her last suitor had been a widowed notary with two small children. Nanna remembered how, after the man's visit, Emma had looked at the family, wide eyed, and asked, "Do I have to accept?"

Much to everyone's surprise Sue immediately responded, "Not unless you think you'd be happier being married than keeping your old aunt company."

Now Sue and Emma sat on the back porch with a mending basket between them. The two looked so much alike they could easily pass as mother and daughter. Walking by the altar in the dining room Nanna glanced at the row of portraits. Ting and Carolien would have to take care of Sue and Emma after she was gone.

***

Soon after they visited Nanna, Jenny took Lam to meet Po Han. Lam seemed nervous, but he relaxed when Po Han said, "I'm glad you're here." Waving at the sofa he added, "Please, sit down. Jenny will make us some tea."

Jenny busied herself with the tea tray while Lam and Po Han talked.

Lam told Po Han about his father's car dealership, his uncle's thriving practice as a prominent lung specialist, and his grandparents' sugar refinery.

"It sounds like you have a wonderful family, Lam. Po Han reached for the cup Jenny offered him. "Now, what about yourself?"

"I went to Chinese school during the war," Lam said. "When the Dutch schools re-opened, I was behind in their curriculum. That's why I'm in the same class as Jenny."

"I see." Po Han lit a cigarette. "And what do you plan to do after high school?"

"My father wants me to go to medical school. He said I can study in Holland if I want." Lam leaned back and crossed his legs.

"I didn't ask what your parents' plans were for your future, Lam. I asked what your plans were after high school. Do you have any?" Po Han fixed his eyes on Lam.

Jenny took a sip of her tea. Across the rim of her cup, she watched Lam shift uncomfortably in his seat.

"Do you want to become a doctor?" Po Han crossed his legs and dropped his hands in his lap.

"Oh, yes. Don't you think it's a good profession?"

"Of course it is," Po Han said. "What would you like to specialize in, Lam?"

"I like to be a surgeon. My uncle says that surgeons make a lot of money without taking the risk of getting infected." Lam smiled.

"Is that why you want to become a doctor, to make a lot of money?" Po Han's thumbs tapped staccato.

For an instant, Lam hesitated. "I'm sure I'll make a lot of money after I study in Holland and open my own practice here." He paused. "My father will pay for all of my studies and, after I graduate, he will buy a practice for me."

"You're lucky, Lam," Po Han rose. "Not everyone is given such a great chance." Walking to the window, he added, "I hope you'll use the opportunity well."

"Yes sir, I will," Lam said to Po Han's back.

Jenny joined Po Han and put her arms around him. "Dad, can we show Lam some of your Holland images?"

"If Lam is interested, sure." Po Han turned and put an arm around Jenny's shoulders.

Lam stared at Po Han and Jenny. Fathers in Chinese families were never affectionate with grown children; love was an inward emotion, not to be expressed in this manner. "I would very much like to see the pictures," he said.

Jenny pulled out sketchbooks and albums while Lam and Po Han moved canvasses around. They spent the next hour poring over Po Han's photographs and paintings.

"Do you think your father likes me?" Lam asked as soon as they were back in the car.

Jenny gazed out of the car window. "What makes you think he doesn't?" she asked, rolling the window down.

Lam hesitated. "Oh, I don't know."

Jenny settled deeper into her corner. "What about you, do you like him?"

"Of course I do, he's your father." Lam exclaimed promptly.

"And if he wasn't, would you still like him?" Jenny smoothed the laced edge of her handkerchief across her knee. Then she folded and unfolded the small batiste square.

"I don't see why not," Lam answered quickly. "He's a nice man. I liked looking at his pictures and listening to his stories."

"Which was your favorite photograph?"

"Oh, I don't know if I have a favorite." Lam took Jenny's hand and pulled her closer. "They were all nice."

Jenny stiffened. Lam's breath was warm on the back of her neck. "Now that I've met all of your family, it's time you meet mine."

"You think so?" Jenny murmured and crumpled her handkerchief into a tight ball. She wasn't at all interested in Lam's parents. When it came down to it, she wasn't that interested in Lam. She squeezed her balled-up hanky but kept silent. If she broke up with him he might brag about what they had done together.

The next day Jenny visited Po Han. "Well, Dad, what do you think of Lam?" she asked, as soon as she entered his study.

"How about a hello, a hug, and a kiss?" Po Han laughed. He got up from his chair and held out his arms.

For a moment, Jenny relaxed in her father's embrace. Then she lifted her face and rubbed her forehead against his somewhat scratchy chin.

Po Han pushed Jenny gently into a chair. "Jenny, it isn't important what I think of Lam. I'm not the one who'll have to live with his beliefs."

Jenny picked up a letter opener and scratched lines into the dark green desk blotter.

"Tell me, girl, what is it you like about Lam?" Po Han's voice was gentle.

The lines on the blotter became a picket fence. Jenny scratched a gate into the fence and large padlocks all across it. If only she could tell her father the truth, but fear of what might happen if he found out kept her quiet.

Po Han closed his hand over Jenny's and took the letter opener out of her hand. "Will you please tell me?"

Jenny scooted her chair closer to Po Han and ran the tip of her tongue across her dry lips. "He's nice, Dad." She propped up her elbows on her knees and dropped her head into her hands. "When he's around, things somehow always turn out okay."

"Really? Like how?" Po Han stroked Jenny's head.

She turned to look out of the window. "The girls at school never tease me anymore. Mom never gives me a hard time when I am with Lam."

"Hmm." Po Han took Jenny's shoulders forcing her to look at him. "Hmm," he repeated and let go of her. He slipped off his desk and pushing his hands deep into his pockets, he started to pace the room.

"I think Nanna and Mom like it that I'm no longer acting like a tomboy, that I wear dresses now and all that stuff." Jenny followed Po Han to the window. She thought of the car, the theater seats, the meals in fancy restaurants. Her pencils were always sharpened, her bike tires always had enough air. If it only could stop there, but her memory continued to the late Saturday evenings spent in her bed.

"Well?" Po Han tilted Jenny's face.

She smelled the tobacco on his hand. "Lam's okay, Dad," Jenny said averting her eyes. "He always takes care of me."

"Okay is not enough to wrap your life around, Jenny." Po Han lit a cigarette. He took a few long drags then asked, "And why do you need Lam to take care of you?"

Jenny shrugged and he added, "You are the best person to take care of you."

CHAPTER 28

Carolien was sitting on the front porch going through mail when Jenny came home from school. "Here." Carolien handed Jenny a light-blue airmail envelope with Els' handwriting on it.

"Thanks." Jenny wormed a finger through a corner of the envelope and ripped it open.

"What does Els have to say?" Carolien asked when Jenny slowly folded the letter.

"They've moved to their own place and she asked what I want to be. Here, you can read it." Jenny passed her mother the letter.

Amsterdam, 27 November, 1950.

Dearest Jenny,

I'm sorry for not having written for so long. As you can tell from the address, we have moved! Yes, we finally have our own house. It's very small, (our living room is the size of your bedroom and our bedroom is not much bigger than Nanna's laundyroom), but it's ours. I'm sure Mother Bouwman is happy to have her house to herself again.

Jan is looking forward to having me cook the Chinese and Indonesian dishes he learned to eat and love. I cooked rijsttafel once while we lived with his parents, but his mother couldn't stand the aroma of the strong spices that are used in Indonesian food.

It has been raining a lot lately and it also turned very cold. I miss home, the sun, the food, and the amiable people. The

Dutch keep very much to themselves and seldom invite friends for a meal. This might be because they have to do everything themselves. Especially during our move, I realized how much I've always taken the servants' help for granted.

Eddie helped us move. Fortunately, we don't live too far from each other. Poor Eddie, he's still having a hard time at work.

How is Nanna? How is everybody, Emma, Aunt Sue, Youngest Uncle, your mother and yourself? Jenny, do you still see your father a lot? Your mother wrote that you are dating a Chinese boy named Lam. You have to tell me all about him. Please, don't let him keep you from pursuing your dreams (which I hope includes studying in Holland).

In another month, the drilling for your final exam will start. I trust that your problems with Bahasa Indonesia have lessened. Have you thought seriously of what you want to be? Holland has excellent universities.

Write soon, okay? Jan said to say hello.
Lots of love, Els.

"Els is right. You should start thinking seriously about what you want to be." Carolien returned the letter to Jenny.

"I want to be a veterinarian," Jenny said, twisting the envelope.

"Now I've heard everything." Carolien brought her hands up to smooth her hair. "I can't imagine that there are too many people who want and can afford to spend money on the health of an animal," she said. "How are you going to make a living, Jenny?" Carolien tapped the porch table with her mail. "Really. Just think about it." When Jenny didn't respond, she asked, "If you want to study medicine, why don't you want to be a real doctor?"

"There are many doctors to help sick people, Mom. But there aren't many veterinarians and I could work for the zoo." Jenny kicked hard at the table legs.

"Do you have any idea how much it costs to study at a university?" Carolien snapped. "Do you expect me to support your foolishness?"

Between Po Han's idealism and Nanna's fascination with nature, she had better make sure that Jenny operated with some practicality. "Just remember, I'm not going to waste any money on having you learn to take care of a bunch of animals," she said and walked into the house.

***

The next afternoon, Jenny visited Po Han. "Yesterday, I got a letter from Els. She's moved into her own house," she said as she prepared the tea tray.

"That's good. It's always hard to live under someone else's roof." Po Han set his paper aside. The late afternoon sun poured through the open windows, but a light mountain breeze kept the study cool. "What else did she say?"

"Oh, she asked if I've thought about what I want to be." Jenny handed Po Han his teacup.

"Thanks. Have you?" Po Han clouded his tea with a few drops of milk. "You're only seven months away from having to make that decision."

"I know." Jenny took a seat on the sofa. "I'd like to be a veterinarian." She peered at Po Han's face over the rim of her teacup. "I could work in the zoo."

Po Han took a sip of his tea.

"But everyone thinks I'm weird. Dad…" Jenny hesitated. "Should I look into scholarships? Do you think I should go to university abroad?"

For a moment they sat quietly. Po Han pensively broke the silence. "If you want to be a veterinarian you might not only have to study abroad, you might also have to live there. Here, people generally don't attach much thought to animal welfare."

Po Han crossed his fingers and tapped his thumbs against each other. "Have you told your mother?"

"Yesterday." Dusk began to settle in the room and Jenny turned the table lamps on. "But she told me I shouldn't do it and she wouldn't help me if I did." Jenny dropped herself hard into a chair. "Would you?"

Jenny studied Po Han's face. There was pain and sadness in his eyes and his jaw was set. He took a deep breath and said solemnly, "Yes, I will."

"Oh, Dad!" Jenny jumped out of her chair and threw her arms around Po Han. "Thanks."

They held each other for a moment before Po Han loosened Jenny's arms. "Let's talk about it." He tapped the newspaper. "The communist party made headlines again. There might be more than one reason why it's a good idea for you to study abroad. It looks like it might get tough here for a while." Po Han lit a cigarette while Jenny returned to her seat. "It seems that the Indonesians are set on making the Chinese scapegoats for their own incompetence and corruption." Exhaling slowly, Po Han's gaze followed the gray ribbons of smoke. "You'll need to go to Utrecht if you want to study veterinary medicine."

Jenny looked away. "Dad, what do you think of me going to America?"

"America?" Po Han frowned. "How did you come up with America? Don't you think that Holland would be a more logical destination?"

Jenny hesitated. "A while ago Mr. Ford said something about his church being willing to sponsor a student who wanted to study in America." Jenny plucked at the fringe of a throw pillow.

"Mr. Ford is your English teacher, right?" Po Han ran his fingers through his hair. "What did he say about sponsorships?"

"I don't exactly remember." Relieved her father seemed open to the idea, Jenny continued. "Do you think I should go ask him?"

"That's a good start." Po Han took a seat on the windowsill. "Jenny, I'm supporting you because I believe that you, like anyone else, have the right to pursue what you believe in with the least amount of hindrance." He fixed his eyes on her. "Please remember that when you talk to your mother."

***

The next day Jenny used her free period to see Warner Ford.

"Come in," he called when she knocked on his door.

"Good morning, do you have a minute?" Jenny hesitated in the doorway.

"Sure, have a seat." Warner waved at the chair across from his desk. "What can I do for you, Jenny?"

Jenny plucked at her skirt and kept her eyes focused on a knot in the woodgrain of Warner's desk. "Remember–when you first came–you told us about your church? You said they had a program that sponsored foreign students."

"Yes?"

"Well, I wondered…"

A broad smile spread across Warner's face. "Is that why you're here?"

Jenny nodded.

"Why are you interested?" Warren leaned back in his chair.

"I've been thinking about what I want to do in the future," Jenny began self-consciously. She was glad that at least part of her prepared speech was coming back. "I'd like to be a veterinarian." Jenny scooted to the edge of her seat and clamped her hands around the wood.

"Hmmm, you wouldn't have a lot of choices to study for that here." Warner walked to a file cabinet and leaned against it. "Suppose you get a degree in veterinary medicine, do you think you'll be able to find a job here?"

Jenny shrugged and bit into her lower lip. "I don't know. Maybe I could work for the zoo."

"That's a possibility. Have you talked about it with others?"

"Almost everyone I've told thinks I'm weird."

"Weird?" Warner exclaimed, but then abruptly halted. "Well, it's natural for a society with a great need for human care to have little to no interest in caring for animals. What do your parents think about your plans, Jenny?"

"My father is supportive, but my mother doesn't like it and won't help me." Jenny looked away during the awkward silence that followed.

"You know, Jenny," Warner finally said, "without your mother's permission we can't do anything. She does have custody and under Indonesian law you won't be an adult until you're twenty-one." Jenny nodded. The uncomfortable anxiety she had been feeling lately expanded in her chest. At first she had assigned the feeling to missing Eddie and Els, but then she came to realize that their presence would not have made a difference to her predicament. They could not have kept the Indonesian Revolution from taking place. Nor could they have changed things between her and Lam.

"Jenny," Warner interrupted her thoughts. "Why don't you tell your mother that we talked and ask her to see me. I'm not promising that I can change her mind, but I'll try to point out that studying veterinary medicine is truly not that terrible."

***

At dinner, later that night, Jenny told Carolien about having met with Warner Ford.

"What makes you think you can take matters into your own hands?" Carolien pushed her plate away. "And who does that American think he is that he can fill my daughter's head with his frivolous ideas? If you're going anywhere, it will be to Holland to study law."

After a moment of silence, Jenny answered quietly. "Mr. Ford didn't fill my head with anything. Remember, I went to see him."

Carolien pressed her lips together and rearranged the fruitbowl.

"Can't you see? It's my life, Mom."

"Why do you have to go to America? You have no one there. How do you expect to be able to make a living caring for animals?"

Jenny shrugged and twisted her napkin. "Please, Mom, at least hear what Mr. Ford has to say."

Carolien wanted Jenny to go abroad, she often imagined Jenny doing the things she once dreamed of doing herself, but she was concerned as well. What would happen if Jenny went to America? On the other hand, what would become of the girl if she were swept into the political upheaval that was brewing in Indonesia? The Chinese were being squeezed between the power struggle of the Indonesian communist, religious, and socialistic parties. What would the future hold?

The next morning, standing in the doorway to see Jenny off to school, Carolien called after her. "Ask Mr. Ford when he wants to see me." She slammed the door before Jenny had a chance to turn around.

During their meeting Carolien listened intently to Warner Ford. He pointed out that Jenny's decision could be construed as a subversive act by government authorities. He also predicted that it would take several months before the American documents would be issued, and emphasized the need for secrecy of their plans.

On her way home, Carolien wondered if Jenny would tell Lam. Most likely, she wouldn't. What would happen to that relationship if the American plan worked? But if Lam were serious about Jenny, nothing would prevent him from following her to America. The Chings could certainly afford it.

***

Jenny read Eddie's first letter of the New Year at her desk. He wrote:

Amsterdam, 15 Jan. '51.
Dearest Jenny,
Finally! I'm working as a surveyor in one of the large building projects! It's a well-paid job. But more importantly, I am on the list to get one of the new two bedroom flats as soon as a complex is completed. Hopefully, we'll be able to move into our own home by the end of this summer. And when you come, the extra bedroom will be yours.
Even though I'm happy to finally have a steady job, I wish I could choose a friendlier work environment. The influx of immigrants from Indie has become a threat to the Dutch on many levels and, as the awareness of this fact grows, their resentment toward us becomes more evident.

Jenny smoothed the thin light-blue airmail paper. What did Eddie mean? Were the Dutch treating him badly? Why? He had fought in their army against the Japanese and the Indonesians. *And when you come, the extra bedroom will be yours.* She imagined them all together. Eddie, Els, Jan Bouwman, and herself. She reluctantly let Peggy Rose into the picture before she stepped out of her daydream. The Indonesian government censored the mail so she had not mentioned her plans in her letters. If she were to receive the scholorship to America, she might never get to see Eddie and Els again.

CHAPTER 29

A howling monsoon storm filled the gutters and poured through the downspouts onto the porches. Nanna could hear the water gurgle against her bedroom wall and she knew it would be spilling onto the porch in clear wide circles. Normally, she'd be out there, moving the long handled scrub brush across the porch tile, loosening whatever dirt had settled into the grout lines and sweeping it into the shallow gutter that ran around the porch.

She lifted a steaming poultice out of an enamel bowl. The strong scent of eucalyptus penetrated her nostrils and, for a moment, cleared her stuffed sinuses. The medicated cloth felt hot against her breastbone. Leaning back into her chair, Nanna closed her eyes and rubbed the heel of her hand against her chest until her wheezing exploded into a coughing spell.

The door opened and Emma entered the bedroom. "Are you okay, Nanna? Can I get you something, a glass of water?" Emma rubbed Nanna's back until the cough subsided into rapid breathing.

"No, thank you. I'm fine." Wheezing, Nanna patted Emma's arm. "Please, go tell Mundi to scrub the porch. The rain makes that job so much easier." Nanna glanced sideways at Emma's portly figure. Strong and efficient, Emma could have made someone a good wife, but she had chased away the few suitors with her sharp tongue and homely appearance. Nanna sighed. Emma was now thirty-three. It still wasn't too late, but the chances of getting married were getting slim. Thank God for

Ting and Carolien. They'd take care of Sue and Emma. Ting's tobacco store did a good business and Carolien had earned quite a reputation as a seamstress. There also was the money the Dutch government had awarded Chip posthumously for his work in the Underground–a Dutch trophy that had been unable to fill the empty seats at the dining table. Nanna knew Ting had invested the funds that she refused to use.

She reached into her cummerbund for a handkerchief. As she blew her nose, she started coughing again. She reached for a spittoon, her hand shaking. Never before had a cold gotten her down this much. Nanna shivered. It was only March. The rains would continue through April.

***

Carolien paced the living room, waiting for Jenny to come from school. Rain battered the windowpanes. Every so often lightening struck and was followed by thunder. Carolien peeked through the curtains. The Ching's car drove up the driveway and Carolien hurried to the front door.

"Nanna's sick," she said before Jenny could greet her. She looked wearily at the Ching's car driving away and asked, "Why didn't Lam come in?"

"His father needed the car." Jenny closed her umbrella. "Nanna's sick?"

"The doctor said she has pneumonia." Carolien tried to keep her panic out of her voice.

"Pneumonia?" Jenny's eyes widened and filled with fear. "Will she die, like–"

"The doctor wants to hospitalize her. But she won't have anything to do with it. She's convinced she'll die in a hospital." Carolien fastened a few loose strands of hair. "Jenny, pneumonia is dangerous and, at Nanna's age, it can be deadly. I want you to go over there. Make her go to the hospital. She'll listen to you."

***

The quiet in Nanna's room was thick and heavy. Sue sat on the edge of Nanna's bed. Ting had pulled up a chair. They looked up and raised a hand when Jenny tiptoed into the room. "She's asleep," Ting whispered. "The medicine has stopped her cough, but she still has a high fever."

A white cloth covered Nanna's forehead. Jenny reached under the blanket for her grandmother's hand.

Ting bent closely over Nanna and said, "Ma, Jenny's here. I'm going to the bathroom, I'll be right back." Then he turned to Jenny and whispered, "She hasn't said a word since yesterday. Sometimes I wonder if she's conscious." Ting added a few ice cubes from a thermos to the enamel bowl filled with water and hand towels on the vanity. "Change the compress when it gets warm," he said before leaving the room.

Jenny took Ting's seat. Nanna's blanket moved with her uneven breathing. "Nanna, it's me, Jenny. I didn't know you were sick. I'm sorry I didn't come sooner." Jenny pulled her grandmother's hand out from under the blanket and placed her face against Nanna's palm.

Ting came back, followed by Emma who was carrying a cup of steaming tea. "Here." Emma handed Jenny the tea. "All we need is for you to get sick too."

While Jenny sipped her tea, Ting suggested that she and Emma stay with Nanna so he and Sue could rest.

Jenny placed her teacup on the vanity table and took a seat on the edge of the bed. Emma stood leaning against a bedpost. "If you want, you can go too. I'll be okay." Jenny smoothed Nanna's blanket.

"You're sure?" Emma suppressed a yawn. "I could use some sleep. I was up all last night."

Jenny nodded.

The alarm clock on Nanna's vanity ticked away time. Jenny had changed the compress several times when Nanna's voice rose softly but clear from the large white pillow. "Don't forget to put the bracing poles under the branches of the mango tree by the creek."

"Don't worry, Nanna, I won't. As soon as the rain stops, I'll get the poles." Jenny rubbed Nanna's thin shoulder. Outside, the rain pelted the windows and sent a mass of water gushing through the metal downspouts. The water lapped against the house.

"Let me tell the others that you're awake. Mom should be here too. Can I get you something?" The task Carolien had given her lay heavily on Jenny's mind.

"Come, lie down. Leave the others where they are." Nanna's voice was soft, but the tone had its usual firmness.

Jenny nestled herself against her grandmother's side. Nanna's sharp wheezing made her feel uneasy. She took a deep breath and whispered, "Nanna, don't you think you should go to the hospital?"

Nanna sighed and looked away.

The door opened softly. It was Ting.

"Get some rest. Jenny's here," Nanna said.

Ting hesitated. "How long has she been up?" he asked.

Carolien and Sue crowded the doorway and peeked over his shoulder.

"We're okay. I'll call if I need help." Jenny sat up. She remained seated after the others left. Shadows shifted soundlessly across the bedroom walls as the night crept toward a new day. Finally the deep rhythmic thuds of the *beduk* followed by the chanting of Muslims saying morning prayers in a nearby mosque announced daybreak.

Nanna stirred. She opened her eyes and looked steadily at Jenny.

"Nanna, will you please go to the hospital?" Jenny stroked Nanna's arm. Nanna didn't answer and she continued. "Can I get you something? Shall I call Youngest Uncle? Or Aunt Sue? Or Mom?"

The Muslims finished their chant and Nanna cleared her throat. "You be a good girl. Remember, Jenny, be a good girl." Nanna spoke slowly. The somber beat of the leather drum accompanied her words.

"Yes, Nanna, I will." Jenny buried her fists into a pillow.

"Good." Nanna let out a deep sigh and closed her eyes. For a moment, it seemed as if she had gone back to sleep, but then her breathing became deeper and more labored.

Jenny bent anxiously over her grandmother and listened to Nanna's gurgling. After taking a deep wheezing breath, Nanna's head fell sideways. Another rattle escaped her throat and an irreversible stillness settled over her.

"Nanna," Jenny called softly. When she did not get a response, she called again, this time louder. "Nanna!" Jenny took her grandmother's hand. It was soft and warm, but when she let go, it dropped. "Nanna!" Jenny shouted, grabbing Nanna's shoulders.

The bedroom door flew open. Ting, Carolien, Sue and Emma crowded around the bed. Ting put a hand on Jenny's arm. "Let go, Jenny," he ordered in a choked voice. All color had left his face.

"She's gone," Carolien said, hardly audible. She turned around and joined Sue and Emma who stood crying at the foot of the bed.

"Nanna. Nanna." Jenny tried to detect a sign of life in her grandmother's still face. She picked up Nanna's hand again. The wrinkles were still loose and the skin felt smooth, like soft leather. She looked as if she was in a deep sleep. Why did Mom say that she was gone? How could Nanna be gone? Jenny couldn't imagine coming to the big house and not finding Nanna on one of the porches or in the garden.

"We have to wash her." Sue adjusted a fold in the blanket.

"We better hurry. It's a lot easier to do it now, before–" Carolien stifled a sob. "Before she's gone all the way."

The room filled with soft crying. Carolien opened Nanna's closet. "Sue, will you lay out her clothes? Em, will you get the water?"

"I need to take care of the funeral," Ting said and left the room.

Sue rummaged through Nanna's clothes. When she turned around, she carried a sarong, cummerbund, chemise, and *kebaja*.

"Jenny, you cannot cry while we wash and dress Nanna," Carolien whispered.

Jenny sent her mother a puzzled look. She had not cried at all. A buzzing sound in her head kept her from feeling sad, angry or lost. The word *dead* seemed to have lost meaning. It was merely a sound that started at the roof of her mouth and ended there, tasteless and colorless.

Emma came back with the bath water.

Carolien blew her nose. "Please remember, you cannot let any tears fall on her," she said to no one in particular.

"Yes, please be careful. Tears will spot her spiritual body," Sue said.

Carolien turned to Emma. "Please see if you can find her box."

Jenny knew her mother was referring to the small silver box in which Nanna kept some coins and loose pearls.

Now, Jenny watched Emma run her hands under and between the neat stacks of Nanna's clothing until she found the small silver box. She turned her head when Emma placed the box on top of the clothes

Sue had stacked on a chair. Death had found its ornaments and now demanded adorning.

Carolien added rosewater from one of the decanters on Nanna's vanity to the bath water. She moved Jenny gently aside before pulling the blanket off Nanna. "Let's start undressing her."

With trembling fingers Jenny undid the silver pins that closed the front of Nanna's *kebaja* and gave them to Emma. Then she unbuttoned the tiny front buttons of Nanna's chemise.

Carolien undid Nanna's cummerbund. Then she and Sue pulled the sarong loose and away from Nanna's body.

Jenny had never seen Nanna, or any other adult, naked. Nanna's thin still body was only a few shades darker than the white bedsheets. Two dark nipples dotted her rib cage. In the center of her flat stomach, the deep dark eye of her navel tunneled into her belly. A thin layer of gray hair spiraled from the small mound between her legs and shielded the birthplace of her sons and daughters.

Emma put a warm damp washcloth in Jenny's shaking hands. "There, start with her face and work your way down," she whispered.

Jenny moved the washcloth across Nanna's face and chest. She returned the cloth to Emma when she couldn't reach further.

"If we do the chemise and *kebaja* together, we only have to turn her once." Carolien reached for the clothes on the chair.

After they finished dressing Nanna, Sue took the largest of the pearls out of the box and placed it on Nanna's tongue. Carolien wedged a rolled handtowel under Nanna's chin. Then they placed the smaller pearls in Nanna's ears and nostrils. Now no evil could enter her body and disturb the spirit while it prepared for its journey.

"Let's comb her hair before doing the coins," Carolien said.

Nanna's curved bone comb was smooth and shiny from many years of use. When Carolien took out the hairpins from the bun on top of Nanna's head, her long straight hair spread like a silver cape across the pillow. Carolien combed Nanna's hair and gathered it back into a bun. "You think she looks all right?" she asked after she fastened it.

Sue and Emma nodded.

Carolien placed each coin in a black velvet pouch and then placed them with trembling fingers over Nanna's closed eyes.

The house filled suddenly with strange voices. Emma peeked through the drawn drapes. "It's Youngest Uncle and the ice vendor."

Carolien turned away from the bed and began to cry.

"There's a car pulling into the driveway," Jenny noticed.

"It must be the cemetery people delivering the coffin," Carolien said.

Jenny stared at Nanna's still body and could not imagine that soon it would be placed in a box and buried somewhere she had never been.

Carolien blew her nose and dried her eyes. "I better see if they need help. You stay with her," she said to Jenny. "You and Eddie were her favorites, you know. You, Eddie, and my brothers were the ones she cared for." Carolien left the room, crying.

Sue and Emma followed her.

Jenny touched Nanna's hand. It felt cool and was no longer soft. After a few moments, Ting entered the room with several strange men who carried a long, narrow, wooden box. Carolien and Emma walked in behind them.

"Jenny, we have to move Nanna. Please get out of the way," Ting said with a hoarse voice.

Carolien took Jenny's arm and pulled her back. "We better get changed into mourning clothes," she said. "You can wear only white for one month. After that, you can wear dark colors as long as you feel you are in mourning." Carolien sniffled.

It struck Jenny that they hadn't done any of this when Chip died. But then, there had been no dead body. Jenny could not help notice how large and red Ting's nose looked in his pale face.

"I hope that it will stop raining so there won't be any standing water in the grave," Ting said to one of the undertakers.

Jenny walked to the coffin. She scanned the face for an expression she recognized and found none. The coins in their velvet bags, taped to Nanna's eyelids, sealed away all familiarity.

***

Jenny stood next to Carolien at the gravesite. The undertakers lowered the coffin into the grave. When they stepped back Ting placed a wooden box on top of the coffin. It held the altar urns Nanna used to hold the incense sticks she burned. Nanna had instructed Ting to dismantle the altar upon her death.

When the others moved away from the gravesite to make room for the workers, Jenny remained. Mundi and Amin, together with two strange natives, shoveled dirt back into Nanna's grave. Jenny wanted to take a shovel and join them. It was the last thing she could do for Nanna. She walked closer to the men until Mundi said gently, "Be careful, *Nonnie.* You'll get all dirty. *Njonja Besar* would not like that." Tears sprang into Jenny's eyes when she heard Mundi refer to Nanna as Grand Madam. She knew that Mundi's dark face was wet not only with perspiration.

"*Non,* your mother's calling," Amin said between two shovels.

"I know." Jenny kicked at some dirt.

"C'mon, Jen." Carolien tugged softly on Jenny's arm.

"Can I just stay here? Until we've got to go?" Jenny stared at the working men.

Carolien sighed. "Sure," she said, and walked away slowly.

Jenny watched the men finish. With each scrape and thud of the shovel, a physical distance grew between her and Nanna, until the grave was covered with a soft mound and the distance was too great to span.

"The ground has to settle before we can put down the sod. Maybe you want to come when we do that?" Mundi scraped his shovel clean.

Jenny nodded. Mundi had gardened with Nanna as long as she could remember. Jenny picked up a stick. Poking into the moist earth, she checked her impulse to reach for Mundi. She wanted to take his hands and put them against her cheeks, but he was a native and she couldn't do that. Jenny dropped to the ground. She curled into a tight ball and burried her face into her arms, sobbing. Nanna was gone.

***

Carolien watched Mundi walk away carrying his shovel on his shoulder. She felt an odd sense of kinship with the native who had grown up in Nanna's household. With only Ting, Sue, and Emma left living in

Nanna's house, it seemed almost ridiculous to have three servants around. But Carolien knew that Rina, Sari and Mundi would remain at Nanna's as long as they wanted to. Caroline tapped Jenny on the shoulder. "Jen, we have to go."

"Okay." Jenny straightened up slowly.

They joined Sue and Emma in the foyer of the undertaker's office while Ting settled the bill.

"What is going to happen now?" Emma looked from Carolien to Sue.

"We need to get home to prepare–" Sue turned wide-eyed to Carolien. "There's no altar. How are we going to perform the rituals?"

Carolien shook her head. Emma's question had not been about rituals. She put an arm around Emma's shoulder. "Don't worry, Em. Everything is going to be all right." Then, turning to Sue, she said, "I don't know. Maybe, by ordering Ting to take the altar down, Mother meant to do away with that stuff."

"You think so?" Sue fiddled with the clasp of her purse.

Carolien looked out of the window across the cemetery. Her unwillingness to yield to tradition had caused Nanna a lot of worry and grief. Yet, in her own way, Nanna had supported her striving for independence.

Carolien sighed. Western influence had not been able to erase the ingrained sense of family responsibility. Now, it was up to her and Ting to make sure Sue and Emma were taken care of and that the family continued to function.

CHAPTER 30

A week before the final exams, Warner Ford called Jenny into his office. Grinning, he waved a manila envelope at her. "It's here! Just in time."

Jenny stared speechless at the envelope. Finally, she stammered, "You–mean–I've been–accepted?"

"Yes. We did it." Beaming, Warner spread several documents on his desk. "It took a good eight months, but here it is. Come, see for yourself."

Jenny stared at the letters that provided travel funds and a year of schooling. She reached eagerly for the pictures that accompanied the letter from her host family. Her heart pounded in her throat as she tried to imagine herself living in the gray two-story house with the jovial man, smiling woman, a boy with a butch cut, and a pig-tailed girl with braces.

Warner told Jenny that he and Harold Thompson, her host father, had been roommates while they went to college in Berkeley. "You'll fit in, no problem," he said cheerfully.

Jenny lay the pictures down. Overcome, she said, "Thank you, Mr. Ford." She wiped the back of her hand across her cheeks and repeated, "Thank you."

"Jenny, I know you'll do just fine." Warner patted Jenny on the back.

Jenny digested the news on the bike ride home. "Mom!" she called as soon as she came into the house. She waved the manila envelope. "Guess what!"

Carolien looked up from her book, then pressed it with both hands against her chest. She looked calmly at the envelope. "What is it, Jenny?"

"I'm accepted. Mr. Ford called me into his office today." Jenny slipped her schoolbag off her shoulder and handed Carolien the envelope. "Mr. Ford would like to see you tomorrow. Can you go?"

"Yes, I will be there."

Jenny tried to scan her mother's face, but Carolien did not look up from the documents. "What do you think, Mom?"

Carolien laid out the photographs on the table. "Looks like a nice family." She tapped at the house in the background. "You probably will share a room with the little girl."

"No. I'll have my own. They said so in the letter." Jenny pulled Ruby Thompson's letter out of the pile of documents. "See, here it is." She pointed at the paragraph.

"Ah, I see. I'll look all of this over while you do your homework. There are a lot of forms to fill out. Also, they'll only sponsor you for a year. What will you do after that?" Carolien pushed the scattered papers into a stack. "Have you told your father and Lam?"

"I haven't told Dad yet. I came straight home from school. But I'm going to Dad's in a little while." Jenny rocked her chair nervously. In the excitement of her acceptance, she hadn't discussed the length of the sponsor program with Warner Ford.

"Have you told Lam?" Carolien dog-eared the envelope.

"Nope." Jenny clutched the chair's back. "Mr. Ford said to keep quiet until all the papers are in order."

"Hmmm." Carolien peered at her.

"I think I'm going to start my homework now," Jenny said, looking away.

In her bedroom, she walked to her closet and looked into the mirror. "It's happening," she said. "It's actually happening. I'm leaving this whole mess." She stretched her arms high above her head.

***

Carolien thumbed through the stack of documents. She had prepared herself for the arrival of Jenny's sponsorship letter. Still, her daughter's excited announcement gave her a painful jolt.

Carolien knew she would miss Jenny, but she had come to realize that it was best for Jenny's future if she left Indonesia.

Carolien read the acceptance letter from the church and the Thompson's invitation to stay with them several times. She still could not understand why Jenny had chosen to go to America instead of Holland. Did Eddie's struggles with racial discrimination have that much influence on her?

When she had expressed her concern to Warner Ford about Jenny's career choice, the young American waved his hand and reassured her. "You're worrying too much, Mrs. Lee. Jenny might leave here wanting to become a veterinarian, but she might very well come back as a lawyer or engineer. It is not uncommon for students to change their minds mid-course." Carolien had dropped the subject. How typically American to have such lack of focus.

Now Carolien separated the forms she needed to fill out. She tried to concentrate but her thoughts kept wandering off. What would it be like without Jenny? Perhaps she should consider moving to Nanna's. There was certainly enough room. She knew neither Ting nor Sue would object to the idea, and Emma would probably be happy to have someone around she could talk to about other than household issues. After Nanna's death, Carolien felt a new compassion for Emma.

***

The final exam moved into the shadow of the preparations for Jenny's departure. She studied feverishly, but most of her excitement and anxiety centered around the progress of obtaining Indonesian traveling documents. She needed a passport and an exit permit. She also needed to get medical clearance from the American doctor at the Catholic hospital.

Each stamp and clearance took hours of preparation and standing in line. But the stack of stamped forms slowly grew and, on graduation day, all Jenny was waiting for was her exit permit.

On the morning the results of the exams were posted, Jenny joined the noisy throng of seniors crowding the announcement board in the school foyer. She was certain she had passed but was eager to find out at which level. Lam held his arms out like a protective shield as they shuffled towards the front.

"Oh. Look. I made it." Clapping her hands, Jenny jumped up and pointed at her examination number. "There. I'm number five. I made the top ten." She turned to Lam. "Did you find your number?"

"Yeah. Here it is." Lam pointed at number seventeen, grimacing. He apparently had not expected her to place that much above him.

Jenny didn't quite know what to say. She finally smiled and said, "Well, the most important thing is that you passed, and you did place in the top fifty percent."

"Yeah, you're right. And, thank God, my parents aren't such performance freaks as yours." Lam canvassed the crowd.

"Let's get out of here. I'd like to tell my parents and have plenty of time to get ready for the party tonight." Jenny tugged on Lam's arm. Her mother would be pleased and proud, her father happy. She couldn't wait to write Eddie and Els.

***

On the drive home from their high school graduation ball that night, Lam took Jenny's hand and pulled her closer. The car took a corner and she fell against him. "And what now, little mouse?"

"What's what?" Jenny was irritated with Lam's nickname for her.

"My parents said that if I got married, they'd pay for my wife's studies as well," Lam said, smiling. "My mother wants to know that someone's taking care of me and my father wants to be assured that I won't get seduced by a blue-eyed blonde and make his grandson a half-breed." Lam laughed.

Jenny's heart began to pound. She pulled away from Lam and laughed awkwardly. "Now, all you need to do is get married."

"Yeah." Lam studied Jenny's face. "Jenny–"

"When will you be leaving?" Jenny interrupted nervously. "Are you going to Leiden or Amsterdam? Have you started the paperwork?"

Lam moved closer to Jenny. "Where would you like to go?"

"What does that matter?" Jenny rummaged through her purse.

"Wouldn't you like to go to Holland together?" Lam leaned forward.

"I'm going to America on a scholarship. I already have my visa and passport." Relieved she had spoken the words, Jenny added, "All I'm waiting for is my exit permit."

Lam fell back against the car seat. He closed his eyes and pressed his interlaced fingers against the top of his head. Then he rolled down the window. His face turned into the cold night air he asked, "Why didn't you tell me?"

"I–I couldn't."

"When will you leave?"

"As soon as my papers are in order." Jenny waited for Lam's reaction but he remained quiet. What's he going to do, she wondered. At this point, what could he do? Even if he told everyone at school–school was over. And she was leaving soon.

When they arrived at Carolien's driveway, Lam helped Jenny out of the car. Jenny walked ahead of him up the back porch steps. When Lam eased the door open, Jenny turned in the doorway, preventing him from entering. "Goodnight." She reached behind her for the doorknob, looking at Lam's shoes.

"Can't I come in for a while?" Lam took a step forward.

"Don't you need to think things over?" Jenny pulled the door closed, her heart pounding. The doorknob felt cold in the hollow of her palm.

"I guess." Lam raised an arm. He ran his fingers through his hair, then dropped his hand into a pocket.

Jenny shifted her weight. The shoe straps around her ankles felt suddenly tight.

Lam held Jenny lightly by the shoulders. She remained motionless when he kissed her forehead. "Goodnight, little mouse," he said and walked away.

Jenny leaned against the door. A light breeze cooled the hot July night. A quarter moon made its way slowly across a cloudless sky. Her mother's tuberoses were blooming and the air was pregnant with their scent. Jenny felt strangely calm. This, she thought, is the beginning of the end.

***

Carolien propped her pillows higher against the headboard and dropped her book into her lap when she heard the Ching's car pull into her driveway. She had been wondering all evening how Lam would take the news of Jenny going to America. Poor Lam, she thought, this must've been a tough day for him. First, Jenny beats him on the rating sheet, then she drops the America news on his head without any warning. The thought of Jenny's placement made her feel proud and excited again. "Jenny!" Carolien called when she heard her daughter come into the house.

Standing in the doorway in high heels, dressed in seafoam green chiffon and tafetta and holding her silver evening bag loosely by her side, Jenny looked like a young woman. She's pretty, Carolien thought, but couldn't make herself say it.

"Come." Carolien patted the place next to her. "Tell me, did you have fun? Did you tell Lam?" She hesitated. "Soon, you'll be gone, you know."

Jenny put her bag on Carolien's bed and, folding her skirt under her, took a seat at the foot end. "The party was great. The band was good. I danced a lot. Everyone liked my dress."

"What about Lam, how did he take it?"

"Like a champ." Jenny laughed loudly. Too loudly, Carolien thought. "He told me his parents wanted him to study in Holland and would pay for his wife's studies as well if he got married before leaving." Jenny chuckled. "Well, he knows now that wife will definitely not be me." She yawned and, stretching, slipped off the bed.

"Jenny, are you sure that you don't want to go to Holland? You are only guaranteed one year of help in America. If you go to Holland, it is certain that you can finish your studies there." Carolien smoothed her covers. "It isn't too late to change your mind, you know."

"Oh, Mom." Jenny grabbed her purse and started toward the door. "Lam will survive and I've made up my mind. I'm going to America."

"Jenny." Carolien clutched her covers.

"Yes?" Jenny turned around.

"I–I'm really proud of you." Carolien reached for the lamp on her nightstand. "G'night now."

"Thanks." Jenny sounded surprised. "G'night," she said into the dark room and closed the door.

Protected by the darkness, the walls, and closed door of her room, Carolien wept.

CHAPTER 31

Jenny looked for Po Han as soon as she and Carolien arrived at the airport. They were early and there weren't too many people in the section cordoned off for international flights.

"Jenny! Jenny." Lam's voice cut through the bustling crowd. Waving a large bouquet of roses over people's heads, he quickly made his way to her.

"You didn't tell me he was coming to see you off," Carolien said.

"I didn't know he was coming." Jenny answered under her breath. When Lam joined them, Jenny asked, "Hey, what are you doing here?"

"Hello, Mrs. Lee, how are you?" Grinning, Lam bowed in Carolien's direction.

"Hello, Lam, I'm fine, thank you." Carolien smiled. Her irritability had suddenly vanished. After she exchanged pleasantries with Lam, Carolien stepped away. Standing aside from the queue, she stared at the entry doors.

Lam placed the roses in Jenny's arms. "Here," he murmured. "I don't want you to forget about us. I'll miss you, you know." Lam bent closer. "Why, why do you have to scamper, little mouse?"

Just then Jenny saw Po Han enter the building. "Dad. Dad!" She pushed the flowers back into Lam's hands and rushed towards Po Han.

Po Han removed his sunglasses and looked across the room.

"I was so worried when I didn't see you." Jenny threw her arms around her father.

Several people turned their heads curiously to watch the Dutch-speaking Chinese girl shamelessly embracing a man.

"Well, I'm here now." Po Han steered Jenny back to the growing queue at the airline counter. "You better get back in line." He nodded in Lam's direction, "What's he doing here?"

"Making sure I won't forget him."

"Hmm." Po Han walked a few steps with her. When he came upon Carolien he stiffly nodded a greeting and turned quickly to Jenny. "You go on. I'll wait for you by the boarding gate."

Jenny froze. Her eyes darted from Po Han to Carolien and back, she hadn't seen her mother and father together in the same room since that day at the courthouse so many years ago. Her mother's stoic appearance and her father's discomfort added to her own mounting anxiety.

"All you have to do is check in, your papers are in order, aren't they?" Po Han wiped perspiration off his forehead.

Jenny nodded and shot Po Han an uncertain look.

"I'll see you in the boarding area." Po Han kissed Jenny lightly on her forehead, then walked away with sure strides.

"Pay attention. It's your turn," Carolien said curtly.

Lam hovered over Jenny while the ticket agent and government official checked her papers.

The Indonesian representative slowly read her name from her passport. "Lee Siu Yin." He paused before reading the next line, "Indonesian citizen."

The official moved his glasses down to the tip of his nose and had a good look at Jenny. "Why is it that you have an Indonesian passport, but don't have an Indonesian name?" Jenny stared speechless at him. Taking a thoughtful crackling drag from a clove cigarette, he returned her look.

The combination of the pungent smoke and the terrifying thought that he had the power to hold her in the airport nauseated Jenny. She steadied herself against the counter and answered in halting Indonesian, "I–have–a Chinese name–because–"

Before Jenny could finish the sentence, Lam moved her aside. He put the flowers down and reached into a trouser pocket. Leaning across the counter, he asked politely in Indonesian, "Can I please see her passport?"

The government official handed the black booklet to Lam.

Lam thumbed the pages, slipping several large bills between them. He paused to study Jenny's picture before handing the document back to the official. "I think you misread the name." He smiled. While the official smoothly removed the money, Lam said in fluent Indonesian, "It's hot and you've been very busy. Perhaps you should take a break and relax for a while." He reached into his pockets again and pushed a few more bills across the counter. "I heard that the airport restaurant serves the best iced coffee in town." The official pocketed the money and took Jenny's passport to another counter.

"What's happening? What are you doing?" Jenny asked Lam in Dutch.

Carolien anxiously worked her way between them. "Is there something wrong?" she whispered also in Dutch.

The airport personnel cast curious glances in their direction.

"It's okay, why don't the two of you rest on those benches," Lam soothed in Indonesian. He spread his arms with a herding motion. "You must be tired of all the standing."

Jenny started to protest, but Carolien took her arm and pushed her toward the benches. When they were out of earshot, Carolien hissed, "Will you ever learn to keep your mouth shut?" Jenny shrugged.

Lam returned to the counter and engaged in an animated conversation with the ticket agent and a government official.

Jenny glanced sideways at Carolien. Her mother often complained about the corrupt nature of the Indonesian government, yet she didn't seem troubled by Lam's behavior. "You don't care that he's bribing them?"

"Do you want to leave?" Carolien snapped.

Jenny stood up to get a better view of the ticket counter. "Thank God, I soon won't have to deal with this anymore."

"I'm glad Lam showed up, at least he's of some use," Carolien said. "Just imagine what would've happened if he hadn't bailed you out. I don't think you could have counted on your father to do the same."

"No," Jenny said softly. "My father wouldn't know how to play any of the games Lam knows."

Grinning, Lam joined them. "That wasn't too bad." He handed Jenny the flowers and the envelope.

"Thank you." Jenny put the envelope in the outside flap of her carry-on and shifted the roses in her arm. "How much did you pay him?"

"Don't worry about it, it wasn't much." Lam waved Jenny's question aside. "Shall we walk to the gate or do we still have some time?"

"I think I'll go to the gate. My father's waiting." Jenny avoided looking at Carolien.

"Oh." As always, the mention of Po Han threw Lam off balance.

Jenny adjusted the shoulder strap of her bag and extended her hand. "Bye, Lam, thanks. Thanks a lot. Take care of yourself."

Lam held Jenny's hand in both of his and forced a smile. "Goodbye, little mouse. Watch out for yourself. There're big cats over there," he said in a husky voice.

Jenny pulled her hand out of Lam's grip and turned to Carolien. "Bye, Mom." The small luggage bag suddenly seemed heavy.

Carolien fingered the leather strap across Jenny's shoulder. "Don't miss the plane in Hong Kong." She let her hand slide down Jenny's arm in an almost stroking motion. "They'll be waiting for you when you arrive in San Francisco, won't they?" Carolien grabbed Jenny's hand.

"Yeah." Jenny blinked to clear the mist blurring her eyes. Her knees were wobbly and she longed to lean into her mother's upright sturdy figure. She started to reach for Carolien, but her hand dropped and she plucked clumsily at her skirt.

Carolien wet her lips. "Write soon," she said in a choked voice, smoothing Jenny's hair with trembling fingers. She squeezed Jenny's shoulder and pulled her suddenly into her arms. They stood for a moment clinging to each other. Then Carolien pushed Jenny gently toward the boarding gate. "Go on now," she whispered. "Go on!"

Jenny felt as if she was sleepwalking down the stairs to the boarding area, but when Po Han's arms closed firmly around her she knew she wasn't dreaming, she was leaving.

Po Han's chin dug into Jenny's scalp.

"Dad," she cried, "I want to go, but I'm so scared." Sobbing against Po Han's chest, Jenny felt his heart pound against the side of her face and smelled his familiar bitter scent.

"You're claiming life, girl." Po Han's voice was raspy but firm. He held

Jenny at arm's length. "And living is a scary business," he added, his eyes boring into hers.

"All passengers for Pan Am flight 462 leaving for San Francisco with a stop-over in Hong Kong are requested to board now," the announcer blared over the microphone first in Indonesian, then in heavy accented English.

Jenny wrapped her arms tightly around Po Han. "I'll miss you," she cried. "I'll be all by myself."

"Then you must be careful." Po Han loosened Jenny's fingers and backed slowly out of their embrace. "Did you say goodbye to your mother and Lam?" he asked, holding her hands.

Jenny nodded. She raised her hand in a wave then turned around. Walking towards the runway, she became a part of the shuffling crowd until she peeled herself free. She lagged until there was no one behind her.

Jenny looked over her shoulder. Carolien and Lam had joined a handful of people standing along the fence line, waving at travelers as they crossed the short distance between the gate and the boarding ladder to the parked plane.

"*Selamat djalan.*" The Indonesian guard wished Jenny a good journey after he checked her papers. She was the last passenger to board.

Jenny waved at Carolien and Lam while the guards closed the gate.

"Don't worry about your mother, I'll take her home. I have the car," Lam called in Dutch.

"Thanks!" Jenny waved again. She walked toward the waiting plane without looking back. Standing in the doorway of the airplane, she caught a waft of cool stale air from the cabin. When she turned around, a hot breeze fanned across her face. Behind the cyclone fence, next to Carolien, Lam jumped up and down while waving his arms above his head. Carolien, dressed in a white dress with large red and yellow flowers, stood still and erect.

Jenny shifted her gaze along the fence to find Po Han. His khaki slacks and shirt blended into the landscape. He leaned into the barrier, clasping the wire at uneven heights. Jenny raised her hand. Her mouth was very dry. She wanted to call out to him, but her tongue stuck to the roof of her mouth and she could not force any words to pass her lips.

"Miss, you must take your seat now. We have to close the doors." An attractive young woman in a light-blue uniform tapped Jenny gently on her shoulder.

***

Carolien's gaze followed the plane even after it had taken to the skies. Her eyes bored into the bright blue until a thin white ribbon was all there was left to see. At least Nanna was spared from losing her favorite granddaughter to the Western world. Staring into the white clouds, Carolien tried to find comfort in the thought, but thinking of Nanna only added to her pain. Her mother, Carolien now realized, had ruled the family with a quiet unfaltering strength that had served as a touchestone for them all.

Carolien glanced sideways. Po Han still stood clutching the wire of the cyclone fence. What was he feeling? What had happened to the happiness that he had told her they would find together? Their eyes met briefly and Carolien could not prevent a wan smile from curving her lips.

Po Han raised a hand in a hesitant wave, then briskly turned and walked away.

Carolien stared at his moving back until he disappeared in the crowd.

"Mrs. Lee, are you ready?" All the confidence Lam had exuded while dealing with the airport officials had vanished as he stood fumbling with his sunglasses.

Carolien gave the empty runway one last look. Jenny had chosen a different future than she had dreamed for her daughter. Carolien sighed. Her own life had not turned out as she had envisioned either. Jenny was going to be fine. She had become the independent strong woman Carolien had always wanted her to be. That part of her dream had come true.

"Yes, Lam, I'm ready. Let's go." Carolien followed Lam through the crowd to the exit doors.

"After you." Lam held the door for her.

Carolien blinked at the sun's reflection off the massive metal flagpole in front of the airport building. The Indonesian red and white flag flapped in the wind. Jenny had just left, but Ting, Sue, and Emma were waiting for her at Nanna's. Her family needed her. Carolien walked past Lam and stepped into the murky afternoon.

CPSIA information can be obtained at www.ICGtesting.com
Printed in the USA
BVOW060257010312

284186BV00002B/1/P